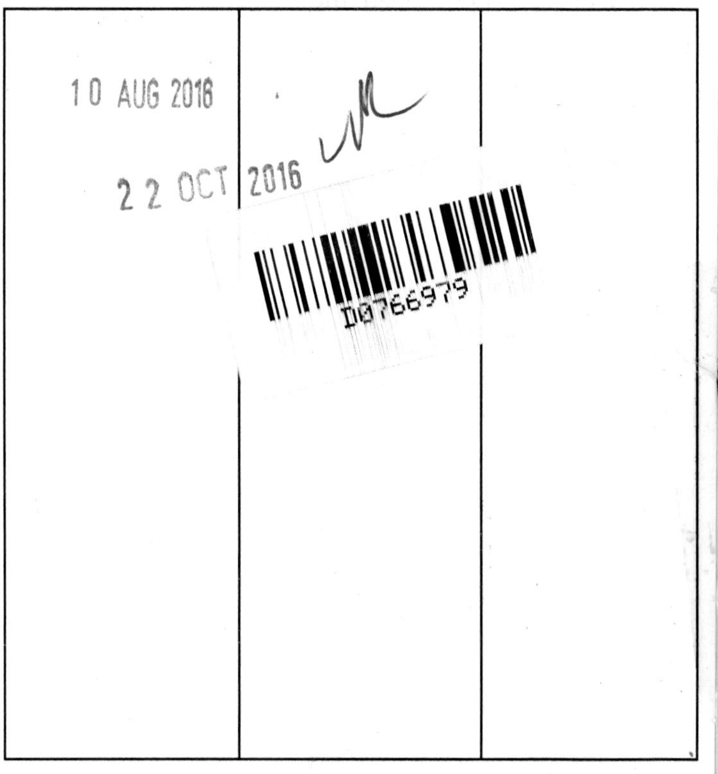

THE BRIGHTER BOROUGH
Wandsworth

"You okay?"

"Yeah." He raised his head, then sat up. The ledge they had come to rest on was safe enough for some of the tension to ease out of him.

She struggled into a sitting position and glared at him. "What did you think you were doing, tackling me that way? You could have been killed."

"I had to save you."

She wiped away a smear of blood and mud on her cheek. "No, you didn't. You'd be better off without me. You could move faster on your own."

"No, I wouldn't be better off without you." He shifted to kneel in front of her and grabbed both her arms. "I never was."

He told himself he deserved the wary look she gave him. He had certainly given her plenty of reasons to not believe him, to be afraid of him, even. He smoothed his hands down her arms, then gently pulled her to him. "I need you, Leah," he whispered. "I always have."

L AWMAN ON THE HUNT

BY
CINDI MYERS

First Published in Great Britain 2016
By Mills & Boon, an imprint of HarperCollins*Publishers*
1 London Bridge Street, London, SE1 9GF

ISBN: 978-0-263-91911-0

46-0716

Our policy is tc
products and m
manufacturing
the country of

Printed and bou
by CPI, Barcel

Cindi Myers is the author of more than fifty novels. When she's not crafting new romance plots, she enjoys skiing, gardening, cooking, crafting and daydreaming. A lover of small-town life, she lives with her husband and two spoiled dogs in the Colorado mountains.

Chapter One

Special Agent Travis Steadman studied the house through military-grade field glasses. Situated on a wooded escarpment above a rushing stream, the sprawling log home afforded its occupants a sweeping view of the snow-dusted Colorado mountains and the golden valley below. Sun glaring on the expanse of glass in the front of the house prevented Travis from seeing inside, but the intel reports told him all he needed to know. The two men and one woman who had rented the house two weeks ago looked like wealthy second-home owners enjoying a quiet mountain retreat, but the FBI suspected they were part of a dangerous terrorist cell.

"One car leaving. Looks like Braeswood and Roland." The crisp words, from fellow agent Luke Renfro, sounded clear in Travis's earpiece.

"I see them," he replied as a black Cadillac Escalade nosed out of the steep driveway. Through the side windows he could make out Duane Braeswood's sharp-nosed profile and Eddie Roland's bullet-shaped shaved head. "They're turning left, toward the highway to Durango."

"Here comes the woman and her driver," Luke said. "I wonder why she didn't go with them."

"Maybe she's going shopping. Or to get her hair done." Travis tried to keep any sign of tension out of his voice, even as he raised the glasses again to focus on the Toyota sedan that halted briefly at the bottom of the drive. He could just make out the silhouettes of the male driver and the woman beside him, but he didn't need the glasses to fill in the details about her. Leah Carlisle was twenty-seven years old, with thick dark hair that curled when she didn't straighten it, which she usually did. Her brown eyes, the color of good coffee with cream, were wide-spaced and slightly almond-shaped, and she could convey a score of different emotions with merely a look. She had a good figure, with a narrow waist and a firm butt, and small but round and firm breasts that were wonderfully sensitive. She enjoyed sex, and the two of them had been really good together…

He lowered the glasses and pushed the thoughts away. Leah's car also turned left, toward town. Maybe she was going to meet up with her partners in crime in Durango. He ground his teeth together, fighting the old anger. To think she had left him to be with scum like Braeswood and Roland.

"Did you say something?" Luke asked. "Transmission's a little fuzzy on my end."

Travis feared he had growled or made some other sound to signal his frustration. He needed to get a better grip. Only Luke, his closest friend, knew about his former relationship with Leah, and he had kept this information to himself.

Travis had admitted to their boss, Special Agent

in Charge Ted Blessing, that he was acquainted with Leah. After all, they were from the same hometown, and it wouldn't take a genius to figure out they had gone to school together. But no one knew he had planned to marry her. "Looks like she's headed to Durango, too," he said.

"Give them ten minutes, then we move in." Blessing's voice, deep and sonorous as a preacher's, shifted Travis's focus to the mission. He and Luke and Blessing and the other members of Search Team Seven were moving in for a "sneak and peek" at the interior of the cabin. They had wrangled a warrant that gave them onetime permission to go inside, look around and plant a couple of bugs that would, they hoped, provide the evidence they needed to arrest and convict Braeswood, Roland and Leah of terrorist activities.

The Bureau suspected the trio had ties to a series of bombings that had exploded at two major professional bicycle races around the world. Blessing and his team had stopped a third bombing attempt in Denver last month, but the bomber had died before he could give them any more information about his connections to these three.

Travis stowed the binoculars and prepared to move down from his lookout position in the rocks across from and above the house. When the signal came, Luke and Blessing would move inside with the rest of the team and Travis would station himself at the end of the driveway, alert for the premature return of the house's occupants.

"Recon Three, you hear me?" The flat, Midwestern accent of Special Agent Gus Mathers came across with the question.

"You're loud and clear," Travis answered.

"Best-case scenario, we've got an hour," Mathers said. "I don't like the looks of that drive—too steep and narrow, and situated in the curve of the road like it is, we won't have much warning if someone comes. You'll have to stall them at the bottom of the drive. Tell them we've got an explosive fuse or something."

"An explosive fuse?" He made a face. "What's that?"

"I don't know, but it sounds good, doesn't it? Something you wouldn't want to interfere with. There's nothing in these folks' backgrounds that shows they know anything about electricity. Just do what you can to keep them back if something comes up."

"Nothing will come up," Travis said. "Even if they drove to Durango and immediately turned around and came back, it would take them an hour."

"Better to be prepared. And let us know if you see anybody else suspicious."

"I know my job." And like everyone else on the team, with the exception of their commander, Blessing, he knew all the players in this case—even ones who were on the periphery or merely suspected of having some tie. The Search Team Seven members were all "super recognizers"—agents who literally never forgot a face. Travis hadn't even realized other people shared his peculiar talent until he had been recruited by the Bureau. He could see someone once, in person or on video or in a still photo, and pick them out of a crowd months later. The Bureau hoped the team would prove useful in identifying suspected criminals before they acted. So far, they had had a few successes, but this terrorist operation was their biggest operation yet.

"Okay, we're going in now." Special Agent in Charge Blessing gave the order.

Travis waited while a utility van with the logo of the local electric company moved slowly down the road and turned into the driveway of the log home. As soon as they reached the house, Luke, Blessing, Mathers and the three other team members inside would pile out and go to work. Mathers and Special Agent Jack Prescott, who had trained with the Bureau's TacOps team before transferring to Search Team Seven, would replace the living room and bedroom thermostats with identical units that contained listening devices, while Luke and Special Agent Cameron Hsung swept the premises for any incriminating evidence. Luke would download the hard drives from any computers onto a portable unit, and Hsung would photograph anything else that looked suspicious.

When Travis was confident the rest of the team was in place, he slipped across the road to the front of the house. Dressed in khaki cargo pants and a long-sleeved khaki shirt with the logo of the electric utility over the breast pocket, he would appear to anyone watching to be a utility worker repairing a malfunction or inspecting equipment. He knelt in front of the electrical box at the end of the drive and pried off the cover. He pretended to study its contents, though he was really scanning the approaches to the house. One hundred yards ahead on the same side of the road, a paved drive led to a glass-and-cedar chalet, the log home's closest neighbor. A retired couple lived there. The intel reports noted that they didn't go out much.

A soft breeze rustled in the aspens that lined the road, sending a shower of golden leaves over him. Another month and they'd have snow here in the high country. Already the highest peaks of the San Juans showed a light dusting. Leah would be happy about that. She had grown up in Durango and liked to ski. Was that why the trio had ended up here, after abandoning the house they had rented in Denver, only a few days before their friend Danny had tried to set off a bomb at the Colorado Cycling Challenge bike race?

"Hello! Is there a problem with the electricity?"

Wrench raised like a weapon, Travis whirled to see a slender man with a head of hair like Albert Einstein step from the shrubbery beside the road and stride toward him.

"Our sensors indicated some bad wiring." He lowered the wrench and delivered the line smoothly, though he had no idea where the words had come from. What sensors? Did electrical wiring have sensors? "We've got a crew up at the house checking it out."

The man glanced up the driveway, a worried vee between his bushy eyebrows. "I saw the van from my house. Did Mr. and Mrs. Ellison give you permission to enter their home while they're away?" he asked.

Ellison was the alias Braeswood had adopted in Denver and was sticking with here in Durango. The "Mr. and Mrs." made Travis wince inwardly. Leah hadn't married the guy, had she? Six months had scarcely passed since she returned Travis's ring.

He realized the old man was waiting for an answer. "It's less disruptive for us to do the work while they're out of the house," Travis said. Undercover Tactics 101: know how to bluff.

The man's frown morphed into a glare. "I didn't ask

whether or not it was convenient for you. Did you get their permission?"

"I'm sure my supervisor spoke to them," he said. He made a show of focusing once more on the interior of the utility box, though every nerve was attuned to the old man and his reaction. All he needed was for this guy to decide to phone the utility company and ask about the group of "workers." Or worse, this nosy neighbor might decide to call Leah or her "husband." Even thinking the word made his stomach churn.

"Does this have anything to do with the power outages we had last week?" the man asked. "I called twice to report them, and the woman on the phone said they would check things out, but you all are the first workers I've seen."

"I'm sorry, I don't know the answer to that." Travis tried to look friendly and humble. "I'm new on the job."

"I thought as much," the man said. "You're going to electrocute yourself if you tear into that box with an uninsulated wrench like that."

Cursing his own ignorance—and the TacOps unit for not doing a better job of briefing him—he dropped the wrench and took out a pair of pliers, the handles bound in green insulating rubber.

"I'm not sure Lisa would be happy to have you all in her house while she's out," the man continued.

So he knew her as Lisa. Close enough to her real name to avoid confusion. Or maybe the old man had misremembered. *No, I'm sure she wouldn't like having us in her house,* Travis thought. He glanced down the road, which was empty, then sat back on his heels and looked up at the man. "I thought I heard they just moved in," he said.

"That's right. They've only been here a couple of weeks. But I made a point of going over to meet them. I think it's always a good idea to know your neighbors."

So he didn't go out much, but he definitely kept tabs on everything. That might make him a useful witness in court one day. "Uh-huh." What could he say to get rid of this guy?

"Her husband was a little standoffish, but she was sweet as could be. As beautiful inside as she is outside."

Yeah, she fooled me into thinking that once, too. He turned back toward the electrical box. "It's been great talking to you," he said. "But I'd better get back to work. We should be out of your way pretty quickly."

"All right." The man leaned closer to peer at him. "Duke G. What does the G stand for?"

"Graham." Travis glanced at the name embroidered into the shirt. He had no idea who Duke Graham was. It was merely the name someone in the props department for TacOps had chosen.

The old man moved back up the road and turned into his driveway. Travis stood and walked up the driveway a short way, until he was sure the neighbor was out of sight. Then he pulled out his phone.

"What is it?" Gus answered halfway through the first ring.

"The next-door neighbor was over here nosing around. I'd hurry it up if I were you."

"We'll wrap it up as soon as we can, but we don't want to abort if we don't have to. We aren't likely to get another warrant."

"Just thought I'd give you a heads-up."

"Thanks." He disconnected, and Travis pocketed his phone and returned to the end of the driveway.

Five minutes later, his knees were beginning to ache from crouching in front of the utility box when a white Toyota sedan came roaring around the curve and swept into the driveway. Travis didn't have time to leap out of sight into the bushes or pull out his phone or weapon before the car screeched to a halt and the passenger window rolled down. Leah stared at him, but said nothing. She appeared stunned.

Her hair was longer than he remembered, and she was maybe a little thinner, but she was still as beautiful as ever. He hated the way his heart ached when her eyes met his. She had dumped him with no explanation and had never looked back. He had thought that betrayal had burned away all the love he had felt for her, but apparently there was enough feeling left that he could still hurt.

He stood and moved toward her. He had one job now, and that was to keep her away from the house until the team finished their work. "Hello, ma'am," he said, his voice flat, betraying nothing.

She gripped the edge of the window with both hands, her knuckles white. She wore red polish on her nails to match the scarlet of her sweater, but some of the polish was chipped. Unlike her. She was usually perfectly put together. "Who are you?" The driver—a burly man who wore a knit cap pulled low over his forehead—leaned across Leah to glare at Travis.

"There's a problem with the power," Travis said, still watching Leah out of the corner of his eye. "We should have it repaired shortly."

"I don't believe you."

Time seemed to speed up after that. The driver reached under his jacket. "Down, Leah!" Travis yelled as he drew his own weapon. She shoved open the passenger door and dropped to the ground as he and the driver exchanged fire. Travis dived for the cover of the electrical box as Leah rolled toward the ditch. The driver revved the car and veered off the driveway, crashing into the underbrush.

In the silence that followed, Travis studied the slumped figure of the driver and decided he had been wounded, or maybe killed. He needed to check on the man in a minute, but first he had to deal with Leah. She crawled to him. "Travis, what are you doing here?" she asked.

"Maybe I wanted to see you," he said. "Maybe I wanted to ask why you couldn't even bring yourself to say goodbye to my face."

Two bright spots of color bloomed on her pale cheeks, as if she were feverish. "I thought it would be easier if I left quietly."

"You left me a letter. A freaking Dear John letter, like some bad movie cliché." The diamond engagement ring he had given her only six weeks before had sat beside the letter, another bullet to his heart.

"I really don't think we should be talking about this." She glanced up the drive toward the wrecked car. "I have to go."

He moved in front of her. "I think it's past time we talked." This really wasn't the best place for this conversation, but he couldn't keep the words back. "I loved you. I thought you loved me. We were going to be married, and then one day I get home and all I've got left of you is a note on the kitchen counter." The note had read *I'm sorry, but I've changed my mind. Please don't come after me. This is for the best. Love, Leah.* The "love" had trailed off at the end, as if her hand had shaken as she'd written it.

She wouldn't look at him, staring instead at the ground. Her hair was coming undone from its ponytail, and she had a streak of dirt across her cheek. "Sometimes things aren't meant to be," she said.

"Are you married to Braeswood now? Or should I call him Ellison?"

She jerked her head toward him, her eyes wide. "No! Why would you think that?"

"The neighbor called you Mrs. Ellison."

"Oh, that. That's just..." But she didn't say what it was. He filled in the blank. Her cover story. The lies they told to hide their terrible purpose here.

"I get that you don't love me anymore," he said, letting that harsh truth fuel his anger. "But I don't understand this. Do you know what Duane Braeswood and his friend Eddie do? They're terrorists. They kill people. It's fine if you want to hate me, but do you hate your country, too?"

She bowed her head and closed her eyes. "I know what they do," she said softly. "And I don't expect you to understand."

"You're right, I don't understand." He leaned toward her, his face so close to hers he could smell her perfume. An image flashed in his mind of her naked, her body soft against his, his nose buried in the satiny skin of her throat, inhaling that floral, feminine scent.

He blinked to clear his head, and the blare of a horn yanked him back to the present. He looked past her, down the road, where the Escalade was barreling toward them. "I have to go," she said, and turned as if to run.

He snagged her arm and dragged her with him into the underbrush, seconds before the Escalade screamed into the drive.

Chapter Two

Travis had a glimpse of Duane Braeswood at the wheel, his face a mask of rage, as the SUV flew by.

He retreated farther into the underbrush. One arm wrapped around Leah, holding her to his chest, he used his free hand to pull out his phone. "Abort!" he shouted as soon as Gus answered. "Braeswood and Roland are here. And two other guys. I didn't get a look at them." They had been only dark figures in the backseat of the SUV.

Gunfire reverberated in the trees before he had the phone back in his pocket. "Let me go!" Leah pleaded, and struggled against him.

"You're under arrest." He pulled a flex-cuff from his back pocket and wrestled it over her wrists.

"No!" she wailed, but he cut off the cry by pulling out his handkerchief and stuffing it in her mouth. She glared at him, her brown eyes almost black with rage.

"Don't worry, it's clean," he said. "The last thing I need is you letting the others know where I am."

He debated binding her ankles also and leaving her out here in the woods, but if the fight moved in this direction, she might get caught in cross fire. Besides, he didn't trust her not to find a way to escape. Better to keep her with him.

He dragged her up the steep slope toward the house. The blasts of gunfire became almost constant as they neared the building, and when they reached the edge of the clearing his heart twisted at the sight of a khaki-clad figure slumped in the drive. He couldn't tell which member of the team had been hit, but knowing they had lost one of their own was enough to make him want to get back at these guys.

He checked his weapon. The Glock wasn't going to be of much use at this range. What he wouldn't give for a sighted rifle right now. He would sit here and pick the bad guys off as they exited the house.

He looked at Leah again. Tears glistened on her cheeks, and he had to harden himself against the pain in her eyes. "Killing a federal agent is punishable by life in prison," he said. "You can be convicted of felony murder even if you didn't fire the shot, simply by your association with these killers."

Something flickered in her eyes—regret? Fear? He once thought he knew her better than anyone, that he could always read what she was thinking. But that was obviously only one of the many things he had been wrong about when it came to her.

He turned away from her to study the house again. Several windows had been shot out. At one, long drapes fluttered in the breeze. The gunfire had ceased, but he thought he heard someone moving around in there. What was the best way for him to help the agents inside? Braeswood and his men would probably expect an attack from the front, but if he could get around back he might be able to reach his trapped fellow agents.

"Is there a back door?" he asked. "Another way inside?"

She nodded.

"How do I get to it?" He pulled the handkerchief out of her mouth so she could answer, but remained ready to stuff it back in if she started to yell.

"There's a path through the woods, on the side," she said softly. She nodded toward the west side of the house. "The door leads into the garage. There's a back door, too, but it leads from an enclosed patio. You can't get to it without being seen from the house."

"Right. Here we go then." He started to stuff the handkerchief back in.

"Don't," she said. "I won't say anything, I promise."

"Since when can I trust your promises?" He replaced the handkerchief in her mouth, ignoring the hurt that lanced him at her injured look.

He took her arm and led her around the house toward the back door, keeping out of sight of anyone inside. His phone vibrated and he answered it.

"Recon Three, this is Recon One. Where are you?" Blessing spoke in a whisper, but his voice carried clearly in the silence around them.

"Outside the house. West side."

"They've got us pinned down on the second floor. Looks like a rec room. Did you say there's four of them?"

He looked to Leah for confirmation. *Four?* he mouthed. She nodded. "That's right. Braeswood, Roland, and two others," he said.

"It's too high up to jump out of the window, though it may come to that," Blessing said.

Leah tugged on his arm. He shook her off, but she tugged harder, her expression almost frantic. "Hang on a minute," he said, and pressed the phone against his chest to mute it.

He jerked the gag from her mouth. "What is it?"

"If they're in the rec room, there's a dumbwaiter," she said. "In the interior wall, behind the panel with the dartboard. It goes down to the garage."

He pressed the phone to his ear again. "Check the panel behind the dartboard," he said. "There's a dumbwaiter that goes down to the garage."

"Won't they know to block it off?" Blessing asked.

Leah shook her head. Travis muted the phone again. "They know about it, but I don't think they'll think about it," she said. "I'm the only one who uses it, when I unload groceries."

"I've got the woman with me," Travis said. "She says she's the only one who ever uses the dumbwaiter—Braeswood and the others won't remember it."

"You don't think she's setting a trap for us?" Blessing asked.

"I don't think so." Maybe that was his old image of Leah, fooling him, but he had to trust his instincts now.

"Then we'll have to chance it." Blessing sounded older. Bone-weary. "If you can, station yourself to lay down cover fire."

"There's a side door in the garage that leads outside. I'll cover you there."

He and Leah repositioned to conceal themselves as near to the garage as he dared, taking cover first behind a propane tank, then behind a section of lattice fencing used to block trash cans from view. He half reclined, bracing his right hand on the fence. "Get down behind me," he ordered her.

"If you have another weapon, I can shoot it," she said, reminding him that he hadn't replaced her gag after his phone call with Blessing.

She knew he carried a small revolver in an ankle holster. She had certainly seen him remove it enough times when he had come home to his Adams Morgan townhome where she had spent many nights. "You may have played me for a fool before," he said. "But I'm not a big enough idiot to give a wanted felon a gun."

Anger flashed in her eyes and she opened her mouth, then apparently thought better of whatever she had been about to say and remained silent. "Get down," he ordered.

She did as he asked, reclining in the dirt behind him. The warmth of her body seeped into him, along with an awareness of the jut of her hip bone and the curve of her breast. He forced his attention back on the door. "Come on," he muttered. "Let's get this show on the road."

Long minutes passed in silence so intense he imagined he could hear the hum from the power line that connected the house with the transformer at the road. He pictured the team assembling in the garage, arriving one or two at a time via the dumbwaiter designed to carry parcels up from the garage to the living quarters. They would wait until everyone was in place before they made their exit.

"Why haven't they come out yet?" Leah whispered, when he judged twenty minutes had passed. Too long.

Braeswood and company would be wondering why things in the rec room were so quiet.

"I don't know," he said.

Just then, the door from the garage eased open. Blessing's face, dark and glistening with sweat, peered out. Then the door burst all the way open and men poured out.

The first bullets thudded into the dirt around them, followed by the sickening sound of ammunition striking flesh. Heart racing, Travis scanned the area and located the source of the shots. Cursing, he fired off half a dozen quick rounds at the man stationed behind the tripod-mounted machine gun on the deck overlooking the garage. The felons must have figured out what was going on in the rec room and stationed themselves to ambush the agents as they emerged from the garage. Travis was too far away to get a good shot at them. All he succeeded in doing was attracting the shooter's attention.

"Go!" Travis shouted, and pushed Leah ahead of him. "Run!" She started running and he took off after her. They fled the hail of bullets that bit into the trees around them and plowed the leaf litter. When she stumbled, he pulled her up and dragged her farther into the woods, running blindly, praying they wouldn't be struck by the bullets that continued to rain around them.

He didn't see the edge of the bluff until it was too late. One moment his booted foot struck dirt, the next the ground fell away beneath him. The last sound he remembered was Leah's anguished scream, echoing over and over as they fell.

Chapter Three

Leah had thought she was ready for death. In the past six months there had been times she had prayed to die. But falling off that cliff, gunfire echoing around her, the ground rushing up to meet her, she wanted only to live. Her hands bound behind her by the cuffs, she had only Travis's strong arms to save her as he wrapped himself around her. She buried her face against his chest and prayed wordlessly, eyes closed against the fate that awaited.

They hit the ground hard. Her head struck the dirt and she rolled, a sharp ache in her shoulder. Stunned, she lay slumped against a tree trunk, aware of distant shouts overhead and the sound of the rushing creek below.

Travis! Frantic, she struggled to sit and looked around. He lay ten feet down the slope, his big body still, blood trickling from a cut on his forehead. Crawling, half sliding on the steep grade, she made her way to him. "Travis!" she called. She nudged him with the toe of her shoe. "Travis, wake up."

The shouts overhead grew louder. She looked up toward the house, but trees blocked her view. Had Duane and the others seen them fall? Would they come down here to look for them? She leaned down, her face close to his, so that she could smell the clean scent of his soap, mingled with the burned cordite from the weapon he had fired. "Travis, you have to wake up," she pleaded. "We have to get out of here before they find us." Duane would waste no time killing them, as she had seen him kill others before. She nudged him with her knee. "Travis, please!"

He groaned and rolled away from her, clutching his injured head.

She scooted after him. "We have to get out of here." She kept her voice low, fearful Duane and the others might hear. The shouts had died down, but maybe they were only saving their breath for the climb down.

He groaned again, but shoved himself into a sitting position and studied her, his gaze unfocused. "Leah? What happened?"

"Duane was shooting at us and we went over the cliff." She glanced up the slope again, expecting to see Duane or one of his thugs barreling toward them. "We have to get out of here before they come after us. Please, untie me." She half turned and angled her cuffed hands toward him. Her shoulder ached with every movement, but she couldn't worry about that now.

He frowned at her, his vision clearing. "I remember now," he muttered. Some of the hardness had returned to his gaze, and she knew he was recalling not just what had happened moments before, but the ugly history between them.

"Please cut me loose," she said. "I can't move in this rough terrain with my arms behind my back like this. I promise I won't try to run away." He was her best hope of finally escaping from Duane Braeswood and his ruthless gang.

Travis hesitated, then shifted to pull a multi-tool from a pouch on his belt and cut the flex-cuff. She cried out in relief, then pain, as she brought her arms in front of her.

"You're hurt." He was on his knees in front of her, concern breaking through the coldness in his expression. "Were you hit, or did it happen in the fall?"

"I landed on my shoulder." She rubbed the aching joint. "I'm just a little banged up. But you took a nasty blow to the head. You're still bleeding."

She reached toward the gash on his forehead. He shied away from her touch. "I'm okay," He shoved to his feet, stumbling a little as he fought for balance. "Where are we?"

"Above the creek that runs below the house."

"Which direction is the road?" he asked.

"That way, I think." She pointed to their left.

"What's in the other directions?" he asked.

She tried to visualize the area, but in the two weeks since they had relocated here, she had spent most of her time in the house, or running errands in Durango. Duane never left her alone, and he would have laughed in her face if she had expressed a desire to hike in the woods behind the house, though she had grown up hiking and camping very near here. "I'm not sure. It's pretty rugged country. Duane had a map in his office of the Weminuche Wilderness area, so I think we're very near there."

"So no houses or roads?"

She shook her head. "Maybe some hiking trails, but nothing else. Wilderness is, well, wild. Undeveloped."

A gust of wind stirred the aspens, and a tree branch popped, making her jump. "We have to get out of here before they come after us," she said.

"Why wouldn't they be more interested in going after the rest of the team?" he asked, even as he ejected the magazine from his gun and shoved in a fresh one. "They don't even know who I am."

"They'll have figured out I'm with you." She stood and brushed dry leaves from her jeans. "Duane won't let me get away."

"Because you mean so much to him." No missing the bitterness behind those words.

"Because I know a lot about the things he's done and I can testify against him." And because he never let anyone cross him without making sure they paid for their betrayal. She started to move past him, but he snagged her arm.

"We're not leaving," Travis said. "We're going back up there."

She stared at him. "We can't go back. They'll kill us."

"I'm not leaving until I'm sure the rest of the team is all right." He holstered his weapon again and started up the slope, tugging her with him.

She gazed longingly down the slope toward the creek. "Try to run and I'll shoot you," he said.

The hardness of the words sent a chill through her. She could scarcely believe this was the same man who had once treated her with such tenderness. She couldn't blame him for hating her, though he would never understand how much she had suffered, too.

They scrambled up the slope, on their hands and knees at times. As they neared the top, he angled off to the side, and she realized he intended to approach the house obliquely. If they were very lucky, Duane or one of his men wouldn't be waiting for them at the top.

When they were almost to the top, he looked back at her. "Stay down," he said. "Don't come up until I tell you."

She wished she had a weapon, to defend herself and to help defend him. But he would never believe that was all she intended. "Be careful," she called after him as he completed the climb to the top, but he gave no indication that he had heard her.

She pressed her body to the ground, willing herself to be invisible and trying to hear what was happening above her. But the only sounds were the rustling of aspen leaves, the flutter of birds in the branches and the constant rush of the creek. A chill from the cold ground seeped into her, making her shiver. She had dressed casually for her shopping trip in town, in jeans and hiking boots and a light sweater, an outfit suitable for hitting the grocery store or the mall, but not for tramping around outdoors, where the fall air held a definite bite.

She wished she had warned Travis about the cameras Duane had positioned all around the house, so that when he was inside he could see anyone who approached from any angle. She should have told him about the two guns Duane carried at all times, and about the razor-sharp knife in his boot. She had seen him cut a man's throat with that knife once, an image that still haunted her nightmares.

Falling rocks and dirt alerted her to someone's approach. Relief surged through her when she recognized Travis returning. He scrambled down toward her, moving quickly. "The others are gone," he said. "Come on. We've got to get to the road and meet them."

She hurried to follow him, slipping in the loose dirt and leaf mold, scraping her hands on rocks. Two-thirds of the way to the creek, he stopped against a tree, both hands searching in his pockets. "I can't find my phone," he said.

"Maybe you lost it in the fall." She leaned against the same tree, a smooth-barked aspen, and tried to catch her breath.

He looked around, then began making his way across the slope, in the general direction of their original landing place. "Help me look," he said. "I've got to call the team and let them know to wait for us."

She followed him, scanning the ground around them, then dropping to her knees to feel about in the dried leaves and loose rocks. "It's not here," she said.

"It has to be here," He glared at the ground, as if the force of his anger could summon the phone. He turned to her. "Give me yours, then."

"I don't have a phone,"

"Don't lie to me. You always have your phone with you."

The woman he had known had always carried her phone with her, but she was a different person now. "Duane didn't allow me to have a phone," she said.

His brow furrowed, as if he hadn't understood her words, but before he could reply, a shout disturbed the woodland peace. "They're down here!" a man yelled, and a bullet sent splinters flying from a tree beside her head.

Travis launched himself at her, pushing her aside and rolling with her, down the slope toward the creek.

He managed to stop them before they hit the water, then pulled her upright and began running along the creek bank. “Is the road this way?” he asked.

“I think so.” She had a dim memory of a bridge over the creek a mile or so from the house.

Crashing noises and falling rock telegraphed their pursuer’s approach. Travis took cover behind a broad-trunked juniper and drew his weapon, but after a moment he lowered the gun. “I can’t get a clear shot and there’s no sense letting them know for sure where we are. Come on.” He tugged her after him once more.

“How do you know your friends will be waiting for us?” she asked as she struggled to keep up with him.

“If they aren’t, we can flag down someone else to help,” he said.

No sense pointing out that the road leading into the private neighborhood of mostly vacation homes didn’t receive a lot of traffic, especially on a fall weekday. If they could avoid Duane and his men, the road did seem the best route for escape. Maybe the only route.

She didn’t know how long they ran, climbing over rocks and skirting thick groves of aspens and scrub oak. They splashed through the icy water of the creek, soaking her shoes and her jeans to the knees, and crawled up the muddy creek bank. Her shoulder ached with every movement and she panted from the exertion, but still the road eluded them. She needed to stop and rest, but they couldn’t afford to give their pursuers any opportunity to overtake them.

“There’s the bridge, up ahead,” Travis said, and she wanted to weep with relief.

“Are your friends waiting for us?” she asked.

“I can’t see yet.” He stopped, bent over with his

hands on his knees, panting. Mud streaked his face and arms, and his pants, like hers, were wet almost to the knees. Blood matted his hair and had dried on his face, yet he was still the handsomest man she had ever known. She had been attracted to the tall, broad-shouldered Texan from the moment they met, in the halls of the San Antonio high school where she was a new student. Though they had gone their separate ways in college, they had stayed in touch, and when they both ended up living and working in Washington, DC, they had begun dating. She had been sure they had been on their way to a happily-ever-after, but Duane's arrival in her life had changed all that.

"I'm going up to take a look," Travis said, straightening. "When I give you the signal, come on up. And don't try anything. I'll have my gun on you."

He had added that last warning to deliberately hurt her, she was sure. "I told you, I won't try to run away," she said.

"Yeah, well, you've lied to me before."

He began climbing the bank. When he was halfway up, the roar of a powerful engine and the crunch of tires on gravel announced a vehicle's arrival. It stopped on the bridge and car doors slammed. Travis moved faster, probably eager to greet his friends.

She saw the danger before he did, the familiar pale face with the hawk nose and the thinning dark hair combed over, dark eyes peering out from beneath heavy brows. Duane didn't see her, focused instead on the man scaling the bank. Fear strangling her, she watched as he pulled a gun from inside his coat and took aim.

"Travis, run!" The scream ripped from her throat, and she lunged toward him as the blast of the gun shattered the woodland stillness.

Chapter Four

Leah's scream propelled Travis to one side, so that the bullet tore through his shirt, grazing his ribs. Pain momentarily blinded him as he rolled toward the creek, landing with a splash in the icy water. More shots hit the water around him until he reached the shelter of the bridge. Plastered against the concrete piling, he waited for more gunfire or for the shooter to climb down after him.

The expected hail of bullets came, but this time the shots weren't intended for him. The shooter had turned his attention to Leah, who huddled behind the thick-trunked juniper as the gunfire tore at the bark. The sight of her trapped that way drove Travis to act on raw instinct. He pushed himself away from the bridge piling, deliberately exposing himself to the shooter above. "Over here!" he shouted, and fired three shots in rapid succession.

When the shooter turned his attention to Travis, Leah ran. But not, as he had hoped, away from danger, but toward it. She catapulted toward him, slamming into him and driving him farther under the bridge. He wrapped his free arm around her and sheltered her between his body and the bridge piling. "Why didn't you leave when you had the chance?" he muttered.

"I told you I wouldn't leave." She touched his torn shirt. "You're hit. You're bleeding."

He pushed her hand away. "Nothing serious." Though he could feel blood seeping from the wound. "How many of them are there?" he asked.

"It depends if Duane left someone back at the house," she said. "There are four altogether—Duane, Eddie and two who just arrived yesterday, Buck and Sam. I never heard their last names. But I don't think Duane would have wanted to leave the house unguarded, so he probably left Sam there."

"Why Sam?"

"I overheard Eddie teasing him about not being a good shot. His specialty is technology." She glanced over her shoulder. "They'll come down the bank in a minute," she said.

"I'll kill them when they do." He readied the gun to fire.

"They'll wait until you run out of ammunition. They won't give up."

A rock tumbled down from the road, gathering momentum as it rolled, landing with a splash in the water. "They're coming down," she said, and buried her face against his chest.

He inhaled deeply, making himself go still. He had to shove aside the fear and call on all his strength. He had no control over what Duane and his thugs did, but he was in charge of his own actions. He raised the Glock and lined up the sights on where he thought the shooter would show himself, then took another breath and let it out slowly.

The echo of the gunshot against the concrete of the bridge made his ears ring, but the sight of the shooter staggering backward let him know he had done some damage. He had no time to bask in this victory, as a second man followed the first, this one armed with a shotgun capable of gutting them both with one shot. Travis retreated farther behind the bridge support, pulling Leah with him.

"We're going to have to run for it," he whispered, his mouth so close he was almost kissing her ear.

She stiffened. "That's crazy."

"Crazy enough to work. And it's our only chance." Already, he could hear someone moving down the other side of the bridge. "Climb onto my back and hang on tight," he said. "If I go down, keep running on your own, but until then, don't let go."

"I'll slow you down," she said. "Leave me here. I'm the one they want, anyway."

He was no longer certain of her relationship to Duane, but he wasn't going to let her go back to that killer. "You're still my prisoner," he said. "I'm not going to give you up to him." He slipped the revolver from the ankle holster, then turned his back to her. "Climb on. Keep your head down."

She jumped onto his back, her arms around his neck, her legs wrapped around his waist. The weight was awkward, but not impossible. "When I give the word, scream as loud as you can," he said.

"Why?"

"Just do it. Scream as if you just saw the biggest, nastiest-looking spider you can imagine." She had always been terrified of spiders.

"All right."

The revolver in one hand, the Glock in the other, he watched the bank to his left. When a second shooter dropped into position there, Travis said, "Now!" and charged forward.

The keening wail she let loose echoed beneath the bridge, a high, sharp note that pierced his ears, but as he had hoped, the sound startled the two shooters as well. They hesitated a fraction of a second, long enough for Travis to gain the advantage. He charged toward the downstream shooter, both guns blazing. The man fell back. At the same time, the upstream man couldn't risk firing, for fear of hitting his boss.

He stuck to the bank at the edge of the water, feet sinking deep in the gravel and mud, staggering as if fighting his way through molasses. Leah had fallen silent, her face pressed against his neck, her fingers digging into his shoulder. He turned to fire at the men, then pulled at her legs. "Can you run?" he asked.

"Yes." She nodded, her hair falling forward to obscure her face.

"Then we're going to run, as fast and as far as we can."

She was swifter than he would have expected, keeping pace with him as they zigzagged through the trees. He led the way up a slope away from the creek, deeper into the area she had identified as wilderness. The shooters had run after them, but they were slower and clumsier, stopping from time to time to fire in Travis and Leah's general direction. After what could have been a half an hour or only ten minutes, the sounds of the gunfire and their pursuers' shouted curses faded away.

Travis risked stopping near a downed pine tree.

Leah collapsed onto the fallen trunk, holding her side and gasping for breath. Several moments passed before either of them spoke. "I've never been so terrified in my life," she said.

He holstered his weapon and sank down beside her. "I think we've lost them for now."

She shook her head. "Maybe. But they'll be back. They'll hunt us down."

"How can you be so sure?" She talked as if she knew these men so well, but how could that be, when she had only been with them a few months? He had known her for years and would have sworn he knew everything about her, and yet he had never seen her betrayal coming.

"They're ruthless," she said. "When Duane decides he wants something, he'll stop at nothing to get it. He'll steal, kill and use people every way you can imagine. He's an expert at it." The grief that transformed her face as she spoke made him want to pull her to him, to comfort her. But he held back.

Instead, he looked around them, at the trees crowded so close together there was scarcely room to walk. The sky showed only in scattered puzzle pieces of pale blue between the treetops. He thought the creek was somewhere to their right, but he couldn't be sure, having lost his bearings in their frantic flight. "Do you have any idea where we are?" he asked.

She shook her head. "I've never had much of a sense of direction, remember?"

He almost smiled, remembering. Her propensity for getting turned around and lost had been one of their private jokes. At the entrance to a mall department store she would address him with mock seriousness.

"I'm going in, but if I don't come out in an hour, you'll have to come in after me."

That particular trait of hers wasn't so funny right now. "Let's hope Duane and his gang don't know where we are, either." He stood and offered her his hand. "It's going to be dark in a few hours. We need to find a safe place to spend the night, but before that, we need to get back to the creek. Without water, we won't make it out here very long."

"Then what?" she asked.

"Then we have to find our way out of here, back to civilization and a phone." And they had to do it while avoiding the men who were out to kill them.

WITH NO WATCH or phone to consult for the time, Leah had no idea how long it took them to locate the creek. But by the time they stumbled and slid down the bank to the narrow stream, she was exhausted and thirsty enough that she was tempted to simply stretch out in the icy water and let it wash into her mouth.

But common sense—or maybe simply an overwhelming desire to stay strong enough to get out of here alive—stopped her. She grabbed hold of Travis's arm to stop him as he knelt at the water's edge. "We have to boil the water before we drink it," she said.

Hair tousled, face streaked with mud and blood, he looked like a man who had survived a street brawl. "How are we supposed to do that? And why?" He looked around. "I don't see any factories or even houses around here."

"The water is full of giardia—a little bug that will make you very, very sick. I had it once at summer camp and I know I never want to be that ill again. If we boil the water or treat it somehow, it will kill the parasite."

He sat back on his heels and scanned the bank around them. "There's plenty of fuel. I don't suppose you've taken up smoking since we last met?"

"No." She scanned the area, then looked back at him. "What kind of supplies do you have on you, besides your gun and ammunition and that multi-tool you used to cut off my flex-cuff?"

He hesitated, then emptied his pockets onto the ground between them—a wallet with his ID, a few credit cards and some cash; badge; the multi-tool; and the Glock and a magazine with ten bullets, plus an empty magazine. The revolver and half a dozen bullets for it. A Mini Maglite, a small notebook and the binoculars. Her mood lifted when she spotted the Maglite. "We can use this," she said. "Now all we need is something to boil the water in. Look around for a tin can."

"We're in the wilderness," he reminded her, as he refilled his pockets.

"Trash washes downstream from other places," she said. "And it lasts a long time in this dry climate." Already, she was headed upstream, studying the bank.

Fifteen minutes later, she had almost given up when she spotted the soda can wedged in the roots of a wild plum growing along the banks. She crawled down and retrieved the can, then stopped to pick the few withered and spotted fruits left in the almost-leafless branches. She hurried with her finds downstream, where Travis was studying a deep pool. "There's fish in here, if I could figure out how to catch them," he said.

"Good idea." She held up the soda can. "If you cut

the top off of this with your multi-tool, we can use it to heat water."

"Did you find matches, too?" he asked, taking the can.

She grinned. "I still remember a few lessons from playing around in the woods as a kid," she said.

While he cut the top from the soda can and straightened out the dents, she gathered dry pine needles and twigs. Atop these, she added shredded paper from his notebook. Then she pulled a pack of gum from her pocket. "What are you going to do with that?" he asked.

"You'll see." She unwrapped the gum and offered him the stick. He took it and popped it into his mouth, then she carefully tore the wrapper in half lengthwise, then pinched off bits out of the middle until only a thin sliver of paper-backed foil connected the two wider halves. "Now I need the battery from the Maglite," she said.

He unscrewed the bottom from the Maglite and shook out the battery. "I see where you're going with this, I think," he said. "You're going to make a spark."

"You got it." Gingerly, she pressed one end of the gum wrapper, foil side down, against the negative end of the battery. "This is the tricky part," she said. "I don't want to get burned." Holding her breath, she touched the other end of the foil to the positive end of the battery. Immediately the center of the foil began to brown and char, then burst into flame. She dropped the burning wrapper onto the tinder she had prepared, and it flared also. As the twigs caught, she began feeding larger pieces of wood onto it.

"Where did you learn that?" Travis asked.

"My best friend's older brother showed us when we were kids. He accidentally set the woods behind his house on fire doing that one time, but mostly we just thought it was a neat way to start campfires. I haven't thought of it in years." She looked around. "I think we're ready for the water now."

"I'll get it." He returned a few minutes later, carrying the first can, along with a second. "I found this," he said. "We can heat twice as much water."

He nestled the water-filled cans among the flames. The metal blackened and the water began to steam. Several minutes later, it was boiling. "It needs to boil ten minutes," she said. "We'll have to guess how long that is." She took one of the dried plums from her pockets. "I found these. If we cut off the bad spots, they should be okay to eat."

"I have to have water before I can eat anything," he said. "But we'll try them later. I had no idea you were so resourceful in the wilderness."

"I told you my family spent a lot of time camping when I was a kid. We lived not that far from here before we moved to Texas."

"Where you acted like just another music-listening, mall-going city kid," he said.

"I was a teenager. I wanted to fit in." Most of all, she had wanted to impress him—and he had seemed so sophisticated and cool. Or at least, as sophisticated and cool as a sixteen-year-old could be. Back then, she wouldn't have admitted to knowing how to start a campfire or forage for wild food for anything.

"Did Braeswood know you were from around here?"

She focused on the boiling water, though she could feel his gaze burning into her. No matter how she tried to explain her relationship with Duane to Travis, he would never believe her. He had made up his mind about her the day she betrayed him. She didn't blame him for his anger, but she wasn't going to waste her breath defending herself. "He knew," she said. She had been shocked to discover how much Duane already knew about her when they met. But that was how he worked. He mined information the way some men mine gold or diamonds, and then he used that information to buy what he wanted.

Travis shifted and winced. Guilt rushed over her. "I forgot all about your wound," she said. "How is it?"

"It's no big deal." He started to turn away, but she leaned over to touch his wrist.

"Let me look," she said. "Now that we have water, I can at least clean it up."

He hesitated, then lifted his shirt to show an angry red graze along the side of his ribs. Now it was her turn to wince. "That must hurt," she said.

"I've felt better."

She glanced back at the water. "Where's that handkerchief you were using to gag me?" she asked.

He pulled it from the pocket of the cargo pants.

Carefully, she dipped one corner of the cloth into the boiling water, took it out and let it cool slightly, then began sponging at the wound. "It doesn't look too deep," she said. She tried not to apply too much pressure, but she felt him tense when she hit a sensitive spot. As she cleared away the blood and dirt, she became aware of the smooth, taut skin beneath her hand. He had the muscular abs and chest of a man who worked out—abs and chest she had fond memories of feeling against her own naked body.

"I think it's clean enough now," he said, pulling away and lowering the shirt with a suddenness that made her wonder if he had read her thoughts.

She handed him the handkerchief. "You can clean that in the creek," she said. "The water has probably boiled enough. If we put it in the creek, it will cool down faster." She pulled the sleeves of her sweater down over her hands, intending to use them to protect her hands from the hot metal.

"I'll get that," he said, and lifted first one can, then the other, off the fire with the pliers from his multi-tool.

She followed him to the creek, where they waited while the water steamed in the cans. "As soon as we drink these, we should heat more," she said. "And try to find some food."

"I'm not comfortable spending the night by the creek," he said. "If Braeswood and his men are hunting for us, they'll know we have to have water. How well does he know the area?"

"He knows it pretty well." She closed her eyes, picturing the maps of the Weminuche Wilderness he had taped to the walls of the room he used as his office. When she opened them, she found herself looking right into Travis's blue eyes. That intense gaze—and the mistrust she saw there—made her feel weighted down and more exhausted than ever. "He had maps of the area," she said. "He planned to escape through the wilderness if the Feds trapped him at the house."

"Why did he come back when he did?" Travis asked. "We should have had plenty of time to search the place and get out before any of you returned from Durango."

"The neighbor, Mr. Samuelson, called Duane. He said some utility workers were up at the house, but they looked suspicious. Duane had made a point of making friends with the old man. He asked him to report if he saw any strangers around the house. He used the excuse that he had a lot of valuables that burglars would want. After he got off the phone with Samuelson, Duane called my driver, Preston Wylie, and told him to take me back to the house and he would be right behind me." If she and Wylie had reached the house first, she had considered asking the strangers, whoever they were, to take her with them. But she dismissed the idea almost as soon as it came to her. She knew Wylie had orders to kill her if she tried to get away. Duane almost never left her unguarded, but the few times he had risked it, he had made it very clear that he would hunt her down and kill her if she ever left him. He had the men and resources at his disposal to find her, probably before she had gotten out of the state. She had resigned herself to being trapped with him forever.

Then Travis, of all people, had pulled her from that car and risked his life to help her get away. Maybe he only saw it as protecting a prisoner, but the result was the same. No matter if he hated her, she would always be grateful to him for taking her away from an impossible situation.

"What can you remember about that escape route Braeswood had planned?" Travis asked. "Are there back roads or trails he intended to follow? A hideout where he thought he could hole up for a while?"

She shook her head. "I don't remember anything. I only saw the map a few times, and I didn't pay much attention to it then. He certainly didn't share his plans with me." If the time had come to flee the house, he would have assigned a guard to drag her along with them, one more piece of baggage he considered necessary, at least for the moment.

"I guess he didn't like to mix his personal relationship with his professional ones," Travis said.

"I think the water is cool enough to drink now." She ignored the gibe and plucked one of the cans from the stream and drained it. Even warm, it tasted so good going down. As soon as she had drained it, she refilled it and carried it back up to the fire. "I'm going to look for something to eat besides those plums," she said.

"I'll come with you." He added his refilled can to the fire and followed her.

"I told you, you don't have to worry about me running away," she said.

"Right now I'm more worried about you getting lost."

"I'll be okay, as long as I follow the creek."

He fell into step behind her. "What are we looking for?" he asked.

"Berries, cattails, more plum trees. There are edible mushrooms, but I don't know enough about them to risk it."

"If I had line and a hook, I could try fishing."

"We could try to make a string from grass or vines," she said. "And you could try my earring hooks."

"Maybe I'll give it a go later, after we've found a safe place to camp."

She paused beside a small shrub and began pulling off the bright red fruit. "What are those?" he asked.

"Rose hips." She bit into one and made a face.

"They're supposed to be full of vitamin C. They taste pretty sour, but they're not the worst thing I ever ate."

He took one, bit into it, then spit it out. "I don't want to know the worst thing you ever ate."

In the end, she collected two more plums, a handful of rose hips and some wild onions. "I sure hope you can catch a fish," she said. "This isn't going to get us very far."

"I'm determined to find a way out of here long before we have to worry about starving," he said. "Let's go back and get the water, then find a place to stay tonight. Then we need to figure out a route away from here."

They headed back downstream. She smelled the smoke from their little fire long before they reached it. Not good, if Duane was tracking them. She hurried to retrieve the cans of boiling water and set them aside to cool. "We'll need to scatter these ashes and cover them with dirt, then leaves, to hide the fact that we were here," she said.

"I'll get a branch or something to dig with," Travis said, and moved off into the woods.

For the first time since they had stopped by the creek, Leah began to feel uneasy. They had remained in one place too long. It wouldn't be that difficult for Duane to follow the creek in the direction he knew they had fled. Another man might have left them to die in the wilderness, but Duane didn't take those kinds of chances. He was successful because he believed in controlling all variables. She was a variable he was most determined to control.

Footsteps behind her alerted her to Travis's return. "The water's cool enough to drink now," she said, gingerly picking up the still-warm can. "Let's empty them and take them with us."

Strong hands grabbed her roughly from behind. The can of water slipped from her grasp as she felt a sharp sting, and then the pressure of a razor-sharp blade held to her throat. Duane's gravelly voice whispered in her ear, "Where's your friend the FBI agent?"

Chapter Five

Travis fought his way through a tangle of vines and was reaching for a stout stick that might serve as a shovel when a strangled squeak made him freeze. It might have been the distress cry of a mouse or a bird, it was so faint, but instinct told him the noise came from Leah, and she was in trouble.

Carrying the stick like a club, he moved as swiftly and silently as he could back toward the campfire. His first view of the area was of Braeswood holding Leah, but this wasn't a loving embrace. Rage momentarily blinded him at the sight of the knife at her throat.

"I…I don't know," she stammered, in answer to something Braeswood said. "He was angry with me. He left."

"Liar!" Blood ran in a thin line down the pale column of her neck. Travis had to grab hold of a tree trunk to keep from lunging forward. Setting the stick carefully aside, he drew the Glock from the holster. All he needed was one clear shot.

"No sign of him, boss." One of the other men—probably Buck—joined Braeswood and Leah beside the smoldering fire.

"Where's Eddie?" Braeswood asked.

Buck made a face. “He’ll be along in a minute. He’s out of shape.”

Duane unsnapped a radio from his belt. “Bobcat Two, do you read me?”

“I’m here, boss.”

“Any sign of those Feds?”

“Negative.”

“You got our location on GPS?”

“Yes, sir.”

“Meet us at the pickup point in two hours with the rest of the team. We should be finished here by then.”

“I’ll be there.”

Braeswood repocketed the radio. “By the time the Feds get back to the house, there won’t be anything left for them to find. And we’ll have taken care of Leah’s friend.”

“Maybe he really did leave her,” Buck said.

“He was here.” Braeswood nodded to the two cans of water nestled in the coals. “He probably went to get more wood or something.”

“He’s wounded,” Leah said. “Why waste your time with him? He’s just another dumb Fed. If you leave now, you’ll be out of the country before anyone even knows.”

“Shut up.” Braeswood shook her. “Don’t think I won’t kill you right now if you don’t stop annoying me.”

“Maybe I’d rather die than spend any more time with you.”

The crack of his palm striking her face echoed through the trees. Her head snapped back and she cried out again. Travis braced against a tree trunk and sighted along the barrel of the Glock, but Braeswood was still too close to her. Travis needed a plan for dealing with the second thug, too. And the third one who might arrive soon.

Leah moaned and slumped in Braeswood's arms, body limp, eyes closed. The sudden weight of her made him stagger back. He nudged her shoulder with the butt of his gun. "Wake up. I didn't hit you that hard."

A noise to their left, like a large animal stumbling through the underbrush, drew their attention. "That's probably Eddie," Buck said.

It probably was, Travis thought. But none of them could see him yet, so he saw his chance. "Luke!" He shouted the name of his fellow team member. "Over here!"

The others froze, long enough for Travis to get off a good shot at Buck, who staggered, then dropped to his knees and toppled over, blood spreading from the bullet hole in his chest. Travis turned his attention to Braeswood, who was struggling with Leah. She had come out of her stupor, which Travis suspected had been faked, and had taken advantage of the distraction to pull away from Braeswood. He still had hold of her arm, but he had dropped the knife, and she kicked and scratched at him, making it impossible for him to draw his gun.

"Braeswood, let her go." Travis stepped from the edge of the woods, his Glock leveled at the terrorist. Braeswood released Leah and went for his own weapon. She fled into the trees to their right.

Travis's first shot missed, as Braeswood dived behind a tree. He returned fire, bullets biting into the trees around Travis, forcing him to take cover also. A few seconds later, a second round of shots narrowly missed him. Eddie had arrived and was firing from behind a fallen pine.

Travis flattened himself in a dip in the ground and debated his next move. He had maybe half a dozen bullets left for the Glock, and a few for the revolver. Not enough to outlast these two. And Leah was out there somewhere, running. If he made a mistake and ended up getting killed, she would be alone, with Braeswood and his men after her.

Stealthily, he began crawling backward through the underbrush. When he judged he was out of sight of Braeswood and Eddie, he stood and ran, choosing a course he hoped would intersect the one Leah had taken.

He heard her long before he saw her, crashing through the woods like an animal fleeing in panic. He increased his own pace and waited until he spotted the bright red of her sweater before he called out. "Leah! It's me, Travis. Wait up!"

She darted behind a tree, then peered out cautiously at him. Tears streaked her face, and her lip was swollen where Braeswood had hit her. When Travis reached her, he pulled her close, crushing her to him. Seeing Braeswood strike her had destroyed his determination to keep some physical distance between them. "Are you all right?" he asked.

She nodded, her face pressed against his shoulder. The subtle floral scent of her perfume tickled his senses, stirring emotions he wasn't ready to examine too closely. "I'm okay," she said, out of breath. "Scared. A little shaken. But okay. What about you?"

The concern in her eyes when she lifted her head to look at him made him tighten his hold on her. "I'm okay." Though the memory of her with that knife to her throat would haunt him for a long time to come.

She jerked in his arms as a crack, like a stick snapping underfoot, sounded in the distance. "They're coming after us," she said, panic widening her eyes. "I told you, he won't give up."

"We've got to keep moving." He took her hand and led the way, moving as fast as they could in the dense forest, following animal trails and the paths of old fires, uncertain of the direction they were traveling. Was it true that people who were lost in the woods tended to walk in circles? Did that mean they could end up accidentally stumbling into Braeswood and the others?

Leah tripped on a tree root and went flying, landing on her hands and knees in the dirt. "I can't keep doing this," she said as Travis helped her up. "I'm too exhausted."

Before long, he would be too worn out to go much farther, as well. His side where he had been shot and his head where he had fallen earlier both throbbed, and he had noticed Leah wincing every time she moved her shoulder. He had been betting they could outlast Braeswood and his men, but maybe that had been foolish thinking. The hatred or greed or whatever force that motivated the terrorist was a powerful driver. "We'll have to find a place to hide," he said.

She nodded and closed her eyes, struggling to catch her breath.

He scanned the ground around them and spotted a dead pine tree, uprooted in some past storm. The roots stretched into the air above the hole where they had once been planted. "Over here," he said, and led her to the hole. It was large enough to accommodate two people. He helped Leah down into the depression, then dragged a tangle of branches and vines over it. After scattering leaves to hide their footsteps, he slipped into the hole behind her and tugged the last branch into place.

"Do you really think they won't see us?" she asked.

"We'll see them first." He grasped the Glock and peered out of their makeshift shelter. If Braeswood or one of his men did try to attack them here, Travis would have the first chance to get off a good shot.

Minutes passed, their breathing growing more regular and even. Then the unmistakable sound of footsteps on the forest floor grew louder. Leah clutched at him, but said nothing. Seconds later, Eddie Roland appeared, followed closely by Braeswood. Both men were armed—Braeswood with his pistol, while Eddie had traded his handgun for a semiautomatic rifle. The two men moved deliberately, studying the ground around them.

"I know they came this way," Braeswood said. "I saw their tracks."

"It's hard to follow anything in this heavy underbrush," Roland said. "We need a dog. They can track anything."

"We don't have a dog, idiot," Braeswood said. "They can't have gotten far. The only place Leah ever walked was on a treadmill."

At the mention of her name, she pressed her face more firmly against Travis's chest. Her silken hair tickled his chin, the sensation at once foreign and achingly familiar. In the silence while the two men above them searched, he became aware of her heartbeat, strong and rapid against his own.

After a while, he couldn't hear their two pursuers anymore. "I think they've moved on," he whispered.

"We should wait in case they come back," she said.

"We will." He settled more comfortably into the bottom of the hole, though he kept his eyes trained on the opening above them, and his ears attuned for any sound of approach. "Try to get some rest," he said softly. "I'll keep watch."

"I'll watch with you," she said, but within moments he felt the tension drain from her body and her breathing grow more even. The physical and emotional stress of the last few hours had taken their toll.

Determined to stay awake, he turned his mind to analyzing the day's events. He had arrived at the log home where Braeswood and his team were hiding with a clear idea of his mission. His job was to capture and arrest a group of terrorists. One of those terrorists happened to be his ex-fiancée, but that didn't make her less guilty of the horrible crimes the group was responsible for.

Now, after a few hours with Leah, he was less sure of the latter. Seeing how afraid she was of Braeswood, and how cruelly he treated her, Travis was beginning to doubt she had gone with the man willingly. He had believed she left him because she had fallen in love with someone else — what else could "changed my mind" have meant? Later, when he had learned she was living with Braeswood, he was shocked and angered that the woman he had loved and trusted had left him for a murderer.

But he had sensed no love between Leah and the

terrorist leader when he saw them together now, only fear. Braeswood had clearly been intent on killing her once he used her to lure in Travis.

So why had she left Travis for a man who only seemed to want to harm her? Before this ordeal was over, he intended to know the answer to that question.

An hour or more had passed when she stirred awake. She sat up, blinking. "I didn't mean to fall asleep," she said, pushing her hair out of her eyes.

"It made sense for you to rest while you had the chance." He checked the view through the narrow opening. Long shadows stretched across the ground, telling him the sun would be setting soon. "Are you ready to head out again?" he asked.

"I guess so. I'm so thirsty." She rubbed her stomach. "And hungry, too."

"We're going to do something about that," he said.

"What?"

"We have to go back to the area where we had the fire, near the creek."

Fear tightened her features. "If Duane retraces his path, he'll find us."

"We have to take that chance." He stood and pushed aside branches to widen the opening to their shelter, then pulled her to her feet.

"Why?" she asked.

"They didn't have Buck or his pack with them when they moved past, so they must have left him there. He had at least one water bottle in that pack, and probably food and other supplies. And he probably has a phone we can use to call for help."

Her expression grew more animated at this news. "I hadn't thought of that. Then yes, we should definitely go back." She started to haul herself out of the hole, but he pulled her back.

"Let me go first."

"Why? So they can shoot you in the head first? At least you can cover me. Don't count on me for the same."

"I can pull you up to the ground," he said.

"You can boost me up from here."

"Are you always this stubborn?"

She smiled. "Always."

Something broke inside him at that remark, some last restraint against his emotions. Not thinking, he pulled her close and looked into her eyes. "I've missed you," he said, his voice rough with emotion.

"I've missed you, too." She brushed her hand along his cheek, then leaned in to bring her lips to his, gently at first, then hungrily, as if he were all the food and drink she craved.

He responded in kind, all the anxiety and anger and despair of their months apart channeled into that kiss. He still didn't know what to think about her betrayal, and he wasn't ready to trust her, but for this moment, stranded with only each other to depend on, he gave in to the need to simply be close to her. To be with her, emotionally, in a way he had never allowed himself to be with any other person.

She pulled away first and regarded him with an expression he read as equal parts wariness and hope. "Does this mean you've forgiven me?" she asked.

"No." He touched the corner of her mouth, which was still swollen from Braeswood's blow. "But I'm not blaming you the way I once did. Consider it a first step in a long journey."

She pulled away. “Speaking of long journeys, we’d better get going.”

He checked the opening, and seeing nothing but still woodland, he boosted her up, then climbed out himself. “Do you know the way back to the body?” she asked.

“I think so,” he said.

In the end, they were able to follow Braeswood’s and Roland’s tracks through the woods. The two men hadn’t been concerned about being followed, and their heavy boots and careless steps made a trail of scuffed leaves, broken branches and even boot prints that led all the way to the little clearing, where the remains of the campfire still smoldered, and one of the cans of water sat, undisturbed, Buck’s body slumped a few yards away.

Leah hurried to retrieve the can of water. She drank half and handed the rest to Travis . “You take it,” he said, returning the can. “I’ll get the bottle on Buck’s pack.”

Already, the body was drawing flies. Travis ignored them and focused on unbuckling the pack from the dead man’s back. He set it aside, then riffled through Buck’s pockets. He found a wallet with three different driver’s licenses, identifying him variously as Bradley Simons, Brent Sampson and Bartholomew Spietzer. He had a couple of credit cards and twenty-three dollars in cash. Travis replaced the wallet and riffled through his other pockets, coming up with a pack of breath mints, some change, a Ruger .45-caliber pistol and an extra clip of ammo, and finally, in his front jeans pocket, a cell phone.

“He has a phone,” he said.

Leah knelt a short distance away. “Can you call someone to come and get us?”

He tapped the phone to waken it, relieved to discover Buck hadn’t bothered locking it, then punched in the direct number to his supervisor, Special Agent in Charge Ted Blessing. The screen almost immediately went black. He frowned and checked the display again. “We don’t have a signal,” he said.

Leah sat back on her heels. “I should have thought of that,” she said. “Wilderness areas don’t have cell towers. Plus all these trees…” She tilted her head back to regard the pines and firs that towered overhead.

“Maybe we can climb to a better signal.” He pulled the water bottle from the pack and drank deeply, then offered some to her.

She shook her head. “I’m okay. But I’d like to know if there’s any food in there.”

“We should move to a safer location before we check it out,” he said. He stood and shouldered the pack. “Whatever is in here, it’s heavy enough.” Anything they didn’t absolutely need, he would discard at the first opportunity. They had to move quickly, and that meant not taking anything that would weigh them down.

He led the way back into deeper woods—not taking the path they had followed to get here, but moving, he hoped, closer to the road. Leah followed, saying nothing. After a while, he noticed she still carried the two empty soda cans. “We might need them,” she said when she saw him looking at them.

“Good idea.” She had come up with a lot of good ideas so far during this ordeal. Another civilian might have been a burden, but she was turning out to be a capable partner. As much as he had loved her before, he wasn't sure he had ever respected her the way he did now.

Chapter Six

It was almost dark before Travis felt it was safe enough for them to stop moving. He had held out the hope of making it to the road before they halted, but navigating among the trees grew dangerous as the darkness deepened. He halted in a small clearing backed by a shelf of rock. "We can't go any farther without light," he said. "And I don't want to risk using the flashlight, in case the wrong people spot it." He didn't bring up the worry that Braeswood and his men might have night-vision goggles or infrared scanners, which would make finding them much easier.

"No, we won't risk it." Leah sank to the ground. Her shoulders slumped and her face was slack with exhaustion.

"Are you okay?" he asked.

She straightened and looked up at him, forcing a smile. "I'm fine. And I'm anxious to see what's in that pack. If we shield the flashlight with our bodies, we can risk taking a look. I'm hoping for food." She rubbed her arms against the night chill. "And maybe a fleece jacket."

Travis slung the pack from his shoulder and dropped it onto the ground in front of her. Then he lowered himself to sit beside her, their shoulders almost touching. He switched on the Mini Maglite and propped it against a couple of rocks so that the beam shone on the pack. Then he opened the top of the backpack and began laying out its contents. First out was a wrinkled black fleece jacket. He handed it to Leah and she immediately wrapped it around her shoulders. "Not only will it keep you warm, it will make you tougher to spot," he said.

She smoothed her hand over the sleeve of her red sweater. "I wasn't anticipating having to flee through the woods when I got dressed this morning."

"Where were you going when you first left the house?" he asked.

"I had an appointment for a manicure." She studied her chipped nail polish.

"How nice for you."

She glared at him. "It was better than being stuck alone with my jailers all the time."

Now would probably be a good time for him to ask her more about her time with Duane, and how she had ended up with the man in the first place. The more time he spent with her, the harder it was to think of her as a terrorist. But he wasn't ready to let down his guard with her yet. And how would he know she wasn't telling him more lies? Better to put off finding out a little longer.

He returned his attention to the pack and pulled out two sandwiches. He sniffed the packets. "Peanut butter and jelly," he said, and handed her one.

"My favorite," she said. "At least right now it is." She tore open the plastic zipper bag.

He unwrapped the second sandwich and took a

bite. Rich peanut butter and strawberry jam on wheat bread—it wasn't steak, but he was definitely going to savor it. Sandwich in one hand, he dug with the other into the pack again. He pulled out a water filter. "That should come in handy." He realized why the pack had been so heavy as it continued to yield treasures: a first aid kit, protein bars, two more clips of .45-caliber ammo, a Mylar space blanket, a plastic garbage bag, matches and cotton wool for starting fires, and another bottle of water. In a side pocket of the bag he found a headlamp and a map and compass. Tension he hadn't even realized he had been holding went out of him. "With these we should be able to find our way out of here," he said.

"Hmmm." Leah had opened the first aid kit and was riffling through it. "Looks like Buck was pretty well prepared. There's all kinds of meds and bandages here." She stopped, and a faint blush edged up her cheeks, visible even in the flashlight's glow.

"What is it?" Travis leaned toward her to see what had caught her attention.

She held up a familiar foil packet, the kind used for condoms. "Like I said, Buck was prepared for anything."

He choked off a laugh, disguising it as a cough. He began putting everything back in the pack. "It's getting dark. We need to make a shelter for the night."

"It's getting colder, too." She wrapped her arms around herself. "We've been having frost at night."

"If we can make a kind of lean-to with branches, it will help hide us and block any wind." He stood and shouldered the pack. "We can wrap up in the space blanket and we should be all right." He grabbed the flashlight. "Help me find some branches."

As Leah helped Travis cut and tear branches from nearby spruce trees, he talked about his plans for the morning. "We'll get an early start, refill both water bottles, then climb until we get cell service," he said. "If we can get above the trees, we should be able to figure out where we are, now that we have a map. The Bureau might even be able to get a helicopter in here to retrieve us."

He made it all sound so easy, but all she could think was *We have to get through the night first.* She wasn't as afraid of Duane as she had been. The sight of Buck lying dead had calmed her, in a way. It had shown her that despite his power, Duane wasn't invincible. Now that Travis had more ammunition and another gun, she believed the two of them had a chance of outrunning and outwitting Duane.

Her uneasiness now all centered on the prospect of spending the long, dark hours in close proximity to Travis. Though the kiss they had shared proved passion still sparked between them, she didn't believe he had really forgiven her. And she still had plenty of reasons for keeping some distance between them, no matter the temptation.

"Here. Take this." He handed her the flashlight and bent and gathered an armful of cut branches. She had put on Buck's jacket, rolling the too-long sleeves up over her wrists. Though the fleece smelled of stale cigarette smoke, she was grateful for its soft warmth as the night air chilled. "Shine the light over there by those rocks." Travis nodded to their right, and she did as he asked. A long-dead fir, the trunk bare of bark and stripped of limbs, lay on its side, the tip caught in the rocks. Travis moved to this area and began leaning the largest branches against the tree trunk. The result was a kind of tent made of soft fir boughs. He stepped back. "What do you think?"

"It looks…small."

"It will be easier to stay warm that way." He took off the pack, opened it, and removed the space blanket. "We'll spread this out to help block the cold from the ground, then wrap ourselves up in it. Here, take this end and crawl in."

She hesitated, but since her only other option was spending the night outside in freezing temperatures, she would have to make the best of it. She crawled into the shelter, dragging the stiff, crackling foil-lined blanket with her. "What am I supposed to do now?" she called.

"Get comfortable, then I'll squeeze in beside you and we'll wrap the blanket around us."

She could have pointed out that on the cold ground in the dark woods, against hard rocks, wearing the same clothes she had had on all day, with no pillows or wine or chocolate or any of the indulgences she considered necessary, the probability of anything close to comfortable was less than zero. But pity parties were best celebrated solo, so she kept quiet. She arranged the blanket under her as best she could, settled her back against the rocks, and tried not to think of the bugs that were probably sharing this space with her. "Okay," she called.

He came sliding in, immediately shrinking the space to the size of a coffin. Unfortunate comparison, she thought. He grunted and turned on his side. "Does your side hurt where you were shot?" she asked, momentarily forgetting her own discomfort.

"It's okay. What about your shoulder and your neck?"

In the rush to escape Duane and everything that had happened since, she hadn't had much time to dwell on what had happened to her. "My shoulder is a little sore, but it will be all right," she said. She put a hand to her throat and felt the line of dried blood. "My neck doesn't hurt, but I hope I don't end up with some nasty infection."

"I can take care of that." He leaned forward and dragged the backpack, which he had left at his feet, up onto his legs. He fished out the headlamp and the first aid kit. The light made a soft white glow in the shelter, illuminating his face and whatever he looked at. He opened a disinfecting wipe and dabbed gently at her neck. "This might sting a little."

It didn't sting. Or if it did, a little sting didn't have a chance to claim her attention, competing as it was with the hot flutterings of arousal that danced up and down her skin at his touch. Apparently satisfied that the wound was clean, he tucked the wipe into a pocket of the pack and took out a tube of antibiotic ointment and began dabbing it onto the cut. "I don't think we need to bandage it," he said. "He didn't go deep."

"He just wanted to scare me." Duane was an expert at that.

Travis's hand stilled and he looked down at her, though the light prevented her from seeing his expression. "You say that like it wasn't the first time," he said.

"It wasn't." She had spent most of her time with

Duane in various stages of terror. It was how he operated. How he maintained control.

Travis busied himself putting away the first aid supplies, then shoved the pack to his feet once more and switched off the light. He settled back against the rock, their bodies pressed together all along that side, but desire had left her, his silence a wall between them.

She didn't have the words to heal the wound she had caused him, so she waited, letting the night sounds fill the void: the rustle of wind in the trees, the creak of a branch, the whisper of some small creature in the leaf litter on the forest floor. Eyes closed, she breathed in deeply of the Christmas-tree fragrance of the cut spruce, and thought of the last Christmas she and Travis had spent together. They had attended the lighting of the National Christmas Tree on the Ellipse, and later enjoyed a concert at the National Cathedral. It had been the most magical holiday in her memory, his love the best gift she could have ever received.

And three months later, it all ended. Duane had stolen that magic from her, and as long as she lived, she didn't think she would have it in her to forgive him for that.

"I've spent the past six months trying to make sense of what happened." Travis spoke softly, but she heard the anger and hurt behind the words.

"It's not something that makes sense," she said. "Not even to me, sometimes."

"I'm ready to listen."

"Are you?" She angled toward him, wishing she could see his face, but the darkness was too complete. She had only her awareness of him, of the broadness of his shoulders and the angle of his arm and the muscles of his thighs where he touched her.

"I saw you with Braeswood this afternoon," he said "You were afraid of him. And he didn't look at you with anything close to love."

"Oh, Duane doesn't love me. He doesn't love anyone but himself."

"Do you love him?" Travis asked.

"Never. I couldn't. I've seen him kill. I know how ruthless he can be."

"Your note to me said you had changed your mind. I thought you meant you found someone else. I believed all this time that you were in love with Braeswood."

"No." She felt in the darkness and found the back of his hand. When he tried to pull away, she laced her fingers with his and held on tight. "I lied. I didn't love anyone else. I don't love anyone else." Though if her feelings for Travis were still love after all that had happened, she couldn't say.

"Why did you lie?" He asked the question in the same tone he must use to interrogate a suspect. *Why did you kill that woman? Why did you swindle those people out of all that money? How could you pretend to justify your crime?*

She sighed and closed her eyes. What could she say that would ever persuade him she wasn't lying now? All she had was the truth. "I didn't want you to come after me."

"Why not?"

"Because he would have killed you."

"Braeswood?"

"Yes." Duane had made her choice very clear—give

up Travis, or he would be dead. Either way, she would lose him. Better to let him escape alive.

He rolled onto his side to face her. Their bodies were so close she could feel the heat of him, smell the sweat and spice fragrance of him. “But you said you didn’t love him. Why did you go with him?”

“It’s a long story.” One she wasn’t sure she could tell without breaking down.

“We’ve got all night.”

Yes, and when she was done, he might hate her even more. “I’ll tell you, if you’ll listen to everything before you judge,” she said.

“I don’t—”

He started to protest, but she put her fingers to his lips, silencing him. “I know you. You want to fix things. This isn’t something you can fix.”

“All right.”

She moved down, the space blanket crackling under her, until she was flat on her back, staring up at the blackness, and prepared to relive a darkness far worse than the absence of light in this shelter.

“HELLO?” LEAH ANSWERED the phone that March afternoon over six months before with her usual efficiency. The display on her cell showed her sister Sarah’s number. “Sarah, why didn’t you call on the office phone? You know that’s the best way to reach me during working hours.” Her younger sister also worked in the Senate Office Building, and the two often got together after work for drinks or to take in a movie. She glanced toward the open door into her boss’s office as she answered her cell phone, but Senator Diana Wilson was engrossed in a phone call of her own.

"Leah, you've got to help." The words came out half choked, so unlike Sarah's usually cheery rush of conversation.

"Sarah? What's wrong? Why are you crying? What's happened?"

"Your sister is perfectly safe. For now." The man's voice on the other end of the line was calm. Too calm, almost like one of those robotic voices that gave directions on voice mail. "As long as you cooperate, she'll remain that way."

"What are you talking about? Who is this?"

"Keep your voice down, Leah. You don't want to upset the senator. Not if you want to see your sister alive again."

The words froze the blood in her veins. Panic squeezed her chest. She had to fight to breathe and couldn't speak. She glanced over her shoulder toward the senator's office again.

"Tell the senator you need to take off work a little early and come to the address I'm going to text you. Come alone. I promise your sister will be there and the two of you can talk."

"I don't understand," she whispered.

But the man had already hung up.

Shaking, she opened the bottom desk drawer and took out her purse, then staggered to the senator's door. Senator Wilson was still on a call, but she raised her eyebrows in question. "I…I'm not feeling very well," Leah said. "I think I need to go home."

Eyes full of concern, the senator nodded. "Take care," she mouthed, and waved Leah away.

She didn't remember leaving the building. She was on her way to the metro station when her text notification signal chimed. The screen showed an address off Dupont Circle. Running now, Leah hurried to the metro station and caught a train just leaving that would take her to Dupont Circle.

Sarah answered the door to the basement apartment where Leah had been directed, but as soon as she had pulled Leah inside, a man she would soon come to know as Duane Braeswood, along with two other men, emerged from a back room, all three carrying guns.

Leah forced herself to be strong, for her sister's sake. "What is this about?" she demanded.

"It's very simple," Duane said. "You have something I want. Cooperate with me and I'll let your sister go."

Leah looked at Sarah, whose brown eyes silently pleaded for help. At twenty-two, she had just begun her first job, working at the State Department. She was engaged to the man she had dated all through college. She was a sweet, optimistic person who had never made an enemy. And right now she looked absolutely terrified, ghost white and shaking so hard Leah could hear her teeth chatter. "All right," Leah said. "Let her go now and I'll do whatever you want."

Duane nodded and one of the other men walked to the door of the apartment and opened it. Sarah looked at the man, then at Leah. "Please let my sister come with me," she said.

"You let us worry about your sister," Duane said. "Unless you want to stay here with her."

Sarah turned to Leah again, tears in her eyes. "Go!" Leah urged. "I'll be fine."

Sarah nodded, then fled, out the door and down the street. Leah closed her eyes, remembering the relief that had flooded through her—a false hope that everything was going to be all right that Duane soon destroyed.

"What did he want?" The words burst from Travis, who had kept his promise to remain silent until now. Leah couldn't blame him for asking. She had asked herself the same question a thousand times in the past six months.

"He wanted a lot of things," she said. "Little things at first. He told me I had to break up with you, but first I had to tell him everything I knew about you." She was glad he couldn't see her face in the dark, glad he couldn't read the shame of those interrogations, when she had broken down weeping and begged Duane to believe she didn't know anything about Travis's work with the FBI. "In the end, he realized I couldn't tell him anything useful.

"He wanted me to tell him secrets about the senator, and to use my influence to find out more."

"Senator Wilson headed the Senate Committee on Homeland Security," Travis said.

"Yes. He asked me to steal paperwork from her office. I refused."

"Did he hurt you?" He gripped her wrist so hard she winced, fury vibrating through him.

She gently pulled away from him. "What he did to me physically didn't matter as much as the other ways he hurt me," she said. "He killed Sarah. He made it look like an accident, but I know he was responsible. He made sure I knew."

Travis swore, and he pulled her close, cradling her in his arms. She pressed her face into his chest and blinked back tears. "You should have called me," he said. "I would have helped."

"I thought you hated me for dumping you the way I did," she said. "And I was so afraid you'd be the next to die. Duane told me he would kill you, and I believed him. I've never met anyone as ruthless as he can be."

"So you gave him the senator's secrets," he said.

"Yes. Though nothing I told him seemed especially incriminating to me. She was an honest woman. I didn't know about any backroom deals or scandals. All I could tell him was about legislation she had proposed and issues she was interested in. But when she resigned three weeks later, I felt so guilty. I thought her resignation was my fault—that Duane had used something I had told him to drive her from office. Then I learned her husband had cancer and she wanted to spend more time with him. I don't think even Duane could give someone cancer."

"Senator Wilson resigned five months ago," he said. "What happened after that?"

"Duane took control of my life. I didn't have a job anymore. I came home one day and he had had someone move all my belongings out of my apartment and cancel my lease. He moved me in with him. He made me sign over everything to him—my car, all my money, even the cabin here in Colorado that I'd inherited when my parents died." Saying the words now made it sound so bizarre. How could a stranger make an independent adult woman do something like that? Looking back, it was as if he had brainwashed her with terror. "I should have fought back," she said. "I should have refused his demands, but I was so afraid." She buried her face in her hands. "Why wasn't I stronger?"

Travis caressed her shoulder. "He knew how to manipulate you," he said. "You probably weren't the first person he had controlled that way."

"It doesn't even seem real now," she said. "After a while I was just…numb. Paralyzed."

"Why did he choose you?" Travis asked. "Was it only because of the senator?"

"I don't know why he chose me," she said. "Though I've thought about that a lot."

"Maybe it was just random," Travis said. "You were unlucky."

She shook her head. "Duane never acts without a reason. He's very methodical and focused. More like a machine than a man at times." A vicious, horrible machine. "Maybe at first it was because of my connection with Senator Wilson. Or maybe it was because of the other things I had. You know I inherited quite a bit of money from my parents. And he was really interested in the family cabin."

"The one on the old mining claim?" Travis asked.

"Yes. You remember when we visited there—it's in the middle of nowhere. It doesn't even have electricity or plumbing. But he asked me dozens of questions about it." When she was a child, her family had spent a month in the remote mountain cabin every summer. She and Sarah had played "prospector," gathering chunks of rocks and bouquets of wildflowers, and her parents indulged in long hikes and lazy afternoons drinking gin and tonics on the cabin's front porch and watching spectacular sunsets. She had never thought of the cabin as having value to anyone other than her family. "When Duane announced we were moving to Colorado, I was sure we were headed there," she said. “But I should have known that wasn’t his style. He likes his comforts, and he has plenty of money to indulge them.”

“Maybe he chose you because he wanted someone he could bully.” Travis’s embrace around her tightened again, more gentle this time.

“I wondered if maybe he chose me because of my ties to you,” she said. “I worried about that. A lot.”

“Because he thought you could give him information about investigations I was involved in?”

“More as a way of getting back at an FBI agent. He hated the Feds. He felt they had singled him out for harassment.”

“He’s right about that. The man is responsible for the deaths of at least a dozen people. And now that I know what he’s put you through…” He kissed the top of her head, the gentlest brush of his lips that brought her close to tears again. He smoothed his hand down her back, caressing, and she stiffened.

“There’s something else you should know,” she said. “About me and…and Duane.”

His hand stilled. Though he didn’t move, she felt him pulling away emotionally. “You lived with him for months,” he said. “He told people you were his wife.” He swallowed hard. “Were you lovers?”

“Not willingly,” she said.

“He raped you.”

“Yes. Though after a while, I learned not to resist. I just…I pretended I wasn’t there.” She felt small and dirty when she said the words, but she fought past that. “I did what I had to do to survive,” she said.

“You were strong.” He caressed her back again. “I’m going to stop him. I promise. He’ll pay.”

"And I'm going to help." She rested her hand, palm down, over his heart, reassured by the steady rhythm of it. "I don't know if I can make you understand what a gift you gave me when you arrested me this morning."

"I was angry with you. I didn't understand."

"And I didn't expect you to. But when you took me away from that house, from Duane and his group, it was as if you broke a spell he had over me. You gave me hope—something I'd lost."

"I should have come after you before now," he said. "I should have realized that note was a lie."

"If you had come after me when I first left you, Duane would have killed you. That's why I never returned your calls or texts, and I avoided all the places we might run into each other. I didn't want to hurt you, but I was terrified of what he might do to you."

"He won't get away with this."

"He's going to keep coming after us," she said.

"Because he knows how damaging your testimony against him could be."

"Partly that, but also because he's a man who doesn't like to lose. I once saw him kill one of his team members because the man beat him at a poker game and made the mistake of laughing about it."

"He thinks you belong to him now, and he doesn't want to give you up."

The words hurt to hear, even though she knew they were true. But she didn't want Travis to believe them. "I don't mean anything to him," she said. "But he won't let the FBI get the better of him if he can help it. And he has a lot of people and resources on his side. It's frightening how many followers he's recruited to the cause."

"What is his cause?" Travis asked. "Or rather, what does he say is his cause?"

"He's convinced the United States government is irretrievably corrupt and headed down the wrong path, so it's up to people like him to correct the course. He's persuaded himself and a lot of other people that he's going to save the country by destroying everything he thinks is wrong with it."

"Including us," Travis said.

"He won't stop until he's dead." A shiver ran through her, and she clung to him even tighter. "Or we are."

Chapter Seven

Travis lay awake a long time after Leah had fallen asleep. Her description of her ordeal—and his own imagination supplying details she hadn't provided—made sleep impossible. He saw the hatred he had nursed for her for what it was now: armor around his hurt feelings. He had thought he was the strong one, carrying on despite her betrayal, yet she was the one who had suffered so much in an attempt to protect him.

He couldn't say what his feelings were for her now. Guilt and relief combined with tenderness and the desire to protect her, but all of that was mixed up with a continued wariness. Too much had happened for them to simply pick up where they had left off. When they were both safe again—tomorrow, he hoped—they both had some healing to do.

Weariness eventually overcame the turmoil in his mind and he slept, and woke to gray light and the first hint of coming dawn through the trees. Leah stirred beside him. "We should go," he said. "We have a lot of ground to cover."

They disassembled their shelter and scattered the branches, then ate a breakfast of protein bars and the last of the plums she had found the day before. She didn't bring up the conversation they had had the night before. He was relieved. Hearing about her ordeal had been difficult enough in the darkness, where he couldn't look into her eyes or see her expression. He didn't know if he was ready to face those things in the daylight.

When they had finished eating, he spread the map between them and, wearing the headlamp, studied the contour lines and landmarks noted on its surface. He had thought he could determine where they were by following the creek from the road, and guessing how far they had walked yesterday. But the crooked blue line branched into half a dozen different streams and drainages as it wound through the wilderness area.

Stumped, he refolded the map and looked around them, at the thick forest that appeared the same here as it had a mile away and a mile from that. "We'll have to climb and try to get above the tree line to figure out where we are," he said. "We're more likely to get cell service up higher, too."

"It would be good if we could find a trail," she said. "There are a lot of hiking trails in the wilderness. It's popular with hikers and backpackers."

He stowed the map in the side pocket of the pack. "Let's get some more water and head west," he said. "That should take us up into the mountains."

"What about Duane?"

"We'll keep an eye out for him. If he comes after us, we'll either run or make a stand, whichever way seems best." He hesitated, then dug the Glock out of the other side of the pack, where he had stashed it when he put Buck's Ruger in his holster instead. "Take this." He handed her the Glock. "Do you remember how to use it?" He had made it a point to take her to the range a few times after their relationship had gotten serious, where they had run through the basics.

"Yes."

"Use it if you have to."

She nodded solemnly, then tucked the gun into the small of her back.

THE GUN FELT heavy and ominous at Leah's back, a reminder that they were still in danger. Travis hadn't said anything this morning about her ordeal with Duane, or about all she had revealed the night before. He had never been one to react emotionally to situations. His calmness had been one of the things that initially attracted her to him. Of course, sometimes his tendency to overanalyze drove her nuts, but she could usually tease him out of any broodiness.

She was in no mood for teasing now. She wanted to shake him and demand to know what he was thinking, but that would only make him clam up more. She would have to wait him out while he processed everything she had told him.

They quickly fell into a rhythm, the aches and pains of the day before fading somewhat as their muscles warmed. After a stop by the stream for more water, using the filter they had found in the pack, Travis took out the compass and studied it. He pointed toward a gap in the trees ahead. "If we head this way and stay mostly due west, we should be high enough in the mountains in a few hours that we can figure out our next move."

She hoped that included finding a cell signal that

would allow them to call in the cavalry, complete with a rescue helicopter, hot food and clean clothes.

An hour passed, then two, with no sign of Duane. If not for the potential danger they were in, it might have been a pleasant day's hike. They passed through groves of golden aspen and fragrant expanses of spruce and pine, serenaded by birdsong and the chatter of squirrels. Once Travis put a hand on her arm to stop her, and pointed out a porcupine a short distance away, quills vibrating gently as it trundled away from them.

After a couple of hours they stopped to drink and rest a bit. "I'm nervous, not knowing what Duane is up to," she said.

"Do you think he spent the night in the woods?" Travis asked. "You said he liked his comforts."

"I think he would leave and gather reinforcements," she said. "He would also be concerned about the FBI getting into the house while he was away, though he probably had men guarding it and carrying away or destroying anything incriminating."

"What was he doing in Colorado?" Travis asked. "Why Denver, and why Durango now?"

Here it was, the questioning she had been waiting for. Now that he had absorbed the details of her captivity, the investigator in him wanted to know what evidence she could supply to help him in his case.

"I have no idea why we came here," she said. "Denver was for the bike race, although that was what he called a peripheral—something extra that wasn't his main goal but would enhance his reputation and make an impact. Those were all his words, not mine."

"So he was involved in the bombings at the bike races?"

"He supplied the bombs and transportation, and worked out all the logistics with Danny. But going after bike races specifically was Danny's deal. He had a grudge against racers. Duane was happy enough to go along."

"What was his main purpose, then?"

"I don't know."

Travis's skepticism was transparent, at least to her. "I don't," she insisted. "He made sure I wasn't in the room when he discussed 'business,' and he always had one of his thugs watching to make sure I didn't eavesdrop or snoop. I thought the less I knew the safer I'd be, though I realize now how foolish that was."

"But coming to Durango had something to do with his main purpose?"

"Yes, but I could never figure out what that was. He often left for a few hours or most of a day. He usually took at least one other man with him, but he never said where he was going or what he did while he was away."

"Did he do that in Denver, too? Go away?"

"Sometimes in Denver he would go away for a day or two. He always left at least one and often two men to guard me. Of course, he didn't call it that. He said the men were there to look after me. But I knew they had orders to kill me if I tried to escape."

"Did you ever try to run away?"

She felt the censure behind the words. She had expected this, too. Travis was the type who would fight to the death for his freedom. He couldn't understand why she hadn't fought harder to leave Duane.

"He killed my sister." She couldn't keep her voice from shaking at those words. "He took everything from me—not only my possessions, but my self-confidence.

I couldn't fight him. I didn't think I had anything to fight for."

"You're strong," he said. "You always have been."

"He made me weak. Haven't you ever felt that way? Helpless?"

He looked away, and despair dragged at her. Of course he hadn't. Travis had never been forced to bend to someone else's will.

"I've only felt that way once," he said, all the challenge gone from his voice. "Only when you left me."

Chapter Eight

"We'd better get going." Travis slipped the pack onto his back and started up a faint path, probably made by animals, that wound through the trees. He didn't want to see pity or disdain in Leah's eyes now that he had revealed his weakness. That's what the admission felt like—a defeat. He had let her get the better of him, and now she knew it. He had spent years learning to hide any vulnerability, yet he had let down his guard with her. Doing so felt like a big mistake. When someone knew your weakness, they could use it against you.

The shuffle of her footsteps on the forest floor assured him she was following. Despite the tough pace he had set all morning, she was keeping up. She had always been stronger than he gave her credit for. Her ordeal with Braeswood proved that. He understood she hadn't really betrayed him. She had only done what she thought was necessary to save him, even though he hadn't needed saving. He could forgive her.

He just wasn't sure he could ever forget.

"We're really starting to climb now, aren't we?"

She sounded out of breath, so he slowed and allowed her to catch up. The trees were farther apart now, allowing them to walk side by side. "If we weren't lost and running from a killer, I might enjoy this," she said. "It's so beautiful. It reminds me of backpacking trips I took with my family." Sadness clouded her eyes, and he knew she was thinking of her sister.

She might see beauty in the wild scenery, but he couldn't forget the danger. "Does Braeswood have a plane?" he asked.

"A plane?" She frowned. "I don't think so. Though he could probably hire one."

"I'm beginning to think that might be the only way he finds us." He glanced up toward the swath of blue visible between the tree tops. "Even then, he would have a hard time spotting us. He made a mistake, not tracking us all night."

"Other people make mistakes, not Duane."

He sent her a sharp look, which earned him a wan smile.

"Hey, I'm just quoting his own words," she said. "He's convinced that's the reason he'll succeed when others fail."

"That kind of arrogance will get him into trouble." Travis filed the information away. Arrogance was a weakness.

She listed to one side, wincing. "What's wrong?" he asked, taking her arm to steady her. "Are you hurt?"

"Just a stitch." She rubbed at her side. "I'll be fine."

"You need a walking stick." Once they started to climb, such an aid would come in handy for both of them. "Hang on a minute." He slid his multi-tool from the pocket of his pants and moved off the trail a little to cut two stout branches to use as walking sticks. He trimmed them smooth, then handed one to her. "You can use it as a club if you have to," he pointed out.

She hefted the stick. "I'll keep that in mind if we meet any bears."

"I'm more worried about two-legged predators."

"It was a joke, Travis. Remember those?"

"Excuse me if I don't feel like joking."

"We're going to get through this. And it helps sometimes to see the humor."

Her attitude amazed him. "You can say that, after all you've been through?"

"Life is full of bad things. Knowing that makes the good things all the more precious. I didn't always realize that on the worst days, but I see it now."

"You aren't saying this is a good day?"

"I'm not trapped with Duane." She started to say something else, then shook her head. "Anyway, we're going to get out of this. We've come too far not to." She moved past him, setting a brisk pace up the trail.

He fell in step behind her, letting her take the lead for a while. The view was definitely better from here, he thought, as he watched her hips sway provocatively as she negotiated the trail. She had always had a sunny, optimistic outlook on life. That she was able to maintain such an attitude after all she had suffered moved him. What had she been about to say just now? That she was glad to be with him again? Not that he had given her much to be glad about. He had arrested her, interrogated her and taken out his mixed-up feelings on her. She deserved better. One more reason they shouldn't be together.

They stepped from the woods into an open meadow, the charred trunks of long-dead trees marking the spot where a wildfire had cleared the area. Wildflowers formed a crazy quilt of color across the rolling landscape, painting the ground with pink and yellow and purple and white. On the other side of the meadow, the terrain rose quickly, transforming from woodland to the rocky slope of a mountain, its peak frosted with pockets of last winter's snow.

Leah stopped and leaned on her walking stick. "We ought to be able to see a long way from up there," she said.

Travis took out Buck's cell phone and checked the screen. "No signal," he said. He studied the peak again, then turned his back to Leah. "Get the map out of the pack," he said. "Maybe I can figure out where we are."

They held the map between them and studied it. Leah frowned. "None of it makes sense to me," she said. "Not without roads or landmarks or something to give me a starting point."

"One mountain isn't enough for us to go on," he agreed. He swept his hand over the closely spaced contour lines along one side of the map. "This place is full of mountains."

"So what do we do?" she asked.

He refolded the map and handed it to her. "We keep walking. If we get high enough, we should be able to figure out something."

"Let's hope the weather continues to cooperate." She peered up at a band of fluffy white clouds that drifted over the peaks. "This is the time of year when afternoon thunderstorms roll in."

"I can still walk in the rain," he said.

"It's not the rain we have to worry about." She moved around behind him to replace the map. "We don't want to be up on bare rock during a lightning storm."

"Then we'd better get moving and hope we can beat out any storms."

After a few minutes of zipping and unzipping compartments and arranging and rearranging the contents of the backpack, she handed him one of the protein bars. "We need to keep up our strength," she said.

"How many are left?" he asked.

"Just one." She glanced at the rocky peak ahead. "There isn't going to be anything we can eat up there."

"As long as we have water, we can go a long time without food." He bit into the protein bar. It must have been in Buck's pack for a while, since it was like chewing beef jerky. Without the beef.

Leah sipped from her water bottle and regarded the protein bar skeptically. "Maybe it would help if I pretended this was something else. What's the best meal you ever ate?"

"The best?" He pondered the question. "I don't know. Probably a good steak somewhere. A big, juicy rib eye." His mouth watered and his stomach cramped at the thought. A steak would be heavenly right now, sizzling and juicy, so tender he could cut it with a fork…

"Mine is lobster," she said. "Do you remember that lobster we had at Chez Antoine? With the lemon butter, and the pesto potatoes." She closed her eyes and made a little humming sound of pleasure that made him forget all about his stomach and think of other appetites, as sharp and urgent as any need for food.

"Yeah, that was some meal," he said, barely able to get the words out. He and Leah had eaten lobster at Chez Antoine the night he proposed. He had given her the ring after the waiter served their chocolate mousse, and the manager had sent over a bottle of champagne in celebration after Leah said yes.

She still had her eyes closed, so he felt free to study her face. The past few months of hardship were written in the hollowed cheeks and faint lines around her eyes, but the maturity of the woman before him now attracted him even more than the youthful perfection he had known in their earlier time together.

A smile curved her full lips. Was she really only thinking about that succulent lobster, or was she, like him, remembering more? Was she remembering the way he had held her close in the back of the cab on the way to her apartment? Or the way they had slowly undressed each other and then made love, not merely as boyfriend and girlfriend, but as future husband and wife? That night, he felt they had already made a lasting commitment to each other.

The day he found her letter telling him she was leaving, his whole world had tilted. Suddenly, nothing in his life made sense, and for a long while, he hadn't trusted his own judgment. The revelations of the past twenty-four hours had left him just as off-kilter and uncertain.

He turned away and stashed his water bottle in the pack once more. "Come on," he said. "We've still got a long way to go."

THE TRAIL SNAKED steeply up the mountain, trees giving way to low shrubs and finally, bare rock as they climbed above the tree line. A haze obscured the landscape in the distance, so that all Leah could see was the forest they had walked out of and the rocky uplift they were climbing toward.

And Travis. She could definitely see him. His tall,

broad-shouldered figure filled her vision and her thoughts. As close as they had been physically in the past twenty-four hours, he still held himself apart from her. She didn't know whether to weep with sadness over the way he was rejecting her or to shake him for being so stubborn. Was it hurt pride that made him so reluctant to rekindle the warm feelings they had once had for each other, or something worse? Did he think she was lying about Duane forcing himself on her? Or about the hold he had over her that had kept her from leaving him?

When they had stopped on the trail earlier, she had almost told him how much it meant to her to be with him again—how during her worst days, thoughts of him safe and memories of the love they had shared had kept her going. But she had held back, afraid of looking foolish or worse, seeing rejection in his eyes.

She had purposely reminded him of the dinner where they had gotten engaged. She had hoped recalling their love for each other back then would soften his attitude toward her. But again he had turned away.

Ten yards ahead of her up the trail, he stopped and pulled out the phone. "Still no signal," he said as she approached.

"No telling where the nearest cell tower is." She scanned the horizon for any sign of a tower, but saw nothing but rocky peaks and a valley of green and gold spread out beyond. Somewhere down there were other people, hikers and campers searching for solitude and adventure in the wilderness, or peak baggers hoping to check another mountain off their life list. One of those people might help them to safety. But she would be hesitant to approach a stranger, fearful of endangering them if Duane came after her and Travis. Or worse, what if the person she approached worked with Duane?

She had learned early on in her association with him that most terrorists didn't provide any visual clues. Duane's followers included housewives and doctors, military men and preachers and successful businessmen. They gave him money and followed his orders and believed he was the means to their salvation.

Travis shoved the phone back into his pocket. "If we keep moving, we're bound to eventually get a signal or reach a road or something."

She nodded, though the wearier and hungrier she became, the more her optimism faded. She didn't want to have finally escaped Duane only to die here in the wilderness.

She pushed the thought away. She hadn't come this far, held on to life this tightly, to lose it now. For a time, Duane had made her feel helpless, even hopeless. She wasn't those things anymore. She was strong. A survivor. And she would survive this ordeal, too.

The higher they climbed up the mountain, the steeper the trek. She labored to breathe in the thin air and lagged farther and farther behind Travis, so that he was forced to stop and wait for her more often. "You're doing great," he said, when she caught up with him near the top of the peak. "We're almost there."

"Almost" proved to be another hour of climbing, but at last no other rock outcroppings or false summits blocked their view. After a last scramble over loose rock and boulders, they reached their goal. Travis, who was hiking ahead of her, stopped and extended his hand to pull her up beside him onto a narrow ledge.

"We did it," he said, wrapping his arms around her. "What an incredible view."

From this elevation, they could see for miles, the world a child's play set spread out before them, with a miniature forest, rocky hills and golden valleys; sun and shadow played across them like spilled paint from a clumsy artist. The scene was both beautiful and intimidating, with no roads or houses or other people as far as the eye could see. How would they ever find their way to safety across such vastness?

"You're very quiet," Travis said. "Are you okay?"

"I'm worried about the weather." She tore her gaze from the view below to stare up at the sky. All morning, the sun had played hide-and-seek with the clouds and the temperature had dropped.

"The clouds don't look serious to me," he said. "We'll be okay."

As if to contradict him, a stiff breeze kicked up, pushing her into him. She had no room to move away, even if she could have found the willpower to do so. His warm, strong arms around her made her feel so safe and reminded her so much of when her life had been good and they had been happy together.

She forced herself not to think of that, or to contemplate the way his arms brushed the side of her breasts or the way her heart sped up as he shifted against her. She turned her eyes again to the view below. "It's like being in a plane," she said. "Everything down there looks so small and far away."

"I can see a river." He pointed, and she followed his gaze to a narrow ribbon of silver threading through the trees.

"We can see other peaks from here, too." She nodded toward the mountains that jutted up around them. "Maybe we can figure out where we are."

"Get the map." He released her and turned so that she could unzip the pack. As she pulled out the map, the wind threatened to rip it from her hand.

"Don't let it go," she said, wrinkling the plastic-coated paper as she clutched it tightly. The map was their best chance of navigating out of here.

"Turn toward the mountain," Travis said. "We'll shield the map with our bodies."

Carefully, she did as he instructed. They huddled together, the map between them, and she tried not to think about the thousand-foot drop at her back. All she had to do was stand still and not move.

Travis studied the map, forehead furrowed in concentration, then stabbed at a blue line on the paper. "That's the Animas River. I think that's what we're looking at."

"That's one of the largest rivers in this part of Colorado," she said. "Do you see anything else familiar?"

"That tallest peak to our north might be Mount Eolus." He indicated the jagged peak that rose above the others in their view. "My best guess is that we're standing on either Mount Kennedy or Aztec Mountain. If we head slightly northwest, that will take us to the Needle Creek Trail." He traced the dashed line that marked the trail on the map. "That will take us to a bridge over the river, and the Needleton Station for the Durango & Silverton Narrow Gauge Railway. We can flag down the train, and in Durango or Silverton I can call for help."

She let his words sink in, then turned to stare across the valley once more. The glinting silver thread through the trees, and the railroad that followed its banks, seemed so far away. And yet so tantalizingly close. As she stared, a thin trail of smoke rose up from the trees.

"There's the train," Travis said. His arm came around her once more and together they watched as the engine with its line of cars emerged from the trees, looking like a child's toy, puffs of white smoke marking its path.

"How long do you think it will take us to reach it?" she asked.

"It's only a couple of miles to the trail on the map, but it's rugged country. We may have to detour more than once. After that, it's only about seven miles to the train station. We probably won't make it to the trail before dark, but we can get close, and finish the trip tomorrow."

"The trains run twice a day," she said. "I remember that from some tourist brochures the leasing agent for the house left us."

"Did you ever ride it when you were a kid?" he asked.

"We rode it a couple of times, when we had relatives visiting who wanted to see the area. The scenery is spectacular, but the most fun for me and Sarah as kids was moving between the cars and hanging out the windows of the open cars to watch the engine as it puffed along the curves." She smiled, remembering the fun of exploring the train with Sarah, their parents and visiting relatives engrossed in the scenery. "I remember one time in Silverton, the town staged a mock shoot-out in the street in front of the depot. It was like traveling back in time."

"We'll get an early start and try to catch the morning train," Travis said.

"Should we try the phone again?" she asked.

He pulled out the phone once more and turned it to show her that there was still no signal. "No towers in the wilderness area," he said. "But my team will be looking for us. We could meet up with them before too much longer."

"How will they know where to look?" she asked. "We must be miles from where we started."

"That's true," he said. "But they won't give up until they find us. In the meantime, we won't wait for them. We've got a hard hike ahead of us. Are you ready?"

"Yes." Her heart fluttered with a mix of excitement and dread. The distance they needed to cover over such rugged terrain still intimidated her, but having a goal in sight and a plan to get there made her feel stronger. Anything could happen over the next twelve hours or so, but they were going to make it, she was more sure than ever.

Another strong gust of wind threatened to knock them from their perch, and raindrops the size of BBs pelted them. "We're getting off the mountain just in time," she said, raising her voice over the drumbeat of rain on the rocks.

"Wait just a minute," Travis said, unclipping the binoculars from his belt. "I want to take a closer look, see if I can make out a trail."

She ducked her head as the rain began to fall harder while Travis focused the binoculars to the north. "How does it look?" she asked.

"Steep. Rocky. But doable if we're careful. I'm trying to see if I can spot the trail…" His voice trailed off, then he swore, the sudden sharp exclamation rocking her back on her heels.

"What is it?" She clutched at his arm. "What's wrong?"

He lowered the glasses, his expression grim. "I found the trail," he said. "There's a big party headed up it. I'm pretty sure it's Braeswood. And it looks like he's brought in reinforcements."

Chapter Nine

Travis ignored the rain pelting his face and soaking his clothing as he studied the line of men snaking their way down the distant trail. Even with the binoculars, they resembled a line of ants. Black-clad ants carrying heavy packs and marching with military purpose up the trail.

"Are you sure it's them?" Leah asked.

"I can't be sure at this distance." Though he had memorized the faces of thousands of people, he had to be close enough to see details in order to use that talent. "But my gut tells me it's them." Casual hikers didn't move that way, or carry so much gear.

She clung to his arm. "Have they spotted us?"

"I don't think so. At least, they're not stopping to look this way." They were covering ground quickly, though. Men on a mission. Hunters out for prey.

He stashed the binoculars and made sure the pack was secure, then took Leah's arm. "Come on," he said. "We'd better get moving."

The rock was slick from the rain, and they were already soaked to the skin from the torrents of water pelting them. "Careful!" he called, reaching out to steady her as she slipped on the loose gravel.

"I'm okay," she said, pushing him away. "Just hurry. We need—"

Thunder, like a cannon shot, drowned out the rest of her words. She screamed as the rain turned to hail, ice pellets the size of grapes bombarding them. He glanced over his shoulder toward the river, no longer visible through the storm. Would the weather slow down their pursuers, or would they press on?

He and Leah had no choice but to keep moving. They had to get down off this peak, and fast. "Come on," he said, moving past her. "This way."

She remained still, rain plastering her hair to her head, glinting on her lashes like tears. "You're planning to move toward them?"

"It's our best chance to reach safety."

"We'll run right into them."

"Not if we're careful. We'll evade them and go around them. There's a lot of territory out there, and they can't cover it all."

She glanced toward the distant trail and the men who were invisible to the naked eye. "They'll know we'll head for the train station. It's the closest way out of here."

"Yes. They'll probably have someone watching. We'll have to find a way to get past."

She seemed to consider this, her expression as serious as if she were weighing the pros and cons of undergoing surgery.

"It's either go forward toward the train station or go back," he said. "It's at least three days' hiking to any kind of road. Maybe longer to safety." He didn't mention that Braeswood might very well have a second crew hiking in from that direction, intending to trap them in the middle.

Another crash of thunder shook the air, jarring her from her stupor. “All right,” she said. “Let’s hurry.”

Descending with any speed proved challenging, with the rain and hail obscuring their vision and making the footing treacherous. The loose rock scree slid from beneath their boots, so that every step threatened to send them careering down the steep slope. Thunder shook them, and lightning exploded behind them, the light blinding and the air sharp with the smell of ozone.

“We’ve got to find shelter!” he shouted, and grabbed her hand.

“We’re on bare rock. There is no shelter.”

He’d been an idiot, ignoring her concerns about the weather. Now they were going to end up another statistic, among the half dozen or so climbers who died each year because their desire to reach a summit overruled their common sense.

“Come on.” He tugged at her hand. “We have to move down.”

They half ran, half slid down the next stretch of bare rock. The hail stopped, replaced by rain in silver sheets, water running in streams down the rock. Thunder crashed in percussive waves, and lightning bathed the air in eerie blue light. The hair on Travis’s arms stood up and the back of his neck prickled. He gritted his teeth, bracing himself for the strike he was sure would come, but it did not.

“Look over there!” Leah stopped and pointed. He followed her gaze to a dark shadow on the side of the mountain.

“What is it?” he asked.

"I think it's a cave. Or maybe a mine tunnel."

Before she had finished speaking, he was pulling her toward it. They needed shelter, and even a hole in the ground might be enough to save them.

They had to walk sideways along a narrow ledge to reach the cave, a shallow opening beneath a rock ledge. It smelled of animals, and a faded, crushed beer can testified that they were not the first humans to use it as a refuge. He ducked inside and Leah followed. She dropped to the ground, panting and wide-eyed. "I've never been so terrified in my life," she said.

"We should be okay now." He stirred a pile of rubbish at the back of the cave with his walking stick—twigs, paper, moss and bark made a messy nest of sorts, but otherwise it was empty.

"Looks like a pack rat." Leah wrinkled her nose. "That's probably the smell, too. Let's hope the rat itself is long gone." She struggled out of the fleece jacket and wrung water from it. "I'm soaked."

"We need a fire," he said. The nest would make a good starter, but they needed bigger wood to burn if they wanted to get enough of a blaze to warm and dry them.

"I guess Braeswood's men wouldn't notice a fire way up here," she said. "Not with all the rain."

Travis raked the rat's nest to the opening of the cave, then took out his multi-tool and began sawing at his walking stick. "What are you doing?" she asked.

"We need the wood for fire. I'll need your stick, too."

She didn't protest, but handed over the stick. Within a few minutes he had a neat pile of kindling beside him. He took the matches and tinder from the pack and quickly had a blaze going.

"Too bad we don't have marshmallows," she said.

"I never liked roasted marshmallows," he said, carefully feeding one of the sticks to the flames. "Though I wouldn't say no to a nice sausage."

"Stop it. You're torturing me."

He sat back, watching the wood catch and the flames flicker bright gold. They had needed this, to stop and warm themselves by a fire, and rest in a place where they felt safe. Even if Braeswood's men did notice them up here, it would take hours of climbing for them to reach this spot, and by then he and Leah would be long gone.

"This feels so good," she said, scooting closer to him and stretching her hands toward the blaze. "I don't know what it is about a fire that's so comforting."

"It's probably genetic," he said. "Our cavemen ancestors looked to fire for protection and warmth."

"Hmmm." She let out a long sigh. "I think the rain is already letting up."

"We'll stay here until it stops and we dry off," he said. "The rest will do us good."

He fed another stick to the blaze. "Besides, we might as well use up the wood I cut."

"I'm going to miss my walking stick," she said.

"I'll cut you another one when we get down to the tree line," he said.

"Who knew you were such a woodsman?" Her smile was gentle and teasing, and he felt the familiar pull of longing for her. He forced himself to look away, focusing on the fire. She wasn't the woman he had known before, and he wasn't the same man. Whatever they had shared before, that was gone now. Trying to recreate it would be a mistake.

"You know what I've been up to for the past six months," she said. "But what have you been doing?"

Missing you. But no point going there. "Working. I was in Denver last month. I took a week this spring to go to Texas and see my folks." What could he possibly tell her that would sound interesting? His life was routine and boring, except for his work, which he couldn't talk about. "You remember my friend Luke?"

"Of course." She smiled—the same smile most women got when they thought of Luke, who was movie-star handsome and had charm to spare. "How is he doing?"

"He's engaged. To a sports reporter he met in Denver."

"Engaged! How wonderful for him. Do you like her?"

"I do." Morgan Westfield was smart and funny and she had courage to spare. "She's a lot like you, really. A strong woman."

She leaned forward to add a stick to the fire. "I'm happy for them, then."

He studied her profile, the smooth curve of her cheek, the slight jut of her chin, the curl of hair around her ear, and remembered the first time he had seen her—in the lunch line at their high school. He hadn't been able to stop looking at her and had followed her to her table and introduced himself. Later, when they were both grown and working in DC, he'd run into her at the Senate cafeteria, and that time he'd vowed not to let her get away.

Maybe some promises simply weren't meant to be kept.

"Will you go back to DC when this is over?" he asked.

She looked startled. "I don't know. I haven't thought about it much." She plucked a piece of gravel from the floor of the cave and rolled it back and forth in her fingers. "I never let myself think about the future when I was with Duane. It was too frightening. Too painful." She shook her head.

"You're smart, and you have good experience. You could find a job anywhere," he said.

"I'm sure employers will be lining up to hire a suspected terrorist." She made a face. "I'm sure I'll find something to do and somewhere to live when the time comes. I can't think that far ahead." She glanced at him. "What about you? What will you do when you're back in Durango?"

"Keep working on the case," he said. "Maybe go back to DC, or wherever the Bureau sends me." He shrugged. "The job doesn't make planning ahead easy." Though one time they had had big plans for a life together. They had been so optimistic and full of faith that everything would work out for the best. Braeswood had stolen that, too.

"I guess it's not so bad, living in the present," she said. "Isn't that what the Zen masters say you should do, focus on the now?"

"If that's what we're really doing." He leaned forward and stirred the coals with the last piece of firewood. "Sometimes I wonder if I'm not just stuck in the past." The past he'd had with her, when they had both been so happy. Knowing what they did now, could they be that happy again, or did that brand of bliss require a naïveté they would never have again?

He felt her gaze on him, and he wished he hadn't said anything. He didn't want to answer any more questions or think any more about mistakes and regrets. He tossed aside the stick. "The rain has stopped," he said. "Are you ready to go?"

"I guess we'd better." She gazed out at the now-sunlit slope. "Maybe we'll get lucky and the rest of the trip will go smoothly.

Travis put out the fire, then led the way down, attempting to pick the best route while still headed northwest toward the river and the train tracks. They moved slowly, having to detour or backtrack twice to avoid cliffs from which there was no safe descent. At this rate, they wouldn't reach the tree line before dark. For now, the sun beat down, quickly evaporating the puddles that had collected during the storm, reflecting off the rock with a brightness that hurt the eyes.

Leah moved even more slowly than he did. He stopped often to check her progress. At one point when he looked back she was sitting and inching her way down the slope on her butt. "I'm going to get down this," she said. "I can't promise it will be pretty."

"Do you want to stop and rest?" he asked.

"No." She gave him a weary smile. "I'm afraid if I do I'll never get going again. I don't remember when I've been so tired."

He knew what she meant. Their brief respite in the cave had done little to relieve the bone weariness that had set in from miles of walking over rough terrain. Being hungry didn't help, either, but no sense bringing that up. The protein bar that served as lunch had done little to end the gnawing in his gut. He drank from his water bottle, then extended it to her. "I can get mine," she said.

"Save your energy. We'll share yours later."

"All right." Her eyes met his, heated and knowing, as if she, too, was remembering when they had shared moments far more intimate than drinking from the same water bottle.

She gulped down water, then returned the bottle to him and heaved herself upright once more. "Let's go," she said. "It's bound to be easier when we get off this mountain."

Less physically demanding, maybe, but hacking their way across dense woodland wilderness, with an unseen enemy gathering around them, wasn't his idea of easy.

They set out again. The sinking sun to their left cast long shadows across the rocks, and pikas, small rodents resembling a cross between a rabbit and a mouse, chattered at them from the granite rubble around them. He stepped down onto a rock that looked stable and it slid out from under him and he crashed to the ground, the impact sending a jolt of pain through him. He flipped onto his stomach and grappled at the ground, seeking purchase on the steep, slick rock. When he came to rest some ten feet down the slope, he was breathing hard, his hands scraped and bloody, a rip in the knee of his pants.

"Are you all right?" Leah called, half running, half sliding toward him.

"I'm okay." He sat up. "Just…be careful."

She stood a few feet above him, worry and weariness clouding her face, but not making her any less beautiful to him. “I’m beginning to get freaked out,” she said. “I just want down off this mountain. I feel so…exposed up here.”

“I know what you mean.” He stood, trying to ignore the ache in his knees and back from the fall and the hours of climbing. All Braeswood and his men had to do was turn binoculars in the right direction and they would spot the two of them up here on this bare rock. He adjusted his pack and turned back down the trail. “Come on. We need to pick up the pace if we’re going to make it into the trees by nightfall.” He would feel better under cover, and they could plan their route for tomorrow.

“There are people who do this for fun,” she said, starting down behind him. “They try to climb every one of Colorado’s 14,000-foot-high peaks. Or every one of the 13,000-foot peaks.”

“Some people enjoy the challenge, I guess,” he said. “And if you did it with the right preparation and equipment, I can see how it might be enjoyable.”

“Count me out,” she said. “When I’m out of here I’m heading to a posh hotel with room ser—ahhhh!”

Her scream, and the sickening cascade of sliding rock and a falling body, tore through him. He whirled to see her flailing for purchase as she bounced down the side of the mountain like a rag doll.

Chapter Ten

Travis launched himself sideways toward Leah's falling body, like a tackle intercepting the ball carrier in a football game. He struck her hard, shoving her sideways and momentarily slowing her fall, but as he wrapped his arms around her and tried to dig his heels into the loose rock, they fell together, rolling and sliding at a terrifying pace. Rocks tore at them and he struggled to keep hold of her, trying to roll to shield her from the worst of the impact. She continued to flail, grabbing at the ground, her face a mask of terror, while he continually fought for purchase with his heels.

In the end, it wasn't their own efforts that saved them, but the bent trunk of a stunted tree that clung stubbornly to a ledge that jutted out over nothing. They came to rest against the trunk, Travis's left foot dangling in empty air. The rough bark of the tree dug into his back, but it was the most welcome pain he had known.

Leah stared at him, her eyes almost black from her fear-enlarged pupils, her skin the color of the snow that lingered in pockets on the peak. "We stopped," she whispered.

"Yeah." He buried his face against her shoulder

and struggled to rein in the tidal wave of emotion that threatened to unman him. Fear that they had almost died, exhilaration that they had survived, rage that they should be in this situation in the first place and a paralyzing terror that he had almost lost her. He could talk about justice and his job and his duty to his country, but in those seconds when his life had been in the balance, the one truth he knew was that everything he had done from the moment he had laid eyes on her at Braeswood's mansion had been for her. She was the reason he was fighting so hard, the reason he was willing to risk everything.

She nudged him. “You okay?”

“Yeah.” He raised his head, then sat up, slowly, keeping his back against the tree. The ledge they had come to rest on was fairly wide and level, safe enough for some of the tension to ease out of him.

She struggled into a sitting position and swept her hair out of her eyes, then glared at him. “What did you think you were doing, tackling me that way? You could have been killed.”

“I had to save you.”

She wiped away a smear of blood and mud on her cheek. “No, you didn't. You'd be better off without me. You could move faster on your own.”

“No, I wouldn't be better off without you.” He shifted to kneel in front of her and grabbed both her arms. “I never was.”

He told himself he deserved the wary look she gave him. He had certainly given her plenty of reasons to not believe him, to be afraid of him even. He smoothed his hands down her arms, then gently pulled her to him. “I need you, Leah,” he whispered. “I always have.”

The touch of her lips and the feel of her arms tightening around him filled him with heat and light, like a powerful drug flowing through his veins. The kiss was both remembered and brand-new, the urgent pressure of her mouth against his own, the tangling of tongues and press of bodies something he had longed for and something he waited to discover.

She fell back, pulling him with her. He straddled her, one knee planted on either side of her hips, her breasts pressed against his chest, her heart like a drumbeat in counterpoint to his own. One hand tangled in his hair while the other wrapped across his back. He kissed her cheek and tasted the metallic tang of the blood drying there, and pulled back. "You're hurt," he said.

"So are you." She smoothed her hand across the dark bruise forming on his forearm where he had slammed into the rock. "But we'll be okay. We're together and we'll be okay." Then her lips found his again, silencing words and obliterating thought. Fear and doubt, aches and pains, didn't matter in the face of their need for each other. He slid his hand beneath her shirt, cupping and caressing her breast, and he pressed his growing arousal at the juncture of her thighs. She arched against him and reached for the pull of his zipper.

Something—the call of a crow or the bite of the wind at his back, or the sharp jab of a rock against his hand when he moved—pulled him out of the drugging fog of lust and need. He wrapped his fingers around her wrist. "I think maybe this isn't exactly the right time for this," he said.

She blinked up at him, then a blush warmed her cheeks. "I guess I got a little carried away," she said.

"Hey, I wasn't complaining." He sat back and helped her to sit also.

"I guess we'd better get going," she said.

"Wait." He pulled her back down and reached around for the pack. "I want to tend to that gash on your face while there's still good light."

He found the first aid kit buried in the pack and cleaned and dressed the cut on her cheek and another on her arm with antibiotic ointment and adhesive bandages. She did the same for a gash on his knee and the cuts and scrapes on his hands. The sun had dipped behind the mountains to the west, taking with it most of its light and warmth. She shivered as the wind gusted across their rocky perch, and he fought the urge to pull her close once more. He was cold, too, now that the rush of adrenaline and passion had faded.

"Come on." He stood and reached to pull her up beside him. "We've got to hurry down and find some place to spend the night."

"Right. The last thing I want is a fall like that in the dark."

Carefully, they made their way down the next steep stretch. Thankfully, the grade became more gradual after that. Soon, they reached the shelter of the trees and a deeper darkness in which the black of trees was barely distinguishable from the black of the air around them. He stopped so that they could catch their breath and to try to orient himself. "I'd rather not turn on the light," he said. "In case someone sees it."

She gripped his arm, fingers digging in. "No. Don't turn on the light. I'm more afraid of Duane and his troops than I am the dark."

"I'll cut us another couple of walking sticks," he

said. "That will help us feel our way and keep our balance."

Even that simple chore took longer in the dark, and he was forced to turn on the light briefly in order to find branches of the right size and shape. He trimmed them quickly and handed one to Leah. "Thanks," she said. "At least now I have a crutch if I sprain my ankle tripping over a rock."

"Don't even think that." He tested his own stick, a stout, knotted length of cedar that would double as a cudgel. "Come on." He wanted to get deep enough into the woods to have good cover when they stopped for the night, but movement was more difficult than he had anticipated. Though the ground was more stable underfoot here, they had to constantly be on guard for tree roots, stumps and other obstacles. When he had banged his shins for the fourth time and she had tripped for the third, he took hold of her hand and pulled her to his side. "We've got to stop," he said. "Before one of us is seriously hurt."

"It's so much darker here than in the city," she said. "Darker than I ever knew it could be."

"I'm going to risk the headlamp again," he said, pulling the light out of the side pocket of the pack and slipping it on. "Just until we find a safe place to bed down."

The light cast a weak golden beam across the forest floor, enough to reveal they were in an area of closely growing trees and dense underbrush. "No wonder we kept running into things," Leah said.

"It's good cover to hide us tonight," he said, directing the light around them. "No one's going to be able to get close without us hearing them."

"I hope you're right."

As they had the previous night, they made a shelter of tree branches in the hollow left by a fallen tree. He spread the space blanket and crawled in, then pulled her in after him and covered them both.

She snuggled against his shoulder with a weary sigh. "I'd trade a year of my life for a cheeseburger right now," she said.

His stomach growled in response. "Try not to think about it," he said.

"It's all I can think about." She turned to face him. Though he couldn't make out her features in the darkness, he sensed her face very close to him. "Distract me," she said, her breath warm against his cheek.

As tired as he was, that plea was all the invitation he needed. He slid his hand beneath her shirt and over her breast. "Does this distract you?"

"It's a start." She squirmed against him and moved her hand around to squeeze his backside. "How about you? Are you feeling distracted?"

He nuzzled her neck, sliding his tongue into the hollow of her throat, savoring the silky feel and taste of her, a mix of salty and sweet. "Distracted from what?" He pressed into her, letting her feel his arousal, then covered her lips with his own.

She opened her mouth at his invitation and tangled her tongue with his, even as she explored his body with both hands. She pushed up his shirt and trailed her fingers across his chest, leaving sensations like the bite of sparks on his flesh.

"I've missed you so much," he said, resting his forehead against hers and fighting to rein in the desire that drove him to take her now, this very minute.

"I've missed you, too." She pushed his shirt up farther and kissed his shoulder, then slid her teeth across his flesh. "I've missed making love to you." She unfastened the top button on his pants.

He stilled, his fingers tightening on her shoulders. "I'm not sure now is the right time," he said.

"Are you worried Duane and his men will find us?"

"I don't think they'll find us tonight. We're too well hidden, and he's already shown he doesn't like to search at night. He probably figures we aren't going anywhere."

"Then why?"

He shifted, trying to get comfortable—impossible, given his current state. He traced the curve of her cheek with one finger, her skin like satin. "Think about it. We're exhausted. Hungry. Filthy, lying on the ground. You deserve better than that."

"I don't care about any of that." She cupped her hand to his face. "Look at me."

"I can't see you."

Her lips curved in a smile beneath his finger. "Then feel." She grabbed his hand and laid it over her heart. "You risked your life today to save me. But it wasn't the first time you saved me. Through the worst of the times with Duane, I got through it by thinking of you. I remembered what it was like to be with you, whether we were walking in the park or making love in your apartment. I remembered how much we had loved each other, and that reminded me that I was worthy of love. A good man had cherished me once. No matter what happened to me, I had had that."

"You deserve better than the way I treated you," he

said, and kissed the corner of her eye, tasting the salt of her tears, his own eyes stinging.

"We can't change the past," she said. "And tomorrow we could die. I hope not, but it could happen. If it does, I want to spend my last night with you. All these other things—the hard ground, my empty stomach, my fear—you can make them go away for a little while."

"I want to make love to you." He wished he could see her face right now, could read the emotion in her eyes. He settled for kissing the corner of her mouth. "But I'm worried about hurting you." She had been through so much—he couldn't think of it without feeling sick.

"You can't hurt me." She slid her hands down his chest and lowered the zipper on his pants. "I trust you, Travis, and I want to be with you. And that's all that really matters right now."

LEAH HELD HER BREATH, waiting for Travis's answer. Would his lingering doubts keep him from bridging this final gap between them? Was she crazy for even wanting this, considering their situation? "I want you," he said, and kissed her, a tender, dizzying kiss that quickly turned more passionate.

Undressing in such close quarters, in pitch blackness, proved a challenge, but one they were equal to. She giggled as he helped her squirm out of her jeans and underwear, and laughed at his attempts to shed his own pants while kneeling over her. Then he leaned away, reaching behind him.

"What are you doing?" she asked.

"I had to get the condom from Buck's pack," he said.

She laughed. "Thank goodness for Buck."

"That pack has saved us more than once the past couple of days," he said.

"Yes, but you have to admit—a condom is not something most people would consider essential wilderness survival gear."

"I think I read somewhere that a condom can be used as an emergency water carrier, or as a waterproof wrap for a wounded hand or foot," he said. "That's probably the reason it was in the pack."

"Sure that was the reason." She took the packet from him and tore it open. "But we're going to put it to better use, I think." She reached for him.

Breath hissed through his compressed lips as she fit the condom to him. She smiled, enjoying this moment of control and suspense, the trembling anticipation of the joy yet to come.

Travis took her by the shoulders and urged her to lie down. He slid alongside her and pulled her to him. The sensation of his warm skin against her, the contours of his body so familiar and welcome, brought a lump to her throat.

He nuzzled her neck and kissed his way across her shoulder, his hands skimming over her torso, like a blind man rereading a familiar text he had enjoyed many times. She arched against him, urging him on.

His mouth closed over her breast and she lay back, eyes shut tight, losing herself in their lovemaking. He still remembered how to touch her, what she liked and what excited her most. And she hadn't forgotten how to make his body respond to her touch—where he liked to be stroked, how he wanted to be held.

They each moved slowly, deliberately, murmuring words of encouragement and endearment, their entire focus on pleasuring and being pleasured. And when he knelt between her legs, poised over her, she was trembling with need for him. She reached up and pulled him to her, welcoming him as if the months apart had never happened, all the hurt and shame burned away in the heat of their passion.

Her fulfillment shuddered through her in a slow wave that left her gasping and grinning like a kid at Christmas.

"You liked that, did you?" he asked, another thrust like an exclamation point at the end of a sentence.

"Y-yes," she said, her voice unsteady.

"I liked it, too." He thrust again. "A lot."

She squeezed her thighs around him and lifted her hips to meet his next advance. They fell into a familiar, urgent rhythm, her need for him spiraling upward once more, her breath coming in gasps. Somehow she had forgotten, or refused to let herself remember, how good they were together. How right.

He came with a cry and reached down to stroke her, bringing her to a quick, second climax soon after. She was still shuddering when he withdrew, discarded the condom and lay down beside her, his head on her shoulder. She trailed her fingers across his shoulders and back, tracing patterns across his smooth, warm skin. "I love you so much," she murmured.

But her only answer came in a soft snore from her exhausted lover.

Chapter Eleven

Travis woke while it was still dark, the familiar yet unexpected weight of Leah against him disorienting him, as if their months apart had been nothing more than an unpleasant nightmare. Yet the hard ground beneath him and the chill around them reminded him of their circumstances, and the dangerous gauntlet they had yet to run before they could truly heal the wounds they had both suffered.

"What time is it?" she asked, her voice holding no trace of sleepiness, though he would have sworn she wasn't yet awake.

"I don't know. Early, I think."

"I slept well, considering." She stretched, and he could imagine her smile, the one that had so often greeted him in the morning after those nights she had spent at his place.

"Me, too." Yet as slumber receded and alertness returned, the aches and pains of the previous days' treks burned at his knees and hips and back. His stomach felt hollow, too. "We should set out as soon as it's light enough to see," he said.

He found the flashlight and switched it on. The thin beam lit their tiny shelter like a candle flame. She sat up beside him, hunched against the tree branches that formed their roof, and efficiently plaited her hair and secured the end with an elastic band. She was naked still, her breasts luminous in the light, and he felt a fresh surge of desire for her. They were both hungry, dirty, bloodied and bandaged. Yet she was still the most beautiful woman he had ever known. He sat also and cupped one breast in his hand. "How are you feeling this morning?" he asked.

"Hungry, thirsty and horny—not necessarily in that order." She grinned at him. "If someone had told me I'd be sitting in a lean-to in the woods after a night of sleeping on the ground, not having had a shower or a decent meal in a couple of days, with a gang of sociopathic terrorists pursuing us, and the chief thought on my mind was how soon I could get you back in the sack, I'd have told them they were certifiable. Does that make me some kind of pervert? Or just really desperate?"

"I think desperate circumstances force us to focus on elemental needs. The fundamental drives of our animal nature." He bent to kiss the valley between her breasts. "Or maybe I'm the same kind of pervert."

She combed her fingers through his hair, then suddenly grew still.

"What is it?" he asked, sensing a change in her mood. "What's wrong?"

"Nothing. I..." She bit her lip and shook her head. "No, I don't have the right."

"The right to what?" He took her hand and brought it to his lips. "Tell me what's upsetting you."

She looked up at him through the veil of her lashes. "After I left you—were there other women? I don't blame you if there were. You're a good-looking man and you weren't attached. I just…I just wondered." Her voice trailed away and she stared at the ground between them, the picture of misery.

He traced his finger along her jaw, her skin soft as satin. "There wasn't anyone else," he said. "Not in my bed. I couldn't. Or at least, I didn't want to." He had been so angry, then hurt, then afraid of having to suffer those feelings all over again if he got too close to anyone else.

"I'm sorry I hurt you," she said. "I made what I thought was the right choice, but so much has happened that I couldn't have foreseen."

He wished she hadn't made those choices, too, but he thought he was doing a good job of handling those emotions. He kissed her forehead. "You were right last night when you said we couldn't change the past."

"What about our future? I know I said I didn't want to think about what I was going to do now that I'm free again, but ever since we talked about it up there on the mountain, it's all I *can* think about. What are we going to do when we get out of here? I'm a wanted felon and you're an FBI special agent."

"So you knew we were looking for you?" he asked.

Her expression clouded. "Duane showed me on the computer—that I had made the FBI's Ten Most Wanted list. He seemed so pleased by the news, while I was horrified. Of course, that was the point—now that I was a wanted criminal, I had one more reason to stay with him. He convinced me that as soon as I left his protection I'd end up in prison, or even sentenced to death for acts of terrorism." She rubbed her shoulders, as if trying to warm herself against a sudden chill. "All

I could think was I was glad my poor parents didn't have to suffer through that—one daughter dead and the other a criminal. And you." She raised her eyes to meet his, their normally bright brown dull and bleak. "I wondered what you thought of me. Your whole life was about upholding the law. This seemed like the final betrayal."

It had felt that way to him, too. The day the bulletin was issued adding her to the list, he'd locked himself in his office and pretended to be engrossed in computer research. But all he'd done for hours was stare at the photo of Leah on the screen. It was the picture taken for her Senate identification badge, with her facing the camera, her hair tucked behind her ears, lips curved in a coy smile, as if she might burst into laughter the moment after the camera clicked.

"Isn't that the woman you were engaged to?" Luke had asked him when they left work that afternoon. It wasn't a question he even had to ask. Like Travis, Luke was a super recognizer who never forgot a face. He'd been with Leah dozens of times over the past month and would never confuse her picture with anyone else.

But Travis knew why his friend asked. This was his chance to either discuss the situation with someone who would listen and keep his confidences, or close off the subject forever. He looked Luke in the eye and chose the latter option—the only one he could live with at the time. "It's not Leah," he said. "It's just someone who looks like her."

Luke studied him a long moment, then nodded. "Okay. That's what I'll tell anyone if they ask."

"Are you going to have to arrest me when we leave here?" Leah asked. She attempted a smile, but failed.

"But I guess you already have. Isn't that what you said when you first dragged me out of the car? That I was under arrest?"

"I'm not going to arrest you," he said.

"I won't blame you if you do," she said. "You're doing your job."

"I was doing my job then. Now I know better. You were a hostage. The government won't pursue the charges against you once they know that."

"I wish I believed that. Even if the government does drop the charges against me, there will always be people who see me as part of Braeswood's group. A terrorist. Associating with me won't be good for your career."

As much as he wanted to deny this was true, he couldn't. Dating a woman who was currently on terrorist watch lists across the country, not to mention the Bureau's own Ten Most Wanted list, could bring his career to a screeching halt, or even mean the end of a job he loved. He levered himself over her and stared down into her beautiful, troubled face. She wasn't a terrorist. He was as sure of that as he was sure of his own name. And he was sure there was no point in wasting time worrying about what being with her might mean to his job. Not when they still had so much to get through to reach safety. "Right now, all I care about is making it safely through today," he said. "And spending the hour or so before it's light enough to start walking doing something a lot more pleasant than worrying." He lowered his body, making sure she felt his arousal.

Her breath caught and her eyes glazed. "Um, that sounds good," she said, and wrapped her arms around him and pulled him close.

He kissed her, a long, leisurely enjoyment of her sensitive mouth. His hands roamed her body, delighting in the feel of her. He skimmed along her ribs and traced the line of her hip. Then his hand stilled and he let out a groan.

"What is it?" she asked, her voice full of alarm. "What's wrong?"

"We don't have another condom."

She let out a shaky breath. "It's okay. I'm still on birth control. It's a hormone implant, so I don't have to worry about missing pills or anything."

"That's great." He smoothed his hand down her shoulder, and tried and failed to keep the discomfort in his voice. "I haven't been with anyone since you left," he said. "So I know I'm healthy. But you…"

She had been with Duane. He didn't want to think about that, but there was no getting around the specter of the villain that in some ways was always between them. But he let her fill in the rest of his objection. He couldn't say the words out loud.

She bit her lip and turned her head away from him, a deep blush staining her cheeks. "He always wore a condom," she said softly. "He was very fastidious about that kind of thing. But I understand if you'd rather not…"

The pain in her voice and the realization that he was making her remember that horror cut him to the quick. He gathered her close. "I want you," he said. He brushed his lips across hers, then drew her into his arms. "I've never stopped wanting you."

She dragged her gaze back to his, some of the light returning to her eyes. "There's no one here but us right now," she said, as much to herself as to him. "Only you and me, with nothing and no one between us."

He had made love to Leah many times, in apartments and hotel rooms and once, in a moment of daring, in a deserted conference room in the Senate building where she had worked. They had known the hesitant excitement of new partners and the frantic urgency of more experienced lovers. But none of those encounters had the intensity of these stolen moments in the pitch blackness of this crude shelter in the woods, when they relearned each other's bodies by touch and taste, aching to fulfill a need that surpassed the fear and hunger and fatigue that was like a black cloud hovering around them. Making love to Leah kept that cloud from engulfing him, at least for a little while.

They lay together for a little while afterward, dozing, until a dusky light began to breach the shelter, filtering down through gaps in the overlain pine boughs. They couldn't put off the tough day ahead any longer. He sat up. "I think it's time to go," he said.

Another woman—another person, he corrected—might have protested, begging for a few more minutes' rest, or complaining of the predawn chill that stung them as soon as they pushed back the space blanket they had been wrapped in and emerged from the lean-to. But Leah only folded the blanket, put on her shoes, then rummaged in the pack until she found their last protein bar. "Breakfast," she announced, holding it up as if she had unearthed a gold nugget.

"You eat it," he said, even as his stomach clenched painfully.

"Don't be so noble." She broke the bar in half and handed him one portion. "If it comes right down to it,

I ought to give the whole thing to you. If I grow too weak to walk, you can carry me. If you faint from hunger, I couldn't do a thing about it."

"Who says I'd carry you?" he asked around a dry chunk of the stale bar.

"You would. You're wired to be a hero."

He grunted and reached for the pack. "I might surprise you."

"All right, then." She stood and looked him up and down. "Maybe you'd just do it for the sex."

TRAVIS DUG THE compass out of the pack and spent a little time orienting them toward the north. Leah looked over his shoulder. "I think they taught us how to use one of those at Girl Scout camp one year," she said. "They took us out in the woods and we had to find our way to a meeting point using a compass and a map."

"Then maybe I should give this to you," he said.

"No way." She held up her hands as if to ward him off. "I never did find the meeting point during that Girl Scout camp. I seem to recall they had to send out a search party."

He laughed and consulted the needle again. "I think I've got this figured out. At least I hope so." He hefted his stick. "North, ho!"

He led the way, pushing through the dense greenery and ducking under the low-growing branches of spruce and fir that crowded this part of the forest. He held the compass in one hand and his hiking stick in the other, using the stick to push aside tangles of vines or branches that blocked their way.

Leah struggled along behind him. She hoped the compass worked and that he was reading it correctly.

Everything about this thick, shadowed woodland disoriented her. Travis had shown her on the map how, if they traveled north, they would eventually intersect the Needle Creek Trail, a well-traveled path that led from the Needleton train station to the popular Chicago Basin backcountry area. "All we have to do is keep walking north," he said.

Right. So easy. She winced as yet another thorn-covered vine whipped back to strike her in the legs, the thorns biting through her jeans. She carefully picked the vine away from her, then hurried to catch up with Travis, who was stomping through the undergrowth with all the finesse of an elephant. "If anyone is following us, they won't have any problem figuring out which way we went," she said.

"Braeswood and his men are most likely between us and the trail." He slashed at another vine with his walking stick.

She shivered. "How many men were in that group you saw yesterday?" She should have asked for the binoculars so she could see the hikers for herself. Even at that distance she might have recognized Braeswood or one of his inner circle of thugs.

"I counted eight." He held aside a leaning sapling and motioned for her to move past him. "They were fully kitted out with high-tech gear, too. Like a SEAL team on a mission." He shook his head. "Why is he going to so much trouble—spending so much time and trouble—trying to find you?"

Did she imagine the annoyance in his voice? She didn't have to be a therapist to figure out what had prompted the question. For a while last night and again this morning, they had both managed to put aside thoughts of Duane Braeswood and her complicated relationship with the terrorist. But he always lurked in the shadows, a phantasm poisoning everything good between them.

As strong and confident as Travis was in every other aspect of his life, in these past few days she had discovered how deeply she'd wounded him. Doubts about her loyalty—and maybe about his own feelings as well—worried at him. He asked the same questions of her over and over out of the very human desire for a better answer, one that would explain the unexplainable. Had she really been Duane Braeswood's unwilling mistress? Had she done anything to attract him to her? The things that had happened to her in the last six months had to have changed her, but had they changed her into a woman he could never really love? A woman who could never love him?

She struggled to find the words that would assuage his fears and bolster her own confidence. "I don't pretend to understand why Duane does anything he does," she said. "There was never any emotional connection between us. People don't mean anything to him. He used me the way he might use an inanimate object. I served some purpose in his twisted worldview, so he kept me around. I was someone he could manipulate and control. Someone he could hurt, and I think he got a kind of pleasure from that."

Travis stopped so abruptly she almost collided with him. He whirled to face her, his face a mask of pain. "He had better hope I'm never in a room alone with him," he said. "When I think of what he did to you..."

She grabbed his arm, her fingers digging into his rock-hard biceps. "Don't do this to yourself," she said.

"Don't dwell on it. It's in the past now. All we can do is focus on getting out of here and doing everything we can to see that he is captured and punished."

He inhaled raggedly and nodded, regaining his composure. She released her hold on him and took a step back, still watching him carefully. "I'm okay," he said. "And we are going to find him and see that he's punished. Your testimony will go a long way toward making that happen."

"I hope so," she said. "I don't know a lot about his operation, but I know some things, and I know the people he associated with. I don't have your memory for faces, but I think I would recognize a lot of them again."

"You probably know more than you think you do," he said. "Enough to put him away for a long time."

He checked the compass, and they set out walking again. "Don't forget that I'm not the only one Duane is after," she said. "He doesn't have any love for the Feds. You ran him down in his home, you took me away and you killed one of his men. Any one of those things could be reason enough for him to have a grudge against you."

"How many people does he have working with him? Were there more than your driver and Eddie Roland, Buck and Sam?"

"There are probably hundreds of people connected to Duane in one way or another," she said. "Some merely send money to support his efforts. Others provide information or access to a location, while others do the actual work of carrying out attacks, building bombs, intercepting intelligence and disseminating propaganda. In many ways, he operates like any head of a large international corporation."

"And Braeswood heads it all?"

"In the United States," she said. "Though I sometimes had the sense that there were other people, in other countries, who wielded power also, to the point where Duane had to answer to them." She shook her head. "But I don't have any proof of any kind of connection like that. In any case, there were always new people filtering in and out of the house. Mostly men, but a few women, too."

"Do you think you could identify them again?"

"Some of them. But I'm sure there were others I never saw. He was always on the phone, talking in a cryptic kind of code about targets and objectives and tasks. He never said anything in my presence that told me what he was really up to."

"How long would you have stayed with him if I hadn't come along?"

She couldn't see his face when he asked this question, but the stiffness of his shoulders and the chill in his voice warned her to tread carefully. "I don't know," she said. "Maybe I would have found the courage on my own to leave. Or maybe he would have grown tired of me and had me killed. There were days I would have welcomed that."

He turned and sent her a sharp look. "What happened to all that optimism and hope you were preaching about earlier?"

"I wasn't preaching. And it's much easier to be hopeful now that I'm away from that prison. I had plenty of bad days. Some truly horrible days." She closed her eyes, struggling for composure. She would never forget the things Duane had done to her, but she didn't want to let them define her.

His hand around her wrist made her open her eyes. He studied her, his expression intense, as if he were searching for something familiar in a stranger's face. "I never realized before how strong you are. I wonder what else about you I overlooked."

Then he released her and turned away to study the compass, then adjust their course toward the path that, she hoped, would take them to safety.

THE JOURNEY BECAME a forced march as they concentrated on putting one foot in front of the other, finding the best route, stopping only to check the compass and once to filter water to fill the water bottles from a small stream. Leah moved steadily behind Travis, never complaining, stopping only when he did. He had loved her and wanted to spend the rest of his life with her, but he had always thought of her as gentle and delicate. He was the strong one in their relationship—the man who was supposed to protect her. Maybe that was a sexist thing to believe in the twenty-first century, but it was a belief reinforced by both his upbringing and his training. He was an officer of the law, sworn to serve and protect.

She was smart, and funny, and incredibly sexy. But he had never known she was so tough and determined. Seeing her this way both awed and unsettled him. What other aspects of her character had he misjudged or failed to see in her? If he had been more in tune with what was going on inside her, would he have picked up on her distress over her sister? Could he have done something to help her? Could he have saved her from the hell she had suffered as the prisoner and pawn of Duane Braeswood? The idea that he had failed her weighed heavy; he wouldn't fail her again.

He stopped to check the compass again; fallen trees, dense underbrush and rocky outcroppings forced them to continually detour off a direct route. Leah moved up beside him, her hand on his arm. She rose on tiptoe and whispered in his ear. "I think I heard voices."

He looked at her sharply. "Where?"

"I can't tell which direction they were coming from. Listen."

He raised his head, straining his ears to pick out any sound beyond the sigh of wind in the branches overhead and the occasional birdsong. Her hand tightened on his biceps and he recognized the low murmur that might be distant conversation.

He pointed ahead and to their left, and indicated they should move in that direction. She pulled him back and spoke again, her mouth against his ear, the words barely audible. "What if it's Duane's men?"

"We won't know until we check it out," he said. The average backpacker wouldn't be able to save them, but they might have food or information about Braeswood's whereabouts.

"Do you still have the Glock?" he asked.

She reached behind her and withdrew the gun from the waistband of her jeans.

"Hide behind a tree here and I'll go check this out," he said. "If anyone comes after you, shoot them."

"No." She shook her head. "We'll check it out together. It doesn't make sense for us to separate. If they do discover us, we're better off facing them as a team."

The stubborn set of her chin and the determined

look in her eyes told him argument would be a waste of time. "All right." He drew the Ruger and checked that a round was in the chamber. "We'll go together."

They moved slowly, carefully placing each step and pausing often to listen to the intermittent bursts of what he was sure was conversation. Whoever these men were—and the low register of the words indicated they were men—they weren't trained in stealth operations. They weren't making any great effort to conceal their whereabouts.

At last they reached a bluff overlooking the river. A well-worn trail meandered along the bank of the waterway, and beside this path two men sat on a fallen tree trunk, eating lunch. Travis was sure these were two of the men he had seen hiking in yesterday. They were dressed in black tactical fatigues, with heavy black packs resting at their sides. He could make out a holstered pistol at one man's hip—possibly another Ruger —and the blued stock of an assault rifle showed in the shadows beside the other man's pack.

"The man on the right works for Duane." Leah spoke softly in his ear. "I don't know his name, but I've definitely seen him before."

Travis nodded and started to move forward. Leah tugged on him, her expression one of alarm.

He indicated they should retreat into the woods again. When he judged they were far enough from the river that the men there wouldn't hear their whispered conversation, he stopped. "We should move around them and cross the river downstream while they're eating," she said.

"Do that and we might walk right into a trap. If they have men guarding the bridge, I'd like to know before we get there. If I can get close enough to hear their conversation I might find out more about who is here and where."

"It's too dangerous."

"The more information we have, the less danger we're in." The primary focus of his job with the Bureau was gathering information. The right knowledge often made the difference when it came to stopping criminals like Braeswood.

She worried her lower lip between her teeth, then nodded. "All right. But we'll go together."

He could have argued that two people were taking a bigger risk than one, that two people made more noise and were more likely to be seen. But he didn't want to be separated from her any more than she wanted to wait behind for him. The memory of Braeswood holding a knife to her throat when he'd left her before still sent a chill through him. "We'll go together," he agreed.

They returned to their previous position on the bluff. The two men had made another tactical mistake, stopping so near the river. The noise from the water rushing over rocks would mask sounds around them. And they were still chatting as they ate, only occasionally scanning the area. As long as he and Leah were careful, they shouldn't have too much trouble getting close enough to hear their conversation.

He touched her shoulder and indicated she should follow him through a thick growth of bushes that filled a drainage leading to the river. This cover would take them almost to the water's edge, downstream and behind the two men. From there, he hoped they would be able to listen in on their discussion. He only hoped the two were talking about their job here in the wilderness, and not their favorite sports team or women.

They crawled through the bushes on their hands and knees, a torturous progress, battling thorns and rocks and snagging branches. Fortunately, a thick layer of leaf litter covered the ground, muffling the sounds of their progress. As long as the two men didn't decide to look behind them and notice the bushes moving, he and Leah should be okay.

Very near the water, he stopped. Though the noise from the river swallowed up some of the two men's words, he could make out enough to get the gist of their conversation. It was, as he hoped, about their duties out here.

"It's a big waste of time." The older of the two, the one Leah had recognized, was a wiry, tanned fellow with closely cropped salt-and-pepper hair. He bit into an apple and chewed as he spoke. "If they aren't dead by now, they will be soon."

"Then we'd better find their bodies," the second man, a younger, beefy blond, said. "The chief isn't going to let up until he knows they're out of the picture."

"I'm going to really enjoy shooting a Fed." The older man mimed firing a pistol.

"The chief wants the woman alive," the blond said. "I think she's the real reason he's going to all this trouble."

"Women can make a man do crazy things, that's for sure." The older man finished off his apple and tossed the core into the grass at their feet. "Though I never knew what to make of the two of them together. He never paid that much attention to her. And she never looked all that happy to be there."

"Oh, I think she was happy enough. The chief is loaded, and some women really get off on the power. She was one of those types. Why else would she stick around? It wasn't like he kept her chained to the bed."

"Now there's an idea," the older man said. "I had a girlfriend once who was into that stuff. You know, bondage and whips and stuff. Pretty hot."

"Maybe when we find Braeswood's woman, we don't turn her over to him right away," the blond said. "Maybe we have a little fun with her first."

Behind Travis, Leah made a choking sound, then stumbled back.

"What was that?" The blond sat up straight and reached for the rifle.

"Something over there, in the bushes." The older man was on his feet, his gun drawn. Travis turned to look at Leah, who huddled in the underbrush, eyes as wide as a frightened rabbit's. He started to move back toward her when the loud crack of gunfire froze him, and a bullet smacked into the dirt inches away from him.

Chapter Twelve

Leah bit down hard on her hand to keep from screaming as bullets slammed into the dirt around them. Travis surged forward and, grabbing her hand, dragged her after him. They didn't bother with stealth this time, crashing through the tangle of vines and shrubs, fighting their way up the slope. The rapid tattoo of gunfire propelled her forward with strength she hadn't known she possessed.

At the top of the bluff, Travis dived behind a large boulder and she followed him, landing with her cheek pressed to the dirt, the frantic pounding of her pulse and ragged breathing drowning out all other noise. Then a deafening blast of gunfire made her jump. She raised her head to see Travis firing down the slope. Braeswood's men returned fire and a bullet nicked the rock beside them, sending shards of granite flying, then all was silent.

"They're too well hidden for me to get a good shot," Travis said.

"At least they stopped shooting at us," she said. She had drawn the Glock and held it pointed at the ground, knowing better than to fire without a clear target.

"They're probably radioing for help," Travis muttered. "It's what I would do in their position."

"They'll try to surround us." The thought made her chest feel hollow.

"Which means we have to get out of here now." He unshouldered the pack, took out the box of ammunition and began reloading the Ruger. "We're going to run hard that way." He nodded to the west. "We're headed for the bridge. The train hasn't stopped there yet—we would have heard the whistle."

"Duane will have someone guarding the bridge," she said.

"Then we'll have to find a way past them." He shoved the gun into the waistband of his pants. "Are you ready?"

She took a deep breath. The first rush of adrenaline had faded, leaving her shaky, but she had to find a way to get past that. She wouldn't sit here and let them take her back to Duane without a fight. "I'm ready."

As soon as they began moving, the gunfire followed them, closer this time, as if their two pursuers were climbing the ridge. They retreated farther away from the bluff, into the cover of thicker underbrush, but continuing to run parallel to the river. She hoped their head start on level ground gave them an advantage.

The going was tough, and fear made it even more difficult to breathe. At the point when she felt her lungs would burst, Travis stopped and pulled her into what she thought at first was a tangle of downed trees. On closer examination, she saw they were sheltered in the remains of a crude log cabin, the kind a miner might have built over a hundred years before.

His arms encircled her, pulling her close. She rested

her head against his chest, feeling the hard pounding of his heart, and some of her panic eased. “What are we going to do?” she whispered.

“We’re going to rest here for a minute,” he said. “We’ll see if they’re following us.”

“They’ll be able to tell where we crashed through the woods,” she said. “They’ll know we’re in here.”

“Most people aren’t trained trackers,” he said. “None of their shots hit us because they weren’t aiming—they were just firing wildly in our general direction.”

They had gotten lucky this time. But what about next time? “If they trap us in here, how long can we hold them off?”

“We have maybe thirty rounds of ammunition for the Ruger, less for the Glock.”

“So not long.”

“That rifle the blond guy was toting will rip through this old wood like tacks through paper,” he said. “If they get close enough, how much ammo we have left won’t matter.”

“You do know how to reassure a woman.”

“Is that what you want? Pretty lies to make you feel better?”

“No. Thank you for being honest with me.” They had always told each other the truth—until she lied to him about Duane. In trying to save him, she had destroyed so much. “I could offer to surrender if they let you go,” she said. “You heard what those two men said—Duane wants me alive.”

“Because he loves you so much.” He spoke the words with a sneer.

“Because he loves that he can control me. Or he

could. Getting away from him, running for our lives here in the wilderness, has shown me what I can do. I won't stay with him again. But I'll make him think I will if it will give you time to get away."

His arms tightened around her. "No. I won't let him or his men have you. Now be quiet and try to rest. We need to listen for them."

She settled against him, but her mind raced, preventing rest. The odds that Duane would let Travis go in exchange for her were slim, but with Travis's cooperation they might be able to trick him. The tough part would be distracting the hunters he had sent out after them. Maybe she could draw their fire here in the ruined cabin while Travis sneaked out the back and circled behind them. Did they have enough ammunition to make that plan feasible? And what about his assertion that the rifle bullets would cut through the old wood as if it weren't there? Her stomach churned along with her thoughts, a stew of frustration. She hated feeling helpless like this.

Travis slipped his arm from around her shoulder and leaned forward. "Listen," he hissed.

Something—or someone—was moving through the underbrush and not bothering to disguise the sound of his approach. Travis put his eye to a gap between the logs, and she found a gap to peer through also. At first, she saw nothing. Then she detected a shaking in the trees. The blond young man emerged, rifle at the ready.

"Come out with your hands up and we won't shoot," he shouted, and her blood turned to ice.

Travis gripped her wrist, whether in reassurance or restraint, she couldn't tell.

"We know you're here," the young man shouted.

"You won't get away." But he had turned his back to them, aiming his words at the general surroundings. She exchanged a glance of relief with Travis. Blondie hadn't seen their hiding place—not yet.

The older man emerged from the woods to the west, his face flushed, his breath coming in pants. "Did you find them?" he gasped.

Blondie shook his head. "They came this way though. I'm sure of it." He scuffed at the leaf mold at his feet. "It's too dry for tracks. What about Will and Jacko? You heard from them?"

"They're doing a sweep away from the river. No sign of anything yet."

"They couldn't have gone far," Blondie said, scanning the area. "No one could in this thick underbrush."

"Come on. They're headed for the bridge." The older man slapped him on the back. "They'll try to catch the train. We'll have them then."

Together, the two men moved away. Leah leaned back against the rough log wall and closed her eyes. For long minutes, neither she nor Travis said anything.

Travis was the first to rouse himself. He moved back to the gap in the logs. "We should keep an eye out for Will and Jacko," he said. "Do you know them?"

"No. But I didn't know the names of a lot of men who worked for Duane. And most of them didn't know my name, either. I was just—the woman." Or "Duane's woman" or one of the other names he called her when he was in a bad mood. She had learned to ignore the name-calling and even most of the physical abuse, turning her mind to other things while he ranted at her, or when he dragged her to his bedroom. Pretending not to be there was a coping mechanism.

But his reminders of how much control he had over her had hurt. When he wanted to get to her, he told her he planned to burn down the family cabin she had signed over to him. Or he told her the car that was still in her name was being used to run drugs down near the Texas border, or that he had spent the money her father left her to buy weapons and bombs.

"He'll have an army waiting for us at the bridge," she said. "We'll never get past them."

"No," he agreed. "They would spot us long before we got there."

"We could go back the way we came, try to make it to a road. They won't expect that." A fresh wave of despair washed over her at the idea of another two or three days in the wilderness, trying to survive on roots and berries.

"My guess is he has people watching the roads, too."

She buried her face in her hands. To find their way to a road, only to be stopped again, was too horrible to contemplate.

"You know Braeswood better than I do," Travis said. "What do you think is going through his mind right now?"

Braeswood's mind was not a sewer she wanted to explore. "I don't really care what he's thinking," she said. "Except that he's probably enraged that we've evaded him so far."

"If we can figure out what his next move is likely to be, we can try to get a step ahead of him," Travis said.

She pondered the idea, reviewing everything she had learned about Duane Braeswood in the past six months. "He's definitely a control freak," she said. "He spends a lot of time planning his operations, as he calls them. He drills everyone and oversees every detail. He brags about never having been caught because he's so meticulous."

"What does he do when something happens that he can't control?" Travis asked.

"You mean like the Feds raiding his home and me running away? He blows up. He does exactly what he's done this time—he throws every resource at the problem."

"Would you say he acts irrationally?"

She considered this. "Not irrationally, exactly. But his reaction is over the top. Out of proportion."

"But he tries to think of every possible angle to solve the problem?" Travis frowned.

"Not exactly, no. He's really smart, but he's arrogant, too. He decides what the problem is, then what the solution is and goes all out to use that solution to fix the problem."

"So he might overlook something."

"He might. But he really is a genius, I think. I don't remember him ever being wrong about a situation."

"No one can be right all the time," Travis said.

"No. But he has a lot of information and resources at his disposal."

"Even so, arrogance is a flaw we can exploit." He settled back against the logs once more, hands resting on his knees. "I'm guessing he's a man who enjoys luxury. That wasn't some little cabin in the woods he was renting."

"Of course. He can afford it."

"He doesn't like being uncomfortable. He doesn't like roughing it here in the woods."

She snorted. "Trust me, he's not roughing it. If he

was in that group we saw headed up the trail, you can bet the others are carrying most of his load, and he'll have the best of everything in his campsite."

"He's called off the search every night."

"We can't count on him doing that tonight. Not when he knows we're so close."

"Still, even with night-vision goggles, it's not easy stumbling around in these woods, especially with a bunch of gear. Better to station sentries along the approach to the bridge and wait for us to come to them."

"Which means we're still trapped."

"Blondie and the older guy only mentioned two other men by name. That's four, plus maybe Braeswood."

"Duane would have at least one man with him as a bodyguard. Probably Eddie Roland."

"So that's seven. I counted eight on the trail when we first spotted them. Eight men can guard the bridge pretty effectively, but they can't guard the whole river."

A shiver of apprehension raced up her spine. "What are you suggesting?"

"The railroad follows the course of the river through the wilderness area," he said. "We can cross anywhere and hit the tracks. Then we lie low until the train approaches and we flag it down."

She stared at him, digesting this information.

"You don't think it's a good idea?" he said.

"We can't just wade across the river," she said. "The water is flowing really fast and it's bound to be ice cold. It's probably deep, too. I mean, there's a reason there's a bridge to the hiking trail. A really big bridge. And getting to the river anyplace but at the bridge is going to be tough. It's in a gorge. The banks are really steep."

"That's why Braeswood won't expect us to attempt it. But there's bound to be a place we can climb down. An animal trail we can follow. And this time of year the water is at its lowest point. We can get across. We're both strong swimmers."

"I can swim laps in a pool," she said. "That's a lot different from swimming an ice-cold, raging river. Especially when we haven't had a decent meal in three days."

"Then you can wait on the bank while I go across and get help," he said. He leaned over and took her hand. "This is our best chance of getting to safety. We can't afford to wait much longer."

He was right. She had already done so many things in the past six months that she never would have thought she was capable of. What was climbing down a cliff and swimming across a cold, raging river when compared to all that? And if they did die in the attempt, it was better than being gunned down by one of Duane's thugs, or worse, going back to Duane. "I'm willing to try," she said. "But you're not going to leave me behind. We'll do this together."

He pulled her close and kissed her. When he released her, he was almost smiling. "The moon is almost full," he said. "That will help us."

"What does the moon have to do with any of this?"

"We'll have to make the crossing at night," he said. "It will lessen our chances of being spotted, in case they're patrolling the bank or scanning it with binoculars."

"So we're going to climb down cliffs and swim the river at night?"

He patted her shoulder. "You can do it."

Right. Maybe she had made a mistake being so stalwart through this whole ordeal. Now he thought she was a superhero!

Chapter Thirteen

Travis didn't need Leah's incredulous look to tell him that what he proposed was crazy. But, as the saying went, desperate times called for desperate measures. "The best chance we have to get away from here safely is to do something Braeswood thinks is impossible," he said. "Yes, the river is cold and the water is fast, but it's not that wide—about the length of the pool back in our gym in DC. I'm not saying it will be easy, but I don't think it's impossible."

The long, mournful wail of a train whistle echoed through the canyon. "There goes our ride," Leah said, a stricken look on her face.

Travis powered up the phone and checked the time. "Eleven fifteen. Now we know what time we need to be at the track tomorrow."

"I thought you said we're crossing at night."

"We are. We'll cross the river at night to lessen the chance of our being seen. Once we reach the other side, we'll have to lie low until right before the train comes. We can't risk one of Braeswood's men spotting us."

"What will happen after we leave here?" she asked. "To Braeswood, I mean?"

"We'll mobilize a team to move into this area. If

we're lucky, we'll get to Braeswood and his men before they realize you and I are gone. With the evidence we've collected already and your testimony, we should be able to put them away for a very long time."

"Do you think the court will believe me?"

"They will." He squeezed her hand. "I believe you."

"You didn't at first."

"I was angry." He shifted to face her. "I let my pride get in the way of what I knew in my heart. When I read your note the day you left, I should have realized something was wrong. I should have followed up and done more to protect you."

She lightly touched the back of his hand. "I wanted you to stay away. If you had come after me, Duane would have killed you. I couldn't save Sarah, but at least I could save you."

"I'd rather have taken my chances and still had you."

She sat back and closed her eyes. "I want to forget about everything that happened, but it's not easy."

"When we get out of here, you should talk to a counselor or a therapist," he said. "Someone who can help."

"Maybe we both should."

He hesitated, then nodded. He wasn't the type to unload his problems on someone else, but his feelings about what had happened to Leah were in such turmoil, maybe talking to a professional would help him sort them out. "That's a good idea," he said. "Maybe we can help each other."

His first instinct was to leap in and fix everything for her, but he understood that in this case, charging in and taking over wasn't going to help. He had to navigate a tightrope between her desire for independence and his need to protect her. "Try to get some rest," he said. "We'll stay here another hour or two, then start walking. We'll try to pick out a place to cross the river while we still have light, then wait until full dark to set out."

She made a small noise of assent, then lay down on her side, her back to him. He leaned back against the logs, the loaded gun beside him, and tried to sleep. They would both need every bit of strength they could muster to get through the night.

THOUGH LEAH HAD slept for over an hour, she didn't feel refreshed by the rest. Disjointed, confusing dreams had plagued her—dreams of running from unseen enemies, or of being trapped in houses with many rooms but no exits. Travis had been in the dreams as well, as a face at the window outside the house, or a voice calling her name. But they were never able to reach each other as she struggled through the dream world.

When she opened her eyes he was watching her. "You were restless," he said. "I thought you were having a nightmare. I wanted to wake you, but I wasn't sure if that was the right thing to do."

She sat and tried to straighten her rumpled clothing. "I read somewhere that dreams are the subconscious trying to solve problems."

"So, did your dream give you any solutions?"

"Not yet. But I can be patient." She glanced out the gap between the logs, at the long shadows of tree trunks stretched across the forest floor. "When can we leave here?" she asked.

"Whenever you're ready."

"Then let's go now." As much as she dreaded the ordeal that lay ahead, she was ready to get it over with.

They left the log ruins and began hiking along the bluff. They headed upstream, staying out of sight of the riverbank itself, but always keeping the sound of the river to their right. They hiked for two hours—what she judged to be four or five miles—then cautiously made their way to the edge of the bluff and looked down on the water. They had been steadily climbing all afternoon, so she wasn't surprised to see the water lay some forty feet below. The setting sun silvered the water where it tumbled over rocks in the narrow channel, but the bank they stood on was already in shadow.

"How are we ever going to get down there?" she asked.

"We'll have to walk along the bank until we find a less steep place or an animal path or something."

He sounded so confident that there would be a less steep place or a path. "What if it just gets steeper?" she asked.

His eyes met hers, calm but determined. "Then we'll walk in the other direction."

Right. What else could they do? She followed him upstream for another half hour, scanning the steep embankment but seeing nothing that looked promising. Bunches of drying grass and a scattering of yellow and purple wildflowers clung to the reddish soil that had collected between the rocks. The embankment on the opposite side of the river, leading up to the railroad tracks, looked just as steep and forbidding.

Travis stopped, and she almost stumbled into him. "I think we can get down here," he said.

She stood on tiptoe to peer over his shoulder and studied the faint line of what might have been a trail, snaking down the slope at a sharp angle. "You're kidding."

"We can do it," he said. "We'll take it slow and use our walking sticks to help balance."

She shivered, as much from fear as from the chill that descended with the setting sun. "What do you think made that trail?" she asked.

"Mountain goats, maybe. Deer? Some kind of animals headed to the river for water."

"Maybe you need four legs to get down something like that," she said.

"You climbed down a mountain yesterday. You can do this."

Right. The whole superpower thing again. They were going to have to have a talk about that sometime, but maybe not now.

"We'll wait for the moon to rise," he said. "Then we'll head down." He moved back toward the cover of trees. "In the meantime, we'll find a place to wait."

"You can wait. I'm going to find food." She turned and started walking back the way they'd come.

"Where are you going?" he asked.

"Some of those bushes we passed earlier looked like raspberries." The idea of anything to eat made her mouth water.

He fell into step beside her. When they reached the cluster of bushes again, her heart sank. Combing through the branches, all they found were a few shriveled berries. They ate the dozen or so bruised fruits, then she plucked some rose hips from the wild rosebushes that grew nearby. "If we had a fire, we could heat water and make raspberry leaf tea," she said, though she couldn't muster much enthusiasm for the idea.

"We can't risk it." He plucked a leaf from a raspberry bush and chewed, then spit it out. "It tastes terrible."

Her laughter surprised her; she hadn't thought she had any mirth left in her. "The look on your face is priceless," she said.

He made a show of looking around them. "What else do you think I should try? Fir branches?" He grabbed hold of a nearby evergreen branch. "Is the tree bark any good? I've heard this place serves an excellent stone soup."

"You'll have to settle for chewing gum." She handed him a stick from the packet she had unearthed earlier in the day. She had been saving it for right before they set out on their river crossing, but now seemed a better time. "I'd forgotten I had this in my pocket."

The gum did little to satisfy their hunger, but the act of chewing and the little bit of sweetness the gum provided felt good. Travis took her hand. "Come on. Let's find a place near that trail to wait for moonrise. And try to watch where you step. We don't want to go tumbling off the cliff."

"That would be one way to get to the bottom quickly."

"Come on, you." He tugged her alongside him and squeezed her shoulders.

They moved a little farther into the woods and settled down against the large trunk of a towering fir, the air perfumed with the Christmas tree scent. "You might as well take another nap," he said, patting his thigh.

She hesitated, then stretched out beside him, her head in his lap. He idly stroked her hair and she remembered another summer afternoon when they had sat like this, on the National Mall, listening to a free concert of classical music. Had it really only been last summer? It seemed a lifetime ago. "This is kind of romantic," she said. "If you overlook the fact that I'd kill for a steak and a shower."

He laughed. "I guess it is—if you overlook those things." He caressed her shoulder. "It's good to see you in a better mood."

"I guess I've still got some fight left in me."

"Good. I have a feeling you're going to need it."

She closed her eyes and snuggled against him. "Bring it on," she said, already sinking toward sleep.

SHE WOKE WITH a start when Travis nudged her. "It's time to go," he said, his voice low.

She sat and brushed pine needles from her clothes, then glanced toward the bluff, and the indentation that marked the beginning of the steep path they had to negotiate to the river. The moon shone like a white spotlight above the trees, bathing everything in a silvery glow.

"Are you ready?" Travis extended his hand.

She took it and let him pull her to her feet. "Probably not," she said. "But sitting here longer isn't going to make me any more ready."

He handed her the stout walking stick she had been using since they had come down off the mountain. "Use this to steady yourself on the way down. If you feel your feet slipping out from under you, sit down right away."

"I'll do that. And pray. A lot."

"That's a good idea, too."

They set out, picking their way down the narrow, steep path. A chill breeze buffeted them, but Leah scarcely noticed, she was focused so intently on placing each step.

In front of her, Travis froze. "What is it?" she asked, her voice a hoarse whisper.

"Look." He pointed and she shifted her gaze some distance ahead of them and to the right. Her breath caught as she stared at a large black bear making its way down to the water, two chubby cubs ambling along after her. The cubs batted at each other and tumbled around their mother's feet. The mother hefted her big body over rocks and around tree trunks, looking back to check on the twins from time to time.

"She doesn't know we're here," Leah whispered.

"We're downwind from her."

"The babies are adorable, but I'm just as glad we didn't meet them in the woods."

"Me, too." He turned his attention away from the bears to her. Moonlight softened and shadowed his features, like a smudged charcoal portrait. "How are you doing?"

"Okay," she said. "The climb down isn't as bad as I feared. The mountain was worse." She glanced toward the river. The rushing current had provided the background noise for much of their day, but the sound was louder now, and the moonlight cast an eerie glow over the foaming rapids. How were they ever going to get across that?

As if reading her mind, Travis said, "We'll walk

upstream a ways, and cross where the current isn't as swift."

"I hope Duane and his men aren't watching us." She shivered at the thought.

"If they were, we would have heard from them by now."

"I guess when it comes to Duane and his buddies, no news really is good news."

They continued down the slope. The mother bear and her cubs reached the river, then meandered downstream. "Maybe she's looking for a better place to cross, too," Leah said.

"Maybe she is."

They reached the narrow strip of gravel beside the water. The sound was much louder here, so that they had to raise their voices to talk over it. "Which way do we go?" she asked.

"I think I saw calmer water downstream."

If not for the danger, this would have been a romantic scene, strolling in the light of the full moon along the riverbank, silvery cliffs towering overhead, silvery water dancing alongside. The rapids gave way to a smoother, though wider and possibly deeper stretch of water. "I think this is the place," Travis said. He slipped off the pack and began unbuttoning his shirt.

"What are you doing?" she asked.

"It's cool enough that if we stand around in wet clothing after we cross, we risk hypothermia. We'll be better off if we wrap our clothes in plastic in the pack and put them on again when we reach the other side." He peeled off the shirt and unzipped his pants, then bent to untie the laces of his hiking boots.

"Okay." Undressing made sense. But the prospect

of crossing the river naked made her feel even more weak and vulnerable.

"Come on," he said. "I want to get this over with."

Reluctantly, she began to strip off her clothing. She turned her back to him, though why, she didn't know. It wasn't as if he'd never seen her naked before. The night air raised goose bumps on her skin as she folded her clothing into a compact bundle.

When she turned around to hand her clothing and shoes to Travis, his gaze was fixed on her. "You should see yourself in the moonlight," he said, his voice husky with emotion. "You're so beautiful."

She couldn't look directly at him, afraid her face would give away all the emotion she was feeling—fear and love and shame and wonder. She watched him out of the corner of her eye and noted the way the moonlight burnished the muscles of his shoulders and arms. The bullet wound on his ribs was still an angry red, but the scar somehow highlighted the beauty of the rest of him—the flat abdomen and muscular thighs, and the thick perfection of his sex.

In this deserted wilderness, bathed in silvery moonlight beside the flowing waters of the river, they might have been Adam and Eve in paradise. Except that they were about to risk their lives crossing that river, and while the moonlight would help guide them, it would also make them more visible to anyone who might be watching.

"Are you afraid?" she asked, blurting the question she had only meant to think to herself.

"Yes," he said. "Any sane person would be. But we're going to do this anyway."

She nodded. "Yes. We're going to do this."

He wrapped the clothing, along with both guns and the ammunition, in the pack's rain fly and then in the plastic trash bag, then lashed the pack shut. "That should keep everything dry," he said. "As long as I don't lose the pack."

"Don't you dare." The thought of having to flag down the train naked made her face heat.

He laughed. "I promise, I'll hang on to the pack. Come here." He pulled her close.

He was warm and solid—and aroused. "Now isn't the time for this," she said, even as she felt her skin heat and her nipples bead into tight peaks.

He nuzzled her neck. "I know, but the sight of you naked in the moonlight definitely turns me on."

And the feel of him naked against her did the same for her. "Save that thought for later." She reluctantly pulled out of his embrace and faced the water. "So what do you think? Just dive in?"

"Wade in. Use the walking stick to brace yourself. If you fall, let the current carry you downstream until you can regain your footing or swim. Aim your feet downstream and watch for obstacles."

"You talk as if you've done this kind of thing before," she said.

"I had to take a water rescue course once, in preparation for a mission." He cut his eyes to her. "Don't ask."

"I wouldn't dream of it." When they had started dating, she had adhered to a policy of not asking about his work with the Bureau. She didn't want to know what kind of danger he put himself in daily.

He took her hand and pulled her forward. "You go

first," he said. "That way I can see if you get in trouble and try to help."

"What if you get in trouble?" she asked.

"I promise to yell loudly." He pulled her tight against him and kissed her, a surprisingly fierce, passionate gesture. "It's going to be all right," he said.

"You're just saying that."

"I don't lie, remember?"

"I remember." She touched her fingers to his lips, then waded into the water.

The shock of the cold stole her breath and forced out an involuntary yelp. She faltered.

"Keep moving," Travis urged, stepping into the water behind her. "The faster you move, the sooner it will all be over."

She nodded, and forced herself to take a shaky step forward, and then another. The icy water pushed against her legs and the gravel river bottom continually shifted beneath her feet, making it difficult to keep her footing. It was so cold. How did those people who took polar bear plunges for charity or for fun ever do it? She planted the walking stick and held on tightly, clenching her teeth against the cold and shaking.

A few more steps and the water was up to mid-thigh, and then up to her hips. Fighting the current, she struggled forward, planting her foot on a smooth rock, bracing with the stick…

Then she was down, water engulfing her, cutting off the scream that ripped from her throat. The cold water rushed over her head and stole her breath, and rocks scraped her backside and arms.

She tried to stand, managing to get her head above water and sucking in a gasping breath. But the current made it impossible to find purchase on the rocky river bottom and her feet continually slipped out from under her. Remembering Travis's advice, she fought to turn her body and aim downstream as the river pulled her along. She popped to the surface again, gasping and shouting for help. Though who would hear besides Travis, she couldn't imagine.

She tried to relax and let the current carry her, focusing her efforts on keeping her head above water, but the constant buffeting against rocks and tree branches sticking up from the river bottom made that impossible. She feared she would be battered to death before she ever reached the shore.

Desperate, she grabbed hold of one jutting branch and clung to it as the water rushed around her. She was too weak to pull herself out of the water, but the momentary pause allowed her to catch her breath and assess her situation.

She was little more than halfway across the river, and at least a hundred yards past the point where she had fallen. She ached with the cold and her fingers were so numb she had trouble keeping hold of the branch she clung to. How long did it take for someone to die of hypothermia? An hour, or only minutes? She raised her head as far out of the water as she could, and spotted Travis standing in midstream, water to his chest, looking down the river. Relief flooded her at the sight of him. At least the water hadn't dragged him under. After she rested here a moment, she would attempt to cross the rest of the way. Soon they would be together on the shore. She raised her hand and waved to let him know she was all right.

In that moment, the branch broke, sending her hurtling into the current once more.

Chapter Fourteen

"No!" The cry of frustration tore from Travis's throat as the current ripped Leah from her anchor. Exhausted and trembling with cold, he'd stopped halfway across the river to get his bearings and had been relieved to see her safe, clinging to the branch of a tree that had lodged in the riverbed a hundred yards downstream. Now anger and fear gave him renewed strength and he dived into the water and started stroking for the far shore. The current carried him downstream, but he kept his eye on his goal and fought to make headway. After another minute his feet struck the bottom and he waded forward, pushing hard.

He didn't allow himself a moment of rest when he climbed out of the water, but ran downstream, in the direction Leah had disappeared. He feared at first he had lost her. "Leah!" he shouted as he ran, scanning the tumbling water for some sign of her dark hair or flailing limbs. The thundering roar of the rapids swallowed up the cry.

He spotted her twenty yards ahead. She was swimming, but making little headway, clearly tiring in her fight against the rapids. He ran farther up the bank, shedding the pack as he moved. Leaving it beside the water, he strode into the icy current once more, setting a course to intercept Leah.

He was still ten yards away from her when she went under and didn't resurface. "Leah, no!" he shouted, and barreled toward her. He plunged under the water at the place he thought she had gone down, but found nothing but the gravel bottom.

He surfaced to take a breath, then dived, again and again, until his teeth chattered violently and fatigue dragged at his limbs. On the verge of giving up, something bumped against his leg —something soft and pale. He reached down and his hand closed around Leah's ankle.

He dived and gathered her body close and dragged her to the surface. Eyes shut, she lay limp in his arms. Not allowing himself to think, he wrapped his arm around her in a lifesaving carry and began fighting his way back to the shore, his body and mind numb to everything but the goal of saving her.

It took every last reserve of energy to struggle up the bank, dragging Leah with him. He lay with his face in the mud just out of the water, shivering, his heart thudding. He turned his head to look at her, her pale skin tinted blue in the moonlight.

"No," he said again. He forced himself up onto his hands, then he crawled to her and put his ear to her chest, listening for her heartbeat. He thought he heard a faint pulse. He pressed his cheek to her lips and felt a faint flutter of warm air. Quickly, he turned her onto her side and began rubbing her back, then chafing her wrists and hands. "Come on, Leah," he pleaded. "Wake up for me."

She jerked and coughed, then convulsed as she

vomited up a flood of murky liquid. He held her, brushing her hair out of her face. "That's a girl," he said. "Get it all up. You're going to be all right."

"Travis." The single word was barely audible, but it hit him with the impact of a shout. He helped her sit up and she stared at him, blinking. "Wh…what happened?"

"The branch you were clinging to must have broken," he said. "The current pulled you under."

She curled her knees to her chest and wrapped her arms around them. "I'm so cold."

"Let me warm you up." He pulled her to him, then they lay together, legs and arms wrapped around each other, until her shivering subsided.

"You saved me," she said after a long while.

"I thought I'd lost you." Seeing her slip under the water had been the worst moment of his life. He shuddered, remembering.

"No. Not yet." She burrowed her head against his shoulder. "I'm so cold."

"We should get some clothes on."

"Where's the pack?"

"I left it on the bank when I dived in after you." He looked up and spotted the pack, sitting fifty yards upstream. Exhaustion pulled at him. It might as well have been a mile away.

"One of us is going to have to get it," she said.

"I know." He heaved himself into a sitting position. "I'll get it."

He retrieved the pack and dropped it beside her, then fell to his knees. He took out one of the water bottles and drank, then handed it to her while he opened the pack. Relief rushed through him as he unfolded the plastic. "Everything is dry," he said.

They dressed quickly. The clothing felt good against his skin. Warmer, though not really warm enough.

"Maybe we should build a fire," he said.

"A fire sounds heavenly." She looked down the riverbank, toward the bridge and the train station, too far to see from their vantage point. "But we probably shouldn't risk it. If Duane and his men found us now, I wouldn't have the energy to run away from them."

"You're right." He shouldered the pack. "Let's find someplace safe to wait until morning and wrap up in the space blanket. Our body heat will warm us."

A few hundred yards upstream, they found a hollowed-out place in the bank half hidden by brush and weeds. They crawled into this and pulled the space blanket around them. Within minutes they had fallen into an exhausted sleep.

LEAH WOKE TO bright light hitting her face. She moaned and tried to turn away from the painful glare, but there was no room in her cramped hiding place. "I was going to wake you soon." Travis spoke from a few feet away, where he knelt before the pack. "The train will be here in a half hour or so."

The train. Their salvation. But to reach it, they had to climb the steep bank to the tracks. Every inch of her ached at the prospect. She pushed aside the space blanket. "How are we going to get the train to stop?" she asked.

"I thought we'd use your sweater as a flag," he said. "It's red, so they'll be able to see it from a long way off."

"My sweater?" She clutched at the garment in question. "You want me to flag down the train topless?"

He grinned. "I'll bet the engineer would stop for that."

At her horrified look, he laughed. "You can wear the fleece jacket. It zips up the front. And once we're on board, you can have the sweater back."

She couldn't think of a solid argument against this plan, so she reluctantly peeled off the sweater and handed it over. While she put on the fleece and zipped it up, he tied the arms of the sweater to a tree branch and waved it experimentally.

"This ought to work. I'll stand on the track and wave it over my head."

"What if the engineer doesn't see you? What if he can't stop in time to avoid hitting you?"

"I remember now. You always were a grouch before you had your morning coffee."

She glared at him.

"The train isn't traveling that fast," he said. "I'll stand where I'm sure the engineer can see me from a long way off." He tugged the space blanket from around her and began folding it. "Are you ready?"

"I just need to shower, brush my teeth, comb my hair and do my makeup, and have some breakfast." She combed her hair back out of her face with her fingers. "Oh, wait. I can't do any of those things."

"There will be food on the train," he said. "And coffee. And restrooms."

"You sure know how to tempt a girl." She shoved herself up. "I'm ready."

He shouldered the pack, then led the way up the steep bank. The trail was straight up, and slippery with gravel, but she managed to pull herself up by gritting her teeth and picturing the cheeseburger she was going to devour as soon as they reached whatever passed for a dining car on the tourist train.

At the top of the trail, Travis put his hand on her shoulder. "Listen."

She stilled, and the low moan of the train whistle reached her ears. Her heart leaped. "It's coming."

He removed the pack and handed it to her, took the flag he had made from her sweater, and walked out onto the track. The slim rails were only thirty-six inches apart, coarse gravel filling in the space between the ties.

The train appeared around a bend up ahead, the engine a black monster, wheels churning, white steam pouring from the smokestack and shooting out from the brakes as the engineer negotiated the curve. Sunlight glinted off the engine's windows, making it impossible to see the engineer. The whistle sounded again, much louder now and more urgent.

Both hands raised over his head, Travis waved the makeshift flag. The train's brakes squealed, shooting out steam, and gradually the engine slowed. Travis joined Leah beside the tracks. Behind the coal car, passengers leaned out of the window to gape at the man and woman beside the tracks. "We must look like a couple of derelicts," Leah said, aware of her unwashed body, messy hair, and torn and dirty clothing. Travis sported a four-day growth of beard and equally ragged clothing.

"They'll just think we're a couple of backpackers." He took the pack from her and slung it onto his back. "Nothing that unusual out here."

"What do we do when it stops?" she asked, as the train rolled slowly toward them.

"I'll show them my credentials." He dug the folder with his badge and identification from his pants pocket.

She slid her hand into his. Now that they were so close to safety—to food and hot water and an end to the physical and mental exhaustion of being pursued by killers—her whole body vibrated with anticipation. She focused on the engine's wheels churning slowly down the track. The engineer leaned out of the window toward them, checking them out. Travis held up his credentials, though Leah doubted the engineer could make out anything about the wallet from this distance.

The engine drew alongside them, the sound of the whistle deafening. Leah covered her ears and moved closer to the tracks, ready to climb on board as soon as the engine stopped. She couldn't see into the cab anymore, though she could hear some of the passengers shouting questions about the reason for the delay. Any second now, they would be on board. Safe.

Then, instead of stopping, the train began moving faster. Fast enough that instead of walking, they had to trot to keep up with it. "Hey!" Travis shouted. "Stop! We need help!"

A stern-faced man in the blue suit and billed cap of a conductor appeared on the steps of the platform leading to the first car behind the coal tender. "You have to board at the station," he shouted above the hiss of steam and the churn of the engine's wheels.

"We need help!" Travis protested.

The conductor shook his head and pointed downstream, in the direction the train had come, toward the Needleton Station. Where Duane and his men were no doubt waiting for them.

TRAVIS AND LEAH STOPPED. Frustration and rage boiled inside him. After all they had been through, this was too much. He grabbed Leah's arm. "Come on," he said. "We're going to have to jump on board."

"What?" But she kept pace with him as he ran toward the cars at the rear of the train. Though the engine had picked up speed, it still wasn't moving more than a few miles an hour. He watched the cars as he passed, trying to judge the distance between the track and the bottom step leading up to the platform at the rear of each car. It was a big leap, but if he could make it, he could help Leah up after him.

Catcalls and abuse assailed them as they ran. An empty plastic cup bounced off his shoulder. "They're not going to let us on!" Leah called.

Travis stopped and held up his credentials. "FBI!" he shouted. "Let us board."

"Hazel, I think that badge might be real," one man said to the wide-eyed woman beside him.

A few hands reached out to Travis from the platform. He leaped, his toe just catching the step, and they hauled him on board, then he turned to help Leah. Two other men leaned out to assist, and together they pulled her up onto the platform.

The other passengers bombarded them with questions. Who were they and what were they doing flagging down the train? Was he really an FBI agent? Why was the FBI all the way out here? They pressed forward to examine the badge and identification Travis displayed, and stared at the disheveled, dirty pair as if they were from another planet.

"Maybe it's a movie," someone farther back in the car said. "Or a television show."

A conductor—maybe the same one who had glared at them from behind the coal tender—pushed his way through the crowd at the back of the car. "Let me see those credentials," he demanded, extending his hand.

Travis handed over the wallet. The conductor studied the picture, then Travis's face. "This doesn't look much like you," he said.

"It looks like me when I haven't spent four days in the wilderness." He took back the wallet and returned it to his pocket. "I've been pursuing a fugitive."

The conductor nodded to Leah, who stood at Travis's elbow. "What about her? Is she an agent, too?"

"She's a key witness in my case," he said.

"What I am is half starved," she said. "Does this train have a dining car?"

"The refreshment car is through here." The conductor turned and they followed him up the aisle. The other passengers gaped at them with open curiosity, the spectacular scenery outside the windows momentarily forgotten.

At the end of the car, Leah stopped before a door marked Ladies. "I'm just going to go in here for a minute," she said. She held out her hand. "May I have my sweater, please?"

"The refreshment car is next," the conductor said. "You can meet us there."

She nodded. "Are you sure?" Travis asked as he handed over the sweater, which was still attached to the tree branch.

Her smile burned through him. "Don't worry. I'm not going to let you get too far away from me again. I'll meet you there in a few minutes. Go ahead and order me a cheeseburger."

Travis followed the conductor across the platforms into the next car, which contained a snack bar manned by two young women in bib overalls. The aroma of coffee and grilled food made him feel a little faint, and it took all his willpower to wait for the couple in front of him to finish before he placed his order.

"You must be really hungry," the young woman said after he had asked for three burgers, two orders of fries, two milks, two coffees and a package of cookies.

"You have no idea," he said, and took out his wallet.

"What's this all about?" A third man joined Travis and the conductor at the snack bar. "Russell Waddell," he said. "Railroad security."

"Special Agent Travis Steadman." Travis displayed his creds, then accepted his change from the snack bar cashier.

"I'll have to ask you to surrender your gun until we get to Silverton," Waddell said. "The young lady, too, if she's armed. We don't allow weapons on the train."

"As a law officer, I'm licensed to carry a duty weapon," Travis said. He didn't bother mentioning the Glock Leah no doubt still carried tucked under the oversize fleece jacket.

"He says he's after a fugitive," the conductor volunteered.

"Here on this train?" Waddell's eyebrows rose.

"I've been tracking him through the Weminuche Wilderness," Travis said. He tore open one of the cartons of milk the young woman handed him and drank it down in a gulp. "As soon as we get into cell phone range, I'll call for backup."

"You won't have cell service until we reach Silverton in a little over an hour," Waddell said. Apparently he'd decided to drop the argument about Travis's gun. "But we have a radio you can use to relay a message to our headquarters in Durango."

"Great. As soon as Leah and I have a chance to eat we'll do that." He glanced toward the back of the car. What was taking her so long?

"She's probably in there cleaning up," the conductor said.

He nodded.

"Your order's ready, sir."

He turned to accept the tray of food.

"Here she comes," the conductor said.

Relief flooded him when he glanced back and saw Leah making her way toward him. But instead of returning his smile, she sent him a tense, worried look. He set down the tray and started toward her. "Leah, is something wrong?"

"Nothing wrong at all."

Travis's mouth went dry when he recognized the man who spoke. Walking very close to Leah, his arm around her, Duane Braeswood offered a smile with no mirth. Instinctively, Travis reached for the gun at his waistband.

"Good to see you again, Agent Steadman," Braeswood said. "Leah and I were just discussing what a coincidence it is that we should all end up on this train."

Chapter Fifteen

Leah's eyes pleaded with Travis for help. He eased his hand away from his weapon. The way Braeswood held Leah, he probably had a gun or knife pressed against her. So much for the rule about no weapons on the train.

"Friend of yours?" Waddell asked. He had probably picked up on Travis's hostility.

Travis forced himself to relax. "We've known each other a long time," he said, trying to sound casual.

"You might say we were once rivals for the affections of a certain beautiful woman." The smile Braeswood gave Leah made Travis's skin crawl.

Leah licked her lips, her eyes glassy with terror. "Duane says he has a private car we can wait in until we reach Durango," she said, her voice strained with tension.

"That's right," Duane said. "Bring your food with you and we'll catch up on old times."

"What about the call you needed to make?" Waddell asked. "The radio is in the engine compartment."

"Making a call like that through a third party could jeopardize national security," Duane said. "Not to mention compromise Ms. Carlisle's safety."

Leah's expression grew more pained. Travis wanted to punch the smirk off Braeswood's face. Waddell wasn't likely to buy a phony excuse like "national security," but for Leah's sake, Travis was going to have to sell the idea. "The guy I'm after isn't going anywhere in a hurry," he said to Waddell. "Rather than try to relay what I want through the people at railroad headquarters, it's probably a better idea to make the call myself when we get nearer Silverton."

Waddell frowned. "If you're sure."

"I'm sure." He picked up the tray and wondered if shoving the food in Duane's face would distract him enough to make him release Leah. But if Braeswood did have a gun in his hand, he might fire it, and gunfire in the crowded confines of the train was bound to result in innocent people getting hurt.

They made their way forward to a car marked Private—Reserved. "Hello, Mr. B." An attendant greeted them at the door.

"Marcie, these are my friends Leah and Travis," Braeswood said. "They're going to be riding with me the rest of the way."

"Yes, sir." The dark-haired young woman flashed a friendly smile. "Welcome aboard. Can I get you anything to drink?"

"Water would be good." Travis followed Braeswood to a small dining table covered with an old-fashioned lace cloth.

"And you, ma'am?" Marcie asked.

"Water is fine." Leah slumped into a chair next to Travis. Braeswood withdrew the gun he had held pressed into her side, though he kept hold of it, resting it on his thigh beneath the table.

"As long as you cooperate, no one gets hurt," he said in a low voice. "Try anything and I'll kill her. And you, too."

Travis ignored the threat, his focus on Leah. He pushed the tray toward her. "We might as well eat," he said.

He thought at first she might refuse, but after a moment, she reached for a now-cold French fry. It didn't matter that the food was cold and not all that appetizing. He was so hungry he could have eaten almost anything. Braeswood said nothing while they finished the meal.

When they were done, Marcie cleared their trays, then returned to stand by the door. Travis leaned across the table and spoke in a low voice. "Whatever you're planning, you won't get away with it," he said.

"I was planning to return to Durango to gather more forces and equipment to hunt down the two of you," Braeswood said. "You've saved me that trouble and expense." He turned to Leah, frowning. "I must say, I'm very disappointed in you. I warned you what would happen if you tried to run away, and now you leave me no choice but to follow through on that promise of punishment."

She glared at him, saying nothing. The smile he gave her sent a fog of red through Travis's brain. It took every bit of his willpower and training not to leap across the table and attempt to rip that sneer from Braeswood's face. "You've wasted a lot of my time and cost me a great deal of money," Braeswood said. "So before I kill you I should try to recoup at least part of my losses. I have a friend who owns a brothel down near the Mexican border where a young woman like you would be in high demand."

Still Leah said nothing, but her face paled and her breathing grew more shallow. Travis sensed her retreating into herself, returning to that pale, frightened woman he had pulled from the car in the driveway of that rented mountain home only three days ago. "You'll never get away with it, Duane," he said, his voice as menacing as he could make it. "Even if you kill both of us, the rest of my team knows you're in this area and they will stop at nothing to hunt you down."

"The Feds are nothing but a bunch of half-trained foot soldiers strangling in red tape and government oversight." Braeswood met Travis's glare with a cool look. "I'll admit, you impressed me a little bit, the way you managed to evade my team back there in the wilderness. But they would have found you eventually, and then your exalted government agency would have pretended you didn't exist, or blamed your demise on your own clumsy efforts. If you're really so interested in seeing justice done in your lifetime, you'd join my organization. We could use a man with your skills."

"Your organization is a bunch of murderers and thieves."

A muscle at the corner of Braeswood's eye twitched, the only indication of any emotion on his part. "Change is difficult," he said. "Watch a butterfly emerging from a cocoon sometime and you'll see how much work and pain is involved. But those who persevere through the brutality will, like the butterfly, soar."

"What a pretty speech," Travis said. "Is that your favorite pep talk for the troops?"

"I do more than talk about change," Braeswood said.

"I work to make it happen. Something you government types don't understand." He checked his watch, an ornate gold Rolex. "We should reach Silverton about one p.m," he said. "I'll have a car and driver waiting there. The town is very remote, and the countryside around there is filled with old mines and Jeep trails. I shouldn't have too much difficulty finding a place to dispose of your bodies."

As if all his talk about exiling her to a Mexican brothel hadn't been enough to frighten Leah, Duane's boast about disposing of their bodies should have been enough to send her into a faint from sheer terror. When she had stepped out of the ladies' room and almost collided with him, she was sure she was hallucinating, mistaking some stranger for the man who had haunted her nightmares for months. Then she had felt the hard jab of a gun barrel biting into her side and heard his voice, his words chilling her more deeply than the river water ever could have. "Hello, Leah. It's so good to see you again."

The shock of seeing him on the train, when she was so sure they were finally safe, had left her momentarily catatonic, but all his boasts of working toward a better world, familiar as they were, had shaken her awake again. The past few days of struggling to survive in the wilderness had shocked her out of the paralyzing stupor she had been in ever since her sister's death. Duane counted on people fearing him. Their fear gave him most of his power, so almost everything he said and did was calculated to make them more afraid. Now that she could see so clearly what he was doing, she wouldn't let him manipulate her with his threats anymore. She had to fight back with everything she had.

The door at the end of the car opened and the conductor entered. "We'll be arriving in Silverton in about half an hour, folks," he said. "Make sure you have all your belongings with you when you depart the train. If you're making the return trip to Durango, listen for the train whistle around three o'clock. That's your signal to head back this way."

"My friends and I have decided to return to Durango by road," Duane said. "I have a driver waiting for us."

"Then thank you again for riding the Durango & Silverton Railway," the conductor said, his face bland. "I hope you enjoyed the trip."

"Yes, it was very enjoyable." Duane took Leah's hand. "Especially since it allowed me to reconnect with my dear friends."

Leah pulled her hand away and glared at him. He was so evil—how else to account for the fact that the prospect of murdering her and Travis didn't upset him in the least. He spoke of his plans to dispose of them in the same tone he might use to describe an afternoon picnic. The conductor appeared not to notice her hostility. "There's still some great scenery between here and the Silverton station," he said. "We'll be passing through Elk Park, then directly after that we'll come to Deadwood Gulch. Quite the view there. The train will slow so you can take pictures if you want."

She waited until the conductor had moved on to the next car before she turned on Duane. "You can't think you'll get away with murdering us," she said. "Too many people will know we were with you."

"They'll know a man named David Beaverton, a successful plastics manufacturer from Ohio, was with you," he said, his demeanor as calm as ever. "If they try to find such a person, they'll learn he died last year."

"Did you have anything to do with his death?" Travis asked.

"He died of a brain aneurysm at age forty. He and I share the same body type and general coloring. I have a contact in vital records who keeps me informed of such useful persons."

"So you stole his identity," Travis said.

The train slowed to a crawl. Marcie approached their table. "Can I get you anything, Mr. B?" she asked.

"No, thank you," he said. "We won't be requiring anything else this trip. Feel free to leave us alone."

"I'm assigned to this car for the whole trip," she said. She glanced out the window. "Not much longer. We're at Elk Park. Sometimes the train stops here, if we have a hiker or someone like that who needs to get off. Most of the time we just crawl through so folks can take pictures of the old bridge."

What had the conductor said? Something about Deadwood Gulch being next on the list? Leah raised her eyes to find Travis's gaze fixed on her. She didn't have to read minds to know what he was thinking—if they didn't find a way to get away from Duane before they reached Silverton—and definitely before he hustled them into his car and drove off into the mountains—they could very well be dead before nightfall.

Rage filled her at the thought that they had endured so much—struggled so much—only to have Duane win in the end. She couldn't let that happen. She wouldn't sit here and not try to do something to save herself and Travis. She shoved back her chair and stood. "I need some air," she said, and headed toward the viewing platform at the rear of the car.

"You need to stay here until we reach Silverton." Duane leaned back, giving her a clear view of the gun in his hand.

"I'm just stepping out on the platform," she said, reaching for the sliding door that led outside. "I feel like I'm going to throw up." Even as she said the words, she braced for the impact of a bullet slamming into her. Duane didn't like it when she talked back, and being in a semipublic place was no guarantee that he wouldn't lash out at her.

"You poor thing." Marcie jumped up to pull open the door for her. "The motion of the train affects some people that way, especially after a big meal. The fresh air will help you feel better."

Maybe Duane was reluctant to shoot Marcie along with Leah. Or maybe he didn't want to alert the security agent, Waddell, when he was so close to making his escape. Whatever the reason, he didn't shoot Leah now, though he kept his hand on the pistol and the weapon pointed in her direction, even as both men scraped back their chairs and prepared to follow. Leah lurched out onto the platform and clung to the railing as the cars rocked from side to side over a rough stretch of track. She stared up at the jutting mountain peaks that looked as if they had been painted by an artist in love with color. Bright yellow cascades of waste rock streaked the steep red and purple slopes, the white of snow in the shaded valleys and on the highest peaks giving way to the scarlet and gold of aspen, the deep green of spruce and pine, and the rust-orange splotches of beetle-killed fir. The air smelled of cinders and smoke and rushed against her skin in a chill wind.

Travis moved in close behind her, his arm around her waist. "You okay?" he asked.

"No." There was nothing okay about having had the last six months of her life stolen by the man who had murdered her sister and many others. Duane had robbed her of the job she loved, the marriage she had dreamed of, the sister she had adored. He had taken her money, trashed her reputation, and turned her days and nights into a nightmare that would probably haunt her for the rest of her life. Getting rid of him wouldn't change any of that, but it might prevent other people from enduring the same misery.

"Get away from her." Duane shoved Travis out of the way and took his place behind Leah, the pistol once more driven painfully into her side. "Make one wrong move and I'll blow your guts out," he said. "It will be a horrible, painful death, I promise."

She turned her head to look at him, careful to make her expression soft and inviting. "You don't have to worry about me, Duane," she said. "I know when I've been beat. I'm only going to stand here and let my head clear and enjoy the scenery."

His eyes narrowed. "Go ahead and enjoy it all you want," he said. "It will be one of the last sights you see."

"It's so incredibly beautiful," she said. "And I can't get over all the gold mines that are still active up here."

"I haven't seen any gold mines," he said, his tone scoffing. Yet she didn't miss the greedy light in his eyes.

"There are lots of them," she said. "I read somewhere that with the price of gold going up so much, a lot of people are working small claims again and making money at it. You just have to look for the openings in the rocks. There's one up there." She pointed up the slope.

"I don't see anything," he said.

"Come stand on the other side of me." She indicated the space where a length of cable closed off the steps leading toward the track. When the train stopped, a conductor would unhook this cable and passengers could file down the steps. "Lean out just a little ways and look straight up the slope, just at the tree line." She demonstrated, angling her body over the cable and gazing up the slope.

Travis moved in behind her once more, his whole body tensed. "I see what you're talking about," he said. "That little wooden structure?"

"Right." She turned to Duane, who had moved to her other side and was leaning, though not very far, and squinting up at the rocks. "Do you see it?" she asked.

"No."

"Lean out more. You need to look at an angle to really see it."

He did as she suggested, one foot almost off the floor as he arched farther over the cable.

"That's it," Leah said. "Perfect." She caught Travis's eye and he nodded. She put a hand on Duane's back and gritted her teeth. She could do this. She could push him off the platform, if it meant saving her own life and Travis's.

Travis lunged forward and grabbed Duane's arm with his left hand. In his right, he held the Glock. "Duane Braeswood, you're under arrest," he said.

Duane jerked like a fish on the line, twisting and turning, kicking out. “Let me go!” he shouted. “You have no authority over me.” The gun fell from his hand and Leah kicked it away. It slid across the metal floor of the platform and sailed into the gulch.

“Stand still, you idiot.” Travis struggled to hold him with one hand. “Take my gun,” he ordered Leah. “If he does anything out of line, shoot him.”

She took the gun and held it with both hands. It was all very well and good for Travis to tell her to shoot Duane, but any shot she fired had an equal chance of hitting Travis himself, especially with Duane fighting against his restraint like a rabid dog.

“No!” Duane shouted, breaking free of Travis’s grasp. He backed up against the cable, his face scarlet, eyes dilated.

“You’re trapped, Braeswood,” Travis said. “You need to come with me quietly.”

“You’ll never take me.” He glanced over his shoulder, at the narrow trestle over Deadwood Gulch, a picturesque, deep canyon with a silvery creek threading through its rocky floor.

Travis took a step toward him. “Turn around and put your hands behind you,” he instructed.

Duane hesitated, then whirled to present his back to the lawman. But instead of standing quietly awaiting the handcuffs, he threw himself over the railing, like a diver intent on plumbing the depths of a lake.

The rumble of the train wheels and the blast of the whistle drowned out any cries Duane might have made when he fell. He bounced awkwardly against the rails, like a mail sack falling from a boxcar, then rolled along the gravel verge and over the edge, falling through space toward the ravine below.

Leah turned away from the horrible sight, one hand clamped over her mouth to cut off a sob. Travis pulled her close. “It’s okay,” he murmured, stroking her back, much as she had Duane’s. “It’s over now. We’re safe.”

Chapter Sixteen

"Did anyone see what happened?" Leah asked when she had recovered enough to speak.

"If they did, we'll know soon," Travis said. "They'll stop the train."

"How could they not have seen?" She pushed away from him and stood on her own, her legs unsteady, but holding her up. "Everyone was looking out the windows."

"But they were watching the scenery, not the goings-on outside a private car," he said.

Instead of stopping, the train began to pick up speed. Already, the trestle over Deadwood Gulch was receding from view. "Should we tell someone what happened?" Leah asked. "Maybe they can…" Her words trailed away. Maybe they could what? No one could fall that far and survive. If the rocks at the bottom didn't kill him, he had likely drowned in the creek.

"I'll report it when we get to Silverton," he said. "If we say anything now, it will just cause trouble for the train company and a lot of innocent people. Come on, let's go back inside." He took her hand and pulled her toward the door.

"Where's Mr. B?" Marcie asked when they returned to their seats at the table.

"He wanted to say goodbye to someone he knew in one of the other cars," Travis said, delivering the lie as smoothly as if he had practiced. He pulled out a chair for Leah, then sat himself.

"Oh." The young woman looked disappointed. Maybe she had been hoping for a big tip from her high-rolling customer. Leah could have told her not to waste her breath. Duane never tipped well. In his vision of the ideal world, the "little people" served the power brokers of the world, privileged to be part of the machine working for the greater good—or his vision of the greater good.

Travis pulled out the cell phone. "I have a signal," he said.

"Thank God," Leah said. "How soon do you think someone can get to Silverton to pick us up?"

"Someone from the San Juan County Sheriff's Office will be waiting for you at the Silverton Station." Russell Waddell spoke from the open doorway at the end of the car. He moved toward them, the door sliding shut behind him. "I radioed ahead for you."

"What did you tell the sheriff's office?" Travis asked.

"Where's your friend Beaverton?" Waddell asked.

"He stepped back to say goodbye to another friend," Travis said. "He's decided not to take the train for the return trip."

A deep vee formed between the security officer's brows. "Is he really a friend of yours?" he asked. "Neither one of you looked very happy to see him."

"His name isn't even Beaverton," Travis said.

Waddell propped one booted foot on the chair Duane had recently occupied. “Level with me, Agent Steadman. Is Beaverton, or whatever his name is, the fugitive you’re after? Do I need to be concerned about the safety of passengers and employees on this train?”

“He isn’t a threat to anyone on this train,” Travis said.

Not anymore, Leah thought. She closed her eyes and again saw the sickening vision of Duane falling into that chasm, toward the shallow creek below. As much as she despised the man, the memory of his death made her shudder.

“What did you tell the sheriff’s office?” Travis asked Waddell again.

“I told them we’d picked up an FBI agent near Needleton and he needed assistance.” Waddell compressed his lips together, as if he had more to say, but was keeping the information to himself for now.

“I appreciate your discretion,” Travis said. He held up the phone. “Now if you’ll excuse me, I need to contact my bosses and fill them in on the situation.”

Waddell gave him a look Leah couldn’t interpret. He straightened and nodded to her. “Ma’am.”

When they were alone again, except for Marcie, who was cleaning up behind the bar in the corner, Travis phoned his bosses and gave them a brief summary of everything that had happened, including Duane’s decision to jump to his death rather than face trial. He listened to the person on the other end for a few seconds, then said goodbye and ended the call.

“They’ll contact the San Juan County Sheriff’s office and arrange for us to be driven back to Durango,” he said. “The rest of the team will meet us there. They'll send a squad into the wilderness area as soon as possible to search for the rest of Braes-wood's men."

"What about Duane?" she asked.

"We'll get a recovery team to the gulch tomorrow to claim the body." He covered her hand with his own and squeezed. "The lawman in me wishes I could have brought him in safely and seen him stand trial," he said. "But the rest of me is glad he's dead. He's harmed too many other people in his life, and I could never forgive him for what he did to you."

"I'll just be glad when this is all over," she said. "When I can get back to living a normal life." If she even remembered how.

The train let out three long, low blasts of its whistle. "We're coming into Silverton," Marcie said.

Travis stood and offered his hand to Leah. She let him pull her up and followed him out to the platform. She spotted the trio of sheriff's officers right away, in their khaki pants and shirts and Stetsons, with silver star badges on their chests. Two black-and-white SUVs were parked just behind them. Travis took Leah's hand and started toward them.

"Agent Travis Steadman?" The tallest of the officers, a trim, lean man of forty or so, stepped forward to meet them.

"Yes, sir." Travis offered his credentials.

The lawman glanced at the folder, then returned it and extended his hand. "Sheriff Bryce Staley, San Juan County," he said. The two other officers moved in beside Leah. "Undersheriff Kinsale and Deputy Lawson."

"Has my office contacted you?" Travis asked.

"Yes, sir," Staley said. "They've filled us in on the

situation and provided instructions on how we should handle everything."

"Just get us to Durango," Travis said. "That's all we really need right now."

Staley turned to Leah. "Are you Leah Carlisle?" he asked.

"Yes, sir." She offered a wan smile. "Thank you for helping us out like this."

He didn't return the smile. His gaze flickered to the officers on either side of her and they each grabbed one of her arms. "Leah Carlisle, you are under arrest for conspiracy against the United States." They forced her arms behind her back and the cuffs closed around her wrists, the metal cold against her skin.

Chapter Seventeen

"What do you think you're doing?" Travis charged toward Leah, but Staley pushed between them. "Calm down, Agent Steadman, or I'll have them cuff you, too. We're under direct order from your boss to arrest Ms. Carlisle. We're also under orders to see that you do not interfere."

"You can't arrest her." The words exploded from him with a force he would have preferred to direct to his fists. Leah's eyes locked to his, clouded with fear and confusion, and he wanted to rip apart the men who held her with his bare hands.

"According to your bosses, she's on the FBI's Ten Most Wanted list."

"She's innocent. She's an important witness in my case."

"You can take that up with your supervisors." Staley nodded to his men and they led Leah toward the black-and-white.

"Where are you taking her?" Travis asked.

"She'll be held in the La Plata County Detention Facility in Durango until she can be transferred to Denver, or until someone from the FBI directs us otherwise," Staley said. He put a hand on Travis's shoulder. "Come on. We've got a long drive ahead of us to meet your team in Durango."

He looked back toward Leah. She stopped beside the sheriff's vehicle and her eyes met his. Where he had expected to see the same fear and hopelessness that had clouded her vision when Braeswood made his threats, he found instead a grim determination. For the moment she was battered, but she wasn't defeated, and neither was he. "I'll make some calls and get you out as soon as possible," he called to her.

She nodded, and then one of the deputies pushed down on the top of her head and she folded herself into the backseat of the cruiser.

THE MEMBERS OF Search Team Seven had appropriated one floor of a nondescript office building on the south side of Durango as their base of operations. By the time Travis stormed into the conference room where the team had convened, he had had plenty of time to nurse his anger and worry over the way Leah had been treated. "What the hell are you doing, arresting Leah Carlisle?" he demanded of his commander, Special Agent in Charge Ted Blessing. "She's a victim here, not a criminal."

"Welcome back, Agent Steadman," Blessing said, his dark Buddha's face as impassive as ever. "I see your temper survived your ordeal in the wilderness."

"You smell worse than my son's entire basketball team after a game," said Special Agent Wade Harris, a fortysomething originally from Montana who had a sixteen-year-old who was apparently a talented defenseman.

"You look as bad as you smell," Special Agent Cameron Hsung said.

Travis ignored the gibes and continued to stare at Blessing. A twenty-year veteran of the Bureau, Blessing never let anything ruffle him. And Travis had never known the man to act rashly. But arresting Leah defied all logic. "I told you on the phone she was innocent," he said. "Braeswood kidnapped and murdered her sister, stole her property, and practically made her his slave."

"All assertions that we will thoroughly investigate," Blessing said. "But the fact remains that until we have proof of any of this, she's a wanted fugitive, a suspected terrorist and a flight risk. We followed the same procedure for her that we would follow with any other person in her position. She'll have ample opportunity to prove her innocence at a later date."

"I vouched for her. Doesn't that count for anything?" he said.

Blessing leveled his gaze at him. "You had a long-term, close relationship with Ms. Carlisle, the nature of which, I note, you did not fully divulge," he said.

Travis didn't flinch. "I told you I knew her, and that we went to school together. I didn't lie."

"Are you familiar with the term 'sins of omission'?" Blessing shook his head. "That's all beside the point now. But I don't think it's unreasonable to conclude that your judgment might be clouded by the fact that you were once engaged to marry the woman."

Travis shot a look at Luke, who shrugged and looked guilty. The two of them would talk later. He turned his attention back to Blessing. "There's nothing wrong with my judgment," he said. "Leah is innocent."

"And she is perfectly safe where she is right now."

Blessing put a hand on his shoulder, his gaze locked on Travis's. There was sympathy in those dark brown eyes, as well as the stern concern of a father for a troubled son. "You've had a rough four days. I'm ordering you to go home and get a shower, a good meal and a decent night's sleep. I want you fresh and ready in the morning to take the train with the rest of us to Needleton Station. We still have a number of Braeswood's associates to pick up."

"You're waiting until the morning?" Travis asked. "Why not go right away?"

"The tourist train is the only way into the area where we believe the men are located. Unless you want to make a multiday hike over rough, roadless terrain."

"Then send the train in tonight," Travis said. "Don't give them all night to get away."

Blessing grimaced. "You can't exactly sneak into an area on a steam train. They'll hear us coming from miles away. We've commandeered a car on the first morning train. We're posing as a group of friends on a hiking trip."

"What about Braeswood's body?" Travis asked.

"We've got a recovery team on the second train that will handle retrieving it," Blessing said. "They'll transport it to the La Plata County Coroner."

"You said he jumped from the train?" Agent Harris asked. "How did that happen?"

The others gathered around him. "Leah distracted him by pointing out a gold mine in the mountains above the tracks," Travis said. "He'd gotten cocky, believing we were subdued and trapped. He let down his guard and I grabbed him. I was trying to cuff him when he fought me off. I had him cornered and was trying to persuade him to come with me quietly when he jumped."

"Any chance he survived?" Agent Hsung asked.

Travis shook his head. "No way. He fell at least four hundred feet into a rocky, shallow creek."

"Without him, we might have a harder time making a case against the others," Luke said.

"Leah can help us there," Travis said. "She lived in the same household for six months. She doesn't know everything Braeswood was up to, but she can identify many of the people who worked with him. And we've got the house outside of Durango. That might turn up documents or computer files that could link Braeswood to his crimes."

"No luck with the house," Harris said. "They torched it."

"Probably cleaned it out before they set the blaze," Hsung said.

"They burned Gus's body along with the house," Wade said, his expression grim.

For the first time since rejoining the team, Travis realized Agent Gus Mathers wasn't with them. Neither was Jack Prescott. He remembered the khaki-clad figure he'd seen lying in front of the house. "They killed Gus?" he asked.

"He was trying to get to the van and they gunned him down," Blessing said.

"What about Jack?" Travis asked.

"He was injured when we fled from the house into the woods," Hsung said.

"He took a couple of bullets," Blessing said. "He'll recover, but for now he's on medical leave."

Travis swore under his breath. Another murder

Braeswood was responsible for. "You need to let Leah out of jail," he said. "She can help us stop these guys before they act again."

"She'll have her chance to prove her innocence," Blessing said. "I want to stop these terrorists as badly as you do, but we're going to do this the right way. No slick lawyer or tabloid journalist is going to accuse us of favoritism or taking shortcuts. When we send these guys away, they're going for life."

He turned to agent Luke Renfro, Travis's closest friend on the team. "Agent Renfro, take Agent Steadman home. He needs to get some rest. And frankly, I can't stand the smell of him any longer."

San Juan County, Colorado, didn't have the population to support a jail of its own, so the San Juan County Sheriff's officers escorted Leah to the La Plata County Detention Facility in Durango, where she was photographed and fingerprinted. She was allowed to take a shower and dressed in loose orange scrubs. She could have wept with joy as the hot water and soap washed away days of sweat and grime, but instead she shed tears of anger and frustration. She had known she was wanted as an accomplice of Duane's, but she had never actually believed the authorities would arrest her. She was with Travis, and he would explain that she was innocent, a victim, not a criminal.

But Travis had been helpless when the sheriff's deputies handcuffed her and led her away. Speaking up for her might even jeopardize his career. She was on her own again, stranded in a strange world full of enemies. She would have to learn how to cope, as she had when she was with Duane. At least here she didn't have to worry about the daily threat of rape and violence—she hoped.

Alone in her cell, segregated from the general population of the jail, she lay on the hard bunk and tried to sleep. Maybe when she woke up, she would discover this was all a horrible nightmare, a variation on the familiar theme of being trapped and helpless. But, exhausted as she was, sleep eluded her. When she had lost Travis the first time, she had grieved hard, but had eventually resigned herself to the loss. He was better off—safer—without her in his life.

Being with him again had made her believe they had a second chance at happiness. To have that chance snatched away hurt even more than the first loss, a sorrow too deep for tears.

"You don't look like I thought a terrorist would."

She sat up and stared at the man who spoke—a young guard with buzzed hair and a prominent Adam's apple. His name tag identified him simply as Lawson.

"I'm not a terrorist," she said.

He ignored her plea of innocence. Probably everyone who came here claimed not to have committed their crime, she reasoned. "What makes you hate this country so much you want to destroy it?" he asked.

"I don't hate this country," she said.

"That's not what I heard."

"When do I leave here?" she asked. She had already had enough of this guy.

"Don't know. I guess the Feds are still arguing over where to send you. Maybe you'll go to Denver, maybe you'll go to Washington—or maybe somewhere else. Wherever you end up, the penalty for treason is the same." He made a slashing motion across his throat.

She knew she shouldn't rise to his bait, but she couldn't keep quiet any longer. "The FBI agent I was with when I was arrested will vouch for me," she said. "He knows I'm innocent."

"Some men will say anything for a pretty face and figure." Lawson looked her up and down. "There's no accounting for taste."

She lay down again and turned her back to him. Duane had said worse to her—much worse. His abuse wasn't anything she would have ever thanked him for, but at least he had helped her develop a thick skin. Something that would come in handy in the days ahead.

LUKE INSISTED ON coming inside the apartment Travis had rented in a complex that housed several of the team members on temporary assignment in Durango. After only four days standing empty, the air in the place smelled stale. "Thanks for bringing me home," Travis said when they both stood in the one-bedroom unit's entryway. "I won't keep you."

"I'll stick around a while." Luke slipped off the light jacket he wore against the evening mountain chill and dropped it over the back of the cheap beige sofa that had come with the furnished unit. "Want me to order a pizza while you shower?"

No. He didn't want a pizza and he didn't want to talk to anyone about what had happened—not even his best friend. But his stomach growled at the mention of pizza, and the prospect of a long evening spent pacing the floor while he worried about Leah was too bleak to contemplate. "Yes, sure," he said. "But what about Morgan?" Luke had met the pretty sports reporter while the team worked a terrorism case in Denver a couple of months ago and the two had been an item ever since. She had followed him to Durango, and they were planning a spring wedding.

"She understands about my work."

Travis narrowed his eyes at his friend. "So I'm work now? Did Blessing ask you to pick my brain?"

"Morgan understands about friends, too," Luke said. "And Blessing didn't tell me anything but to bring you home."

"And to make sure I stayed here. Don't worry. I'm too beat to go anywhere." The only person he wanted to see was in jail and the sheriff wouldn't let him anywhere near her. He might as well stay home and rest up for tomorrow.

"Hit the shower," Travis said. "I'll call for the pizza."

Half an hour later, showered, shampooed and shaved, wearing clean clothes and feeling better than he had in days, Travis dived into the large sausage and pepperoni pizza Luke had ordered. "I had dreams about a pizza like this while I was out there," he said, wiping sauce off his chin. "And steak and cheeseburgers and cherry pie."

"I've always been partial to peach pie, myself." Luke polished off the last bite of crust from his first slice of pizza.

"I've never been so hungry in my life," Travis said.

"Were you ever worried you wouldn't make it?" Luke asked.

"The first night was bad, when we knew Braeswood's men were chasing us. But once we spotted the train and knew which way to go, it was just a matter of slogging it out."

"How did Leah do?" Luke asked.

"Leah was amazing. I know grown men—trained agents—who would have cracked under the pressure she was under, but she didn't. She never complained, either. She just kept going."

"Not what I expected," Luke said. He moved a piece of pizza onto his plate and contemplated it.

"You told Blessing she and I had been engaged, didn't you?" Travis asked.

"It was going to come out," Luke said. "Maybe not right away, but a reporter would have dug it up eventually. And I thought the information was relevant. Blessing did, too."

"Yeah. I probably would have done the same in your position."

Luke gave him a questioning look. "None of my business, but are you two an item again? Even after she dumped you?"

Were they? He wanted to try again with Leah, but was that even possible? "She dumped me because she was afraid Braeswood would kill me," Travis blurted. He hadn't meant to discuss this with anyone, but now the need to tell someone overwhelmed that reticence. "She stayed with Braeswood because he had kidnapped her sister. He took over all her assets and made her a prisoner. Then he killed her sister and made her believe if she left him, he would hunt her down and kill her."

Luke let out a low whistle. "She told you all this?"

"I believe her, Luke. And her sister is dead. I remember reading the obituary a few weeks after Leah left." His first instinct had been to call Leah and offer his condolences, but then he had realized he had no idea how to reach her. Her apartment had been rented by a stranger, and her cell phone number no longer worked. She had made it clear that she wanted nothing to do with him and had done everything to make sure he couldn't find her. "I should have known something was up when she broke our engagement," he said. "That wasn't her. She was always so open and straightforward. If she had really wanted to leave me, she would have told me to my face, not in some 'Dear John' letter left on the kitchen table."

"So why didn't she tell you to your face?" Luke asked. "Why didn't she ask you to help her, instead of running away like that?"

"Because she was afraid for her younger sister. She thought if she did everything Braeswood asked, he would leave Sarah alone. He did let her go after Leah turned over everything she owned to him. But he arranged for Sarah to have an 'accident' not long after."

"How do you know it wasn't really an accident? One with really bad timing?"

"Apparently Braeswood got a charge out of telling Leah what he had done to her sister. It was another way he played with her mind and made her believe he had total control over her life."

"Why did he pick on Leah?" Luke pointed a slice of pizza at him. "What's the connection?"

Travis shook his head. "I don't know. She worked for Senator Wilson, who was head of the Senate Committee on Homeland Security. Braeswood used Leah to try to get to the senator. But if that was all he wanted, he didn't have to keep using her the way he did. Maybe he wanted something in her assets. Her parents left her a lot of money and property when they died. Or maybe he saw her one day and was attracted and decided she would be the target of his sick game."

"We need to find out why he targeted Leah," Luke said. "It could be important."

"I'm not going to let it drop, if that's what you think," Travis said. "But first, I have to get the charges against her dismissed. She's no more a terrorist than you or I. And she can be a big help to us in this case. She knows Braeswood and the people he worked with better than anyone at this point."

"If she knew about his planned attacks and she never turned him in to the authorities, that could be a big strike against her," Luke said. "Enough to get her some serious jail time."

"She didn't know any of that," Travis said. "He made sure she was kept in the dark."

"Still, it's going to be tough," Luke said. "No judge or other elected official wants to look like he's soft on terrorists."

"She's not a terrorist!" He slammed his fist on the table, making their water glasses jump.

"Okay. Calm down." Luke sat back, looking thoughtful. "I've got a lawyer friend we can call. He might be able to persuade the courts to release Leah on bond."

"Call your friend," Travis said. "But you said it yourself. No judge wants to be seen as going soft on terrorists."

"It would help if we could get Blessing on our side," Luke said. "A special agent in charge vouching for her would carry a lot of weight."

"Fat chance of that," Travis said. He sat back also,

suddenly bone weary. "Blessing is the one who gave the order for her to be arrested in the first place. He's never going to back off of that."

"He might surprise you," Luke said. "He plays by the book, but he's not above writing new chapters when it suits his purpose."

AFTER LUKE LEFT, Travis wouldn't have believed he would sleep a wink. He lay in bed, imagining Leah in a stark cell, with no blanket or mattress and a lightbulb that burned twenty-four hours a day. Here in his own comfortable bed it seemed a betrayal for him to get a good night's sleep.

But sleep he did. He woke at six when his alarm blared, took another shower, had two bowls of stale cereal for breakfast and went to meet the rest of the team at the train station. He recognized a few of the workers—the conductor, Russell Waddell and Marcie—from the previous day's trip, but they made no show of recognizing him. They had probably been thoroughly prepped on the importance of secrecy.

The five active members of Search Team Seven and four other agents brought in to help with this mission rode together in an open gondola car near the rear of the train. In keeping with their cover story of a group of friends on a hiking trip, they had stashed loaded backpacks in the cargo hold and wore stout boots, hats, cargo pants and long-sleeved T-shirts under light fleece jackets.

"This is incredible scenery." Cameron Hsung swiveled his head from side to side, trying to take in everything as the train chugged out of Durango, headed for the mountains.

"It gets better the farther we go," Travis said. But he could muster little enthusiasm for the journey. The thought of hiking through the woods again made every part of him ache, and every step would be just one more reminder that this time Leah wasn't with them.

"How are we going to find the guys we're looking for?" Wade Harris asked as the train chugged along beside the highway, blasting its whistle at every crossing.

"Agent Steadman, perhaps you'd like to address that question." Special Agent in Charge Blessing, dressed like the others in hiking gear, wearing mirrored wraparound sunglasses that made him look more like a Secret Service agent and less like a vacationer, turned to Travis.

"You'll recognize them," Travis said. "And not just because you've probably seen some of them before. They're wearing black tactical gear and they move like trained fighters. Not to mention your average hiker isn't armed to the teeth. These guys have sidearms and semiautomatic rifles, and I suspect at least some of them are wearing body armor."

"How many of them are there?" Luke asked.

"We think at least eight," Travis said. "The last time I saw any of them was the day before yesterday. They were chasing us and we managed to evade them. We overheard two of them stating the plan was to watch the bridge for our approach, since that was the best way to get to the train, and the train was our fastest ticket out of the wilderness. They knew we had no food or supplies and that we were getting desperate."

"You could have walked out the way you came in," Blessing said.

"That would have taken days," Travis said. "But I

imagine Braeswood was smart enough to have men watching that route, too."

"I can't believe he went and offed himself," Wade said. "After all these months of us chasing him, he went and cheated us out of putting him on trial. Where's the justice in that?"

"Ending up on the rocks at the bottom of a ravine isn't exactly an easy way to go," Luke said.

"Tell the truth, Travis." Cameron Hsung leaned forward to address Travis. "When you had him backed up to the drop-off, weren't you tempted—at least a little—to give him a little push?"

Travis had thought Leah might push Braeswood. He had a clear image of her hand on his back, the determination mixed with pain in her face. Maybe he should have let her do it. After the torture Braeswood had put her through, it would have been fitting.

But he wasn't wired that way. He had been taught to protect all life, even that of the criminals. So he had moved in quickly to put on the cuffs. Just not quickly enough. "I wanted to make him go through a trial and endure the public scorn he deserved," he said. "That would have been a fitting punishment. Then I wanted to see him rot in prison for the rest of his life."

"It would have been good to find out what his plans were," Blessing said. "It's possible he's already set in motion other acts of terrorism and his followers will carry them out." He directed one of his patented stern looks at Travis. "Do you think Ms. Carlisle can tell us anything about Braeswood's planned activities?"

If Travis said yes, it might be Leah's ticket to freedom from jail, at least for a little while. But he wouldn't lie to his boss. "She says Braeswood tried to keep her in the dark about his activities. He had thugs who guarded her, and he conducted his business meetings away from the house or in his home office, where she wasn't allowed to go. The best she can do is give us an idea of his whereabouts for the past six months, and identify people he associated with. That might lead us to other sources of information."

"Agent Renfro and I did some research last night and the story she gave you checks out," Blessing said. "At least as far as the surface facts. She did resign from her job and sign over all her property to Braeswood, or more accurately, to one of the shell corporations we suspect he had set up to launder money for his terrorist activities. Her sister died in a car accident three weeks later. It was a one-car accident that local police labeled as vehicular suicide, but I found notes by one investigator that noted the evidence was inconclusive and, in his opinion, suspicious."

"Did anyone ever follow up on that?" Travis asked.

Blessing shook his head. "You know how it is. An overworked department has better things to do than follow up on every bit of information that doesn't line up quite right, especially if no family members or press are on their backs about it."

Travis looked at Luke, who held out his hands in a gesture of contrition. "I had to check it out," he said. "For your peace of mind, as well as ours."

Good thing he had, too. Travis owed his friend one. "Does this mean you'll go to bat for Leah?" he asked Blessing.

"We'll do what we can," Blessing said. "The Justice Department is a separate entity. They're under no obligation to listen to us."

But they will, Travis thought. *They have to.*

Chapter Eighteen

The sun had already disappeared behind the canyon walls when the team members returned to the Needleton Station late that afternoon after the last tourist train had departed, a row of shackled prisoners in tow. They had taken Braeswood's men by surprise. Only one had escaped through the woods, and local authorities and train personnel had been alerted to be on the lookout for him.

The chase had been cathartic for Travis. Once on the hunt, his aches and pains had vanished. He had been able to home in on the area where they had seen the men and positively identify each of them. The outlaws fought back against the agents, but only briefly, outmatched and outnumbered. The days in the woods had taken their toll on Braeswood's men—they looked like refugees of some tragedy, unshaven and dirty, their clothes rumpled and torn. Travis realized he must have looked like this when he'd emerged from the woods. No wonder the train passengers had stared.

No passengers stared as they boarded cars for the return trip. Federal authorities had commissioned a special train consisting of only two passenger cars and an engine to take the prisoners back to Durango. Instead of a conductor, Russell Waddell met them at the top of the platform in the first car. "You're looking a little different today, Agent Steadman," he said with a grin.

"I imagine this is more excitement than you usually see on your tourist train," Travis said as the prisoners filed past.

"You might be surprised," Waddell said. "Our main focus is on tourist traffic, but we've hauled everyone from Hollywood stars to construction equipment and a whole herd of bighorn sheep."

"No sheep today." Travis nodded to the row of disheveled men slouched in the train seats. "Though I think most of the fight has gone out of them."

"What happened yesterday, after you got to Silverton?" Waddell asked. "Did you arrest Beaverton, or whatever his name is?"

Travis tried to keep the pain he felt from his face. He didn't like remembering the scene in Silverton, or the look on Leah's face as the sheriff's deputies hauled her away. "It's a long story," he said. "But Mr. Beaverton won't be causing any more trouble."

As the train whistle sounded and the cars lurched forward, he dumped his pack in an empty seat with several others, then made his way to the front of the car to sit beside Luke. "I thought we were headed back to Durango," Luke said. "But we're traveling the wrong direction."

"I think we're stopping off at Deadwood Gulch to pick up the recovery team," Travis said.

"The place where Braeswood jumped?"

"Yeah." A man had to be crazy to do something like that.

They fell silent, Travis staring at his own reflection in the window against the blackness outside. All day he had been distracted by the mission, but now his thoughts turned to Leah. What was she doing right now? Did she think he had abandoned her again?

The train slowed, then jerked to a stop with a loud exhalation of steam from the brakes. After a few moments, they heard voices, and a quartet of weary men filed into the car. They conferred among themselves, then they moved down the aisle, toward Travis. "Are you Agent Steadman?" one asked.

"I'm Travis Steadman."

"Shawn Peterborough." The man offered his hand. "San Juan County Search and Rescue. We contracted to bring up a body from Deadwood Gulch."

"Was he in bad shape?" Luke asked.

Peterborough shook his head. "He wasn't in any kind of shape. We couldn't find him."

Travis stared, trying to let this information sink in. "What do you mean, you couldn't find him? I saw him fall from the train into that gulch. Nobody could survive a drop like that."

"We didn't find anything—no blood, no footprints, nothing," Peterborough said. "We spent all day combing through the area for two miles on every side. Nothing. Your guy is gone."

That was impossible. "Maybe an animal dragged the body away," Travis said. "A wolf or a mountain lion."

"We don't have wolves here," Peterborough said. "And mountain lions store their prey near the kill site. We would have found it."

"He couldn't have survived a fall like that," Travis said.

"I've seen stranger things happen," Peterborough said. "If he landed in a deeper part of the creek, in softer mud, and if he was very, very lucky..." He shrugged. "He might have walked away with a few bruises, maybe a broken bone or two."

"Son of a—" Travis bit off the curse. "He can't have gotten away. He can't have."

"If you want, we can go in tomorrow with a search dog," Peterborough said. "But the trail will be pretty cold by then. We'd have to get lucky to find anything."

"Nothing about this mission has been lucky," Luke said.

"Yeah, well, even if your guy survived his fall and walked into the woods, he's not going to last long out there alone with no supplies," Peterborough said.

"I'm sure he had a phone," Travis said. "He wouldn't have had to walk far toward Silverton to be able to call for help. He could even follow the train tracks to town. It's only a few miles from the gulch."

"Provided the phone wasn't damaged in the fall, and he was in any shape to climb up to the tracks," Peterborough said. "I made some calls, and no one in town reported a man wandering in from the wilderness."

"Maybe they didn't notice him, with all the tourists and everything," Travis said. "And Braeswood already had a car and driver waiting in Silverton. He could have met up with them and been out of town before the train left to return to Durango."

"If he did make it out of here alive, we'll find out sooner or later," Luke said. "He won't stay quiet for long."

"That's what I'm afraid of," Travis said. "When we do hear from Braeswood again, it won't be good."

AFTER TWO NIGHTS in jail, Leah had decided that being patient and cooperative wasn't getting her anywhere. She was fed up with the guards' condescending attitudes and their assumption that she was guilty of the charges against her. She didn't want to hear any more excuses about why she was being held here in the middle of nowhere, with no access to a lawyer or any outside visitors. She refused to believe Travis hadn't at least tried to see her, so her jailers must be keeping him away, the way they were keeping away the reporters and others who had tried to speak with her.

"You have to let me see a lawyer," she said when a guard responded to her shouts for help on the morning after her second night in the stark, uncomfortable cell.

"You'll see a lawyer whenever you get to Denver or DC or wherever they decide to send you," the guard—a portly redhead whose name badge identified him as Erickson—said.

"You can't just hold me here forever," she said.

"We can do whatever the Feds tell us to do," Erickson said, and turned away.

"Then bring me some paper and a pen," she called after him.

"Why?" He turned toward her again. "Do you plan to write your memoirs?"

"I'm going to write a letter," she said. The *Denver Post* wouldn't pass up the chance to publish a letter from a notorious fugitive who'd been captured, she was sure.

Maybe she would write to Travis, too. She would apologize for dragging him into this mess, and tell him she loved him. She hadn't had the courage to say the words out loud when he was awake when they were in the wilderness, but she wanted him to know them now. Whatever happened, whether they were able to ever be together again, she wanted him to know she loved him, and she always had.

The writing paper never materialized, however. Instead, about ten o'clock Erickson returned with another officer, who unlocked her cell and motioned for her to step out. "Someone here to see you," he said.

"Who is it?" she asked as he led her through the double doors that separated the cells from the rest of the facility.

But he ignored the question and motioned her to walk in front of him down the hall, into a gray, windowless room that contained a table and a single chair.

He left her in the room, locking the door behind him. She sat in the chair and looked up at the camera mounted in the ceiling. Was someone watching her now, the way a scientist watches a rat in a maze, waiting to see how the animal will react to various stimuli?

After what felt like an hour had passed, but was probably only ten minutes or so, the lock on the door snapped and the doorknob turned. She stood to greet her visitors. A distinguished-looking black man in a dark suit entered first, but it was the second man who commanded all Leah's attention. "Travis!" she said, and started toward him.

She would have hugged him, but he held her at arm's length. "How are you doing?" he asked, looking her up and down.

"I'm okay." She glanced down at the baggy orange scrubs and rubber flip-flops they had given her to wear. "At least I'm cleaner than the last time you saw me."

"Ms. Carlisle, I am Special Agent in Charge Ted Blessing," the black man said, "with the Federal Bureau of Investigation. Special Agent Steadman and I have some questions for you about your association with Duane Braeswood."

She looked from Travis to Agent Blessing and took a step back. So they were here in an official capacity, not because Travis hadn't been able to stay away. No wonder he was being so distant and formal. She returned to the chair and sat, smoothing her palms down her thighs. "I'm happy to answer any questions you have," she said. "But shouldn't I have a lawyer present?"

"You're entitled to a lawyer," Blessing said. "We will see that one is provided when we question you in our offices later this afternoon."

She turned to Travis, afraid to jump to any conclusions. "Are you taking me to Washington?" she asked.

"We have offices here in Durango," he said. "But for now, you're being released into my custody, pending disposition of the charges against you."

She wet her lips, choosing her words carefully, and decided to address her next question to Agent Blessing. "What is the disposition of the charges against me?"

"We've petitioned the US attorney's office to drop the charges against you in exchange for your cooperation with us in this case."

The breath rushed out of her and she was glad she was sitting down. "I'm happy to cooperate," she said again, though inside she wanted to whoop for joy.

"Come on." Travis offered his hand. "Let's get you out of here."

Ten minutes later, she stood on the street in front of

the jail with Travis and Agent Blessing. She still wore the orange jail scrubs, and was aware of the stares of passersby. But her own clothes, which they had offered to return to her, were too filthy to contemplate putting on again. "We'll get you some new clothes," Travis said as he opened the back door of the car for her.

She had hoped he would ride in the backseat with her, but he slid into the front passenger seat, and Blessing drove. The short drive across town was largely silent, with the men exchanging a few bland comments about the scenery or the weather. Neither of them said anything to her, as if she weren't even there.

She stared at the back of Travis's head, wishing she knew what he was thinking. Was he trying to distance himself from his involvement with her because he worried what their relationship might mean to his career? In the hours they had been apart, had doubts about her innocence grown? Or was he merely concerned with looking professional in front of his boss?

Yet he had said she was being released into his custody. That meant he was responsible for her, didn't it? Why would he accept such responsibility if he didn't believe in her?

At some point during the long drive, she dozed, lulled by the warm sun on her face and the car's comfortable backseat. She woke when the car stopped in front of a small apartment complex, the front of the building landscaped with beds of flowers and groupings of evergreens. "We have a meeting with someone from the US attorney's office at three," Agent Blessing said as Travis opened the car door.

"Yes, sir," Travis said. "We'll be there." He climbed

out of the car, then opened Leah's door for her. "Come with me."

She exited the car and followed him up the walkway toward the building. Blessing drove away and Travis took out a key and led the way to a door on the second floor. "I rented the place furnished," he said. "So it's not much."

"Where are we?" she asked, confused.

"This is my apartment," he said.

"Why did you bring me here?"

"'Released into my custody' means I'm responsible for you. You have to stay with me." He frowned at her. "I thought you understood that."

"So I'm your prisoner."

"No." He shoved open the door and motioned for her to go inside ahead of him.

He was right when he had said the apartment was plain. The front room was small and decorated in neutral colors and nondescript furniture—the kind used in midgrade hotel rooms. But it looked comfortable and it wasn't a jail cell. She stood a few feet inside the room, unsure what to do next.

Travis closed the door and stood still also, looking as unsure as she felt. "You're not my prisoner," he said. "I don't want you to think of it that way."

"I'm not free to leave," she said.

"Do you want to leave?" He looked pained.

She turned away. "I don't know what I want," she said softly. But she did know. She wanted him to look at her with eyes of love again. She wanted to feel his arms around her and hear him tell her that everything would be all right.

He moved toward her, but stopped when he was still

a few feet away. “I know this isn’t the best situation,” he said. “It’s not what I want, but it’s the best we can do right now. It was a compromise to get you out of jail.”

She nodded, tears clogging her throat. She swallowed and found her voice. “Thank you for getting me out of there,” she said.

“We’re going to get the charges dropped,” he said. “We captured most of the men who were with Braeswood in the wilderness and at least two of them are cooperating. They confirmed that you weren’t involved in Braeswood’s terrorist activities, and that they were sent to hunt you and me in the woods.” He laid his hand on her shoulder, the weight of it so heavy—physically and emotionally—she feared her knees might buckle. “Agent Blessing checked out your story, as much as he could, and he believes you’re innocent now, too. The US attorney will listen to him.”

“Is Agent Blessing your boss?” she asked.

“Yes. He’s a hard man, but a fair one.”

“Did he order you to look after me? Is this your punishment for associating with a wanted fugitive?”

“A punishment? What are you talking about?”

“It’s clear you don’t want to be seen with me,” she said. “You’ve scarcely looked at me since we left the jail.”

He moved closer still, one hand remaining on her shoulder, the other under her chin, nudging her head up to look at him. “I couldn’t look at you without wanting to touch you. I had to be careful in front of Blessing and others who might be watching. There were reporters outside the jail, you know.”

She shook her head. “I didn’t know.”

“They were across the street, taking pictures. Until

the charges against you are dropped, we have to be careful. If the press thinks you received preferential treatment because of your personal relationship with an FBI agent, it could jeopardize not only your freedom, but the whole case. Do you understand?"

"Yes." Everything he said made sense, difficult as it was to hear.

"But we don't have to be careful now," he said. "We're alone." He bent and covered her lips with his own.

The kiss began gently, but she wrapped her arms around him, pulling him close and letting him feel her desperate need of him. "I was so afraid," she whispered when at last they broke the kiss.

"It tore me apart, seeing them take you away in cuffs," he said. "I hated thinking of you in that cell, alone and afraid."

"I wasn't afraid of jail," she said. "At least, not much." She stroked her fingers along his jaw. "I was afraid I'd lost you."

"You haven't lost me," he said. "Never again." He kissed her cheek, then drew away. "I bought you some clothes and things. They're in the bathroom. You can take a shower and get dressed and when you come out, I'll have lunch ready."

"That sounds good," she said, suddenly aware of her uncombed hair and baggy orange scrubs.

In the bathroom she found jeans, a gauzy blouse, new underwear, a pair of leather flats and silver hoop earrings. She smiled, touched that he had not only remembered her size, but the styles she liked. In the shower, a new bottle of her brand of shampoo and vanilla-scented shower gel awaited. She let the water run until it was steamy, then indulged in the luxury of standing under the spray until she had washed away the scent and feel of the jail. When she finally emerged, her hair blow-dried and her face freshened with the powder, mascara and lipstick he had also purchased, she felt like a new woman.

Travis looked up from the table he was setting and smiled. "You look like you feel better," he said.

She hugged him. "I feel great. Thanks for the clothes and makeup. And the earrings." She touched the silver hoops. "You still remember what I like."

He looked pleased. "Sit down," he said. "I don't know about you, but I'm still making up for all those lost meals."

She sat in the chair he indicated and he set a plate in front of her—a bacon-wrapped fillet, baked potato and green beans. "I'd pour you a glass of wine, but we probably shouldn't show up at the courthouse this afternoon smelling of alcohol," he said.

"This looks fabulous." She inhaled the aroma of the steak, and her mouth watered.

He sat across from her. "Dig in."

For long minutes, neither of them said anything as they ate. Finally, her hunger abated, she set down her fork and looked at him. "What's going to happen this afternoon?" she asked.

"Your attorney will be there." He wiped his mouth with a napkin. "My friend Luke knew a good criminal defense attorney, so we called him. Reg Kosinski. He's meeting us there. He'll present the motion to drop the charges. Agent Blessing will say his piece and hopefully that will be it."

"Agent Blessing said he wanted to question me."

"Yes. You can ask your lawyer to sit in on that if you want, but once the charges are dropped, it shouldn't be necessary. All we want is to hear your story and anything you can tell us that might help us find and convict Braeswood."

She froze in the act of reaching for her water glass. "What do you mean find Braeswood? Isn't he dead?"

Travis shook his head. "The search-and-rescue team we sent into Deadwood Gulch couldn't find any sign of him."

"But he jumped from the train. How could he have survived a fall like that?"

"The search-and-rescue guy I talked to thinks he could have made it." He took a long drink. "Anything you can tell us will help us figure out his next move."

"I'll do my best." She shivered. "I hate to think of him out there somewhere." She wouldn't feel safe until he was locked up for good.

"Don't worry," Travis said. "I won't let him hurt you ever again."

"It's strange, being away from him after so long," she said. "I'm thrilled, but I'm a little nervous about starting over. I have so much to do. Find a job, an apartment and a car. I don't have any money or anything. It's a little daunting."

"You're strong and you're smart. You'll get through this."

"I will." She took a deep breath. "I just have to figure out where to start."

"Blessing thinks there's a chance we can recover at least some of your assets from Braeswood. And I'll help you with anything else you need."

"I can't let you do that," she said. "You shouldn't—"

He reached across the table and took her hand. "I'm going to help the woman I love," he said. He rubbed his thumb across her knuckles, sending heat curling through her. "The woman I want to marry."

Her breath caught and she stared at him. "What are you saying?"

He reached into his pocket and pulled out a ring. The diamond solitaire glinted in the sunlight through the window behind her. He slid the ring onto the third finger of her left hand. "I believe this belongs here," he said.

She stared at the ring, as she had stared at it so many times in the weeks after their engagement. "You kept it," she said.

"I did."

"I was sure you'd be so angry with me for returning it that you'd sell it or throw it away."

"I had to keep it," he said. "Just in case I got the chance to win you back."

She didn't remember rising from her chair and moving around the table toward him, but the next thing she knew she was sitting in his lap, his arms around her. "Leah Carlisle, will you marry me?" he asked.

"Yes." She kissed him, joyful tears wetting both their cheeks. "I love you," she said. "I never stopped loving you."

"No," he said. "And we will never stop."

Charges Dropped Against Suspected Terrorist

The federal government has dropped all charges against a woman who had been suspected of participation in a terrorist cell responsible for dozens of deaths around the world. Leah Carlisle, 27, was placed on the FBI's Ten Most Wanted List earlier this year after a link was established between her and suspected cell leader Duane Braeswood. Ms. Carlisle was captured in a raid on Braeswood's compound in rural La Plata County last week. "We have evidence that Ms. Carlisle was not, in fact, a member of the terrorist cell," said FBI Special Agent in Charge Theodore Blessing in a statement to the press. "Rather, she was kidnapped and held hostage by Braeswood and kept a prisoner until she managed to escape during the raid on a rental home where Braeswood and his followers were staying. She has fully cooperated with authorities and is providing valuable information we hope will lead to the arrest and conviction of Braeswood and his followers."

FBI Special Agent Gus Mathers was killed in the raid on the Braeswood compound, and another agent was wounded. Several members of the suspected terrorist group escaped, including Braeswood. A subsequent fire destroyed the home where the group had been staying. Six members of the group were captured in the Weminuche Wilderness. Braeswood and one other of his associates are still at large.

* * * * *

She studied him for a second and he glanced at her. "Something wrong?"

"No, nothing. I've just never met. . .well, someone like you before."

"Someone like me," he mused. "What does that mean?"

"You're a cowboy."

He flashed her a smile. "What gave it away? The hat, the boots, the saddle in the back, or maybe it's the subtle whiff of cow lingering in the air?"

"All of the above," she said, but her voice revealed she knew he was teasing her. "Of course, in my line of work it pays to be observant."

"And I bet you don't miss much."

COWBOY SECRETS

BY
ALICE SHARPE

First Published in Great Britain 2016
By Mills & Boon, an imprint of HarperCollins*Publishers*
1 London Bridge Street, London, SE1 9GF

ISBN: 978-0-263-91911-0

46-0716

Our policy is to use papers that are natural, renewable and recyclable products and made from wood grown in sustainable forests. The logging and manufacturing processes conform to the legal environmental regulations of the country of origin.

Printed and bound in Spain
by CPI, Barcelona

Alice Sharpe met her husband-to-be on a cold, foggy beach in Northern California. Their union has survived the rearing of two children, a handful of earthquakes, numerous cats and a few special dogs, the latest of which is a yellow Lab named Annie Rose. Alice and her husband now live in a small rural town in Oregon, where she devotes the majority of her time to pursuing her second love, writing. You can write to her c/o Harlequin Books, 233 Broadway, Suite 1001, New York, NY 10279, USA. An SASE for reply is appreciated.

This book is dedicated with love to
Amalia Anina Mauro LeVelle

Chapter One

Sierra Hyde yawned into her fist as she nursed a glass of white wine at a long mahogany bar. The music, the booths on the back wall and the big mirror behind the bottles all reeked of familiarity.

Her main interest, however, wasn't the establishment, but the solitary woman sitting alone at a dark booth near the back of the room. Her name was Natalia Bonaparte, age thirty-three. Occupation: job counselor. Frequent glances at the diamond watch sparkling on her wrist suggested whomever she was waiting to meet was late, but Sierra already knew this. Her job was to catch a photo of the man who joined the woman. According to Sierra's client, Savannah Papadakis, that man was going to be Savannah's estranged husband.

Yeah, well, it better be him because trailing Natalia was getting tedious and it had only been two days. The woman had a pretty active after-hour party life.

"Will you have another?" the bartender asked as he ran a rag along the bar. Sierra looked down at her glass and realized she'd imbibed half the wine. "I'll have a ginger ale this time," she said. With any luck, her client's husband would show up, she'd get a few photos and be on her way back to New York City within the next few minutes. She needed a good night's sleep after the disco stakeout last night.

He left to pour her drink right as the door opened. Sierra darted a quick glance. Two young guys barely old enough to legally walk through the door held each other up as they staggered to the bar and plopped down on either side of Sierra.

"Hey, pretty lady," one of them said. The guy's breath reached her nose before his words reached her ears and she instinctively flinched.

The bartender showed up with the ginger ale and took orders for two beers, while Sierra declined to let her new "friends" buy her one, too. The door opened again, sending a renewed jolt of cold January air into the bar. A man about the right age sauntered in. His perfectly groomed head of white hair caught every stray beam of light as he looked from the bar to the tables, past groups of revelers, until his gaze stopped on the far corner where Sierra knew the blonde sat. He seemed to momentarily frown before crossing the room to join her. The woman greeted him by lifting one of her hands, which he kissed. Sierra witnessed all this by watching their hazy reflections in the mirror that backed the bar.

The two drunks were both leaning closer to her, making her thankful she hadn't taken off her jacket. She had to get rid of them if she was going to get the pictures and escape this place.

"Those gals over there are giving you the eye," she whispered to the one on her left. She nodded at a table a good distance away, where two women pushing forty sat talking over martini glasses. As far as Sierra knew, neither one was even aware the guys at the bar existed.

"Them?" the one on Sierra's left said after turning to stare.

"Too old," the man on her right said. "Besides, they ain't looking at us."

"Sure they are," she said as she took a pair of tortoiseshell glasses out of her pocket and slipped them on her face. "They just look away whenever one of you turns around."

"You know, dude, there's nothing wrong with bagging a couple of cougars," the other guy said with a speculative note in his voice.

"But we can't abandon this little gal," the one on the right insisted.

"Sure you can," Sierra said. "I'm about to leave, anyway."

He grinned and cracked his knuckles. "That case, I call dibs on the brunette."

Both men wobbled their way toward their new targets. Heaving a sigh of relief, Sierra once again focused on the mirror's reflection. The lighting in that booth sucked. Details were hard to see.

She turned casually on her stool, glanced at the two women, who had apparently invited the drunks to sit down with them, and looked at the blonde's table as she activated the camera hidden in the nose bridge of the frames of her glasses. She counted out a dozen shots, then got to her feet, put a twenty on the bar and made her way to the restroom, which meant she walked right past the booth. To her relief, the candlelight on their table was adequate at close range, and she took several pictures while passing, mostly of the woman, though the point was to get them both in the frame.

After washing her hands, Sierra retraced her steps,

this time angling for a better shot of her two subjects. As she snapped a photo, the man called the bartender over. She darted him a startled glance. He looked right through her and she continued walking. She'd been so sure! But that accent…

Spiro Papadakis had been in the States for over a decade, but according to his wife, his Greek accent was still pronounced. This man sounded like the Jersey shore. He looked up at her as she passed and their eyes met. He blinked and looked away. She'd seen several photographs of her target and there was something familiar about this guy despite the voice.

Well, she'd download and study the pictures later. For now, her job here was done and she walked outside. Freezing rain pelted her face as she made her way to her car. Her phone chirped but she didn't recognize the caller ID and answered cautiously. "Yes?"

"Is this Sierra Hyde?"

"Yes," Sierra said as a sound from behind caused her to glance over her shoulder. She'd been a PI for almost five years now and liked to think her instincts picked up anything unusual in her environment. For a heartbeat she studied the facade. The lake behind the tavern was huge and black, and sent a layer of mist swirling around the painted wooden fish over the door. There didn't appear to be anyone else around.

She turned her attention back to her caller. "Who is this?" she asked as she traversed the crowded lot to the very back corner, where she'd parked.

"My name is Pike Hastings," a male voice said. "I'm sort of related to your sister, Tess."

"I know who you are," she said as she spotted the bright red bumper sticker promoting her choice of candidate for the upcoming mayoral election. She beeped the car open and settled behind the wheel. “You’re Mona’s son.”

“That’s right. I know we’ve never met—”

“Oh, my gosh, are you calling about Tess?” Sierra interrupted as she closed the car door behind her. “Has my little sister shown up? Does her dad know? Is she okay?”

“Yes, no, hard to say. Yes, she showed up, but here at my place. One minute she says call her dad, the next she refuses to let me do it. I’m not sure how she is except for a head cold and what looks to me like a major case of the jitters.”

“You’re in Montana, right?”

“No, the family ranch is in Idaho. About Tess, like I said, something has her spooked but she insists on talking to you and me together. Can you come right away?”

“Of course,” Sierra said.

“That’s great,” he said, and there was no missing the relief in his voice. “I took the liberty of buying you a plane ticket. I’ll email it to you. The only flight I could get you on leaves at five tomorrow morning from New York, I hope that’s okay.”

Sierra suppressed a groan. There went the night’s sleep she’d been hoping for. On the other hand, Tess had been mostly out of touch since a couple of weeks before Halloween. Sierra was so relieved to hear she was alive and breathing—even if it was in Idaho—that she would have walked there if she’d had to.

“I’ll pick you up at the airport,” he added.

“That isn’t necessary,” she assured him. “I’ll rent a car.”

“I insist,” he said. “The ranch can be hard to find and the roads are kind of tricky this time of year and your phone might not work," he told her. "We don't exactly have the same cell coverage you're used to. Trust me on this."

"Okay," she said, and added her thanks before clicking off. Almost immediately, a sound outside the window made her look up and she gasped. It took her a second to make out the squished-up features of one of the drunks from the bar.

"Hey, baby, you're voting for the wrong guy," he said with a wide sweep of his arm toward the back of her car. "Jakes is a loser. Vote Yardley!"

She smiled and nodded and hit the door lock. No way was she rolling down the window. She started the car and hoped she didn't back over one of his feet.

"Hey, come on back inside!" he squawked and reeled away. Did that comment about the mayoral candidates for New York City mean he had to drive all the way back to the city tonight? She sincerely hoped the bartender confiscated his keys and called him a cab.

Jumpy now, her mind racing with everything she had to do in the next seven hours, she drove out of the parking lot and headed home. A glance in the rearview mirror reassured her no one followed.

It crossed her mind that she didn't know why it had even occurred to her to check.

PIKE HASTINGS WAS glad the predicted winter storm hadn't materialized...yet. He arrived at the airport in Boise a half hour before Sierra's flight was due to land and made the loop, keeping an eye out for a woman who fit her description. He'd never met her, had never even seen a picture of her. She shared only a mother with Tess, and Tess had warned him that while she had inherited her mother's genes, Sierra had not. She'd told him only to look for a tall woman with red hair and an attitude.

As descriptions went, it wasn't a lot to go on, but he figured they'd find each other without too much trouble. He eventually parked in the loading zone in front of the airline on which he'd booked her flight and got out of the SUV. Within minutes, a woman headed out of the building pulling a carry-on, impatience written all over her face.

But what a face. One in a million women could claim skin like hers: creamy, glowing, perfect. Large green eyes the color of spring ivy might look frustrated right now, but there was nothing wrong with their shape, just as her lips formed a lovely curve and her auburn hair fell in a glistening sheet to frame her jaw. She wore a black suede jacket and matching riding boots, skintight black jeans and a white shirt. A brilliant solitaire diamond glistened at her throat and a large leather handbag that could double as a saddlebag hung over one shoulder.

A large man with a mustache walked behind her. He wore a baseball cap pulled down over his eyes, but Pike could see that he was staring at Sierra's seductive shape just as intently as Pike had. The man seemed to become aware of Pike's gaze and he put his hand up to his eyes and veered away as though embarrassed to be caught staring. Pike could have assured him just about any man would have ogled a bit.

"Sierra Hyde?" Pike said, stepping forward. She turned as though just becoming aware of him, pocketed her phone and maintained eye contact as Pike approached. He tried to see himself through her eyes and wondered what conclusions she might be making about him. He could only hope they were as flattering as the ones he'd drawn about her.

"You must be Pike," she said, holding out her hand and shaking his with a firm, no-nonsense grip. "My phone works," she added.

"Wait until we get out in the middle of nowhere," he said with a smile.

"No doubt. Funny how dependent we get on our gadgets."

Tess had said her sister was a private eye and he bet she was good at what she did. She didn't look as though she'd tolerate being anything but good.

"Let me help you with that," he said, reaching for her suitcase. "Please, go ahead and take a seat."

She seemed almost reluctant to let him help, but did as he asked. He deposited the suitcase in the back of the SUV as she climbed into the passenger seat. "Did you have a nice flight?" he asked as he pulled away from the curb. She had turned to look back at the terminal and took a second to look forward again. Was there something back there? He glanced into his rearview mirror and saw nothing but a sea of cars. "Is everything okay?" he asked.

"Yes," she said, avoiding eye contact. "And my flight was fine. How is Tess?"

"Pretty miserable," he said.

"Has she told you anything?"

"No. But I was referring to her head cold as well as her emotional state."

"She hasn't even said where she went after she left home all of a sudden?"

"Not a thing. I only heard from her once in all that time and that was right before Christmas. She texted me but never responded when I texted her back."

"That's about the same thing that happened to me, too," Sierra said. "But I'm surprised she tuned you out. I know you've done your best to visit her every few months and get along with her dad. She even came out to your ranch once or twice, right?"

"Yes. And I've flown to LA. She's a nice kid who seemed to get lost in the shuffle."

Sierra nodded, the assessing look back in her eyes. "Frankly, I'm surprised she wants me to come at all. She's been angry with me for years."

"I wouldn't take it personally. She's just kind of confused. And I, for one, am very glad you're here," he added. "I can tell she's scared of something, but she insists she wants to talk to both of us. I was hoping you two had made some inroads with each other."

"I wanted her to come stay in New York with me after our mom died," Sierra said, "but Doug was her legal guardian and he insisted she stay with him in LA. There wasn't much I could do about it. I think Tess thought I didn't want her. And I don't know… I was about eighteen at the time and she was what, six or seven? I'd seen little of her since before she started kindergarten. I tried to stay in touch but after her dad hooked up with that woman—" She paused and cast him a quick look. "Sorry, I forgot for a second that Mona is your mother."

"I'm under no illusions when it comes to my mother," he assured her. "She left about five minutes after I was born and never looked back. Don't worry about offending me."

"Well, in that case, let's just say Mona got caught up in what was left of Doug's Hollywood glamour. She didn't want Tess around, or me, either, for that matter. Unfortunately, Doug is about as perceptive as a cantaloupe.

Tess was problematic and he dealt with it by ignoring her. Those two people are hopeless as parents, but I'm still surprised that they didn't do more to find her when she walked out in October."

"Mom said that Tess stormed off in that car Doug bought her. She was eighteen, legally an adult. I think it was easier for both Mom and Doug to throw up their hands. And you have to remember this was right after Mona caught good old Doug fooling around at his restaurant and kicked him out. When Tess left the next day I think Mona said good riddance to both of them." He shook his head. "People, right? Give me a horse any day."

She studied him for a second and he glanced at her. "Something wrong?"

"No, nothing. I've just never met…well, someone like you before."

"Someone like me," he mused. "What does that mean?"

"You're a cowboy."

He flashed her a smile. "What gave it away? The hat, the boots, the saddle in the back? Or maybe it's the subtle whiff of cow lingering in the air?"

"All of the above," she said, but her voice revealed she knew he was teasing her. "Of course, in my line of work it pays to be observant."

"And I bet you don't miss much."

"I'm not sure if I do or not. Exactly how far into the middle of nowhere is your ranch located?" she added as they left the Boise city limits.

"About two hours north of here." He was aware of her disappointment upon hearing that. "Listen, there's not all that much to see between here and there," he added.

"Why don't you close your eyes for a while so you'll be fresh when we get there?"

"I couldn't do that," she said.

"Why not?"

She shrugged lovely shoulders. The gesture seemed out of character for her, like a tiny little beachhead of uncertainty. "It would seem, I don't know, too familiar, I guess."

"Don't worry. If you snore I won't tell a soul."

"I do not snore," she said.

He smiled at her. "Go ahead. Close your eyes. I'll turn on the radio so I can't hear any little snorts or grunts—"

"I don't snort or grunt, either," she said, but this time she laughed. "Okay, I'll try to get a little sleep. My eyes feel like sandpaper. Wake me up before we're actually there, okay? I'd like to orient myself."

"Sure thing." He fiddled with the FM station until he found easy listening music that shouldn't keep her awake, but realized almost instantly it would take a brass marching band to accomplish that. One second she was sitting kind of stiffly in her seat, tilted cautiously toward the window, and the next her head had rolled forward until her chin touched her collarbone. She didn't look all that comfortable, but he resisted the urge to shift her. Something told him she was not the kind of woman to touch, even innocently, while she slept.

SIERRA OPENED DOOR after door along a darkened hallway. Each held the very same man, a guy of about fifty with a shiny bald head. "Have you seen Tess?" she asked each in turn and they all responded negatively in Greek. There was only one door left and she put her hand on the knob. At that moment the earth shook and she tumbled out of her dream and into an SUV.

Pike Hastings looked at her. "Sorry. I tried to rouse you when we hit Falls Bluff, but you were out like a light. I figured nobody could sleep through the cattle guard. It can be a little rough if you're not used to it, though."

She turned to look behind her, but there wasn't much to see. In fact, there wasn't a whole lot to see no matter which way she looked. Just mountains, fences, trees, a long line of power poles straight ahead and an endless stretch of rolling pastures. For a woman used to towering skyscrapers and hordes of people, it was disconcerting to see so much…nothing.

"Is this it?" she said. "Is this your ranch?"

"You sound disappointed."

"I'm sorry," she said quickly. "It all looks very…peaceful."

"It can be," he agreed.

She studied him again. He'd taken off the cowboy hat when he got behind the wheel, so she could see his profile clearly and there was nothing about it anyone could fault. The occasional flash of his dark blue eyes as he addressed her was pretty darn galvanizing as well, as was the clarity of his expression. He did not look like the kind of guy who lied or cheated or bamboozled, and she should know—she'd met her fair share of all of the above.

Of course, that could just mean he was really good at dissembling, but she kind of doubted it. Wearing jeans and a leather jacket, he looked decidedly casual and yet also as though he could fit in almost anywhere. This was a trait she valued as a detective. It was fine to stand out when you needed or wanted to, but you also had to be something of a chameleon to get the job done.

The drive down the more-or-less straight road seemed to stretch on forever. Here and there crossroads led toward the mountains and she caught glimpses of buildings, perhaps houses. "Is this all Hastings land?"

"It is."

"Do you live in one of those buildings they have in old Westerns?"

"What kind of building do you mean?" he asked with a sidelong glance.

"You know, a bunkhouse."

"No, I live in a barn," he said.

"In a barn!" She sounded incredulous and he smiled.

"Yeah, a barn."

"With animals and everything?"

"Yeah," he said, with another quick glance. "This your first ranch?"

"You can tell?"

"I just guessed." He drove up a hill and suddenly the view changed as a small valley spread below them. Bisected by a shimmering gray river, the acreage on the peninsula that the U-shaped bend in the river created looked stark and icy and terribly remote. A big, old, wood house sat in a protected alcove. Surrounded with covered decks, the house appeared well cared for. What looked like work buildings sat off at a distance. Pale winter light glinted off the frosty shore of the river.

"My father's place," Pike said.

"Is this where Tess is?"

"That's right. She's afraid to be alone."

Sierra gestured at the half-dozen vehicles gathered in the back. "All family," Pike said. "And I'll be damned, Frankie must be here. That's his truck. Haven't heard from him in a couple of weeks, which in and of itself isn't unusual. Of course, him being here probably means he's brought some kind of trouble."

"Frankie is one of your brothers?"

"The youngest. Gerard is the oldest, then Chance and me and Frankie."

"It's hard to watch someone you love struggle with life, isn't it?"

Pike didn't answer right away and then finally he allowed himself a sigh. "I guess that's one way to put it. Of course, he wouldn't think of himself like that. He's just a little more…creative…than your usual cowboy. And lord knows he doesn't back down for anyone." He shook his head and added, "I shouldn't be talking about him."

She looked past his long lashes and the intensity of his gaze, peering deep into him. "I didn't mean to prod," she said after a moment. "Tess is my only relative and I rarely see her. Apparently I'm rusty when it comes to concepts like family loyalty."

"I don't know. You dropped everything and flew here with very little warning," he said. "Sounds to me like you know exactly what loyalty is about."

"This might be my last chance to make it all up to Tess," she said quietly with a quick sweep of her eyes. "Ever since she disappeared, I've been thinking I should have tried harder."

"Well, you're here now," Pike said. "And that's what counts."

As they pulled in beside the other vehicles, the back door opened. Another tall man, who looked enough like Pike to identify him as one of the brothers, waved from the opening and strode across the yard to meet them, joined by three dogs. One looked like the Lab her father had had for years, and the other two looked like border collies. Sierra didn't consider herself to be much of an animal person, though she could enjoy the simple adoration that shone in a dog's eyes. And you had to admire their perpetual good moods.

One of the dogs jumped on her as she got out of the vehicle, planting muddy paws eight inches above her waist, and she winced as her dry cleaner's disapproving face popped into her head.

"Get down," Pike admonished. He produced a clean cloth from one of his pockets and held it in front of her, staring at the mud, obviously flummoxed by how to help her without invading her privacy as the smear was right across her breast area. She took the cloth from him and wiped off as much as she could.

"Sorry," he said.

"No problem." It had been stupid to wear suede. She'd just figured there'd be more concrete and less dirt.

"Silly dog," the approaching man said as he rubbed the mutt's ears with his left hand and offered Tess his right. "You must be Sierra. I'm Gerard. We're real glad to have you here. I know Pike has been worried about your sister."

"I think everyone has," Sierra said. "Where is she?"

"Upstairs, finally getting some sleep," he said.

Pike hit the side of the blue truck. "When did Frankie arrive?"

"Dad said he sailed in about forty-five minutes ago. He's been waiting for you to get back. He wants to talk to everyone at once."

"Just like my sister wants a family confab," Sierra said. "Must be something in the air around here."

"Is everything okay with Frankie?" Pike asked as he opened the tail of the SUV and took out Sierra's suitcase.

"I'm not sure," Gerard said. "Let's go find out."

Chapter Two

They entered the house as the family almost always did, through the mudroom into the huge kitchen that, as usual, smelled of wonderful food. Roast chicken today, Pike thought, the aroma as welcoming as a holiday hug. From there, they walked into the dining room, and then on to the entryway, where the front door was framed by glass panels. Double doors opened from the entry into the den or office, called different things by different family members but well accepted as the spot where most family discussions took place.

Today a fire burned in the rock fireplace in an effort to stave off the cold air pressing against the windows. For Pike, the chatter of those gathered was like any other sound on this ranch—from the running water of the river to the wind in the tree boughs, the thunder of horse hooves against the summer earth or the faraway braying of cattle. They were the sounds of his past and future, his home.

What did Sierra think of all this? Probably found it confusing as hell. He could picture her in a SoHo loft or a Park Avenue condo, but he couldn't quite fit her into this ranch. He knew there were few things more confusing than meeting a roomful of people who knew each other very well and of whom you knew practically nothing. He also got the feeling that Sierra wasn't the shy type and would cope just fine.

But Sierra pulled on his arm. "Whatever Frankie wants to tell you has nothing to do with me," she said. "I want to see Tess."

"I'll take you to her room," Pike said.

"But your brother is waiting."

"He'll make it a while longer. Let's go see if Tess is awake." He took her muddy jacket and laid it across a chair while quietly perusing the trim white blouse with an almost men's-wear starkness that gave way to some kind of sheer material around the hem. The shirt fit Sierra like a glove and revealed she was much curvier than he'd first thought.

He motioned for her to go ahead of him up the broad staircase leading from the foyer. "The room at the end," he said, directing her to the bedroom in which he'd spent his childhood. They found the door ajar, but the room was dark because the shades had been pulled. It was also warm and steamy. The hum of a humidifier in the corner explained that. The congested sound of Tess's breathing drew Sierra to cross to her sister's bed and stand looking over her slumbering body.

Pike watched her for a minute or two until he felt a hand on his arm. He turned to find Gerard's soon-to-be wife, Kinsey, standing beside him. She jerked her head toward the hallway and he held up a finger. A second later, he touched Sierra's shoulder. She looked beyond him to Kinsey and followed them out into the hall.

After a hasty introduction, Kinsey brought them up to speed on Tess. "I imagine you're disappointed to fly all the way here and find your sister asleep. Dad insisted we call the doctor this morning. Of course, the doctor said you can't really treat a head cold except with steam and acetaminophen and stuff like that. By the time I got back upstairs to start the humidifier for Tess, she'd fallen asleep and didn't even open her eyes as I set things up. She really needs this rest. I could hear her pacing in the guest room half the night."

"I'm not disappointed," Sierra insisted. "What guest room are we talking about?"

"The one at our house," Kinsey said. "Pike and Tess came for dinner last night and Tess wanted to lie down. When she dozed off, I told Pike I'd look after her and he should go home. Unfortunately, she didn't stay asleep long."

"I see," Sierra said. "And you live close by?"

"About a half mile up the river."

"Come downstairs with us and hear what Frankie has to say," Pike suggested.

"No, I'd rather stay here in case Tess wakes up. I have some emails to write, anyway."

"I'll get your suitcase," Pike said.

"Thanks."

"She has a very interesting face," Kinsey said as they walked down the hall. "Good bones, great eyes."

He knew her comment referenced the fact that Kinsey had spent most of her life painting portraits. Since moving to the ranch, she'd developed an interest in still life and scenery as well, and the house she shared with Gerard was filled with her work. She was a small woman with light brown hair and an easy, engaging smile. Come June, she'd marry Gerard.

"She's gorgeous," he agreed. "She doesn't look anything like Tess, though, which I expected but still came as a surprise."

"She doesn't act like Tess, either," Kinsey said.

"Well, she's twelve years older and they haven't lived together for even longer than that. Besides, remember, Tess's latest female role model was my mother."

Kinsey rolled her eyes. She hadn't met Mona, but Gerard had obviously filled her in. All four brothers had different mothers. In fact, Grace, his dad's wife of less than a year, was actually number seven, or lucky number seven as the patriarch of the family fondly called her.

"Do you know what Frankie wants?" Pike asked as they started down the stairs.

"No, but I get the feeling your father does."

She continued into the den while Pike dodged out to the kitchen where they'd left Sierra's suitcase. He lifted it easily and ran up the stairs.

He found Sierra sitting on an upholstered chair in the darkened room, one long leg folded up under her, head resting on her fist. Their hands touched as he gave her the suitcase and she smiled up at him as she murmured her thanks.

He left without uttering a word, but he didn't want to. Instead, he kind of wanted to stand in the doorway and keep watch. He'd spent his entire life around men until the last year or so. He'd always considered himself a man's man, happiest out on cattle drives, sleeping under the stars.

However, even though Tess had brought tension into his life, he also found her company refreshing. And now Sierra was here and he'd known her all of three hours, but there was something about her, too. Something competent and self-assured, qualities he responded to in anyone and that were downright sexy in a beautiful woman. He knew his link to her was flimsy at best and she'd be gone in a day or two, but he could already feel that he would miss her. For a few moments, while walking down the stairs, Pike wondered if anybody kept her warm at night.

Frankie sat on the fireplace hearth, but as soon as Pike finally entered the room, he sprang to his feet. It was obvious he was excited and Pike took a deep breath, hoping it was for some positive reason and not because he was about to go to jail for something.

Like all the Pike men, Frankie was tall, but his build was a little more wiry than the others and his hair was lighter, especially in the summer. Now, in the midst of winter, it had darkened to Pike's color, but he wore it longer. He also tended to dress a little more *GQ* than anyone else, and today wore dark gray slacks and a light gray shirt that mirrored his eyes.

"Dad has an announcement to make," Frankie said, but Harry Hastings shook his head.

"This is your show, boy. You're the driving force behind it all."

Frankie made eye contact with everyone gathered around him. "I wanted to reveal all this after calving season and before summer work piles up on us, but the producers are anxious to do a little preliminary work. Besides, there's never a time where everything gets quiet and boring around here, especially not lately, right?"

He paused to grin and glance at each of them in turn. Pike had to agree it had been a hectic few months.

"What producers? What are you talking about?" Chance asked from his seat beside Lily. Charlie, her five-year-old son, was still at kindergarten, but Chance gripped Lily's hand in his and it appeared he wasn't letting go. Good for him. When your soul mate comes along, what else can you do but grab on to her and hold tight?

Frankie took a deep breath. "As you guys all know, November is the one hundredth anniversary of the incident at the hanging tree."

He was referring to the bank robbery of the ghost town, or what was left of it now, and the subsequent capture and execution of three of the four thieves. They had paid for their crimes with their lives by dangling from the end of ropes strung up to the big oak tree out on the plateau. The fourth robber had disappeared along with the spoils and had never been identified or caught.

"About a year ago, I met this guy in Pocatello," Frankie continued. "I mentioned the ghost town on our land and the robbery. He'd actually read a diary written by someone who used to live in Falls Ridge, as the town was called back then. He confessed he'd had a life-long fascination with the events that had the killed the town almost overnight.

"Anyway, it turns out he makes documentaries and he wants to do one about Falls Ridge and the bank robbery and the tree and all that. He says there's been some discussion about the mystery guy who got away, so they'd cover that aspect, as well. Originally, they were going to come on out and start filming in late April, but their backers want winter shots and interviews with all of us so the release can be timed to coincide with the anniversary of the events."

His announcement was met with studied silence. "Dad?" Gerard said at last. "This sounds like a good idea to you?"

Pike watched as his father stood up and walked over to Frankie. It crossed Pike's mind that his father probably couldn't have cared less about hosting a bunch of television people and raking up the past. It probably didn't seem like a good idea at all to him, but on the other hand, when was the last time anyone saw Frankie get interested in anything but making trouble? Consorting with legitimate filmmakers was a far cry from his usual scenarios. Assuming they were legit, of course.

"I don't think it will have much impact on most of us," his dad now said. "I researched the company—it's won a couple of awards and is respected within the industry. They showed us a tape of a show they did on a nesting pair of bald eagles—looked like high-quality work and they're bonded and have the right licenses. They've got network backing… Anyway, unless someone can point out some reason to walk away from this that I haven't seen, I say we get Frankie to give them a call."

"I agree," Pike said, throwing in his hat. Not for a minute did he think having movie types around wouldn't get in the way of ranch life and schedules, but so what? "Let's shake things up a little," he added when he glanced at Chance and Lily. After what they'd gone through back in October, he knew the last thing in the world they would want is any kind of stress, but Chance rallied and threw in his agreement.

Lily, however, had a question. "Did you tell them part of the ghost town burned down last year?"

"Yeah," Frankie said. "It's not a problem. Before the real filming takes place, I'll take some machinery up there and move stuff around. Frankly, what happened there adds to the drama of the place."

At this Gerard stood up. "What do you mean 'what happened there'?"

"Not about your wife and daughter, Gerard. That will

get mentioned because it's part of the history of the place now, but no one wants to dwell on a personal tragedy like that."

"And what about what happened to Lily up there, and Kinsey?" Chance asked.

Lily shifted in her seat. "Jeremy died there, Frankie, and Jeremy was Charlie's father. Do we have to muck up all that again?"

"Listen," Frankie said as things began to slide south. The ambience of a moment ago had begun to sour. "What happened here in the last year is part of this family's story, but it's not part of the bank robbery. Our experiences have to be acknowledged but they don't have to be the focus. No one wants that."

Harry Hastings clapped Frankie on the shoulder as he looked at each person in turn. "The production people will be here in a couple of days. They want to scope things out. How about we go that far and if issues arise, we reassess things. I personally think Frankie is right. This show will not be about our recent tragedies."

They all agreed that sounded reasonable. Everyone obviously liked the idea of an escape hatch, a back door, so to speak.

"Gary Dodge, he's the documentary guy I told you about, is interested in Kinsey doing some artist renditions of how the town looked and how an angry posse might have appeared."

"I've done a little commercial work," Kinsey said. "This sounds exciting to me."

"And Dad has agreed the crew can stay in this house with him and Grace."

"We have room at our house, too," Kinsey said as Gerard put an arm around her. They looked at each other and exchanged silly grins, then Kinsey spoke again. "Since everyone is here, it might be a good time to tell you that we're getting married a lot sooner than we originally planned."

"But I thought you wanted a late spring wedding," Frankie said.

"We did. But since our baby is due in June—"

She didn't get any further than that. It seemed to Pike that everyone in the room started speaking at once. Half of them were on their feet, slapping Gerard on the back or hugging Kinsey.

Pike took a vacant chair. The house vibrated with the winds of change, from the two women upstairs to all the news and excitement downstairs. He didn't usually dislike change, but he had to admit that today there was a chill inside him that he couldn't explain. He thought of the way Sierra had turned at the airport to look behind them as they drove away and the chill deepened. As if paralleling her unease, he turned now to face the door and found Sierra standing in the opening. She gestured at him and he immediately went to join her.

"Finished emailing?" he asked.

"Finished before I started. My phone doesn't work, just as you predicted, and I don't know the password for your Wi-Fi."

"The password is *ridgeranch*, all lower case, one word," he said. "I know, it's not terribly original. How long have you been standing there?"

"Most of the time," she said. "I didn't want to bother you."

"So, you heard Frankie's plan?"

"I did. It sounds pretty exciting."

He narrowed his eyes as he gazed down at her face.

She was only half a head shorter than he; a tall, shapely woman who he suddenly realized had not come down here out of curiosity or boredom. "What's wrong?" he said quickly.

"Tess's breathing is really loud. I'm worried about her."

"Head colds aren't any fun," he said.

"I tried to wake her and she was limp and didn't even open her eyes. Kinsey said she hadn't given her any medications, right?"

"Beyond acetaminophen, no."

"She spent the night at their house," Sierra said, a new element of fear in her voice.

"Yes, but—"

Kinsey walked into the foyer followed, closely by Grace. Though a generation apart, both women were small of stature, dainty and pretty in their own way, which made sense because they were related. In a twist of fate, mother and daughter had been reunited. Sierra towered over them. "Is Tess all right?" Kinsey asked.

"I don't know," Sierra said. "She seems so out of it. Did you talk to her this morning?"

"Of course. Like I said, she had a restless night. I drove her over here late this morning because Pike had left early to get to the airport. She didn't have a lot to say, but she was awake and coherent."

"What are you thinking?" Grace asked.

"I don't know for sure," Sierra said. "She was alone while you were on the phone, right?"

"Yes. By the time I found the humidifier and got upstairs, it had been about thirty minutes," Kinsey said. "She was sound asleep and then you guys arrived."

"If she took something it must have been within that

thirty-minute window. But where would she find something to take?"

"I'm pretty sure she didn't bring anything with her from LA," Pike volunteered. "She was traveling light and didn't have any money. She didn't even have the car Doug gave her. God knows how she got here. She wasn't saying."

"Who would know if she found something at this house?"

"I would," Grace said.

"We'd appreciate it if you could look," Pike said.

"Of course I'll look. We'll all look. Come on."

They hurried up the stairs. "We'll start with the bathrooms," Grace said. As the three women started their search of drawers and cabinets, Pike went into his old bedroom and opened the drapes. He sat down beside Tess and picked up her limp hand.

He'd had a college roommate years before who partied himself into a stupor every single weekend, and that was the last time Pike had seen someone so oblivious. He shook Tess's fragile shoulders and called her name. Her eyes opened briefly, she sort of smiled and faded back away. He searched the garbage can and the night table for some indication of what she might have taken.

And then he picked up the phone and called the doctor. By the time Sierra, Kinsey and Grace arrived with ashen faces and a brown prescription bottle, he had already lifted Tess into his arms and was exiting the room.

"An ambulance is on its way," he told them. "I'm going to meet it on the road to cut down travel time. What did you find?"

"Some of your father's sedatives are missing," Grace

said with a concerned face. "I don't think very many, but I don't know for sure."

"We're not taking any chances," Pike said. "She's going to get her stomach pumped."

"I'm coming with you," Tess said. He nodded once and they all descended the stairs in a hurry, Tess stopping to accept the blanket and pillow Kinsey pushed into her arms. A moment later, in Kinsey's car now since Pike's still had a saddle in the back, they tore up the hill and down the long, long roadway, Tess prone in the backseat, her head on Sierra's lap, the blanket tucked around her still body.

THEY MET THE ambulance in a pull-off. The EMTs were at the door with a gurney within seconds, hooking up Tess to bags and drips, calling her name. Sierra stood off to the side with Pike, both of them trying to stay out of the way. Pike handed over the prescription bottle and soon after the ambulance took off with sirens wailing while Pike and Sierra climbed back in Kinsey's car and followed behind.

"Where are they taking her?" Sierra asked.

"The urgent care center in Falls Bluff. The doctor will meet us there."

"Why would she do this?" Sierra asked as tears burned her eyes. She didn't know if they were tears of anger or hurt. "She asked me to come, so why would she choose now to drug herself? Is it to punish me?"

"Don't borrow trouble," Pike said, sparing a hand to cover her arm. In the rush to leave the house, she'd forgotten to put her jacket back on and now, with the warmth of his touch, she realized how cold she'd become. "Tess did know you were coming, true, but she also knew it would take most of three hours to get to the ranch from the airport. Kinsey said she heard Tess pacing all night. Maybe she just wanted to get some sleep. If her motives were any more than that, wouldn't she have emptied the bottle?"

Sierra stared at him for a few heartbeats. "I guess so," she admitted. She rubbed her forehead with her fingers. It was difficult to believe that it had been less than twenty-four hours before when she followed Natalia Bonaparte out of New York to that bar and waited for her companion to show up.

A sudden thought popped into Sierra's head, a flash of intuition, perhaps. Was it possible the man last night had been Spiro Papadakis, after all? What if he'd recognized Sierra that first time she walked past their table? Hadn't she detected a glimmer of recognition on his face when their gazes met? Perhaps he'd been spying on his wife spying on him! He could have seen Sierra and his wife meet somewhere. Could it be that he'd learned to hide his accent and sound like he was fresh from the Atlantic City boardwalk at least for a second or two? Had he, in fact, fooled her?

As a non sequitur went, this one was a doozy, but it often happened that way: get your mind flooded with one problem and an insight into another problem floats in to announce itself.

Her laptop was in her carry-on. As soon as they got back to the ranch, she could download the photos onto the computer and then email the images to Savannah. All she'd told Savannah last night was that she wasn't sure if it was Spiro or not and to be prepared for photographs. She'd also asked about accents but hadn't gotten a response yet.

"You've gotten kind of quiet over there," Pike said as

they finally left the riverside road and drew close to a small town proclaiming itself Falls Bluff. Icy rain slithered down the windshield as Pike drove to the urgent care center. The town hardly looked big enough to support such a thing, but that's probably the exact kind of community that needed an emergency facility the most.

"I was thinking," she said. "Not just about Tess, but about a case."

"Does that case have anything to do with why you looked over your shoulder this morning at the airport?" he asked.

She turned to face him as he pulled into a parking spot. "I'm not sure if it does or not," she said, then opened her door. She couldn't believe how her knees wobbled when she stood or the way her heart suddenly raced.

What if she lost her little sister before ever really finding her, or ever really helping her? The thought was intolerable.

Pike shrugged off his jacket and slipped it over her shoulders as she stepped onto the sidewalk. His arm around her suggested he saw or sensed this sudden bolt of numbing fear, and she welcomed his support as they hurried inside.

Chapter Three

Pike leaned against a wall, hands clasping his hat against his chest, legs crossed at the ankles, waiting for Sierra to arrange medical coverage for her sister. No one knew if Tess had insurance, so Sierra had said she would pay the bill with a credit card. Of course, they could call Tess's father and ask him, but Sierra was reluctant to do that until after they spoke to Tess, and right now that was impossible.

Eventually, Sierra joined him in the waiting room and they sat down beside each other. Pike leafed through a magazine. Sierra just stared toward the door leading to the treatment rooms.

After what seemed like an eternity, Dr. Stewart showed up and greeted Pike like the longtime family friend he was, then sat down. Pike introduced Sierra and explained the relationships. There were so many confusing this-person-married-that-person and divorced-a-year-later explanations that some men might have been baffled, but Mason Stewart was one of Henry Hastings's oldest friends and he knew all about Harry's seven wives.

"She's doing well," he said. "After we got everything out of her stomach, we administered activated charcoal and a cathartic to cleanse the rest of her system."

"Is she conscious?" Sierra asked with a tremble in her voice.

"Yes. Talking is tricky for a while because we numbed her throat, but I expect her to recover as expected. Give her a few minutes and you can speak to her. I have to warn you, she seems very agitated."

"She's been that way for the past day or two, ever since she got here," Pike said.

"Do you know why?"

"Not yet. That's why Sierra came to Idaho. We need to talk to her. Something has her spooked."

"Doctor, I have to ask this," Sierra said softly. "Is there any indication that Tess purposely overdosed?"

"She knew you were coming, right?" he asked.

"Yes. My arrival was imminent."

"Let me just say this. Blood tests and stomach contents show she didn't take a whole lot of the sedative, but she hasn't eaten much of anything, it seems, for quite a while, and she is a slightly built girl. Two of those pills will knock Harry out for twelve hours, let alone a kid weighing less than half his weight. If you're worried about suicide, you should get someone to talk to her, but she insists it's just a case of being desperate to get some sleep, and I'm tending to believe her. I'd like to keep her for a few hours but we're not equipped or staffed to have her all night. I don't know if you're aware of this, but Grace actually worked here as a nurse a few years back."

"Pike's stepmother?" Sierra asked.

"Yes. I feel good sending her home knowing Grace can help look after her. I'm going to call her and bring her up to speed. Give the kid a couple of days to recover from all this, okay? Keep things as mellow as you can."

"Absolutely," Pike said and wondered how on earth they would accomplish that feat.

Dr. Stewart stood and they rose, too. "She wants to see you both. Normally I'd suggest she rest, but I don't think she'll be able to relax until she shares whatever has her upset, so you might as well get it over with. We'll let you know when she's ready."

Once again they sat. If Pike had known Sierra longer, he would have tried to comfort her. It seemed almost natural that he should take her hand or put an arm around her. Instead, he decided to distract her with a question. "Tell me about your last case."

"What?" she said as though she'd been thinking of way different things than work. "My case?"

"The one you had to leave to come here."

She shrugged. "I have a client who is separated from her husband. She wants a divorce. She's the one with the money. She signed a prenup that gives him a good hunk of cash if the marriage dissolves unless she can prove he cheated on her."

"And you were employed to gather evidence."

"Yes. So, she got wind he was seeing a woman out of town. I followed that woman to Jersey to a seedy bar. When a man who looked like my client's husband joined the woman, I snapped pictures, but then I decided he was the wrong guy. Now I'm wondering if I made too quick a judgment."

"Why?"

"Gut feeling, I guess."

"Is that why you seem worried about it?"

"I suppose. It's weird, really. There's no reason to second-guess myself, I just do sometimes, and when that happens it invariably proves I noticed something, you know, like subliminally."

"Did you contact your client already?"

"Emailed her, yes. She doesn't like to talk on the phone. She always emails me unless we meet face-to-face, which only happened once. I'll have to look at the pictures again when we get back to your place."

He looked into her green eyes, eyes as clear as ocean-washed bottle glass. What he saw were things he admired in a human being: passion about their life and convictions, truthfulness and the desire to help. "Do you like your job, Sierra?" he asked.

"Most of the time. How about you?"

He smiled. "Most of the time."

The nurse announced they could go see Tess. Sierra didn't need any more encouragement. She walked briskly down the hall, still wearing Pike's jacket, which, while way too big for her, looked sexy as hell on her lithe body. Her legs in the jeans and boots were shapely, tantalizing, and just to prove how long this day was getting, he found himself wishing the two of them were on an island somewhere, on a beach, lots of bare skin and warm sunshine…

"She's in here," a nurse said and the fantasy died a timely death.

Tess was an elfin-like girl with huge violet eyes and sun-streaked short blond hair. She could be very friendly and sweet or she could be testy and secretive, but the last two days were the only time Pike had seen her scared and he hated it.

Sierra immediately leaned over Tess and hugged her, then smoothed her hair away from her face. Tess looked pale and wasted and about ten years old instead of eighteen. Pike took her hand and squeezed it.

"I'm sorry I messed up," Tess said. Her voice was even more hoarse than it had been and her nose was red.

"Don't worry about it," Sierra and Pike said in unison.

"I take Dad's pills sometimes, but they must be different."

Pike bit back recrimination. They could talk about being stupid on another day.

Sierra lowered her voice. "Tess, sweetheart, what's going on?" she asked gently. "What's the matter?"

Pike scooted a chair close so she could sit down. He stood on the other side of the bed.

Tess's eyes filled with tears and she shook her head.

"Start with where you went when you left your dad and Mona's place," Pike suggested.

"Danny," she said.

"Danny? You mean you ran off with that guy you met last summer?" Sierra asked.

Tess nodded.

There was a look on Sierra's face and a tone to the way she'd said "Danny" that rang a few alarm bells in Pike's head. "Who's Danny?" he asked.

More tears rolled down Tess's wan cheeks and she sobbed into her hands. Sierra offered the tissue box and met Pike's gaze, but she didn't say anything. They waited until Tess calmed down. By now she was sitting up as she was apparently unable to handle the tears and congestion in a prone condition. Her breathing was raspy.

"My—my boyfriend."

"They met at the beach," Sierra explained. "He's a lot older than she is and—"

"He's dead," Tess mumbled.

Sierra sucked in her breath. Pike leaned forward. "How did he die?"

"Someone—someone shot him." She buried her face in her hands and cried so hard her whole body shook. Pike hadn't expended much energy in his life being unsure of himself, but he had to admit that in the face of all this grief he wasn't certain where to start.

"Who shot him?" he asked at last.

Tess shook her head.

"Drug dealers?" Sierra asked. "Tess, was he dealing again?"

"I didn't know he was doing that anymore," Tess mumbled. "After I found out, he promised he'd quit because it scared me. And then we were in the car that Dad bought me, you know, the blue one? We were going to go for a hamburger. He said he had to talk to a friend and he parked outside a yellow house. He took the keys and left me in the car. I waited and waited but he didn't come back out, so I went up to the porch. I heard someone yell from inside and then the door opened and Danny was standing there. He looked straight into my eyes. And then…and then I heard a shot and Danny just collapsed like someone let all the air out of him. I knew he was dead before he hit the floor. A man was standing behind him with a gun in his hand. I—I ran away. I didn't have the car keys, so I just ran and ran."

The last part had come out all in one breath while her voice got more and more ragged until, at the end, they almost had to guess what she was saying. After a few seconds of stunned silence, she added, "The man who killed Danny looked right at me."

"Who was he?"

She shook her head. "I don't know."

"What did the police say?" Sierra asked. "Why didn't someone call Pike or me?"

"I didn't go to the police."

"Oh, Tess."

"All I wanted to do was blow LA. I didn't know where else to go so I came here. But what if he finds me? He has the car so he knows my name, he could find out about me, he could come here and kill…and kill me."

"We have to call the Los Angeles police and your father—"

"No, please, no," Tess begged.

She was shaking so hard by now and crying so pitifully that the nurse showed up at the curtain. "Is everything okay in here?" she asked.

"Maybe some water and another box of tissues," Sierra said, putting an arm around Tess. The nurse hurried away and once again Pike and Sierra exchanged bewildered looks. He could imagine what she was thinking because he was thinking it, too. Tess was in trouble and it was up to the two of them to make it go away.

"You'll be safe at the ranch," he assured Tess as she sipped the glass of water the nurse delivered. "We've had our share of trouble and we know how to take care of ourselves and our own. You'll be safe. One of us will be near you all the time."

This seemed to calm her, and eventually she drifted into an uneasy sleep.

"May I speak with you outside the room?" Sierra whispered to him. They walked down the hall a few paces, then stopped. Sierra looked exhausted and he felt for her.

"I understand where you're coming from," she said in a very soft voice. "I want to make it all go away for her, too. But we can't hide an eyewitness to a murder. She's going to have to grow up real fast starting very soon, because she's right about the murderer knowing who she is.

Who's to say he won't come gunning for her next? And you and I have both lived enough to know that safety is an illusion."

"She needed something to hold on to," Pike said. "It was all I could think to offer." He ran a hand through his hair. "But I know what you mean. You're right."

"We need to inform Doug, too. Tess is going to need her dad's support in the months to come. I get the feeling Doug is a path-of-least-resistance type of guy."

"He'll listen to me," Pike said, and he knew it was the truth. He'd bent over backward to be decent to the guy, both for Tess's sake and, truth be told, for his mother's.

"And I need to talk to the police and find out what's going on," she added. "Trouble is, I don't know if any of this can be adequately accomplished over the phone."

"What are you suggesting?"

"I'm not sure yet. We'll have a chance to talk to Tess when we drive back to your ranch. We have to make her see she has an obligation to Danny and society and to herself, too."

He nodded and tried to look positive about their chances, but Pike realized he might actually know Tess better than Sierra did. He'd be stunned if she agreed to return to LA without a fight.

"NO WAY," TESS SAID. A few hours had passed and she sounded more like herself, though obviously close to the end of her rope from the stress of the past several days. Her nose was still red and her eyes watery.

"Be reasonable," Sierra said gently and reiterated her conviction that they needed to inform Doug and the police in person.

"I won't go," Tess said. "Pike said I'm safe here, and I believe him."

"You have to talk to the police," Sierra said for about the fifth time. "They'll have questions only you can answer."

"I'll tell you everything I know. You talk to them."

"And leave you here alone?"

"I won't be alone, I'll have Pike. And while you're in LA, you can see my dad and tell him what happened. If he cares. He probably doesn't. Oh, and you can go to Mona's house and get my things."

Sierra had to admit she was a little startled by Tess's refusal to budge. She herself lived in a world of cooperation with law enforcement. She could hardly imagine Tess shirking this basic responsibility. On the other hand, Sierra had seen a man shot dead once, too, and it had shaken her down to her bone marrow. She tried again. "Your dad won't listen to a word I say so there's no point in my talking to him. And Mona is not going to let me rifle through her house looking for your stuff."

"Then Pike should go."

"But if you aren't going to explain things to the police, I have to. Even then, they'll probably have someone in Idaho come debrief you or even send one of their own investigators. And that's a best-case scenario. When they catch the murderer you'll have to testify at his trial. If you don't, they could issue a warrant and make you return."

"I'll do whatever they want as long as I don't have to go back to LA. And if one of you has to talk to Mona and Dad and the other one has to talk to the cops, then both of you go."

By now they were coming over the hill into the main house's yard. The house was well lit, shining like a

Christmas-card picture with the clear skies overhead full of twinkling stars. In a way, Sierra hadn't really believed such quaintness still existed.

Grace met them at the back door, fussing and nervous, and for a second, Sierra thought it had to do with them bringing Tess back to this house, but she soon realized she was mistaken.

"It's those television people," she said. "Frankie said they wouldn't come until the weekend but then they got wind a storm is expected and they decided to drive here straight away." She waved an irritated hand and turned her attention to Tess. "Oh, you poor thing. Come with me. We're going to get you all comfy in the downstairs room. I already moved the humidifier close to your bed. I'm going to spend the night with you. It'll be like a slumber party! But don't you worry, Frankie and your Uncle Harry will be on alert. Pike called and gave us a heads-up. You're safe here with us."

"I'll stay with her—" Sierra began, but Tess had already allowed Grace to put an arm around her and lead her down a short hall. Sierra gazed up at Pike, who smiled at her.

"Feel like you've fallen down a rabbit hole?"

"Kind of," she admitted. "I can't believe how stubborn Tess is being."

"She's had quite a day, you know."

She shook her head, a reluctant smile playing with her mouth. "Are you always so kind?"

"Not always, no."

"She's settling in," Grace said a second later when she returned. "She asked if she could stay here with us while you and Pike take a short trip to LA to 'fix things.'"

"I would never ask such a thing of you," Sierra said, horrified.

"Don't be silly. Tess is Pike's sister so she's one of ours. There are more than enough of us to keep an eye on her and I mean that in every sense. You have to remember, she's visited here before, stayed in this house, cared for the horses. She feels at home here in a way, don't you think, Pike?"

"No doubt," he said.

"Exactly. And remember, last summer you took her all around, to see the ghost town and the old gold mine and the hanging tree and the lake up in the mountains? That gives her a sense of place and nothing makes a frightened person more comfortable than a sense of place."

"I wouldn't argue with you," Pike said diplomatically.

"You know what family means to me, Pike. Everything. Go do what you have to do. I'll try getting her used to the idea she's going to have to return to California." She looked closely at Sierra and shook her head. "You look almost as tuckered out as your sister does."

"I'd be happy to sleep in Tess's room," Sierra said.

Grace shook her head sadly. "It's too small for three of us and Dr. Stewart asked that I stay with her through the next couple of nights."

"Then another room?"

Grace was the soul of hospitality and Sierra could see it pained her to have to shake her head. "I'm so sorry. The television people will be here until about midnight and they're taking all our extra rooms. I don't know why they couldn't wait to get here until morning like ordinary people. Pike, I didn't offer your place for lodging, so you have room there for Sierra. Now you get her home and tucked in before she falls over."

Sierra opened her mouth to protest, but what was the point? Grace was doing what the doctor ordered and the truth was she was so tired that her ability to process any more information seemed doubtful.

"I believe Gerard put Sierra's suitcase in your SUV so it's ready to go," Grace added, directing her comment to Pike. "He said to leave Kinsey's car here and he'd pick it up later. And Sierra, I spot-cleaned your jacket. It's hanging in the closet—Pike, get it for her, will you? I don't know what to say about your boots," she added.

"I'll brush them, they'll be fine," Sierra assured her.

"I hope so. Gerard told me what happened. I don't know what got into that dog. Give me a minute and I'll put soup in a thermos so Pike won't have to cook."

They left a few minutes later, laden with soup and freshly baked bread. Sierra had finally given Pike back his jacket, and hers, while clean as a whistle and way better fitting, wasn't as comfortable as his had been.

"What exactly did Grace mean when she said that thing about family meaning everything?" Sierra asked as they walked to Pike's vehicle.

"Don't most people feel that way?"

"Yes, but there was another quality in her voice."

"Grace is actually Kinsey's mother as well as her mother-in-law. Kinsey was raised by her grandmother after her grandmother killed her father."

Sierra stopped walking. "Wait, are you saying Grace's mother killed Grace's husband?"

"That's what I'm saying. Of course, it didn't go down so cut and dried. She was eventually exonerated but it tore the family apart for over two decades."

Sierra continued walking, and when they reached the SUV she sank into the passenger seat with a sigh. "I'm so tired I could sleep standing up," she commented, and as the headlights swept the dark road ahead, she closed her eyes and didn't open them again until the vehicle slowed down.

Pike pulled up in front of a red barn. Illuminated pillars stood on either side of a large double door. As she watched, a plump yellow dog nosed its way through a dog flap, yawning and stretching and wagging its tail. The dog moved to Pike's side of the car and when he opened the door, he spoke to her.

"Hey, Daisy," he said, and ran his hand along the dog's head. "Did we wake you up?"

"This is the barn you live in?" Sierra asked as she got out of the car, wary lest this dog jump on her, too. But Daisy seemed to only have eyes for Pike and attached herself to his side as he retrieved Sierra's suitcase and unlocked the door.

"Yep. Come inside. It's freezing out here. Those film people are right, we're going to have snow by the weekend."

He switched on lights and she found herself in a huge open space with rafters high above the floor. A wall covered with all sorts of shelves housed books and all sorts of other things, including a small painting of Pike wearing glasses, sitting on a hay bale, his expression inscrutable.

"Kinsey's work," Pike said. "If you sit down for too long, she draws or paints you."

"She's good."

"Yeah. And before you think I'm the kind of guy who goes around framing pictures of himself for display, Kinsey gave me that for Christmas and placed it right where it sits."

"Aw, shucks," she said in a passable Texas accent. "It never crossed my mind you were that kind of guy."

There were a few open doors off the long wall and Sierra saw part of an office through one doorway and the edge of a bed through another. The kitchen was at the south end of the barn, the living area set up in the middle. The second floor was open and accessible by a broad wooden stairway. A wood-burning fireplace was currently unlit while a fuzzy dog bed occupied one cozy corner.

Daisy had retreated to her cushion, her gaze fastened to Pike but darting to Sierra now and again as though keeping track of the competition. "Your dog can't take her eyes off you," Sierra said.

"She's practicing for motherhood, I guess."

"She's going to have puppies?" When Pike nodded, she added, "When?"

"A couple of weeks. The vet said it's her first litter."

"You don't know if she had puppies before?"

"No. I've only had her three months. Found her Halloween night. She'd been hit by a car and was out on the road. Thankfully, she wasn't too badly hurt, but no one claimed her and now she's mine."

"She's a yellow Lab, right?"

"Mostly. There might be something else in there, too, who knows. Have a seat. It's kind of late to start a fire in the fireplace but I'll turn up the heat and put the soup on the stove."

"Let me help you," she said, knowing that if she sat on the comfortable-looking sofa she probably wouldn't get up until morning.

"Sure."

In the end, she sat at the counter and drank a glass

of wine he poured her while he heated minestrone soup and toasted slices of bread. She liked watching him move around the kitchen. She'd noticed how fit and handsome he was the minute she saw him—it was just impossible to miss. And now, when the hard day had honed some of his edges while softening others, she admitted to herself he was a very hot guy.

"Are you dating anyone?" she asked.

He spooned steaming soup into a bowl and set it in front of her. "Not currently. Why? Would you like to sign up?"

"I'm kind of over long-distance dating," she said.

"I take it you aren't…involved with anyone?"

"Nope. My last boyfriend moved to France when his company transferred him. We tried to keep it together, but it didn't work. How about you? Any cowgirl's heart go pitter-patter when she sees you?"

"Well, there's a kid about Tess's age at the feed store who has had a crush on me for about five years."

"Do you like her?"

"Patty? She's a nice girl, but she's a kid. I like women."

"Tall women?" she asked, then took a sip of the soup while keeping her gaze on him. Grace was a good cook.

"Yeah," he said as he sat across from her with a bowl of his own. He pushed the basket of bread her way and added, "I'm partial to redheads with green eyes."

"That describes me," she said with feigned surprise.

He looked at her as though just noticing her appearance. If she hadn't seen him checking her out a half-dozen times that day, she might have fallen for it. Another grin and he laughed.

"Well," Sierra said, "besides the distance issue, we have another problem. How are we going to handle Tess?"

The spoon was halfway to her lips when a large black shape landed on the counter near her elbow. She threw up her hands and the spoon went flying.

"Sinbad, get down," Pike demanded and Sierra finally realized the shape belonged to a svelte black cat with yellow eyes. The cat meowed and jumped to the floor, where it proceeded to walk away as though offended.

"How many animals do you have?" she asked.

"Just these two, who hang around inside the barn. Of course, there are a lot of others outside. This is a ranch, remember?" His gaze dropped to her bosom. "And you have soup all over your blouse.

Sierra looked down at her shirt and winced. The dry cleaner's image appeared again.

Pike replaced her spoon with a fresh one and they finished the soup with idle chatter until Pike sighed. "Looks like you and I are going to LA."

She nodded. The thought of more travel wasn't exactly comforting right at that moment.

"Let's get it over with, okay? I can arrange plane tickets for tomorrow."

"Okay. Make the flight late enough that I can talk to Tess in the morning and get details about everything she saw and heard."

"Yeah. I have some ranch work I need to finish up, as well. I'll see if I can get an evening flight. You have to feel like a dead man walking. Let me show you to your room."

Sierra nodded. The promise of lying down was the only thing still keeping her on her feet. He toted her suitcase for her, depositing it on top of a dresser in a small room bright with white paint and pine walls. "There's a bathroom behind that door in the corner. This house is wireless. I know you had business you wanted to take care of. The password is *PIKESPLACE*, one word, all caps."

"You seriously need to work on creating secure passwords," she said with a smile. "However, work can wait until tomorrow, too," she said, but kind of knew she'd get started on it before she fell asleep.

"This can't wait," Pike said and stepped close to her. Staring down into her eyes, he touched her cheek, tilted her chin up, leaned down and kissed her. His lips were vibrant and fabulous and the kiss way more impactful than she would have guessed. It took all her willpower not to pull him back when he moved a few inches away.

"Been wanting to do that since the first moment I saw you," he said, his voice as warm as a caress.

"Me, too," she admitted.

He kissed her briefly again. "Good night, Sierra. Sleep well."

Sierra stripped down to her underwear and hurried under the blankets. The barn was chilly. She'd retrieved her laptop, turned it on and waited for it to boot. The bed was soft and comfortable and the pillow felt like a little cloud. The memory of Pike's tender and unexpected kiss spread contented tendrils throughout her body. Consciousness lasted about ten more seconds before she fell asleep in the glow of the computer screen.

Chapter Four

Sierra woke up early to find the black cat staring at her from his perch on the nightstand. She sucked in a surprised gasp of cold air that startled the creature. He jumped to the floor and disappeared out the door and she showered and dressed quickly.

She felt rested but a little at odds. She'd been dreaming, she realized, and though she couldn't recall the content, she did know it hadn't been pleasant.

Her first thought was of Tess and she picked up her phone and opened her bedroom door. Then she saw the time and decided not to call yet. Instead she wandered over to the painting she'd seen the night before, the one of Pike wearing his glasses.

Kinsey had caught the intelligent glint in his eyes and the angular shape of his face. Sierra had seen each of the brothers and they were all handsome, virile men, but they were all different, too. In the past, she might have been attracted to Chance or Frankie, who each exuded a hint of wild spirit close to the surface. Pike was not usually the kind of man toward whom she gravitated. He was a serious guy with a quiet, strong core; too intense for her, or so she might once have thought. But now he occupied all the spare nooks in her mind.

She used her phone to take a picture of the painting, and then she shot another of a framed map of the Hastings ranch. The place was huge, but at last she saw where the houses were in relation to one another, where the so-called hanging tree ruled a portion of a plateau and the location of the ghost town. She was turning away when a small bronze statue of a man standing beside a horse caught her attention and she snapped a photo of that, too.

A clicking sound announced the arrival of Pike's dog, Daisy, who seemed to be smiling as she wagged her tail. "You look like you're going to pop pretty soon," Sierra told the dog. Was that the first animal she'd ever addressed as though she could understand the words? Maybe.

Eventually, she started a pot of coffee and settled down on the sofa to read emails and to study the photos she'd taken at the bar.

"OUR PLANE LEAVES at six o'clock tonight," Pike announced when he found Sierra sitting on the couch fooling with her laptop. "Do I smell coffee?"

"I put on a pot, hope you don't mind," she said. "Come look at something."

He joined her on the sofa. Whatever soap she'd lathered with hadn't been found in his shower, he was sure of that. Nothing he owned smelled quite like flowers mixed with sunshine. A pair of eyeglasses sat on the table in front of her. "I didn't know you wore those," Pike said.

"They're clear glass. There's a camera in the bridge piece."

He smiled. "Very James Bond."

"They work pretty good. My dad's old cohort taught me to use them when I was a kid."

"Was he a private eye?"

"Nope, he was Dad's campaign advisor, Rolland Bean. Everyone called him Rollo."

"Was your dad in politics?"

"He was on the city council. Then he ran for mayor of Dusty Lake, New Jersey, and lost in a landslide. Rollo and his creepy son, Anthony, kind of disappeared after that."

He smiled at her and leaned in closer. There was a smile twitching her lips as she spoke and he wasn't sure if it was because of old memories or the fact they were mere inches apart. "Why do you say his son was creepy? Creepy in what way?"

"Hmm. Well, his eyes were two different colors. One brown, one gray, which was kind of cool, but he was always lurking around, buttering up the adults, you know, then acting superior to the kids. And he was sneaky mean." She fussed with the machine and brought up two photos on the screen. "Tell me what you see."

"A man in two different places," he said. One photo showed a guy standing at a counter, looking back over his shoulder. The other one showed the same guy sitting in low light. "Who is he?"

"The one ordering coffee is Spiro Papadakis. He's the husband of the wealthy client I told you about."

"The one who wants to protect her money in a divorce," he said.

"That's right. A day or two before, Savannah—she's my client—hired me. Her girlfriend swore she saw Spiro at a New Jersey bar with the woman in this picture. It so happened the girlfriend knew the woman he was with because they'd worked together at a junior college a few years back. Savannah didn't want me to follow Spiro because she was afraid he'd make my tail and use that against her, so I opted to follow the woman. The first night she went to a retro disco place in New York City, met a guy there and flirted like crazy. I finally left when they did. She went to his place and since he was twenty years too young to be Spiro, I went home. They were so hot and heavy with each other that I thought for sure the girlfriend had been mistaken, maybe not about Spiro but about Natalia. Anyway, the next night Natalia drove out to Dusty Lake, New Jersey, and went into Tony's Tavern, which is the same place the girlfriend saw her at a few days before. Natalia waited there for the man who looked like Spiro to show up. It seemed I had everything I needed until I heard the guy speak. Spiro is Greek and by all accounts has a pretty distinct accent. The guy in the bar sounded like a longshoreman. I thought I struck out."

Pike put on his glasses and studied the photo. "There's damn little to identify either one of them. No scars, no distinctive anything."

"Just their watches," Sierra said. "His is hard to see, but hers looks like diamonds."

"Real diamonds?"

"Who knows? As a counselor she can't make that much money, but she lives in a nice place and her clothes are fabulous. She doesn't strike me as a girl who wears fakes."

"What does Savannah say about the pictures?"

"I don't know yet. I just emailed a whole slew to her." She opened her email and clicked. "I copied the email to myself. This is what I sent."

He whistled. "That's a lot of photographs."

"If nothing else, I'm thorough," she said with a chuckle. "Now listen to this. Savannah responded to the accent thing and that's what makes it interesting. She said Spiro was an actor back in Greece and still dabbles in small productions. According to her, he can adjust his voice. So now I'm back at square one."

"This is fun, isn't it?" he said.

"You mean like putting together a puzzle?"

"Yeah."

She smiled at him. "It can be." She closed the laptop and studied him for a moment. "You look pretty damn sexy in those glasses."

He picked up the tortoise frames and settled them on her face. It was hard to imagine a look she couldn't pull off. "You're kind of cute yourself," he said, and they exchanged bemused smiles. He wasn't sure why he felt so comfortable with her. By all rights, she should make him uneasy. They were two worlds colliding and yet there appeared to be a little pool of commonality between them.

"I'm going to rustle up some breakfast and then we'd better head over to the house and get things moving," he said.

She grinned at him. "I don't believe I've ever seen anyone rustle before. Mind if I watch?"

THIS TIME THE unexpected vehicle parked beside the main house was a bright blue van with the initials LOGO on a plaque attached to the door. It bore a Washington State license plate.

"Looks as though the television people arrived," Sierra said.

They went inside to find three men standing around the granite counter sipping from mugs of coffee. Pike's dad was facing them, hands on his waist, frown on his long, lean face. Tension was thick in the air.

Tess, nose dripping but looking better than the day

before, sat nearby on a stool. She wore the same fuchsia T-shirt she'd worn the day before, though it appeared to have been freshly laundered, and pink loafers. It occurred to Sierra that the girl had run away without a change of clothes.

Introductions were made, all too fast to remember for more than a few seconds. The man in charge looked about fifty, with gray on his temples and wire-framed glasses. He introduced himself as Gary Dodge.

"Is something wrong?" Pike asked.

Gary said, "Not really," at the same time Pike's dad said, "Hell, yes. They've got legal troubles!"

"Now, that's an overstatement," Gary said in a calm, reassuring voice. He spread his hands on the counter and addressed Pike, obviously anxious for a different perspective. "We have one former disgruntled employee who tried to sue us for wrongful termination. He lost, but since then weird things have been happening and we're about one-hundred-percent positive he's behind it all. He's made things…difficult…for us lately, with nuisance calls and sporadic crazy behavior, but we don't believe he poses a threat to anyone's safety."

"You told me his behavior was getting more erratic," Harry said.

Gary swallowed and nodded. "Yes, I wanted to be honest with you. Listen, we're all set to go on this project. We've done a year's worth of groundwork and no one wants to walk away. It's true that last August this guy somehow canceled our caterers on a desert shoot and we went thirsty and hungry for a day. And last month he broke into our headquarters and destroyed a couple of computers and ransacked the safe, trying to destroy this project. But we always have backups and nobody has ever been hurt."

"I don't know," Pike said. "It seems to me people like this keep upping the ante. Why haven't the police stepped in?"

Gary's eyes shifted to his hands. "We haven't called them," he said.

"Why not?"

"Because we can't prove anything and we don't want the bad publicity."

Or their insurance and backers to get nervous, Pike thought. He kept that to himself. "So, what's the upshot?" he asked.

"We'd like to go ahead with everything as it's planned. Your father is understandably nervous about the possibility this guy would make trouble for you. I've been trying to explain that, so far, he's only made trouble for us."

"There are women and children living here," Harry said.

Gary cleared his throat. "Listen. We'll only be here a couple of days. What if we hire a protection agency to secure this place?"

"More people?" Grace said from the stove where she was frying sausages. The tone of her voice made it clear what she thought about that idea.

"Just a couple."

"I don't know," Harry said. He turned his gaze to Pike. "What do you think?"

Pike shrugged. "What does Frankie say?"

"He says since when does a Hastings get scared of a lunatic? The boy is anxious for this project, you know that."

"He isn't the kind to back down from a challenge,"

Pike said and, addressing Gary, added, "Personally, I appreciate your disclosure, but I don't think we need anyone to watch our backs in the winter. There are a lot of us here and we're all experienced with weapons and, lately, with our share of homicidal maniacs. Come the fall when we're up to our ears in ranch business, that's a different story. Let me talk to Frankie. Where is he?"

"He and Oliver went out to your barn," Gary said. Then he jammed his hands in his pockets and added, "I hesitate feeding fuel to the fire but there's one more thing you have to know."

"Now what?" Harry barked.

"In the interest of transparency, the talent we had lined up to do the voice-over had a stroke earlier this week. He's pulled out of the project."

"What does that mean for us?"

"It doesn't mean anything for you right now. It means that we shoot the winter scenes as planned and then I start looking for someone else."

"One issue at a time," Pike said. He smiled at Sierra and Tess and started out to the barn.

Lily arrived home from driving her son to the end of the road to catch his school bus as Pike left the mudroom.

"Things still tense in there?" she asked.

"Kind of."

"Oh, goody."

He patted her fondly on the back and walked to the barn, where he found Frankie talking with a fourth man, who introduced himself as Oliver. This guy was a head shorter and a decade older than Frankie. A bag of camera equipment hung over his shoulder and all three ranch dogs sat by his legs staring up at him.

"Dad still fussing?" Frankie asked.

"Some. What's with the dogs?"

Oliver laughed. "I gave them an old cracker I found in my camera bag. Now they're my new best friends."

"Surest way to their hearts is through their stomachs," Frankie said with a grin.

Pike told Oliver that breakfast was almost ready over in the house, and Oliver loped off, dogs trailing behind him. "Let's ride over to the feed barn and make sure the tractors are ready in case the storm they're predicting comes and we need to haul hay to the cattle," Pike said. "We need to talk about the documentary, anyway."

They saddled their horses and headed out, talking as they rode. Frankie was adamant. "Everything is going to be fine," he said.

"What about the loss of the actor who was going to do the voice-over?"

Frankie shrugged. "Oliver says they'll find someone else. I'm not worried about it."

"Then let's just tell Dad we think the project should continue."

"I agree. He's just being cautious."

"That's in his job description," Pike said.

By the time the day had passed, he had started to sort out the documentary people. From what he gathered this advance team consisted of Oliver, who was the camera-man, Gary the producer, an assistant producer named Ogden and a story consultant named Leo. In other words, Pike figured out at last, LOGO was an acronym for their first names. Did that mean that this crew was pretty much the whole company?

"Just about," Gary said when Pike asked. "We hire freelancers for other positions on a as-needed basis. Like, we have an historian working for us right now and today we engaged your soon-to-be sister-in-law, Kinsey Frost, to produce a series of sketches and paintings to illustrate past incidents." He paused and smiled. "I want to thank you and your brother for convincing your father to give us a chance."

"You might think about hiring an investigator to uncover the truth about your sabotages," Pike said.

"Yeah. I actually talked to Ms. Hyde this afternoon and she gave me the name of a guy who works in Seattle."

Pike arranged for Frankie to stay in his house to keep an eye on Daisy while he was gone, and before too long it was time to drive to Boise. Five hours later, the plane touched down in Los Angeles, and an hour after that, thanks to traffic, they walked into the lobby of the hotel Pike had booked for them. They agreed to meet for dinner in thirty minutes.

As it happened, a half hour later they arrived at the elevator at the same time. "Nice hotel," Sierra commented as they rode down to the lobby.

"I stayed here the last time I came to see Tess."

"Not at your mother's house?"

"No, I take her in small doses."

"Her and Doug both."

"Actually, Doug is better than the husband before him. The only good thing that man ever did was die young."

She laughed. "And leave your mother a big old house and a boatload of money."

"True."

The restaurant downstairs had a free table, so they decided to eat there and both ordered a pasta dish and a glass of wine. "So, what did your client say about the photographs?" he asked her.

"She just emailed me that the guy in the bar was her husband."

"Wow. End of case."

"Well, no, actually, just the beginning. We're going to meet when I get home to figure out the next step. She'll need more intimate photos than the ones I shot if she needs to make her case to a judge."

"Is she hard to deal with?"

"A little. Like I said, she has a phone phobia so we seldom talk, and she's something of a recluse. She was Miss Georgia a couple of decades ago. I think that's how she nabbed Spiro. If I can catch her husband in a really embarrassing situation her lawyer might be able to convince him to sign away his rights to the prenup and she can be done with him even faster."

"Do you do many divorce cases?"

"My share. A lot of what I do is computer work. Background checks and things like that. By the way, I should have mentioned that I called the Los Angeles Police Department this morning and spoke to a Detective Hatch. I told him everything Tess told me and he said he would start looking into it so he'd have some news to share when I go see him tomorrow."

"I thought you didn't think this was a conversation to have over a phone," Pike commented.

"I didn't. But unless we want to be down here for more than a day or two, I decided the police had to be told in advance. Plus, if they're sitting on a homicide while their star witness hides away in Idaho, they're bound to get upset."

"I agree," Pike said. "Did he mention any dead drug dealers?"

"Nope. Said there were only two local unidentified

bodies and they were both female, but who knows what he found out today."

The rest of dinner probably appeared relaxed to an onlooker, but there were rivers of tension flowing underneath. Beyond the stress of the coming commitments, there were undercurrents of awareness between the two of them. Pike couldn't help but be hyperaware of Sierra's lips as she spoke, of the way she chewed, the way she leaned forward to hear what he was saying. There was the memory of their very brief kiss and the lack of any kind of restraint between them, to say nothing of lingering eye contact.

So it came as a little bit of a disappointment when she kissed him good-night on his cheek and thanked him for her meal. He pulled on her shoulder as she started to unlock her door and she turned around, her eyes questioning.

"When do we see Detective Hatch?"

"I thought we were going our separate ways," she said. "The police department isn't far from here. I can take a cab while you drive out to Mona's house. I assume you have to ask her where Doug went after she kicked him out?"

"I do, but I'd rather we stick together. I'm as anxious to hear what the police say as you are. And if we're going to fight for what's right for Tess with her father, we should show a united front."

"That makes sense," she said. "I told Hatch eight o'clock."

"Fine." He ran his fingers along her silky jaw. "That's not really why I detained you, you know that, right?"

Her smile shot through him. "I kind of figured. But I

also think we should get some sleep. Let's give ourselves a little time to catch our breath."

"How about a friendly kiss good-night?" he asked.

She smiled. "That couldn't hurt, could it?"

"No, that couldn't hurt," he agreed and touched his lips to hers. He'd intended it to be light and informal, but the fuse that was lit between them changed things. She raised her arms to circle his neck. Her breasts beneath her sweater pressed into his chest. Her lips parted, and her mouth was warm and inviting. He'd never been so intensely aware of a woman as he was of her.

"I could get addicted to you," she whispered when at last they separated.

"That's fine with me," he murmured, his lips against her cheek.

"We live such different lives."

"Is that what's worrying you?"

She nodded as she touched his face. If she wanted him to slow down, she was going to have to send clearer signals. "I'm not against a casual affair as long as everyone understands that it's terminal," she said softly, her fingers caressing his ear.

"And you don't think I can handle that?"

Her lips touched his again. "I'm not sure. I don't even know if I can. I think I need to say good-night, Pike. I'll see you in the morning."

"Good night," he said and waited until she'd opened the door and retreated inside, sparing him one last smile before the door closed.

DETECTIVE RICHARD HATCH was a guy of about forty with a framed photo of a woman and three young children sitting on his desk. His fair hair was cut in a buzz cut, his skin was tanned a light brown, suggesting he spent time at the beach when off duty, and his crisp white shirt would probably look more in place back east than in the easy breezy climate of Southern California.

Sierra had dressed in her black jeans and newly brushed boots. She wore her leather jacket over a white tank. Pike looked down-home comfy and incredibly good in his usual garb of boots, jeans and a shirt. The clothes might be ordinary, but the man inside them was so well put together that he elevated them.

She decided she was fixating on all these details to keep from being nervous about what she was about to hear Hatch say.

He spread his hands on his desk. "I got nothin'," he said.

"Nothing? What does that mean?" Sierra asked.

"It means no dead body, no evidence of a shooting, no street news."

"What about Danny Cooke?"

He thumbed through a small stack of papers. "Daniel Robert Cooke. Twenty-seven years old, born in Detroit, Michigan. He's been in and out of trouble his whole life. The nature of the crimes escalated as he got older. You know, he shoplifted when he was eight, robbed a bowling alley when he was thirteen, used a weapon in his next robbery. In and out of jail, lots of drug charges. Moved out here about nine months ago. He's been a guest in our jail a few times, all drug related, all in and out. Don't know when he started dealing for sure."

"Did you find anyone he did business with, or who may have known him on a personal level, like as a friend?"

"No. But I spoke to his landlord, a Mr. Fred Landers,

who happens to live in the adjoining duplex. He bought in to the community a long time ago and then watched it get overrun with gangs. Anyway, he saw Danny and your sister leave that afternoon. This was after an altercation between them. He didn't hear what was said, just that there was an angry exchange of words and that apparently it wasn't uncommon. He said Danny was shouldering a backpack the landlord had seen your sister carry on occasion. They drove off in a blue car.

"Three hours later, he saw Danny drive into the duplex driveway and get out of the car alone. He walked into the house and the landlord heard the usual noises. Then Danny came back out, threw a few things into the car and took off. The landlord had a weird feeling about things so he went over and found the apartment empty with the key on the table. It wasn't the first time someone had run out on the rental and since he'd been more or less expecting something like that to happen, he wrote if off to the drugs he knew Cooke used."

"Was he positive it was Danny who returned?" Sierra asked.

"He said he was. I don't know. Sometimes people just see what they expect to see. The view from the window he admitted looking out of wasn't great."

"Why had he been expecting something to happen?" Pike asked.

"Danny talked constantly about returning to Detroit. The landlord figured they must have had a big fight and Danny abandoned Tess somewhere, taking the car and moving out before she got back to the apartment. By the way, the landlord thought your sister used drugs, too."

"She doesn't. I checked her arms."

"Maybe weed?"

"Maybe. She says no. Did you check on whether Danny made it back to Detroit?"

"Talked to his mother this morning. She hasn't heard from Danny in a year or more and says she doesn't expect that to change. She's heard no word he's back in town."

He set the papers aside and folded his hands. "We went to the house you told me about, the one where your sister claims Danny Cooke was killed. We found absolutely nothing suspicious. The woman who lives there, Inez Ruiz, is an elderly lady with poor hearing who's resided at that address for twenty years. It took us forever to get her to answer her door. Says she's afraid of what's outside. Forensics gathered samples from the area right inside the house, but without further evidence, this will get low priority. You're familiar with how big-city departments are run, Ms. Hyde. It's not like television. Things take time and when there's so little to go on—no body, no witnesses—"

"Except my sister," Sierra interjected.

He nodded. "Yeah. Except a kid who may or may not use drugs, who was living with a known drug dealer and who waited a week before telling anybody what she saw. Ms. Hyde, I think your sister is the victim here. The victim of a boyfriend who wanted her car and not her. I suspect Danny is alive and well and knows that he scared her enough to keep her quiet."

"Would you mind if I go to the neighborhood and ask a few questions?" Sierra asked. "I understand where you're coming from, but she described Danny's death in such painful detail, I have to give her the benefit of the doubt."

"Knock yourself out, but be warned. This is a high-crime, gang-regulated part of the city. Tread lightly. And I know it's painful, but keep an open mind when it comes to the possibility that your sister was high and either thought she saw things happen that didn't, or is lying because she lost her car to her drug-dealing boyfriend."

"Thanks," Sierra said, her voice tight. She glanced at Pike, who hadn't said a word past the introduction. "Do you have anything you want to ask the detective?" she asked.

He sat forward. "Has anyone found her car?"

"Well, no one has looked for it because it wasn't reported stolen. Your sister or her father, whoever is the legal owner, should file a report."

"Okay," Sierra said.

"One last thing," Pike added. "Are you sure you got the right house?"

"The house where the reported shooting took place?"

"Yes," Pike replied. "Tess seemed relatively vague about exactly where it was."

"I went on the information I was given," the detective said. "Middle of the block, North Ash, red door. I'm pretty sure we got the right place." He stood up and offered his hand to each of them in turn, then slipped Sierra an index card. "These are the addresses and the names of the people I spoke to. I'll keep my eyes open and stay in touch. You do the same."

"Thank you," she said. She and Pike left the department in silence, both lost in thought. Did Tess use drugs? Had she imagined the whole thing or had Danny faked his death to end their relationship? Even more painful was the thought that Tess might have lied to her and Pike.

Sierra wasn't sure what the truth was, but she knew she better find out.

Chapter Five

Through mutual agreement, they decided the morning might be best spent trying to find out where Doug had gone after Pike's mother kicked him out of her house instead of tackling a gang-orientated neighborhood that probably wouldn't come alive until later in the day.

The traffic was grueling and the only thing that made it halfway tolerable was the fact that Sierra sat next to him in the car. She was fooling with her phone and at last she looked up. "It's twenty degrees in New York and twenty-eight degrees in Idaho," she announced. "And it's seventy-eight degrees here."

He smiled as he gazed at the sky. Under a veneer of smog, it was indeed clear and bright. He didn't tell her he'd take cold, crisp air any day to this, but that was the truth. "I think we better plan on leaving by tomorrow night or we stand a chance of getting frozen out of Boise," he said. "I read the anticipated storm is due to hit by Friday night."

At last they pulled into Mona's driveway. The house was circa 1950, a big old mansion of a place surrounded by grounds that kept two gardeners busy three days a week. It was a good thing that Mona's previous husband had left her cash as well as the house.

"This is the first time I've been here," Sierra said. "Tess sent me pictures a few years ago. It's a great old place."

"It is that. I'm surprised you never came to visit your sister, though."

"Well, neither Mona nor Doug exactly rolled out the welcome mat. Like so many families nowadays, like yours, for instance, ours was a little complicated. I had my father and Tess had Doug. My mother was our commonality and when she died, well, things got tricky. If we'd been closer in age, maybe I could have shared my dad with her, but it just didn't work out that way. But oh, brother, I loved visiting Dad every summer. He and Rollo always seemed to have something going on."

"Rollo. He's the man who taught you about the camera glasses," Pike said. "The one with the creepy son."

She smiled. "Yeah."

"Sounds like you still miss him."

She fingered the stone at the base of her throat. "You're right, I do. I should have found other ways to stay close to Tess. Maybe I was too judgmental about some of her iffy friends."

"Like Danny?"

"Exactly. She told me about him once and then never mentioned his name again. That's after I came unglued when she said he did drugs and sometimes sold them."

"Did you try to talk to Doug about him?"

"I tried. He wasn't listening. It was right before Mona kicked him out of her house."

Pike shook his head.

"Yeah, well, beating myself up isn't going to change anything, so I'd rather concentrate on fixing what can still be fixed," Sierra added. "But I do have to ask. How did someone like Mona end up giving birth to someone like you?"

"Mona grew up in a small town close to Falls Bluff," he told her as they wound their way up a heavily landscaped path to the patio by the side door. "She and Dad had a fling after Chance's mother left. When she got pregnant she came to Dad for money to end it. Her only goal was to become a movie star and that did not include a baby. Dad said if she would stay long enough to give birth to me and hand me over, he would finance her in LA for one entire year. Mona took the deal. They got married and then divorced within two months. I grew up with three brothers and a few stepmothers thrown into the mix."

"But Mona never acted, did she?"

"Not in films. A little stage work at first and then she transitioned from being an actor to being an actor's wife."

"Parents do a number on kids sometimes, don't they?"

"I can't complain. The ranch is great and I have people who love me. Can't ask for much more than that."

"I suspect you're an easy guy to love," Sierra said.

He stared down into her hypnotic green eyes, made all the more brilliant by the plethora of greenery around her. His gaze traveled to her peachy lips and she smiled. "This isn't a good time for hanky-panky," she said with a soft laugh.

"'Hanky-panky'? Where in the world did you dig up that old expression?"

"My dad used to say it about certain political figures."

"One tiny kiss," he said and completed the act before she could protest. The next thing he knew, he heard his name.

"Pike! Is that you?"

He turned to look at the house and found his mother standing at the open door.

Thanks to a rigorous diet and exercise program, to say nothing of yearly appointments with a plastic surgeon, Mona DeVry was not only holding her own at age fifty-one, but in the right light, could also easily pass for someone a decade younger. Fine, blond hair brushed the shoulders of a flowing white caftan as she crossed the cement porch to give him air kisses on either cheek. Pots overflowing with flowers couldn't compete with the floral scent of the perfume wafting around her in a delicate cloud. It might only be eleven in the morning, but as usual, her makeup was flawless.

"You look great," Pike told her.

She immediately touched her cheeks, pleasure glowing in her eyes. "Do I? Oh, good. Why didn't you tell me you were coming? You know Tess isn't here, right?"

"Yes, I know. I need to talk to Doug."

"Douglas Foster is a two-timing rat," she said, but there wasn't much malice in her voice. "Why do you want to talk to him?"

"Tess is in Idaho at the ranch. We need to discuss what's going on with Doug, and Tess would like us to bring back the stuff she left here. Do you know where I can find Doug?"

"Tess moved to Idaho?"

"More or less."

"Why would any woman want to go there?" She turned her attention to Sierra and added, "Oh, are you from Idaho? I'm sorry if I offended you."

"No, I'm not from Idaho," Sierra said.

"This is Tess's sister, Sierra," Pike added. For some reason he'd just figured the two women had seen each other in passing or at least a photograph. The lack of communication between Sierra and Tess's California family was mind-boggling to him.

"Nice to meet you," Sierra said.

"I bet," Mona said, irony dripping from her voice.

"Mom," Pike warned.

"I've asked you not to call me that, Pike," she said. "You're far too old for anyone to believe you're my son. And as for you, Sierra, well, all I know about you I learned from Tess and Doug. To one you're an angel, to the other a demon. I bet you never hear conflicting stories about me."

Pike shook his head but Sierra smiled. "That's true, I don't.

"Do you know where Doug is?" Pike asked again.

"Did I hear someone say my name?" a man called from the doorway. It struck Pike that both Mona and Doug had announced themselves and then proceeded to make an entrance like the patio was a stage.

Tightening the belt of a black silk robe around his waist, he sauntered out onto the patio. Back in the day Douglas Foster had been a force to be reckoned with, an approachable, handsome flirt who was also a competent actor. He'd carried a detective series for most of two seasons before he imploded and ended up in rehab. Most people would still recognize him as the voice of a popular insurance company and from guest spots on other shows. He owned a restaurant in LA, but to Pike it appeared his life seemed geared toward the next big break.

However, the only question on Pike's mind at the moment was what was he doing at this house, seemingly wearing nothing but a robe and slippers? "You two are back together?" Pike asked. "I thought he was a two-timing rat."

Douglas grinned, revealing his trademark dimples. In his fifties now, he still exuded a boyish charm.

Sierra spoke up. "Aren't you going to say hello to me, Doug?"

"Sierra, always a pleasure," he said without really looking at her. "I assume you two are here to see Tess."

"Not exactly," she said.

"Then what do you want? I don't know where she is. She hasn't bothered to call me or answer any texts. Frankly, I kind of gave up on her. In fact, I wondered if she was with one of you."

"Is that why you constantly pestered us about her whereabouts?" Sierra replied. The sarcasm wasn't lost on Doug, who frowned.

Pike interceded. "Tess is on my ranch in Idaho, Doug. We're here to talk to you. We're also here to collect some of Tess's things."

"Take her stuff, I don't care," Mona said. "I'll pack it up for you, or at least the maid will. Last I saw of Tess she was driving away with her druggie boyfriend."

"You never told me that," Doug said, and he did look surprised.

Mona shrugged. "Didn't I? Must have slipped my mind. Well, no matter. That girl has been a problem from the day her hormones kicked in. I, for one, am glad she's gone." She took Doug's hand and sidled up against him. "Now we can concentrate on you and me."

"But if you knew she was with that loser, you should have told me."

"I'm telling you now!" Mona said, sounding bored.

"Tess ran off with Danny what's-his-name. He probably talked her into driving to Idaho to sponge off Pike."

"Not exactly," Pike said calmly. "According to Tess, Danny never left LA because someone killed him right in front of her."

"He's dead?"

"We think so."

"Is that a bad thing?" She shook her head. "No, don't bother answering that. You'd better come inside." She sighed dramatically and added, "Doug, be a dear and whip up a pitcher of mimosas."

WHILE PIKE TRIED to reason with Doug and Mona, Sierra read the lineup of new texts from Tess. A couple mentioned items she wanted them to be sure to bring from Mona's house, but most were plaintive cries for information concerning Danny. Sierra was stuck saying the same thing every time: No news yet, I'll let you know when we find out anything.

They left after surveying Tess's room, which was crammed with teenage stuff, enough to fill a moving van. Sierra pointed out what Tess considered essential to Mona's maid, Lindy, who nodded but wrote nothing down.

All in all, it was a relief to be alone again in the rental with Pike. "Did you get the feeling Doug was more upset about his missing car than his daughter?" Sierra asked three hours later as they drove toward the neighborhood where Tess and Danny had rented a duplex.

"Well, he was still making payments on the car," Pike said with irony. "At least he's reporting it stolen. Are we close yet?"

She peered down at the map on her cell. "A couple

more miles. Doug obviously agreed with the cops—no body, no murder. It's easier that way. Turn left up here."

She heard a ding on her phone. Tess again: Anything new?

Nothing, Sierra texted back. Was it possible Tess was making this up, or had been drinking or using something and had imagined everything? That's what she wanted to ask, but not in a text.

"My mother seems to think Tess made up the story about Danny to get attention," Pike said in an uncannily parallel feed-in to her own thoughts.

"Do you?"

"No," he said thoughtfully. "How could she have described the house they went to so clearly the detective found it without trouble if she hadn't been there?"

"Just because she knows about the house doesn't mean she couldn't have gone there another time." Sierra thought for a second and added, "Although, why would Tess visit the house of an elderly deaf woman in the first place?"

"She saw something, I'd bet my life on it. But trying to get attention is the kind of motive Mona understands."

It was the kind of motive almost anyone who has had to fight for recognition understands, Sierra knew this. And sometimes the feelings that prompted such behavior weren't conscious ones. "Go straight now, I think we're almost at the duplex."

"Great neighborhood," Pike said as he slowed down when Sierra pointed out the building. He pulled to the curb and they both looked at the ratty place built ten feet from the sidewalk. The two units were joined in the middle with driveways to either side. The unit on the left had a very old pink Cadillac pulled into the carport. The unit on the right had a battered truck and a stack of flattened cardboard boxes littered on the porch as though someone was in the process of moving in. "Looks like Mr. Landers got himself a new tenant," Pike said.

They got out of the car and approached the owner's unit. The door opened about four inches, held in place with a chain on the inside. An older man with a pointed nose looked out.

"Yeah?"

"Mr. Landers, my name is Sierra Hyde. My sister is Tess Foster. She lived in the adjoining duplex…"

"I know who she is," he said. "Her and that no-good Danny Cooke lived there for almost three months. Argued all the time. The cops been to see me. Told them all I know. Want my opinion, the girl is better off without Cooke."

The door closed abruptly.

"Now what?" Pike asked.

"Now we drive to the house Tess described. The detective said it's 1008 North Ash off South Vermont Avenue. It's east of here."

While Tess's old neighborhood had looked shabby and unloved, their new destination seemed to be taking them deeper into an almost alternate world. Iron grills and heavy bars protected windows and doors on small businesses, dark alleys looked like death traps and hordes of young men hung out in front of pawnshops and tattoo parlors. A young woman walking with a child in footie pajamas looked like the personification of innocence until the woman turned and Sierra saw that years of meth use had rotted half her teeth and emaciated her body.

Graffiti was everywhere, lots of it undecipherable without knowing the prevailing gang slang. The thought that Tess had run down these streets by herself in the dark to escape Danny's murderer made Sierra's heated skin break out in a chilly sweat.

They found North Ash a few moments later and parked across the street from 1008. If you didn't count the inordinate number of broken-down vehicles in driveways, torn drapes hanging in dirty windows and dead, lifeless yards, the place looked more or less ordinary. The house in question was a small square stucco structure painted a light yellow with two windows facing the street. The door opened off the driveway and it was indeed red. There was a newish small white car in the driveway that looked out of place here.

A knock produced another chained door, but this time a middle-aged woman peered through the crack. She didn't look old enough to fit the detective's description of the home owner. Sierra said, "Is Mrs. Ruiz here?"

"She's here but you don't want to talk to her," the woman said.

"Actually, we came to ask her about a night eight days ago."

"What time of night?" the woman asked.

"Nine o'clock, more or less."

The woman undid the chain and opened the door a little wider. She had a pleasant, round face with a worried expression and was wearing a pair of bright yellow plastic gloves. Sierra and Pike introduced themselves.

"My name is Camila Sanchez. Inez Ruiz used to go to my church before she became too scared to leave the house. I clean for her once a week and I check on her every morning. She can't talk to you about the other night."

"Because of her hearing?" Pike asked.

"That's one reason. The hearing aids don't work so

good and she can't communicate that well with most people. But more than that, Inez goes to bed at seven thirty every night of her life. She goes into her room and locks the door and doesn't come out again until I help her get up and dressed the next morning. Good thing there's a little half bath off her room. Someone told you a lie if they said they saw her at nine at night. It would never happen."

Sierra took out her cell phone and found a photo of Tess taken last summer. "Do you recognize this girl?"

Camila studied the picture, then shook her head.

"By any chance, did Mrs. Ruiz mention that the police had come to see her yesterday?"

"The police! Why would they come here? Oh, it's Raoul, isn't it?"

"Raoul?"

"Her worthless grandson."

"I'm not sure about Raoul. The police came because of a report that there was a shooting."

"Where?"

"Here," Sierra said. "In this house, right by this door." They all looked down at the linoleum.

"Police swabbed the floor looking for blood residue," Pike said.

Camila's forehead furrowed. "You know, funny thing, I noticed the floor had been cleaned last week."

"What do you mean?"

"These floors don't get all that dirty because Inez doesn't go outside and not many people visit, so I only clean them every few weeks—truth is I hate to mop. But last week it looked like they'd been scrubbed clean. I just figured it was my imagination."

"We need to tell the police this," Sierra said.

Camila shook her head. "I would rather not talk to the police."

"It might turn out you can't avoid it," Sierra said. "But for now, why did your thoughts turn to Inez's grandson when we mentioned the police?"

"That one," she said with distaste, "is in and out of trouble all the time. He's a loose cannon."

"Does he visit Inez?"

"No. Not since I changed the locks when I found out he was using her house to crash. Him and his drug friends. Poor Inez didn't even know he was doing this. I was just glad she'd started locking herself in her room. I don't trust that boy."

"Let me get this straight," Pike said. "Raoul would wait until his grandmother had locked herself in for the night and then sneak into the house and spend the night here?"

"Him and his friends. Eat her out of house and home. Most of the time I guess they just slept it off. but sometimes they partied. I know because I picked up the garbage. I wanted to turn him in, but Inez would have hated that...and, well, ever since my own kid had a run-in with the law, I just try to steer clear of making trouble."

"What does Raoul look like?" Sierra asked.

Camila shrugged. "A punk." She turned into the room and asked them to wait. A moment later, she returned with a photo that looked to be several years old. "This is Inez on her eightieth birthday. The man there is her late son, and the boy standing to his left is Raoul."

Sierra and Pike studied the boy's image: very short dark hair, calculating eyes, gang tattoos, superior sneer. "Do you think it's possible Raoul might have started coming back to this house at night?"

"How could he? I changed the lock."

Pike leaned to check out the front door. "The lock doesn't appear to have been tampered with," he said. "Hang on a second," he added and stepped off the tiny porch, disappearing around the house.

"Can you tell me where Raoul lives?" Sierra asked. "I mean when he's not here."

"I don't know. Maybe with friends, maybe he has a girl once in a while… I seen him hanging out up on Vermont near the Tip Top bar a time or two. You might ask around up there."

Pike showed up again. "The laundry room window has been jimmied open," he said. "Where does Mrs. Ruiz keep her keys?"

Camila gestured at an ornate hanger by the front door from which three or four keys hung. "Right there."

"So you're thinking Raoul might have come in through the laundry?" Sierra asked.

"He'd only have to do it once, take the key, get a copy made, put the original back in place and from then on, he'd be home free." He turned to Camila and added, "Do you want me to secure that window before we go?"

"Would you, please? Guess it's time to change the lock again."

"Are there tools in the garage?"

"I'm not sure." She handed him a key from the little hanger. "You can check."

He left again. Sierra pocketed her phone. "I'm going to have to tell the police everything I learned. I don't want to cause problems for you, but they need to know. They'll send forensics back to process this doorway and everything else and they'll need to talk to Mrs. Ruiz.

You and her attorney should be present to help her. May I give them your name and number?"

"Yes," she said with a resigned sigh. "Go ahead."

"And it's probably too late, but don't throw anything away. Just keep all the trash you find in a plastic bag in the garage, in case there's evidence."

IT WAS DARK by the time they got to the Tip Top. The streets were bumper-to-bumper, the sidewalks more or less empty. "There's nowhere to park," Pike said.

"Let me out and I'll ask around about Raoul. You can circle the block. I'll call your cell in a few minutes so you can pick me up." He slowed down the car. She noticed his expression as he scanned the sidewalk. "Don't worry about me, I'll be fine," she added.

"This is a pretty rough part of town," he said.

"Maybe, but I'm no cupcake." She impulsively squeezed his hand before opening the door and getting out of the car. She hurried to the sidewalk to avoid getting hit and prepared herself to enter the dingy bar in front of her.

Before she could take more than a few steps, a group of five men exited the dive and stopped short when they saw her. She avoided eye contact. She could take one on one, but five against one weren't odds she liked.

The men circled her and there was nothing she could do but look into their eyes. That was a sobering experience as she sensed a group mentality concerning single women on "their" turf. A little frisson of fear rippled down her spine that annoyed the heck out of her. She was used to handling herself, but in all truth, she had to admit that the situations in which she usually found herself were a little less raw than this.

She suddenly missed Pike's reassuring presence, but

shook off that feeling. Since when did Sierra Hyde depend on a man?

"Anyone here know Raoul Ruiz?" she asked with a resolute effort to exude confidence.

One of the men had a knife scar running across his throat and a superior way of looking down his nose as though detached from what was going on around him. The power and anger radiating from his eyes could probably melt concrete.

He turned in a bored, I've-had-enough-of-this-broad way and walked back inside the bar. The others looked at each other, avoiding eye contact with Sierra, and one by one they followed on Knife Scar's heels, leaving just one guy behind.

Unfortunately, the one who remained was huge. Not tall, really, just a shining example of steroid abuse. He wore a red muscle shirt over bulging abs and pecs and a blue bandanna around his head that almost hid the fact that he had no eyebrows.

"Was it something I said?" she asked Muscle Guy.

"They think you're a cop," he replied.

"Do you?"

"Maybe. Difference is, I don't care."

"Do you know Raoul Ruiz?"

"I might."

"Have you seen him recently?"

"Maybe."

"But you're not going to say."

"Brother don't rat on brother to the cops."

"I'm not a cop. I'm a private detective."

"Not from around here."

"No," she said. "I'm looking for a guy named Danny Cooke. I thought maybe Raoul would know where he is."

The man stared at her, wheels obviously turning in his head. "What's in it for me?"

"All I got on me. Fifty bucks," she said.

"Beat it, broad," he said loudly and then added in a hushed tone, "Meet me down the alley."

Was Sierra really desperate enough for a lead to follow this behemoth into a dark alley? Turns out the answer was yes.

Chapter Six

Sierra saw her would-be informant's bulging shape lurking behind an industrial Dumpster as she turned down the alley after giving him a head start. She was keenly aware this could go awry and she thought of all the hours spent at the gym. Hopefully she wouldn't have to find out if they paid off.

She stopped a few feet shy of him. "All right, spill it. What can you tell me about Raoul?"

"Dude's a doper."

"And Danny Cooke?"

"Mr. Detroit? Runs a little operation. Weed, crystal, blow, stuff like that."

"When did you see Ruiz last?"

"Earlier this week, driving a blue girlie car."

"Did you see Danny?"

"No."

"Did you speak to Ruiz?"

"Some."

Sierra looked toward the entry of the alley. Her gut was telling her time was running out. "Did he talk about a murder?"

"Murder? No!"

"Did he mention killing someone?"

"What are you talking about? All he said was him and Shorts were leaving town."

"Who is Shorts?"

"A guy."

"Where were they going?"

"Didn't say."

"What's Shorts's real name?"

"Don't know. He just wears shorts all the time." He twitched a little and licked his lips. "Give me the fifty bucks now."

As a lead, this one didn't show much promise. She could tell Detective Hatch about it, though, and maybe he could locate this Shorts person. It all seemed like a long shot.

Suddenly a voice came from behind them. Sierra hadn't heard anyone approaching, but she whirled around to find Knife Scar pointing a gun at her. His gaze flicked from her to Muscle Guy. "How long you been squealing to the cops?"

Sierra doubted that pointing out the difference between a police offer and a private detective would afford her any latitude in her current situation. She stood trapped between two men and knew her chances of outrunning either of them weren't good even without the added factor of the gun.

"Listen, dude, I didn't tell her nothing," the walking muscle insisted.

Knife Scar ignored him. "I'm trying to think of the best way to kill you both. There are so many options." He pointed the gun at his friend's head, then lowered it to aim at Sierra's gut. "I kind of like the thought of starting with you."

With her mind racing for a way out of this, she came up blank. If he moved closer she might have a chance to disarm him. Sure. Probably not, but it was all she could think of. Before she could figure out how to close the distance between them, he was suddenly flying through the air. With a thud, he landed on his back five feet away.

Pike moved quickly to stand over him, jaw tight, fists rolled. He kicked the guy in the side and hauled him to his feet, twisted his arm behind his back and slammed him against the building on the other side of the alley. He took the gun from his hand and pressed it against the guy's thick neck.

Sierra swallowed the last few minutes of terror as Pike kept the guy pinned against the building. The sound of heavy breathing was about all she could hear, but she knew that sooner or later, this guy's buddies would come looking for him and they would be sorely outnumbered. She looked around to see that her informant had fled.

Pike looked into her eyes. "You through with him?"

She thought of trying to question him and decided she'd pushed her luck as far as she wanted to. She nodded and then thought twice and stopped him. She reached into her pocket and produced several plastic cable ties. "Tools of the trade," she said. While Pike held him at gunpoint she tied his hands together. They walked the thug over to the Dumpster, threw back the lid and forced the man to climb into the garbage, where he stumbled to keep upright. Pike pushed him down and slammed the lid. They fled down the alley to the echo of his bellowing.

Once out on a street, they sprinted a couple of blocks to the rental. Pike locked the confiscated weapon in the trunk and they took off without looking back.

BY THE TIME they got to their hotel the adrenaline had started to wear off. "I'm ordering room service," she announced outside her door. "You're welcome to join me."

"That's the best offer I've had today."

"Well, you did waltz into that alley in the nick of time. The least I can do is feed you." She leaned back against her door and ran a finger along his chin. He had a truly delightful face, serious, sexy, playful, his expressions charming and fascinating. "Anything in particular you want?"

"You," he said.

She smiled. "Give me forty-five minutes."

"Is that a promise?"

"I'll let you know in forty-five minutes."

SIERRA SAT DOWN at the table and took out her cell phone, annoyed to see her hand shake. The scene in the alley might have ended differently if Pike hadn't come looking for her. It might have also played out differently if she'd been armed, but she hadn't left New York with the intention of having to shoot anyone.

Tess answered with palatable anticipation. "Sierra? Did you find him?"

"No," Sierra said gently.

"Not even his—his body?"

"Not even his body." She took a deep breath. "Tess, I need you to be very honest with me, okay?"

There was a pause before Tess replied. "I have been."

"Don't get offended. Just answer a couple of questions. Were you and Danny arguing the night he died?"

"Yeah. He could be a jerk. It was no big deal."

"He wouldn't want to scare you, would he?"

"What do you mean?"

"I mean that your car is missing. Could he have faked the shooting—"

"No! What a thing to say. He would never do that to me! Whoever killed Danny has my car."

"Okay. Is it possible you went to that house another time and—"

"No!"

"Let me finish. Is it possible you remember that house for another reason?"

"No!"

"Had you been drinking or doing drugs?"

There was silence for a heartbeat, then a sigh. "I had a shot of brandy, maybe two. I was getting a cold and Danny said it would help."

Sierra reflected for a second. The girl weighed less than a hundred pounds, but a couple of shots, if that's all it really was, wasn't enough to cause her to hallucinate a murder. "Okay, is it possible Danny was shot but not killed?"

This time the answer was even slower to come. "No," she said, but for the first time, there was a note of uncertainty in her voice. "I thought he was dead. He was so still."

"But you had no time to check him, right?"

"I had to go," Tess said, her voice shaking. "The other man had a gun. I was—I was…scared."

"Okay, okay. Calm down. I'm not done looking. We'll be home tomorrow night, okay?"

"Okay."

"It might be late so you don't have to wait up."

"Okay. But I will."

"I know. Are you sleeping?"

"Some."

"Good." They hung up a minute or two later and Sierra sat there to steady her nerves for a moment before calling Grace's phone and filling her in on the situation.

"Don't you worry. I'll make sure she has a warm glass of milk before bed. She'll be fine," Grace said. "Her cold is getting better and I heard her humming today."

As Sierra went in to take a shower she felt pretty sure Tess wasn't humming now. Some big sister she was turning out to be.

SHOWERED, FRESHLY SHAVED and whistling, Pike knocked on Sierra's door. She opened it quickly, and his breath caught. Her red hair was damp again and combed straight back from her face. She wore a slender grass-green kimono trimmed in pink, belted at the waist, plunging at the neckline. The diamond in her necklace rested in the hollow of her throat. It was the only jewelry he'd ever seen her wear.

Every single time he saw her, she seemed to seep a little deeper into his pores. "You look amazing," he said.

She smiled. "I haven't had time to get dressed yet."

"Don't hurry on my account," he told her.

She smiled again. "I have an idea."

"I have an idea, too," he said, and took her hands. "It's been forty-seven minutes, you know."

"Mine is about Raoul Ruiz," she said as he pulled her against his chest. He kissed her neck, pushing aside the damp hair, inhaling her.

"Mine isn't," he said. He found her mouth and kissed her. She was so soft and warm and welcoming. He kissed her over and over again, his body screaming with anticipation. He'd never wanted a woman the way he wanted her. "You are driving me crazy," he whispered against her ear.

She pulled away from him and looked into his eyes. "Oh, Pike. Are you sure? I can't promise you anything—"

"I'm not asking for promises," he interrupted. "All I want is the here and now."

"Are you sure?" she asked as she cupped his face in her hands and kissed his lips. Her half-closed eyes made his breath catch. "Are you positive?" she added, her lips brushing his cheekbone, his temple.

He lowered his head and kissed her throat. Was he positive? Hell, no. But he was certain that he was willing to take his chances. There was no other option. He could no more stay away from her than indefinitely hold his breath. The future would just have to take care of itself. "Trust me," he said.

There was a knock on the door and they looked at each other. "I'll get it," he said, and reluctantly released his grip on her arms. A waiter rolled a small table into the room and asked if he could set things up for them. Pike signed the bill, handed the kid a twenty and told him they'd take care of it themselves.

He turned his back on the covered trays. His growing hunger couldn't be sated with food. He went back to Sierra and led her to the bed. "Dinner is going to be late," he said, sliding the kimono down over her shoulder, kissing the exposed skin.

She raised his head and stared into his eyes. "This is all happening so fast," she said.

"I feel like I've known you my entire life," he whispered as he sat on the bed and pulled her beside him. He continued to kiss her throat as he cupped her silk-covered breast.

"I've never known anyone like you," she whispered.

"I'm just a cowboy," he said.

"I'm not talking about that," she murmured. "I'm talking about your heart."

"Currently beating off the charts because of you," he murmured as he slipped the kimono farther down her arm and the belt gave way. He'd never seen or touched a more sensational, creamy, beautiful woman in his life. Her breasts were firm but soft, her stomach flat, hips flaring from a small waist. It took her about thirty seconds to tear off his clothes before they fell together back on the bed. For a moment, he paused, just looking at her face, devouring her beauty, and then she touched him, and after that, everything happened at once.

She was everywhere. Under him, on top of him, seemingly insatiable, arousing parts of him in ways he'd never expected. He strove to be the best lover he'd ever been and then he forgot to worry about it and it seemed she did, too. Instead, they stopped being two people and became one, perfectly in sync, both giving, both taking until the climactic moment that culminated in the beginning of the rest of his life.

He knew he shouldn't think like that. He did so, anyway. Thoughts were private and free. It was uttering them that exacted a price.

At last they lay spent, arms and legs entangled, her head resting on his shoulder. He ran his fingers up and down her arm. He couldn't believe she was lying here with him, that for this moment, she was his.

"You okay?" she asked.

"Almost."

She tilted her head back to look at him and smiled. "You are something else."

"The feeling is mutual."

"No, I mean it. I've never been with a man who was more sure of who and what he is. It's spellbinding. It's fascinating."

He kissed her succulent lips and knew he would never grow tired of the feel and scent of her.

"You hungry?" he asked after a while.

"Getting there. I need to make a call first."

"Tess?"

"No, I called her after we got back today. Now I need to call Camila, Mrs. Ruiz's housekeeper." Her voice sounded anything but businesslike, more sleepy and contented than exacting. "It just occurred to me that she might know Shorts's real name or know where he lives. She may be able to give us a lead to follow tomorrow."

"The intrepid private eye, always at work," he said, sitting up.

She smiled at him. "Not always," she said, and pulled him back down beside her. "Where do you think you're going?" she whispered while nibbling his ear. Her breasts felt weighty and soft against his arm.

"Nowhere," he said, smoothing the hair away from her forehead and kissing her eyelids. "Nowhere at all."

BETWEEN ONE THING and another, Sierra didn't get around to calling Camila Sanchez until morning, while Pike took a shower in his own room. After grabbing coffee and bagels in the lobby, they slid back into the rental. Pike took the wheel again.

"Head east toward Victorville," Sierra told him as she showed him the map on her phone.

He waited until commuter traffic thinned out before saying much. "Okay, tell me what Camila said."

"She knows Shorts because he's one of the punks who hangs out with Raoul. His sister lives on a piece of property this side of Victorville. It's about two hours from here, maybe more with traffic. She wasn't sure what the woman's name is, but she knows Shorts taps her when he needs cash. And if he was traveling, he would need cash, right?"

"Sounds reasonable. How are we supposed to find her?"

"We look for an auto-wrecking place this side of the city."

California had endured a drought for the past few years. Pike was used to the unending vistas of the plateau at home, and in this way, the golden, rolling near-desert struck a familiar chord. Not that the scenery mattered. Being anywhere with Sierra by his side was far better than being anywhere else without her. Even driving out into the desert in a rental car became something of a joyful event with her along. He warned himself he was falling too hard and too fast. He reminded himself of the ground rules: ultimate termination of the relationship. And then he glanced over at her, her face half covered with sunglasses, her pink lips spread into a smile, and he knew all the warnings in the world were inadequate.

"What's the plan, boss?" he asked as they neared their destination.

"We look for a bunch of old cars. Camila says the sister's husband owned a wrecking yard before he ran his motorcycle into the side of a semitruck."

They drove until they hit the beginning of the city and then they were downtown. "We must have come too far," Sierra said.

"Look up auto-wrecking places on your cell."

"I did. There's nothing listed back the way we came. But Camila said it was before the town. We have to go back."

He turned around and they retraced their route. When they figured they were too far away, they turned again. "It must be off the road," Pike said. "Look for anything suspicious."

Five miles back toward Victorville, Sierra suddenly said, "What was that? Turn around, go back."

He did as she asked and pulled over on a dirt road to find a sculpture he'd been mildly aware of the other two times they'd passed it by. Up close and standing still, he could now see it had been created by welding together old car parts. It was hard to tell what it was supposed to be, but a plastic sign from the hardware store tacked onto the base said Closed. Pike lifted the corner of the sign and discovered it covered another one: Mac's Place.

"Doesn't sound much like an auto-wrecking yard," he said.

"This has to be it. Camila said the sister's husband died about two years ago. I guess she closed the place down. We'll see if she can tell us anything about Raoul."

They drove for a half mile before coming across a tall chain-link fence surrounding a scattering of abandoned cars that quickly turned into a sea of windshields twinkling in the sunlight. At the hub of this chaos sat a faded aqua double-wide trailer backed by a series of sheds, barns and workshops. Everything had a deserted air except for the trailer, from which they could hear the muted sound of music when they stepped out of the car.

It was much cooler here than in LA—probably no more than forty degrees. Access to the double-wide was by way of a ramp. Their knocks went unanswered until the shrill bark of a dog heralded the sudden opening of the door by a woman in a wheelchair. A small terrier darted out and ran around their legs while the woman spoke, but who could hear a word she said? She adroitly wheeled herself back into the room and switched off a CD player. The sudden silence was pierced only by the yapping dog.

"Olive, shush," the woman said.

The dog immediately stopped barking, trotted back inside the trailer and jumped onto the woman's lap. Dog and owner looked a lot alike: both smallish, both dark blond and both sporting dark, soulful eyes.

"Are you an auto-wrecking business?" Sierra asked.

"Used to be, kind of. Only if Mac had heard you call this place that, he would have had issues. He thought of it more as a reclamation center for dead cars. Anyway, didn't you see the sign? Don't tell me it blew away again. I'm not open."

"Your sign is there but we're not here to ask about cars," Sierra replied. She introduced herself and Pike.

"I'm Polly MacArthur," the woman said. "What can I do for you?"

"We're here because we're trying to get a lead on the whereabouts of a man named Raoul Ruiz. We heard your brother, Shorts, knows him."

"Listen," she said, "ever since my Mac skid his bike under that truck and put me in this chair for the rest of my life, Shorts, aka Dwayne, has been conning me for drug money. This last time he came, he was with a guy I didn't know. Dwayne said he'd conned this man for a ride because his truck was dead in the water. Big surprise. It hasn't run good since Mac is no longer around to tinker on it. Anyway, this time Dwayne didn't ask for cash."

"He just came for a visit?"

"Hell, no," she said with a laugh. "Dwayne isn't exactly a conversationalist. He told me he knew this dude who's rebuilding a 1968 Mustang. He said he remembered Mac had an old wrecked one out on the lot somewhere. He wanted to go take parts off the car and sell them to his pal. Maybe he was embarrassed to beg money off his crippled sister with another guy sitting a few yards away, I don't know. What I do know is it's by far the most enterprising idea Dwayne's ever had, so I said sure, why not, knock yourself out."

"Did you get a good look at this other man?"

"No. He never got out of the car. He kept his face averted, but I could tell he was listening to our conversation."

"Did you notice any tattoos?" Sierra asked, thinking back to the photo Camila had showed them. Raoul Ruiz had several tattoos.

She thought for a second. "Yeah, now that you mention it. He had his arm outside the car and he was wearing a tank. There was a sun, I think. You know, a circle with flames shooting out. I couldn't see what was in the middle."

"When were your brother and this other man here?"

"About five days ago."

"Have you heard from your brother since then?"

"No, but I don't expect to. He'll come around again when he runs low on money."

"So they took the parts and left?"

"Yeah."

"Did your brother mention a car trip he and the other guy might take?"

"Those two on a trip together? That just defies imagination, sorry."

"Okay. How long were they out in the yard?"

"Must have been about thirty minutes. I didn't even know they'd left until Olive barked and I opened a window to see the blue car taking off down the road, kicking up a cloud of dust in its wake. They didn't even stop at the house."

"Did you expect them to?" Pike asked.

"It would have been a decent thing to do," she said. "I guess Dwayne got what he was after, but they left without returning the key or locking the gate behind them."

"Could you tell what kind of car it was?"

She laughed. "You aren't married to a guy like Mac for twelve years without picking up on stuff like that. It was a sky-blue Chevy Volt, this year's model or last."

"Did they walk out on the lot or drive?" Sierra asked.

"They drove. There are almost five acres crammed with old wrecks. Nobody goes out there anymore but I figure the roads must be in pretty good shape."

"May we drive out there, too?" Sierra asked.

Polly tilted her head and regarded them for a second. "Is Dwayne in trouble?"

"I don't know," Sierra said. "He's simply our only link to Raoul Ruiz and we need to ask him a few questions concerning a third man named Danny Cooke. And yes, Raoul had access to a blue Chevy Volt."

"The Cooke name is familiar for some reason," Polly said.

"He's a penny-ante drug dealer."

"Figures. Sure, go ahead. Like I said, the gate is unlocked."

Chapter Seven

"Talk about a needle in a haystack," Pike said as they drove along a road that threaded its way between two rows of every kind of abandoned, rusted, wrecked vehicle known to man, then doubled back and started again going the other direction in a series of parallel tracks.

"Well, I know what a Mustang looks like," she said. "My dad used to drive one."

"Do you really think they were looking for car parts out here?" Pike asked.

"No. What I think they were doing is stowing Danny Cooke's body in one of these cars and then continuing their trip to who knows where."

"But which car?"

"The police will have to go through them all," she said. "They can use a cadaver dog. Anyway, we don't have time. We need to be back at the airport by what time?"

"Check-in is at five. We can't leave this place any later than about twelve thirty. We still have to drop by Mona's house to pick up the bags she promised to pack with Tess's things." At least he hoped she'd actually done it. He made a mental note to call her to make sure.

"We also have to deliver the guy in the alley's weapons to Detective Hatch and try to explain what might have happened to Danny," Sierra said.

The weed-infested road looped through the aisles of cars like a line at a Disneyland attraction. They reached the far end of it, admired a cactus standing on the other side of the seven-foot chain-link fence topped with a row of razor wire and turned around. On the way back Pike suddenly stopped the car. "There's a Mustang," he said, gesturing at a pale green rusted-out coupe that hadn't been visible going the other direction.

He opened the rental door and got out. Tess did the same. "What are you doing?"

"There are actually four or five Mustangs in various states of disrepair," he said, surveying the aged metal hulks in front of him. A couple barely looked like cars. "I don't get the feeling Shorts and Raoul are the smartest guys in the world. What if they actually used the Mustang as the dump site?" He started making his way through the car parts to get to the first almost-complete car that was missing all its doors, its engine hood and both fenders. He scanned it quickly and shook his head.

Moving along, he paused and sniffed the air. "Sierra, do you smell something terrible?"

She joined him. "I know that smell. That's rotting flesh."

"It's not that strong. Could be a coyote or a stray dog," he said.

They both stared at the green Mustang. Someone had put a rusted wheel rim off a big truck on top of the trunk sometime in the past. As Pike lifted it off, he heard Sierra warn him not to, but it was too late. With the weight removed, the trunk sprang open. Both he and Sierra recoiled at once but not before the horrible image of a dead man wearing red shorts burned itself into their eyeballs. Pike caught the glistening human-sized shape of black plastic wrapped with duct tape underneath the dead man.

Holding his breath, he closed the trunk and replaced the rim. He grabbed Sierra as he backed away. The trunk was sealed again, but the putrid odor hung heavy in the dry air, and they drove away with the smell of death in their nostrils.

SEVEN HOURS LATER, they boarded their plane. Pike had upgraded their tickets to first class and they sank into recliner-like comfort. He was thrilled when the sheriff had allowed them to return to Idaho after an afternoon of answering questions and explaining what they'd seen and who they'd talked to within the past twenty-four hours.

Poor Polly MacArthur had been called upon to identify her brother's remains. "Looks like Dwayne helped Ruiz move Cooke's body to the wreck, then Ruiz knocked him out," Sheriff Keith Rogers told them. He sounded like he was fresh from Texas. "The ME says it appears he was shot at close range with a foam rubber cushion of some kind buffering the sound. Danny Cooke was wrapped in the plastic, his empty wallet thrown in for good measure. We're searching the country for Raoul Ruiz and the blue Chevy. I talked to Detective Hatch in LA like you asked me to. He said to tell you your sister needs to come back ASAP and tell her story in her own words."

"Ruiz probably ditched the Chevy knowing Polly MacArthur could identify it," Sierra said.

"Probably."

"Oh, and Polly mentioned a tattoo on Ruiz's arm."

"Yeah, she told me about it," he said, checking his notes. "Ruiz is a wanna-be member of a gang called Border Brothers. It consists of undocumented immigrants, usually from the same area of Mexico. The tattoo is a sun with an Aztec god in the middle and an acronym… Anyway, he was actually born in LA, so I'm supposing he got the tat as a sign of solidarity. Most likely it differed slightly when viewed up close and personal."

"Wasn't it kind of risky leaving Dwayne's rotting corpse in his own sister's backyard, so to say?" Pike asked.

"She hasn't been out there since her husband's death," the sheriff replied. "It's cool enough to keep the smell down for a while."

They landed after an uneventful flight during which they held hands and attempted to let go of the day's anxieties. Upon landing, they were greeted by blowing snow as they crossed the parking lot to Pike's SUV.

Two and a half hours later, they rattled over the cattle guard onto Hastings land, but it was a distinctly muted sound. Pike pointed out tracks of another vehicle that were quickly being covered by the falling snow. Someone else in the family must be out and about. Pike was glad he'd put studded snow tires on his vehicle.

As always, he felt the pull of this ranch deep in his soul, and to be coming home with Sierra by his side seemed to fill crevices he hadn't even known existed. Another cautionary warning flashed in his brain, but he stuffed it into a corner with all the rest.

"Do you think the advance documentary crew is still here?" Sierra asked. They had just passed the road to Pike's barn and the desire to veer off in that direction was impossible to deny. He hadn't made love to her since that morning and all he truly wanted in his heart of hearts was to take her into his bed in his own house. He wanted memories of her there, visions he could call on when the day came for her to leave.

But his priority right now had to center on Tess. He'd called his father and told him of their grisly discovery and asked that Tess not be told until he and Sierra were there to do it, but until then, not to let her out of their sight. She had to know the facts because they would soon be public knowledge and she had to be prepared. There was a cold-blooded killer on the run, a man who had murdered a friend he'd enlisted to help him get rid of the body of his drug dealer. Would a man like that leave an eyewitness like Tess alive to talk about him? As far as Pike could see, Dwayne's sister was lucky Raoul hadn't decided to eliminate her, as well. The fact that he hadn't shown his face probably saved her life.

"Hey, over there," Sierra said gently as she tapped his thigh. "I lost you."

"Sorry, I was thinking," he admitted. "But in answer to your question, I doubt the crew will still be here. A storm like this will be around for a few days. We're likely to lose power. I imagine they hightailed it out before it hit."

However, the LOGO van was still parked by the main house. The snow was deeper down in this little valley by the river, and the landscape had turned white. After just two days in seventy-degree weather, the twenty degrees they faced getting out of the SUV felt like a walk-in freezer.

Though it was almost midnight, they found Grace in the kitchen, sitting at the counter working a crossword puzzle, and she looked up when they entered. Disappointment flashed across her face and the pit of Pike's stomach fell. "What's wrong?" he said.

"I was hoping you were your father."

"Why? Where's Dad?"

"He and your brothers rode out to find those television people, who went to shoot pictures of the falling snow before dinner and never came back."

"What? In a storm?"

"We couldn't talk them out of it. They saddled up and rode off like they were the characters in an old Western. Your dad has been gone for hours now."

"Did you call him?" Pike said as he took out his cell."

"Of course. We've been in sporadic communication, but you know what reception is like out here—iffy at best. Last I heard they were going to go film some cattle hunkering down for the storm because Frankie said that's what the cameraman wanted to shoot. But who knows where they are now. I'm sure they're fine—"

Pike's phone rang and that startled all of them. He glanced at the screen and answered. "Frankie?"

His brother's voice was broken. Mountains, weather, valleys and inadequate cell towers all contributed to communication issues they were used to, but this was especially frustrating. "Speak up," Pike said and listened. The only words he was pretty sure he caught before the connection died were *injury* and *tree*.

He related this information and then Grace's phone rang. "It's Harry," she announced and answered immediately. Her smile turned into a frown as she clicked off the phone. "The call was dropped," she said and immediately started texting him.

"I'm going after them," Pike said.

"Do you think that's a good idea?" Grace asked, but he could tell by the way her eyes lit that she was yearning for him to do just that.

"I heard the word *tree* and the only tree around here those documentary people were interested in was the hanging tree. And I'm pretty sure I heard *injury.* I'm going to hook the trailer up to the biggest snowmobile and head out. Grace, could you get the emergency medical kit and maybe heat up a couple thermoses of something hot to drink?"

"Of course," she said and hurried out of the kitchen to get the kit.

Pike turned to Sierra. "I hate to leave you."

"I understand, it's okay. I wonder where Tess is."

"Grace will know." He took her hands and kissed her fingers. "I'll be back in a few hours. You can sleep here or go back to my place."

"I'll stay here," she said. "Tess said she'd wait up."

"Okay."

There was more he wanted to say because she had made him into a giant sap in the last three days. Instead he stared into her green eyes. "You're going to tell her what we found?"

She nodded. "She has to know. There are plans to make."

"Give her a while to digest everything first, okay?" he said.

She smiled and squeezed his hand. "Yes, I know. I will."

He kissed her again, turned away and walked back outside, but not before stopping in the mudroom to borrow the appropriate cold-weather gear and a flashlight from his dad's supply. Outfitted in gloves, a hat and a heavy jacket, he made his way to the equipment barn.

"SHE'S UPSTAIRS," GRACE said when Sierra inquired about Tess. "Lily went up there hours ago with Charlie and Tess went with them, saying she wanted to text friends and read. Her cold has still got her down, but something else is on her mind. She's been very quiet since your call, but I couldn't get her to open up."

"I know she's going to take the news of Danny's death hard," Sierra said.

Grace screwed the top on the thermos. "Of course. Poor dear."

"May I ask why Lily lives here and not with Chance," Sierra added. "I know it's none of my business, but I'm curious. It's obvious they're crazy about one another."

"Yes, they are, but there's Charlie to consider. His father…died…not too long ago. Lily and Chance are getting married this fall, but until then, Lily asked if she and Charlie could live here with me and Harry, and we were delighted to say yes." She handed Sierra the last thermos of soup, which Sierra tucked in a basket with the other two and a stack of tin cups. "There are some blankets in the chest in the downstairs bedroom. Will you get them?"

"Of course," Sierra said and did as asked, but her thoughts were frantically running from the barn with Pike to upstairs with Tess. She felt split in two pieces. She took the basket of broth and the blankets out to the barn to give to Pike, who tucked them in the trailer before folding her in his arms. "I'll be back," he said, brushing her hair away from her face and kissing her forehead.

His embrace was difficult to leave. Never had another human being's arms created such a conflicting oasis of sanctuary charged with awareness. "Be careful."

He kissed her. "Good luck with Tess."

"Thanks, I'm going to talk to her now." He turned to the machine and she added, "I want to thank you."

He turned back to her, his expression surprised. "Thank me? For what?"

She reached up and touched his cheek and shook her head.

"Sierra," he said, lifting her chin so their gazes connected. "Thank me for what?"

"For today," she finally said.

"Today? If I hadn't opened that trunk—"

"Then I would have. Not for that. For being there, for being with me, for letting me be…I don't know, me. You know?"

He smiled at her and pulled her to his chest.

"I know you have other things to think about right now," she added. "Lord knows, I do, too. But I just—"

He effectively cut this speech short by kissing her again. "We'll finish this later, okay?"

She nodded. "Okay."

"Because I'll be back."

"I know."

He stared into her eyes for a long moment. What did he see? She wasn't sure. She just knew what she saw in his and it shook her down to her soul. A moment later, he started the snowmobile and a moment after that he was gone.

She retrieved her suitcase from his vehicle on the way back to the house and carried it inside, where Grace was just finishing wiping down the drain boards. "The downstairs bedroom is empty now if you and Tess want to use it," she said.

"Thanks," Sierra said, still distracted. She figuratively straightened her shoulders and shook off the last few minutes. "If it's okay with you, I'm going to go talk to Tess and then maybe I'll catch up with some work on my laptop in the room with the fireplace. I don't think I could actually sleep."

"I know what you mean. I have some darning to do so I'll be in there, too." She laughed and added, "Don't look at me that way, young lady, people still do darn good woolen socks, you know."

"I didn't know," Sierra said with a smile. "But I do now."

Sierra went to the room where she'd seen Tess only three days before and found it dark. She peeked inside and discerned a shape beneath the blanket. Obviously, Tess had fallen asleep so Sierra closed the door but didn't latch it. There was no way she was going to wake her sister to tell her about Danny. Sierra knew the hard way that getting upsetting news the moment you awaken sucked big-time. She'd learned about her father's heart attack with an early morning phone call from his girlfriend.

A door opened across the hall and a very pretty, small woman in her midtwenties with light brown hair peeked out. Lily, Chance's fiancée, smiled. "Are they back yet?" she whispered.

"No," Sierra said.

"I heard something outside."

"That was Pike riding out on a snowmobile. He got a call from Frankie. He thinks someone may be injured at a place called the hanging tree."

"One of our men?"

For a second, Sierra just stared at her, uncertain how to respond, and then her head cleared. "You mean one of the Hastingses? No, I didn't get that feeling, but really, I'm not sure now that you ask."

"I sure hope not."

"Yeah," Sierra said. "Me, too."

THE QUICKEST WAY to the plateau was a trail beside a stream that ran down the hillside behind the house. But that trail was accessible by foot or horseback alone, not with a snowmobile and certainly not one pulling a seven-foot-long trailer. He would have to use the roads, although he could cut through a field or two to shave off some time.

It was likely his father and brothers would do their best to build a fire to use for warmth and as a beacon. His cell needed a charge after the busy day he'd just had, but it should have a call or two left in it. He'd save it for the chance that he'd misunderstood Frankie's garbled message and went to the wrong place.

The ride was grueling. The snow was almost two feet deep in places, piling up against fences. The cattle were mostly in more protected fields and were likely staying in the brush to escape the snow; they could take care of themselves, although tomorrow the task of delivering hay would begin in earnest. It was the city slickers he needed to worry about now.

An hour later, so cold he'd lost most of the feeling in his legs, he spotted the glow of an open flame. As he drew nearer, he could see a fire had been built under the partial protection of the old hanging tree. Indistinct shapes surrounded it.

He stopped shy of the tree and for a second he just sat there looking at the scene in front of him.

Cast in the subdued glow of struggling flames and overlaid with blowing snow, things looked surreal—almost like a still shot from an old film. His father and two of his brothers stood at the perimeter of the light, firearms drawn. Their demeanor telegraphed watchfulness. The crew huddled close to the warmth. One was prone on the ground, the camera guy was shooting pictures and two leaned against the mammoth tree that would become the object of their film. The reins of the three horses his dad and brother had ridden were tied to the exposed curve of a gnarled root. The animals looked appropriately cold and dejected as only horses could look when they'd rather be somewhere else, say a cozy barn. There was no sign of the crew's four horses and Pike hoped they had the sense to make their way home.

"What the hell happened here?" Pike asked as he approached Frankie on foot.

"Someone shot off a gun," Frankie said.

That stopped Pike in his tracks. "A gun? Out here?"

"Yep. They seem to think it's their old employee out on a rampage."

"But you don't?"

Frankie shook his head. "Seems unlikely."

"Anyone hurt?"

"Gary. As I understand it, they were on their way back from filming a group of miserable cold cows when they stopped here to get some shots of the snow falling through the branches of the hanging tree. Oliver said they were all on horseback, just kind of hanging out discussing things, when they heard a shot fired from somewhere close by. Gary's horse reared up and dumped Gary out of the saddle. He tried to brace his fall and injured his left shoulder. Don't know if it's a break or what. In fact, every last man was thrown to the ground except for Ogden, who managed to stay mounted until his horse jumped a gully, then he had to walk back here to find out about the others. We showed up after they got Gary settled, but we need a transport to get Gary back to the house without further injuring him."

"What about the gunman?"

"Dad and Chance rode around looking for any evidence of another person out here, but the storm had covered all tracks by then and it's just getting nastier by the second."

"There's no one around right now to be shooting anything," Pike said. "Not on this land. And who goes out target practicing in a blizzard? Did you find a bullet or a casing?"

"No."

"Is it possible they heard branches crack and thought it was a gun?"

"Anything is possible, although these guys aren't idiots. Anyway, it's academic right now. We need to get them out of here."

Pike caught his brother's arm as he turned. "First tell me how Daisy is. I didn't have a chance to stop by the house. No puppies, yet I assume?"

"Not yet. By the way, how do you keep her off the sofa?"

"I don't," Pike said.

They distributed the hot broth Grace had sent and set about transporting Gary to the trailer hooked to the back of the snowmobile. The ride to the ranch would need to be slow because of his injuries and because the machine would be hauling several people and the weather just kept deteriorating.

He'd tried numerous times to phone someone at the house. He knew Sierra's phone didn't work out here, but Grace's and Lily's both did. No one responded to calls or texts. Not being able to reach anyone combined with the mysterious shot that had spooked the horses created a restless unease that raced along Pike's spine.

He approached Chance. "You know about Tess's boyfriend, don't you?"

"Yeah. Dad told me."

Pike knew it defied imagination to think that Raoul Ruiz, a city boy by all accounts, had driven to Idaho, found this ranch, bought himself a rifle, made his way out into the snow and taken a shot at a film crew—how would he know they were even here?—on the brink of a well-publicized winter storm all to get Tess alone with no one but other women to defend her. It wasn't impossible, however, and since no other explanation popped to mind, that's what he was left with.

If that was the case, Raoul hadn't figured on Sierra Hyde, who Pike didn't doubt was no slouch with a firearm. Neither was Grace, for that matter. "Maybe her boyfriend's killer is behind this," he told Chase.

"I hadn't thought about that," Chance said doubtfully.

"I know it's far-fetched, but no more so than a vengeful ex-employee running around on unfamiliar ground taking shots. I want to get back to the house. If I take your horse and go down the hill, I can be there in half the time."

"Take Dad's, I'm going with you. Lily and Charlie are in that house, too, and weirder things have happened around here."

A few minutes later, Pike and Chance headed across the plateau to find the trail that would lead them down the hill to the oasis in the U-shaped bend of the river, where their father's house had been built decades before.

Pike didn't know if Chance's heart was lodged somewhere in his throat, but he knew his was.

Chapter Eight

After Grace finally had a short conversation with Harry, she fell asleep in her chair. Sierra fielded a few emails, promising existing and potential clients she'd return to New York as soon as she could. But there was still the matter of Tess and another trip to Los Angeles to take into account. Savannah Papadakis had kind of disappeared and Sierra was secretly relieved. She'd deal with all that later.

Sierra closed her eyes. The day had been long and grueling and she was tired down to her bones. Her thoughts got more and more scattered until, in a haze of darkness, a man ran toward her on a city street. She attempted to step out of his way but he veered to intercept her and knocked her to the ground. Breathless, she looked at him as he sat on top of her. He now wore a Giants football uniform and he was screaming at the top of his lungs. She couldn't understand what he was saying because of his helmet, so she snatched it off his head. Old, bald and wizened, he stared directly into her eyes. "You idiot," he growled and disappeared.

Her eyes flew open. She took a couple of deep breaths as she reoriented herself. The dream had seemed so real, the insult more like a warning. The fire still crackled on the grate; Grace still slept in her chair. The wind outside rattled tree limbs against the windows, but that was the only sound. Sierra checked the time on her laptop and saw she'd only slept a few minutes. Was it the residue of her dream that made her uneasy or something else?

Without thinking it through, she put aside her equipment and got out of the chair. She climbed the stairs and walked down the hall to Pike's old bedroom, where she'd seen Tess asleep when she first got back. As she approached the door, the angry bald man flashed in her brain.

She pushed open the door. Nothing had changed. There was still a bump in the bed, the lights were still off, the room was deathly silent.

Silent.

Where was the sound of a sleeping human with a head cold?

She flicked on the overhead light and approached the bed, realizing way before she threw back the covers that the shape she'd assumed was her sister was in reality two pillows under a blanket. There was also a piece of paper and Sierra, struggling not to tremble, sat down and read a hastily scrawled note.

Sierra and Pike,

I heard from Danny! He's alive. He was hurt, but he managed to escape. He's come to see me but he's afraid he's being followed. He asked me where we could meet. I thought about the barn, but now everyone is running around all worried about those television people so I'm going to saddle up and meet Danny at the old mine. He told me not to tell anyone where I was going but to bring Sierra along

because he wanted to thank her for taking care of me. But I heard a storm is coming and your plane could be delayed so I'm leaving this note instead and going on by myself. I have to see him. He's all I have. Don't worry about me, okay?
Love you guys, Tess.

For a second, Sierra just sat there, head reeling. Where was this mine Tess was talking about? She sprang to her feet and raced downstairs. Her pounding footsteps must have awakened Grace, who was yawning into her fist when Sierra came into the den.

"Oh, no," Grace said when she met Sierra's gaze. "Now what?"

"May I use your phone?" Sierra said. "Mine doesn't work out here and Tess is gone."

Grace handed Sierra the phone as Sierra handed Grace the note Tess had left. Tess did not respond and Sierra left a message. She turned to peruse the gun cabinet. "Do you have the key for this?" she asked.

"It's in the desk drawer," Grace said as she looked up from the note. "God in heaven. How could I have missed Tess leaving?"

"It sounds as if she took advantage of the commotion surrounding the guys saddling up and taking off."

"But I was supposed to be looking out for her," Grace lamented. "And who in the world texted the girl?"

"Well, Danny is dead, there's no two ways about that," Sierra said as she snatched the key from the middle drawer and hurried back to the cabinet. "Someone else wanted to get her alone and I'm guessing it's the guy who murdered Danny. His name is Raoul Ruiz. Do you know what mine she's talking about?"

"There's only one and it's in the ghost town. Sierra, you can't go alone. You don't even know where it is."

"You'll tell me."

"We could get Kinsey or Lily—"

Sierra took Grace's hands. "Listen to me. If this is Raoul, who knows what he'll do. Kinsey is pregnant. I am not asking her to go out in this weather. Lily has Charlie to protect and I am not asking her to leave him. They need you at this house just in case. That leaves me. So draw a map while I go change into jeans. Then help me saddle a horse. Can I use the Glock in the cabinet?"

"Take whatever you need. Ammo is in the drawer."

Sierra affected a five-minute change into warmer clothes, then gratefully accepted a borrowed wool jacket and gloves. As Grace saddled the horse, Sierra recalled the photo she'd snapped in Pike's barn, the one of the Hastings Ridge Ranch. Her phone might not get reception, but she could bring up photos. She'd sent the photo to her laptop and now wished she'd thought to study it on that larger screen. Even the smaller version helped orientate her, however, and that would have to do.

"Won't the dogs try to follow me?" she asked Grace as the three animals milled around the horse.

"In this weather? No way, but I'll lock them in the mudroom just to be safe. You be careful, now."

It took two tries for Sierra to swing herself onto the saddle. She'd only ridden a few times in her life, and then during daylight hours on placid horses. This was the craziest thing she'd ever done, she knew that, but she also couldn't think of an alternative.

"Here's a flashlight," Grace said. "This is the map, but I'm no artist like Kinsey. I put a compass heading for when you reach the plateau. If you go out the back gate and head toward the hills and trees, your horse will find the trail and get you up to the plateau. With any luck, you'll run in to the menfolk and one of them will help you. Otherwise, veer off toward the right and just keep going until you get to the old ghost town, then ride all the way to the end. That's where the mine is. And for goodness' sake, be careful or Pike will have my head. I'll send him or someone else along as soon as they return."

"Go inside and arm yourself," Sierra replied. "Keep the doors locked. And you might call Kinsey and tell her the same thing," she added, shoving the gun in her waistband.

She took off into the night, fingers figuratively crossed, heart racing. Grace had turned on the floodlights and that helped her find the gateway to the creek. And sure enough, the horse began the winding climb on sure feet. The trees overhead slowed down the snowfall and Sierra held on for dear life as the path became steeper. Her mind kept racing to the mine she had to find, and what had become of Tess, who had not recorded the time on her note. Who knew how long she'd been gone, but if she'd left right after the Hastingses had gone looking for the crew, it had to be hours now, more than enough time for her to have reached this mine and for Raoul to have done heaven knows what to her.

It seemed to take forever and then some to reach level land, and she looked through the falling snow in an effort to find some sign of life. Disappointed beyond words—she really had hoped she'd run in to Pike out here, or if not him, then one of his brothers or their father—she kept riding, trusting the horse to know the lay of the land and find footing. Common sense suggested the ground was uneven under the snow, but the horse kept moving and her gait was such that Sierra was relatively comfortable in the saddle. She didn't dare kick the horse into a run because she wasn't sure if she'd be able to stop it. Better to get there in one piece sometime tonight than risk a broken neck and never arrive at all.

For a girl used to crowded sidewalks and subways, this lonely night with only one big heavy-breathing horse and a sky full of snow for company seemed to stretch into eternity. Using the flashlight, she checked the compass heading and saw that she was as close to right on as she could get without micromanaging every step. The horse actually seemed to know the way, and Sierra formed a growing admiration for the way the big red beast kept her head down and one foot in front of the other.

Robbed of any landmarks, she had no reference points. They could be walking in giant circles and, if not for the compass, she wouldn't know. Eventually, so cold her teeth had stopped chattering, she felt rather than saw a change and shined the flashlight to the right. A large dark building was discernable through the snow. Eureka! She'd found the ghost town, or at least she assumed she had. The light played over additional shapes and she felt more confident. Soon, spectral buildings appeared on either side of her and she guessed she was riding down Main Street. The road took a curve and then the buildings petered out, and after a while longer, a hillside appeared at the edge of a large clearing that was scattered with hulking pieces of what must be old mining equipment.

In the face of what appeared to be a rocky outcropping, she saw a darker area shaped like an arc. This must be the entrance. Grace had said that it was covered with a locked door, but Sierra saw no evidence of one. Tracks in the snow suggested activity within the last few hours.

"We found it," she whispered through blue lips to the horse. Her numb legs almost collapsed as her feet hit the ground. A sound from close by sent her heart into her throat and she twirled around, flashlight illuminating nothing but snow at first, until a large shape materialized and hastened toward her like a banshee out of a horror film.

She reached for the Glock but paused at the sound of a throaty snort. The apparition turned into a horse, and it came to within a few feet of her then stopped. Its breath shot out in a cloud as it stamped a foot on the snowy ground and whinnied.

Sierra grabbed the reins of the horse's bridle. The animal was still saddled. It seemed likely that this was the horse Tess had ridden to come here, so that must mean she was still in the mine.

She had to wonder: How did a person unfamiliar with this land find his way to the mine? She thought back to the map. She hadn't noticed other roads, but there must have been at least one. Was it reasonable to expect Raoul Ruiz to be able to navigate out here on a night like this? On the other hand, she recalled the tracks in the snow when they got to Hastings land. Who had driven through that gate when everyone on the ranch was either inside a house or out rescuing the film crew on horses?

She led both animals to the opening of the mine because she wasn't sure what else to do with them. What if they were needed for a quick getaway? What if they wandered off to find someplace more hospitable? How would she and Tess get back to the ranch? The flashlight revealed a few boards jutting up through the snow. Presumably, they were all that was left of the door. The light also revealed an iron rod embedded in the rock right outside the entrance. Maybe it had supported the door. She looped the reins around the iron. The horses could stand inside if they wanted or stay outside—their choice. Satisfied with her solution, Sierra shined the light into the mine and took a deep breath.

There weren't too many things that seriously rattled her, but underground cavities were one of them. And somehow, this ancient, abandoned, man-made mine was twice as terrifying as a cave Mother Nature created. She flashed the light around once, trying to orientate herself, knowing she would have to be careful with both noise and light as she got deeper and hopefully closer to Tess.

The mine tunnel was heavily shored with lumber. Were there bats in here? Probably not, since it had been closed until just recently. No wonder it smelled like a grave. On the other hand there might be fissures leading to the surface through which bats could enter. She could almost feel them in her hair—obviously she'd seen too many Scooby-Doo cartoons as a kid.

Sags and even areas where the lumber had failed altogether made piles of dirt and rock. The tunnel itself appeared pretty straight as far as the light penetrated. A railroad-like track ran along the ground.

Sierra took off her hat, shook off the snow, took the Glock from her waistband and turned off the light. Moving as quickly and silently as she could, she kept her gloved hand touching the wall as she progressed. In all the years she'd been an investigator, she'd actually only pulled out her gun once, maybe twice. Guns tended to escalate a problem and were a tool of last resort for her.

But this felt different. This felt like the Old West and it was hard not to juxtapose her present situation with all the old Westerns she'd watched with her father. For a second she thought of those long-ago bank robbers thundering out of town with their loot, a posse not far behind. For the first time it seemed real.

The air quality abruptly changed and the wall disappeared. She chanced the light again. The tunnel had turned and within fifteen feet, the track on the ground split into two and veered off at right angles to each other.

Again she walked in darkness until she felt air all around her. On came the light. She'd been worrying about which track to take, but now she saw that the spur was actually blocked by a cave-in. While that made the choice easier, it also reminded her how fragile this world was.

The clear tunnel began a rapid decline deeper into the earth. She moved slowly, worried that her feet in the thin-soled boots might slip on the pebbles that littered the ground. She kept listening for voices—Tess's or anyone else's for that matter—but the place was eerily silent, the air cold and dank.

The tunnel wall disappeared and she once again used the light. A deep crevice on her right side looked like nature's handiwork and stretched on along the side of the tunnel. The tracks hugged the opposite wall and continued until they disappeared around another turn. She set off once more, this time walking on top of the track to stay far away from the crevice. She strained to hear any sound that signaled a living human being, refusing to even consider the possibility that Tess lay dead up ahead.

At the place where the tunnel turned sharply to the right, she paused. There wasn't a noise to be heard. She had to have light before chancing a change of direction. The tunnel evolved here into a wider cavern. The crevice she'd noticed earlier was still here. There were a couple of empty mining carts and old metal tubs scattered about, as well as additional tunnels branching off what seemed to be this central area. Near the edge of the rift, she spied a pile of rubble consisting of dirt and rotting timbers. Was it the result of another cave-in?

The light illuminated a splotch of red beneath the rubble. Closer examination revealed a red knit hat. If it wasn't the one she'd seen hanging in the ranch mudroom, then it was its twin. Next to it, she found a pink loafer, and her heart sank as she fell to her hands and knees and shone the light into the seemingly bottomless gash in the earth.

She played the light against the opposing wall, which appeared relatively smooth. Then she aimed the light straight down on her side of the chasm. There was a narrow ledge down there, two or three feet wide. Another pink shoe lay amid additional rubble. There was no sign of Tess.

Had she been knocked into the bowels of the earth or had she been taken away from this mine? If the sole purpose was to silence her forever, then her body probably lay down at the bottom of the rift.

As Sierra stared at the pink shoe she heard a sound from behind and turned her head.

"SHE DID WHAT?" Pike said when he and Chance got back to the house. They'd found Grace asleep while sitting at the kitchen counter, a rifle on one side of her and an empty pot of coffee on the other. Hollow-eyed, she'd roused herself as they entered from the mudroom, obviously embarrassed to have been caught napping on guard duty. Chance mumbled that he'd be right back and left the kitchen, headed for the second floor to check on Lily and Charlie.

"Tess left a note," Grace repeated, her eyes moist and her voice gravelly. "She said Danny texted a message asking her and Sierra to meet him. She didn't want to wait for Sierra. She remembered the old mine you'd shown her, so she suggested that to this supposed Danny. In her defense, it was dark and cold out, but the storm hadn't fully hit yet. Anyway, Sierra read the note Tess left and decided to go after her."

"How is Sierra going to get there in this weather and at night?" he asked. "She's never even been there before. And can she actually ride a horse?"

"I think she can do almost anything she puts her mind to," Grace responded and he had to agree. "And as for getting there, she had a map of this ranch on her phone. I gave her compass headings. Frankly, I was hoping she'd meet up with you along the way."

"How long has she been gone?"

"About two hours."

"She must have ridden past the tree while we were still out there. In this weather she could have been thirty feet away."

"This is all my fault," Grace said with tears in her eyes. "I was responsible for watching Tess and I failed."

He patted her shoulder. "You know people can be sneaky when they want to be. It's just as much our fault for not telling Tess the truth about Danny so she wouldn't fall for some con. None of that matters right now. I have to go after them."

"Wait for Chance to go with you," Grace said.

"No time. Tell him to stay here until the others arrive and then come. I'll text when I have an idea where they are."

He rushed into the mudroom, where he reclaimed the

shotgun he'd laid aside and grabbed a flashlight from a basket. Out in the barn, he saddled a fresh horse and snagged a coiled rope that hung on a post. Within minutes, he rode back up the creek, following what had turned into a muddy trail.

The trip was a grueling issue of mind over matter. It was three or four in the morning by now and he was exhausted and yet panicked at the same time. The wind had picked up enough to cause the snow to blow almost parallel to the ground. The ghostly moans as it snaked through the old town made the hairs stand up on his neck.

At the mine entrance, he found two saddled horses dragging reins in the snow. At the sight of him and another horse, they made low grunting sounds in their throats. The wild look in their eyes reflected tension and they skittered away from him as the sound of an accelerating engine reached Pike's ears. It had to be a snowmobile leaving via the old road that ran parallel to the town and eventually looped around to the main ranch access road.

He should have waited for Chance. Cursing the fact that he was alone, he rounded up the horses and looped the reins around a piece of equipment. He knew the snowmobile tracks would linger for a while even in this snowfall. He'd have to hope he could find them after making sure Tess and Sierra weren't in need of help.

He looped the coil of rope over one shoulder and his saddlebag over the other, as it contained some emergency supplies, including a flask of water. Wielding the flashlight in one hand and the shotgun in the other, he entered the mine.

It had been absolutely forbidden to enter this place when he was a kid. That hadn't stopped him and his brothers from doing just that, however, and they'd spent many a secret afternoons investigating its tunnels, shafts and the natural underground chambers. He flashed the light and then from memory made his way to the central area, moving swiftly but with caution, unsure what he'd find.

He knew there were natural-occurring fissures and he also knew that deep shafts had been dug decades before to access veins of gold. He remembered where the tunnel branched and discovered a cave-in had more or less sealed the way.

Once again he fought the craziness of the possibility that someone like Raoul Ruiz would orchestrate the chain of events that had occurred this night. True, he didn't know the man, but he knew about him and it seemed implausible. Wasn't he more the walk-up-to-you-and-shoot-you-in-the-face kind of guy? Other explanations evaded him, however. He wasn't satisfied with any answer he could come up with or even the questions. So what? Time to hunker back into rescue mode and stop trying to figure it out.

He found the main cavern empty aside from the tracks and abandoned mining equipment he and his brothers had played on as kids.

A weak light shone on the ground near the edge of a chasm. A flashlight had been dropped next to a pile of rubble. His gut twisted in a knot. People don't abandon a light source in a place as dark and treacherous as this unless they'd been forced to. As he fumbled with the reclaimed flashlight, its weak beam caught something twinkling in the dirt. Kneeling down, he picked up a fine gold chain adorned with a single diamond pendant. He battled the creeping ache that he'd never see Sierra alive again and buttoned the necklace into his shirt pocket.

Further investigation of the rubble revealed dirt and boards and a red knit hat caught under a rafter as though it had been knocked off its wearer. There was no sign of a body under the rubble. A pink shoe lay abandoned a few feet away. He wasn't sure about the cap, but he knew the shoe belonged to Tess.

When they'd been young boys, he and his brothers had marched fearlessly through this mine. Now he moved with caution and determination. He lay on his belly and scanned the ledge below with his flashlight. A woman lay facedown too near the fragile lip for comfort. The light glowed on her red hair, leaving little doubt as to her identity.

"Sierra!" he yelled.

For a moment he was sure she moved, but in the next instant he realized it was an illusion caused by the trembling of his own hand as he grasped the flashlight.

He closed his eyes for a second and listened to the suffocating silence.

Chapter Nine

Pike shook off momentary despair and went to work. As kids they had once rigged a harness and lowered danger-loving Frankie into this pit. He'd reported that the ledge ate its way back into the earth, creating a sort of overhang about fifteen feet down. Pike uncoiled the rope from his shoulder and looped one end around an abandoned mining cart that was wedged against an outcropping of rocks. He quickly moved to the crevice and slipped over the side. Hand over hand, one foot wrapped around the rope, he made his way down until he landed a foot or so from Sierra's still form.

He took off his gloves and kneeled beside her, resting two fingers against her throat. The world realigned itself as her heartbeat leaped to his touch. He had no way of knowing if anything was broken. The inadequate light didn't reveal any obvious issues, but he wasn't sure.

As a precaution, he moved her a few more inches away from the edge, but he couldn't take her far as headroom tapered off quickly. Moving her revealed she'd been resting atop Tess's other pink shoe. Using the flashlight, he scanned for any sign of her.

Way back, deep under the overhang, a shape caught his eye. He stared at it until he was able to discern human features: dirt-matted hair, arms and legs all squeezed into a cranny. Tess had to have wiggled herself into this position, which meant she'd been alive after the fall. He got down on his stomach and dragged himself toward her. It was a tight fit and a huge relief when he was finally able to reach out and touch her arm. The light revealed cracked fingernails and rocks imbedded in her scratched hands.

"Tess," he called softly.

Her eyes fluttered open. He could barely see her features, but he could tell her expression went from frightened to relieved and back again in a single breath. "Pike!" she spluttered.

"What happened? Are you okay?"

"Are they gone?"

"Who?"

"Two guys. They…they threw me down here. They must have thought I went all the way to the bottom but my foot hit this ledge and I grabbed on. I don't know how I managed to climb up here. I just kept picturing that black hole…"

"They're gone," he assured her, though he had no way of knowing if they would come back or even if both of them had left. "Can you shift yourself so I can help get you out of there?"

"I'll try," she said.

A moment later, he was able to grasp her shoulders and pull her farther toward the edge. Her coat was torn, her hair knotted. Her runny nose had smeared dirt across her cheeks. He handed her his bandanna. "Did all this happen when you fell?" he asked.

"Yeah," she said as she mopped her face. She looked down at her left foot and he directed the light. Her sock was torn and her foot was swollen. Tears appeared in her eyes. "It hurts."

He felt it gingerly, stopping when she cried out, but then her gaze traveled past him. "Sierra! Pike, when did she get here? What happened to her?"

"I was hoping you could tell me," he said.

She shook her head. "Where's Danny? Did they use me to trap him? I have to find Danny."

"Right now, we have to help Sierra," Pike said, scooting back to lift Sierra's hand and touch her face.

Tess crawled over to join him, dragging her injured foot. "Sierra, please, wake up."

To Pike's infinite relief, Sierra's eyes opened, but she blinked and furrowed her brow. He helped her roll over and sit. She moaned and clutched her head. He cradled her shoulders. "You're hurt," he said, feeling the top of her head and finding a noticeable bump. His hands ran down her arms, over her legs. "Does it hurt anywhere else?"

"It hurts everywhere," she whispered. "Pike, what happened?"

"You don't remember how you got down here?"

"No." She paused for a second. "No. I was looking for Tess." Her confused gaze switched to her sister. "Oh, my God, sweetheart, are you okay?"

"I don't know where Danny is!" Tess said as tears made more muddy tracks down her cheeks.

Pike and Sierra looked at each other, then Pike put an arm around Tess's shoulders. "We should have told you over the phone and then none of this would have happened. Danny is dead, honey. You were right, a man named Raoul Ruiz apparently killed him."

"How do you know? How can you be sure? What if—"

"We're sure," he said with just enough firmness to cut through her emotion. "We'll explain everything later. Right now we need to get you and Sierra off this ledge and out of this mine. You're both frozen and it's a long way home. Can I count on you?" Tess nodded.

The only place the ledge was open enough for a person to stand was right near the rim. He helped Tess first. She couldn't put weight on her foot and tumbled against him, but he managed to prop her against the rocks, where she held on with a white-knuckled grip. Then he fashioned a loop in the end of the rope, tied a bowline knot and pulled it tight.

Now came the tough decision. How did he get both of these women up to the top? Did he leave the dazed one down here to wait her turn, hoping that she wouldn't fall over the edge? Or did he leave the one who couldn't even stand?

Sierra apparently sensed the dilemma. "Her first," she said through chattering teeth.

"Her first what?" Tess demanded.

"I have to go up to the top in order to pull each of you to safety," he said.

Tess clung to him a second. "Please don't leave us."

"I'm not leaving you. Wait for me to give you an all clear, then put the loop around your body and more or less sit on it. Use your good foot to keep yourself off the rock face. I'll pull you up."

He put his gloves back on, noticed Tess's other shoe nearby and grabbed it. It was for the injured foot so he tossed it aside. He turned his attention to Sierra. "Let me help you stand so you're ready when it's your turn." She leaned against him as he gently helped her to her feet. To his relief, she seemed pretty steady as she backed against the rock face beside Tess. He looked into her eyes a long moment and her lovely lips curved into a jittery smile.

"Cover your heads in case I knock dirt and rocks down as I go up," he said.

He hated leaving them twenty feet below, but there just wasn't any other way to get them out of here. He handed Sierra the good flashlight and took the weak one for himself. It didn't take light to get up to the mine floor on his own—it just took brawn.

Once he'd made it to the top, he took a couple of deep breaths. "Okay," he called, as he flicked on the weak light so he wouldn't trip and make a mess of things. He let the rope back down. "Make sure you hang on. You hear me, Tess?"

"I will," she called, but her voice sounded a hundred miles away.

He coiled the rope around the rock for extra leverage and began pulling to take up the slack. When he felt the rope tighten, he began the chore of hauling another person up a rock-and-dirt wall. For the first six feet, Tess was deadweight, but as she finally reached the side of the chasm, he felt the tension slacken as she apparently got her good leg under her and used her hands. Still, it was a great moment when he pulled her safely over the last of the edge, picked her up and carried her to the rock.

"Your turn," he called to Sierra.

Within minutes, he had grasped her under the arms and hauled her the last distance. Arm and arm, they staggered to the rock upon which Tess sat and, for a minute or two, hovered there in the ever diminishing glow of their one good flashlight.

"Look at my poor shoes," Sierra finally said as she

straightened her legs to reveal her shredded black suede boots.

"They're done for," he said.

"They cost three hundred dollars."

He stuck out his foot to display tooled brown leather. "So did these."

"They look fine."

"Well, they're country boots. Yours are city boots."

"They used to be," she said. "Now they're garbage."

He picked up her hand and squeezed it and she smiled at him. The smile fled as she apparently heard an approaching noise at the same time he did. Tess whimpered and shrank against the rock. Someone was coming down the tunnel toward them. He put his finger against his lips and Sierra turned off her flashlight. Without that modest beam of light, the cavern seemed to close in around them, trapping them between the deep shafts and beyond the only exit. He picked up the shotgun.

The way he figured it, someone had meant for both women to disappear. The apparent roof collapse at the rim of the crevice indicated an accident. Without Tess's note, who knows when they would have looked for her here, but when they did, her abandoned shoe would suggest an explanation for her disappearance. Sierra's necklace would do the same for her. But why had the fake Danny asked Tess to wait for Sierra to accompany her? Was he aware that Sierra knew his identity? That had to be it.

And now? Had they come back to make sure the women had both died? Had they had second thoughts about the plausibility of their plot?

He hugged the wall and took a peek out into the main shaft. He could see lights, which made the people approaching pretty good targets. "Stop where you are!" he yelled.

"Pike!" a man responded.

"Gerard?"

Within seconds, all three of his brothers finally came into clear view. He'd never been happier to see them.

"You didn't text..."

"I forgot," he admitted.

"Did you find them? Are they okay?"

"More or less," he said.

"What can we do to help?" Gerard asked.

Frankie clapped Pike on the back. "Are you kidding? The professor here is the clever one in the family. I bet he's got this all figured out."

"Yeah," Pike said and grinned. "Sure I do."

SIERRA OPENED HER EYES. For a moment, she wasn't sure where she was or how she had gotten there. The room was dark, but that could be because of pulled shades. She sat up, which made her head ache, and looked around. Tess slept in the other twin bed. They were in the downstairs room Grace had insisted they use.

They were safe.

Now she remembered. Awakening on the ledge, Pike holding her, the impossibly long, cold ride home, Tess's grief, Grace's gentle care.

And more. She remembered more.

The door opened and Pike appeared. He smiled when he saw her and crossed the room. He hadn't shaved for over twenty-four hours and it looked as if he'd slept in his clothes. All in all, sexy as hell.

He sat down next to her. "How are you feeling?" he whispered.

She shrugged as she glanced at Tess. "How is she?"

"Grace thinks her ankle is sprained. She put a splint on it just in case something is broken. We can't get out of here yet because of the storm. You up to coming with me so we can talk?"

"Absolutely," she said and pulled down the sheets to find that she was wearing her own nightclothes, which meant she wasn't wearing much.

"I guess I better put some clothes on," she said.

His lingering gaze and sudden wistful smile shot through her body. "Need any help?"

She leaned into him and touched his face with her own. His breath was warm against her chilled skin and he smelled like coffee and cinnamon. Delicious. She kissed his lips and for a second they just sat that way, content just to be together.

"Here," he whispered against her cheek and she pulled away to see that he held her diamond necklace. Her hand flew to her throat—she hadn't even noticed it was missing. "It was broken, but I fixed it," he said, and fastened it around her neck.

"Where did you find it?"

"In the mine. You have a red mark on the back of your neck. Someone must have ripped it off."

"My father gave me this," she said softly. "Thank you for fixing it."

He kissed her nose. "Up to rising now?"

"Yep." Various aches and pains announced themselves when she stood. They were explained by the bruises on her legs and arms. One knee hurt and her elbow was stiff. She found clean jeans in her suitcase, then pulled them over her hips and her green sweater over her head, wincing as the neckline tugged on her hair. Pike was suddenly there to smooth the sweater on its way and kiss her forehead.

"They hit my head before they threw me off the edge into the rift," she murmured.

He clasped her shoulders. "Do you remember what happened?"

"Bits and pieces."

They quietly left the bedroom and entered the empty kitchen. The view outside was blinding white—obviously it was still snowing.

"Is it a terrible storm?" she asked as she drew herself a glass of water.

"We've had worse. This one seems to be winding down already." He patted the stool. "Sit down, tell me what you remember."

She sat down across the island from him. "I remember seeing Tess's shoe on the ledge. Then there was a noise and a bright light. I turned around in time to see a man in a ski mask. He grabbed your Glock from my hand, struck me in the head and said something as I staggered away."

"What did he say?"

"I don't know. It was hard to understand him because of the mask, but it's more than just that." She paused for a second, thinking.

"What is it?" he asked. "Do you remember something else?"

"I was just thinking about a dream I had right before I found out that Tess was missing. Someone in a football helmet pinned me to the ground and called me an idiot." She bit her lip. "I don't think it was a premonition or anything."

"What happened next?"

"It all happened in the blink of an eye. He lifted me

off my feet. The next thing I knew, I landed like a ton of bricks. I thought for sure every bone in my body was broken, but I was able to roll farther under the overhang. My eyes felt like they were spinning off into the dark. Then I heard voices and I realized there were two men up there. I think they were arguing about making sure I was dead. And then it sort of slipped away until all of a sudden, you were there."

He took her hand and rubbed her knuckles with his thumb. "What happened last night when you went to help your father and brothers find the film crew?" she asked.

"They were where I thought they'd be. A gunshot had spooked their horses. A couple were injured, the producer worst of all."

"A shot!" she said. "Doesn't that seem kind of coincidental considering what was going on a mile or so over in the mine?"

"It does to me."

"How injured was the producer? Isn't his name Gary?"

"Yeah. Between Tess, him and you, Grace had her hands full. You have a slight concussion, Gary tore his rotator cuff when he put his hands out to stop his fall and a couple of the others are a little banged up, too."

"Did they see anyone at all?"

"No. They're convinced that the ex-employee who attempted to sue them tried another sabotage."

"Why would someone like him target Tess? And how would he even know about her in the first place?"

"I don't know," he said. "Unless there's a snitch in the crew."

"You mean someone on the film crew could be in cahoots with the ex-employee?"

"Yeah. It's no secret what Tess saw happen in LA. Everyone in the house is talking about it. For instance, who knows what a snitch might have overheard Grace telling my father, or what Frankie might have said in passing."

"Oh, man, I never thought of that."

"There's nothing to be done right now but keep a watchful eye. Do you want some tea or something to eat?"

"Tea sounds good," she said. "Did you guys find anything else in the gold mine?"

"Not really. There were a few shoe tracks too large to belong to you or Tess. It looks to me like someone's intention was to make your falls look like an accident. There was a lot of fresh rubble strewn around as though there'd been a collapse. It might have worked if the two of you hadn't been lucky enough to hit that ledge."

Sierra shuddered.

"Chance and Frankie looked for some indication of the snowmobile that I heard when I first got there," he continued. "They found a few tracks and deduced it must have headed to the main road, so that's where they went. They found additional tracks and a spot where a heavy vehicle had gotten stuck in the snow and then dug out. There were no people or machinery left behind, but it seems pretty clear someone brought a snow vehicle onto ranch land and contacted Tess to facilitate an ambush."

"If Raoul isn't behind this, why pick on Tess?"

"Maybe she seemed like a weak link to the snitch," Pike said as he got up to microwave a couple of cups of hot water. He dug tea bags from a canister.

"Did you look at the text Tess thought Danny sent?"

"I couldn't because they stole her phone. She did notice it wasn't his usual number."

"Probably a burner."

"Yeah," he said, handing her the hot cup.

"Some of this doesn't make sense," she added and rubbed her forehead. "Things aren't logical but I can't think clearly enough to figure out what's wrong."

"I can't, either," he admitted. "I'm brain-dead."

"Have you had any sleep?" she asked.

He smiled down into her eyes. "Not much."

"Maybe we should go…take a nap. Together, you know?"

He leaned down and kissed her. "I would love nothing more," he whispered against her lips. "Unfortunately, I have to meet up with Gerard and Chance to feed the cattle."

"How do you accomplish that in this weather?"

"We grow and store hay during the summer for times like this when field grazing is inaccessible. Then we load the hay onto a trailer and pull it out into the fields with a tractor. One of us drives and the two who pulled the shortest sticks get to ride on the back with pitchforks and drop the hay to hungry, frostbitten cows. It's kind of fun in its own weird way."

Her expression looked incredulous. "I have work to do anyway," she said at last. "I haven't heard from Savannah in a while."

"Let me get your laptop for you," he said. "I saw it by the fireplace." He dashed out of the kitchen and was back with the laptop within seconds.

"By the way, I called the local law," Pike said as he handed her the computer. "They said they'll send someone out to check the mine when the weather calms down."

"I'll call the LAPD," she volunteered as she hit the button to power on the laptop.

"Do you miss New York?" Pike asked.

She nodded. "It's my home. Have you ever been there?"

He shook his head.

"Will you come visit me?" she asked.

"Is that an invitation?"

"Absolutely. It'll be fun to show you around. Spring is lovely."

"I bet," he said. "We'll have to get through calving, then I'm all yours."

"And then there's summer," she added, staring up at him. "I admit it's humid, but who has to go outside?"

"Summer is a busy time on a ranch," he said. He put his hand on her shoulder and added, "But I'll make time."

"Good. And then you have to see fall in the city. There's a big election this year for mayor. It'll be wild."

"Fall," he said. "Autumn is beautiful here."

"I bet."

He curled a piece of her hair around his finger. "Did you inherit your dad's interest in politics?"

"Not really. The guy I'm voting for is Maxwell Jakes. He's practically a shoo-in, mostly because the other guy is a first-class sleazeball. My dad would have approved, though. He was a one-party kind of guy and Jakes is the right party."

The sound of clomping came from the direction of the back bedroom and they both turned their heads. Tess appeared, awkwardly wielding a pair of crutches.

"Hey, look at you," Sierra said. Bruised, cut, bandaged and pale, the poor kid looked like she'd been through a wringer. For the first time that morning, Sierra wondered how she looked after the previous night's ordeal. "You have crutches lying around?" Sierra asked, glancing up at Pike.

"Dad said it was cheaper than renting them every time one of us hurt something," he said. He looked at Tess and added, "How are you feeling?"

"Kind of empty inside," she said.

"I'm sorry I had to tell you about Danny like I did."

"It's not your fault. I'm the one who snuck away. I'm the one who put both you guys in danger, something even my dad pointed out. I need a tissue. My nose is running."

"When did you talk to your dad?" Sierra asked as Pike slid a box of tissues toward Tess.

"Before I went to sleep," Tess said, dabbing at her nose. "You were already dead to the world. Aunt Grace said Dad deserved to hear from me before he heard from the police, so I woke him up and told him everything that's been happening." She looked down at her hands. "He says he wants me to come home."

"Of course he does," Pike said. "Would you like a cup of tea?"

She shook her head. "No thanks."

"Honey, can you remember anything else about the men in the mine?" Sierra asked. "Maybe something about their voices, for instance?"

"They didn't talk to me."

Pike turned his gaze to Sierra. "Do you remember something?"

"I'm not sure," she replied. "I told you one of them spoke to me. I don't know what he said. I'm not sure what's bothering me about it."

"I thought I was safe here," Tess blurted out, hugging herself and looking around the cheery room and shuddering. "I'm not safe anywhere, am I?"

"Tess—"

"I don't want to go talk to the LA police."

"We know," Sierra said. "Maybe, because of your foot, they can send detectives here to interview you."

Tess looked around the room again. "I don't want to stay here but I don't want to go there. I don't want to see the man who killed Danny, not ever, ever again."

"What about your father?" Sierra asked gently.

"He doesn't *really* want me to come," Tess said.

"Tess, you're his daughter."

"I'm just someone who gets in his way," she scoffed.

"Don't worry about it right now," Pike advised. "Come sit down."

"No thanks. I'm going to go sit by the fire," she said and Pike opened the door for her to make her way through to the dining room.

"Should we have warned her about the film crew?" Sierra asked after she left. "Where are they anyway?"

"Out in the barn shooting pictures of the horses and interviewing Kinsey and Gerard. I don't see any reason to feed Tess's active imagination. I know I'm the one who brought up a snitch in their ranks, but it's hard to really believe."

"I guess."

He pulled her to her feet and looked into her eyes. "Don't worry about her," he said.

Sierra leaned her head against his chest. "Things are going to get worse for her before they get better," she said. "Even if the LAPD sends detectives here to interview her, sooner or later she's going to have to go back for a trial."

"I know," Pike murmured. "In the end, she's going to have to face Raoul Ruiz." He kissed her forehead and she tilted her head so their lips could connect. The kiss was long and smoldering, and Sierra kind of lost track of herself as she ran her fingers through his hair.

The swinging door behind them ended the kiss. Harry Hastings stood framed in the doorway. His eyebrows inched up his forehead as he gazed at them, then he walked to the refrigerator.

"Time to meet up with my brothers," Pike said against Sierra's cheek and he kissed her a last time. "Later, Dad." Sierra watched him leave until Harry cleared his throat and her gaze swiveled to him. He took a can of soda from the fridge.

"Can I get you anything?" he asked her before he closed the door.

"No thanks," She glanced down to find she couldn't get an internet connection. "Drat," she murmured.

"Is there a problem?" he asked.

"The wireless must be down. May I restart your modem?"

"Lily already tried that this morning, didn't work. It's gotta be the tower outside of Falls Bluff. It's not uncommon after a storm like this, should be fixed in a day or so."

With a sigh, she closed the computer top and drummed her fingers. It seemed like forever since she'd checked email or anything else.

"Things move a little slower here than what you're used to," Harry added, pausing by her side. She looked up at him, trying to find some resemblance to Pike. Maybe around the eyes and certainly in height, but otherwise, she thought Pike resembled Mona more than his dad.

"I've noticed that," she said.

He rapped his knuckles on the countertop. "Do you use Facebook and Twitter?" he asked.

"Yes. Do you?"

"Waste of time," he said.

"Not in my line of work. What people post about themselves can be pretty revealing. Saves me a lot of legwork sometimes."

He laughed. "I bet. A lot of it's malicious nonsense, though."

"But it helps keep me in touch when I'm away. I like to know what's going on at home when I travel."

"That's right," he said slowly. Though the expression on his face was friendly, there was a glint in his eyes as he added, "You come from a long ways away."

"Yes, I do," she said.

"Not just in miles, either, right?"

"What do you mean?"

"Attitudes," he said. "Expectations. The ability to find contentment. People are different in a big city than on a little chunk of countryside, where they're outnumbered by cattle a hundred to one."

"I've heard it said that people are all the same deep down," she said.

He looked her straight in the eye. "You are a smart, accomplished woman, Sierra Hyde, but if you believe that, you're also naive. Well, I'd better get back. Tess is waiting for me to teach her how to play poker."

Sierra narrowed her eyes as he left the kitchen. She wasn't positive but she was pretty sure he'd just tried to tell her something important.

Chapter Ten

It was a subdued gathering that met for a late dinner around the big dining room table. People were just plain exhausted, injured, preoccupied or a combination of all three. Even the normally jovial film crew ate the beef stew Grace and Lily had labored over in introspective silence.

Pike examined each of them as they ate and he was hard-pressed to see a man among them who would attempt murder. It was one thing to feel sympathy for a former coworker and help him create nuisances; it was another thing entirely to help plot the murders of two innocent people. Sierra had said something wasn't logical. She was right. But what was it?

Toward the end of the meal, Gerard cleared his throat. "Today we found out that Leo is qualified to conduct wedding ceremonies," he announced. "I asked Kinsey what she thought about getting married right away, you know, like tomorrow."

"And I said tomorrow would be great," Kinsey said.

Lily squealed. "That's fantastic!"

"Will you be my maid of honor?"

"Of course I will," Lily said.

"And Pike," Gerard said, "will you stand up with me?"

"You bet. Do you have a license and all that?"

"We arranged everything a month or so ago," Gerard said. "License, rings, the whole shebang. Leo being able to marry us made the timing perfect."

"I got ordained online so I could marry my cousin and her husband last year," Leo explained. "Doing this sure beats the heck out of watching it snow."

"And it will be fun to have the wedding before Sierra has to leave," Kinsey added.

"That would be nice," Sierra said with a quick glance at Pike.

"This is wonderful news," Grace declared with moist eyes. "Let's have the ceremony in the evening, okay, so I have time to get things ready."

"Perfect," Kinsey said. "Thanks."

"I'm the one who should be thanking you," Grace said softly. "All those years ago I named you Sandra and when you came back into my life, you were Kinsey. At first I was sad you kept that name and then I realized it didn't matter—what mattered was *who* you were and that we had a chance to get to know each other again." Her eyes suddenly grew wide. "But Kinsey, your grandmother won't be here for your wedding. We both owe her so much."

"Not to worry," Kinsey said. "I spoke to her this afternoon. She urged me to go ahead. We'll fly to New Orleans when the baby comes. That's all she really cares about."

"Then it's perfect," Grace said. "Oh, Harry, there's going to be a wedding on the ranch and then a baby! And it's all happening tomorrow!"

"Not all of it, at least not tomorrow," Kinsey said, patting her stomach.

"I couldn't be happier for you both," Pike's dad said. His gaze shifted to Sierra and he smiled at her. She glanced down at her plate and pushed a piece of carrot around with a fork.

Then the old man turned his attention to Charlie and patted his knee. "Come here, boy," he said and Charlie gleefully joined the man he considered his grandfather. Pike glanced at Chance and Lily as they watched this sweet little scene unfold and he knew a second wedding wasn't far off.

Did he ever think about marrying? Maybe in a vague, someday sort of way, at least until recently. He glanced at Sierra. She was still pursuing the carrot with her fork and didn't meet his gaze.

They all pitched in and cleared the table and did the dishes before they began wandering off to read or go to bed. Though the electricity was on and the television worked, the satellite receiver wasn't functioning, no doubt due to how much snow had accumulated in the dish. Not that he minded. Snowed-in days were good times to draw close, to talk to others in the family and reconnect. He was looking forward to taking Sierra home to his barn, and he found her in the back bedroom with Tess. The two sisters were sitting side by side on one of the twin beds, Sierra's arm around Tess's shoulder. Tess's eyes were bloodshot and her cheeks tear-streaked.

He sat down on Tess's other side to lend support. Eventually, Tess excused herself to go wash her face and that left him and Sierra sitting alone.

"All the talk about a wedding got to her," Sierra said. "She's built Danny into the love of her life. I think I'd better stick close to her tonight."

Disappointment flared, but he knew she was right.

"Yeah, I can see that. Did you get a hold of Detective Hatch this afternoon?"

"Yes. He was shocked that Raoul Ruiz might have traveled here to silence Tess."

"It seems strange to me, too," Pike said.

"Yeah. Well, Hatch assured me that Tess doesn't have to fly back to LA for questioning yet. They'll send detectives to interview her here or even in New York if she decides to come home with me."

He stared at her a second as though surprised. "Have you decided when you're leaving?"

"As soon as I can," she said. "I have obligations… You know how it is. I haven't talked to Tess yet about coming with me."

"This seems sudden," he said softly.

She studied her hands for a second before darting him a quick glance. "Did you notice the way your father looked at me?"

"He likes you," Pike said.

She shot him another look. "I don't know if he does or not, but I do know he doesn't think I'm good enough for you."

"That's crazy. If anything he thinks you're way out of my league."

"I don't mean not good enough in the sense that I'm not smart enough or something. Earlier today, he started talking about New York… It sounded like he was reminding me that you and I are from two different worlds."

"So what?" he said. "There's nothing wrong with that."

"It got me thinking," she continued, still avoiding his gaze. "I don't fit in here. I'm not the kind of woman your father wants for you."

He took both her hands in his. "Sierra, even if that

were true, and I'm not saying it is, I'm not a kid. My father doesn't get to decide who I care about or spend my time with."

"But the thing is, I see his point."

"We talked about our relationship right from the start," he said. "There were ground rules. I haven't meant to cross them—"

"It's not you," she interrupted. "It's me."

"What are you talking about?"

"We were supposed to keep this thing between us light and breezy and then today I invited you to New York to experience every little season. Why did I do that?"

"Why?" he repeated. "Because we like each other? Because we want to spend time together?"

"No, Pike. The real reason is deeper and more self-serving. I think I wanted to see how you fit into my world. I can't imagine living here, but I don't think you can live any other way. These people…I don't even know what I'm doing here."

"You're helping Tess—"

"Am I? What exactly have I done for her?"

He squeezed her hands. "*We* are both trying to keep her alive. *That's* the major reason you are here." He lifted her chin with his fingers and lowered his voice. "Don't jump so far ahead when it comes to us. I promised you I could handle things and I will. No one has to move anywhere or live a life they don't want."

"Ah, Pike, all the good intentions in the world don't mean a thing when your heart gets involved. You know that."

His brow furrowed. "What exactly are you trying to say?"

She closed the gap between them and touched her lips

to his. His hopes swelled and then shrank as she whispered, “I need to step back.”

“From me?”

“Yes.”

“Is everything okay?” a voice asked from the doorway, and they both turned to see Tess standing there. She hobbled over to them using one crutch and the furniture for support. She looked from one of them to the other. “What’s wrong with you guys?”

“We’re just tired,” Sierra said. “Everybody in this house is just flat-out exhausted.”

Pike knew it was time to leave. He stood up, ruffled Tess’s hair and walked to the door. “See you guys tomorrow,” he said, his gut clenching at the look in Sierra’s eyes. Her gaze dropped to her hands and he closed the door.

What had just happened?

He ran into Chance in the mudroom, where his brother was pulling on rubber boots. “Man, I hate going back to my place all alone,” Chance said. “Lily wants to wait to get married until this fall but I don’t think I’m going to make it that long. I want her and Charlie at my place with me.”

Pike sat down beside his brother. “Let me ask you a question,” he said.

“Sure.”

“You used to play the field.”

Chance nodded. “Yep.”

“I think I need some pointers on how to do it.”

Chance laughed. “Isn’t it too late for that?”

“What do you mean too late?”

“I just got the impression that you and Sierra had something special going on.”

"I've known her less than a week," Pike said.

Chance smiled. "I remember the first time I saw Lily. That was it for me, but everyone around here, including you, recognized it before I did."

"It's not like that with me and Sierra," Pike said.

"Yeah." Chance clapped him on the back, added a good-night and went out the back door into the cold, snowy world. Pike followed a few minutes later, and not long after that pulled up in front of his barn on the snowmobile. The headlight illuminated Daisy, who had heard the engine and had come outside to wag a greeting.

He trudged through the snow and kneeled down to pat her and she followed him inside. Once in the kitchen, he poured kibble into her bowl and the cat's, refilled water dishes and grabbed himself a beer.

He sat down on the sofa and looked around the huge space. He'd never really thought too much about it, but in the back of his mind he knew he'd built this place for a future family. There should be kids in the loft rooms giggling themselves to sleep, a woman by his side who shared his values and hopes.

He heard Sierra's voice in his head. She said his family didn't approve of her. What if the truth was that she didn't approve of them?

A streak of black announced Sinbad's presence as he jumped onto the back of the sofa and curled his tail around his own feet. Daisy's toenails clicked against the wood floors as she crossed the room to join them. It took her a few seconds to haul her pregnant body up onto the couch beside him, where she turned around twice before settling with her head in his lap. He smoothed her soft ears and she looked up at him with huge brown eyes.

He'd done the dumbest thing in the world when it came

to securing happiness. He'd fallen for a woman who'd warned him a relationship with her would be "terminal." She'd known the minute she stepped foot on this ranch that she would never dream of staying. She'd been open and honest about it. He'd been the delusional one.

"Well, you guys," he said, looking at his critters. "Looks like it's you and me."

SIERRA WOKE UP to find Tess's bed was empty. She looked out the big window that faced the icy river and found the sun shining. The glare from the snow was amazing. City snow wasn't quite this white and pure. Ordinarily, such beauty coming on the heels of the last two days would have lifted her spirits, but today it was going to take more than a change in the weather.

For a second she lay there. This room was close to the kitchen and she could smell the aroma of a baking cake—Kinsey and Gerard would be married this evening and apparently Grace was getting an early start.

Had she really broken things off with Pike last night? Silly question—she knew she had. And she also knew he would not push or cajole her into rethinking her decision. For better or worse, the deed was done.

And yet the thought that he wasn't hers anymore to touch or kiss was hard to swallow and impossible not to regret. She got out of bed, washed up and brushed her teeth, gathered her hair in a ponytail and put on the green sweater. Her first priority of the day was to make sure Tess was safe and then make arrangements to fly home using the open-ended ticket Pike had purchased when she came here days before.

The smell of cake was too sweet for so early in the day. She comforted herself by thinking of the deli down the block from her apartment. The day after tomorrow, she'd feast on bagels and lox and drink coffee so strong it had the power to kick-start the lousiest day. She'd have to settle for toast this morning, though she couldn't fault the ranch coffee. It was as strong as the stuff she bought. But how did these people survive the afternoon without a cappuccino or espresso?

Tess was seated at the counter eating cereal and doodling on some paper as Grace took the first of three round cake pans from the oven. "Sleep well?" she asked as she set each on a rack.

"Yes, thanks," Sierra said.

"Liar," Tess said. "You tossed and turned all night."

Sierra sat across from her sister. "I was having dreams."

"About falling?" Tess asked, her eyes suddenly fearful.

"No. I dreamed a bald guy was poking a stick at me through a window blind. I tried to stop him and he bit me. Stupid stuff that just made me restless." She looked at the paper upon which Tess had doodled. "What are you doing?"

"Grace said I could decorate Kinsey's cake. I was thinking of flowers with little silver balls in the center. Or we could bake sugar cookie hearts and frost them and then stick them on the cake. I saw it in a magazine and it was cool."

"You have an artistic streak so whatever you decide will be perfect. Listen, honey, we need to talk about what you want to do on a long-term basis," she added. "It's time for me to go home and get back to work."

"You're leaving?" Tess asked.

"I have a job to get back to. I was thinking you could come with me."

"To New York? I don't know."

At the sink, Grace leaned forward to peer out the window. "Who's that?" she murmured. She turned to look back at Sierra. "A car just pulled in. I know Harry got up early and plowed the ranch road, but I didn't know the roads from town were clear."

"Maybe a neighbor," Tess said.

Grace looked out the window again. "I don't recognize the car."

Tess craned her neck to look, but Sierra touched her sister's hand to reclaim her attention. "I want to book a flight as soon as possible. If you want to come with me, I need to get you a ticket."

"I don't know," Tess said.

"The other option is you stay here with Pike," Sierra added.

"I guess I should talk to him."

"That's a good idea."

"The man getting out of the car looks vaguely familiar," Grace said as she continued staring.

"Maybe he's with the local police," Sierra offered. "Pike said they would come out here to investigate when the weather cleared."

"It's not a police car and the man isn't dressed like an officer. In fact, his clothes are all wrong."

Sierra popped to her feet. All she could think was that it must be trouble. A knock sounded on the door. She fought the urge to grab a butcher knife and went to open it.

For a second she just stared at the familiar features, almost unable to reconcile this man's presence on the Hastings Ridge Ranch. He was dressed in pressed jeans and alligator loafers—no socks. His concession to the cold seemed to be a blazer and his graying blond hair was slicked back from his tanned face. "Doug?"

"I thought I'd never find this godforsaken place!" he said under his breath. "It's freezing out here. How do people live like this?"

"Does Tess know you're coming?"

"No, I wanted to surprise her."

"Dad!" Tess squealed from the kitchen, obviously recognizing his voice. "Is that really you?"

Doug smiled broadly, his dimples all but twinkling as he stamped the snow off his loafers and sidled past Sierra. "Do I hear my girl?" he called as he strode through the mudroom.

Sierra closed the door. In the kitchen, she found Doug kneeling in front of his daughter, examining her foot without touching it. He looked like a handsome doctor on a soap opera. "Does it hurt?" he asked. "Has it been X-rayed?"

"We've been snowed in. It really hurts, though."

"It appears to be a bad sprain to me," Grace said from the sink. "I wrapped and iced it but now that the roads are clear and you're here, maybe you could drive her into Falls Bluff to the urgent care center."

"Of course I will," he said as he stood.

Sierra realized Doug and Grace had never met and performed introductions. "I remember your TV show," Grace said. "I was a big fan."

"Thank you," he said graciously.

"Are you doing anything right now besides those clever insurance ads?"

"I have my fingers in a few things," he said, then hitched his hands on his waist and looked around the kitchen. "This is such a cozy cabin. And that cake smells delightful."

"It's a wedding cake," Tess said. "Gerard and Kinsey are getting married tonight." She showed him her doodling and added, "I'm going to decorate it."

"Very cute," he said and turned back to Grace. "How do I wangle an invitation to this wedding?"

She laughed. "We'd love to have you. In fact, where are you staying while you're here?"

"I'll get a room in town—"

"Nonsense, you're Tess's father. There's plenty of room here."

This rambling house was no more a "cozy cabin" than a cruise ship was a rowboat, but saying there was plenty of room right now was something of a stretch. With four people in the film crew, her and Tess and now Doug, even this big house was popping at the seams.

"Why are you in Idaho?" Sierra asked, alarmed at how chilly her voice sounded. Her experience with this man had led her to believe he did very little that wasn't self-serving, but there was no reason to be rude to him, especially when she knew her current bad mood had more to do with herself than with him.

"How could I not come when I heard how distraught Tess was? A girl needs her father after an ordeal like the one she suffered, right, honey?"

Tess smiled and Sierra began a slow thaw toward the man. Maybe he'd come to his senses and realized the very real danger still looming over Tess. For her sake, Sierra sure hoped so.

Doug looked toward the swinging door. "I heard there was a film crew here," he said.

"The movie people are setting up for the wedding out

in the barn," Grace said. "All except for Gary, the producer, who's still in bed because he tore his rotator cuff and he's having trouble sleeping."

Doug nodded. "You mean Gary Dodge. Fine man."

"Are you friends?"

"Never met him, but I pride myself on thorough research. So the others are outside, huh? Maybe I'll go shoot the breeze with them."

"But what about my foot?" Tess asked. "I think I should get an X-ray now so I'll have time to decorate the cake when we get back."

"Sure, sure," he said. "We will, but there's no rush, is there?"

"Well, there kind of is because of the cake and everything. I was hoping we could talk about things."

"Lots of time for that." He tousled the top of his daughter's head, smiled at Grace, avoided Sierra's gaze and left the house.

Grace's gaze shifted to Sierra. Sierra glanced at Tess, who had turned on the stool to watch her father's retreat. Her furrowed brows and down-turned mouth made her appear older and more jaded than she had just a few minutes before. Longing to see Tess smile, Sierra trotted out her cheeriest voice. "Have you decided how you're going to decorate this cake?"

"No," Tess said.

Sierra bit her lip and brought her voice down a bit. "Listen. I know you want to catch up with your dad, but I'd be happy to drive you into Falls Bluff to have your foot X-rayed and you guys can visit later."

"No thanks," she said listlessly.

"I thought your foot was killing you."

She shrugged.

"Hmm. Well, I wanted to tell you that if you decide to come to New York with me, we'll turn my office into your bedroom. You can paint it any color you want. And there are lots of colleges and programs—"

"Just stop!" Tess interrupted, anger flashing in her eyes. "Don't worry about me, okay? I can take care of myself. I don't need anyone else." She grabbed her crutches and hobbled back to the bedroom, slamming the door behind her.

Sierra looked after her sister with wide eyes.

Grace squeezed her hand. "Give her time, dear. It's not your love and acceptance that she's looking for."

AFTER RETRIEVING HER COMPUTER, Sierra made her way to the room with the fireplace, glad to find it empty. She desperately wanted to book a flight home. Until Tess made up her mind about her future, that wasn't going to happen.

Being stuck inside this house, where everything reminded her of Pike, was difficult. Part of her waited with bated breath for him to walk into a room and the other part of her dreaded the moment she'd look into his eyes. She knew she'd hurt him and even if it kept him from deeper hurt ahead, it felt lousy.

No use thinking about that now. Instead she was relieved to find that the internet was working again, and she focused her attention on wading through emails, none of which were from Savannah.

Wasn't that kind of strange?

Next she accessed a news website to catch up on what was happening at home. The garbage company was threatening a strike and two Yankees were accused of wife-swapping, but the big story had to do with the murder of a call girl named Giselle Montgomery and the burgeoning scandal involving evidence that she had been linked to one of the mayoral candidates. No surprise that it was the sleazeball candidate, Ralph Yardley. Sierra mentally patted herself on the back for supporting Jakes. No one had accused Yardley of the actual murder, as he had an ironclad alibi involving a fund-raising dinner he attended with his wife. The innuendo was that he could have hired someone to take care of Giselle if she had threatened to reveal an affair.

The poor woman had drowned and her body had been found in the Hudson River. There was evidence she had been dumped, the report stated without going into details.

There was also a tantalizing sidebar piece that linked the murdered call girl to the notorious Broadway Madame, who was only notorious because nobody knew exactly who she was. Sierra thought for a moment about the difference between her city's news and the news out of Falls Bluff. New York City may have a seedy underbelly, but it was here in the country that she'd been thrown down a chasm and left for dead.

She took care of a few loose ends with clients, made a lunch date for later in the week with a couple of girlfriends and wrote Savannah an email asking if everything was okay. She didn't look up until Gary entered the room. He held his arm kind of funny due to his injury. "Morning," he said, looking around. "Where is everybody?"

"Grace said your crew is out setting up for the wedding in the barn."

"In the barn?" He looked surprised. "It's cold out there. Why don't they have the ceremony in this beautiful room?"

"I don't have the slightest idea," Sierra said. "Gary, there's something else. The police will be here pretty soon now that the roads are clear. They have to be told about your old employee on the off chance he's somehow behind what happened. If you don't tell them, I'm afraid I'll have to."

"I'll talk to them," he said. "Damn."

"Sorry."

"Can't be helped. Nothing good ever comes from trying to ignore reality, does it?"

"No," she said softly. "Not really."

A few seconds later, Doug waltzed into the den and did a double take when he saw Gary. He held out his hand and strode over to him. Gary looked nervous for a moment as though afraid Doug would jar his arm, but Doug seemed to recall the injury and dropped his hand. "Just the man I wanted to see," Doug said. "I've heard good things about the quality of your projects, Gary."

"Thank you. Have we met?"

"No, I don't believe so. I've heard of you, though. My name is Douglas Foster."

"That's why you look familiar. You were in that detective show years ago. What are you up to now?"

"I'm the voice for Safer Insurance Company. Maybe you've heard my ads."

"Sure, yeah." Gary narrowed his eyes. "They're excellent." He chewed on his bottom lip and added, "How coincidental that you're here."

"Not entirely," Sierra said. "Doug is Tess's father. He came when he heard what happened to her at the mine."

"Poor kid was really roughed up," Gary said. His gaze shifted to Sierra and she got the feeling he was willing her not to mention his disgruntled former employee and the possibility he'd been behind almost killing Doug's daughter. Probably worried about attorneys and more lawsuits. She had no intention of saying anything so she produced a reassuring smile.

Doug nodded. "Yeah, she sounded terrible on the phone. I just had to come and offer support. But it's great that you're here. I'm fascinated by your project concerning this ranch and its lurid past."

Gary stared at Doug for a few moments, assessing him, apparently, because Sierra saw in his eyes the moment he reached a decision. "It might be even better luck than you think," Gary said. "Unforeseen circumstances with our voice-over talent have left us without a narrator."

"Nothing serious, I hope."

"Actually yes, he had a stroke."

"Oh, you're talking about Patrick Nestle. Great guy. I heard about the stroke."

"His withdrawal has left us in a little bit of a bind. I need to check with my crew right now. Do you have time this afternoon to talk or would you prefer your agent be present?"

"No need for my agent at this point," Doug said. "Sure, I have the rest of this day. Just let me know when you want to sit down for a while."

"I don't want to get in the way of you and your daughter—"

Doug interrupted him with a laugh. "Tess? Oh, she'll understand. There's always tomorrow."

"Good." They exchanged business cards, Sierra supposed so they'd have each other's cell phone numbers, and Gary left to find breakfast. Doug shoved his hands in his designer-jean pockets, rocked back on his heels and smiled.

"You know, I don't think I really believed it till just now," Sierra said, closing the laptop and shaking her head as she stood.

"Believed what?"

"You. Why you're here."

"I'm here for Tess."

"Like hell you are. You're here for you. You're here on a job interview. Tess was simply your ticket in the door. And the worst part is that she knows it. You almost had me fooled, but she saw right through you."

"You don't know what you're talking about," he scoffed and started to turn.

"Don't walk away just yet," Sierra said, and he paused. "You and I have never been friendly and that's okay. I don't need you or your reputation or your money. But Tess does. For better or worse, she is your kid and she loves you."

"Is that why she ran away with that druggie and didn't bother calling?" he said with a sneer.

"You know, it just may be. Danny was quite a bit older than her. Maybe she was looking for a father figure."

"That's a bunch of mumbo jumbo."

"Doug, please," Sierra said, lowering her voice and reining in her frustration. "Tess witnessed the cold-blooded murder of somebody she cared about. Whether or not the murderer was behind what happened here in the mine, she has to go back to Los Angeles and finger the man she saw kill Danny. After that, she'll be the star witness at his trial and because she's your daughter and you possess a certain amount of fame, she'll be under scrutiny. She's going to have to cope with all of this. I have offered to help her, so has Pike, but in her heart of hearts, she wants you."

"No, she doesn't," he said and damn if he didn't look as though he actually believed it.

"Sierra is right," Tess said from the doorway, where she balanced on the crutches. Her face was blotchy, her eyes red. Sierra knew that the incident in the mine had terrified Tess even more than she'd let on and that dealing with the growing fear of another attempt wore on her mind. Sometimes she could shrug it off and pretend things were okay, but now and again, things just snapped.

And then her dad had come and a leap of hope for his support had been dashed on the sharp edges of his ego.

"Tess," he said.

"I thought you came here because you loved me but you really came for a job, didn't you?"

"You're just saying that because Sierra said it."

She shook her head. "No, I'm not. I knew it the minute you couldn't wait to ditch me so you could hang out with the film crew." Her lips quivered. "It's not like you haven't done the same thing a hundred times before."

"Tess, you're exaggerating—"

"Am I? A crazy, drugged-out lunatic tried to kill me. I bet you wish he'd succeeded. Then I'd be out of your hair forever. I wish I would have died with Danny!"

"Tess!" Doug said, his eyes almost spinning. "Don't talk like that, please, honey."

"It's the truth," she sobbed. "I wish I were dead."

Her declaration practically ignited the air in the room. Doug's expression turned even more bewildered and when he finally spoke, his voice sounded shaken. "Oh, Lord, what have I done? How do I fix this? Tell me what you want."

"I want you to love me," she whispered.

Sierra took a step toward comforting her, but Doug

held up his hands and shook his head. It was he who walked to Tess's side and draped an arm around her shoulders. "I've always loved you, baby," he said as he helped her to the sofa, where the two sat down. Tess's trembling hands worried the bottom hem of her sweater as Doug continued talking softly to her. "Sometimes I'm a tad selfish, I know that. But hurting you…well, that was never my goal. If you want, I'll help you face whatever lies ahead."

"I don't know how you can," she said.

"Listen. Mona and I split up, this time for good. I'll rent us an apartment with great security. We'll get to know each other again. Trust me just this one more time. Give me another chance, please, Tess."

She stared at him for several seconds and then nodded.

"Good. We'll leave right now if you want."

"What about Gary and the documentary?"

"Gary will understand. We can meet later if he's still interested. As of right now, you are the main priority."

"Then I'd like to wait until after the wedding," Tess said. She looked up at Sierra. "Are you okay with this?"

"Absolutely. I'll give you the contact information for the detective we talked to at the LAPD. All I want is for you to be safe and happy, Tess."

"We'll drive in for that X-ray now," Doug said.

An unexpected tap on Sierra's shoulder surprised her and she whirled around. Two hands caught her arms and steadied her. She looked up into Pike's eyes and a jolt of pain shot through her chest. It was obvious to her that he'd rather be anywhere on earth than standing next to her.

"We need to talk," he said as he lowered his hands and backed away.

She followed him from the room.

Chapter Eleven

Despite the dark circles under her eyes, Sierra looked as gorgeous as ever to Pike. Her creamy skin glowed, begging him to extend a hand and touch her. Instead he spoke. “Robert is here to talk to you. He’s waiting in the kitchen. He’s also sent a crew out to the gold mine.”

She blinked. “Who is Robert?”

“Sorry. Officer Robert Hendricks. He’s an old friend.”

They were standing in the foyer and Sierra glanced back at the sofa at Tess. “Does he want to see us both at the same time?” she asked.

“No. He said you go in first and then Tess. When did Doug show up?”

She lowered her voice. “A couple of hours ago. Tess must have told him about the documentary, probably including the fact that they’d lost their actor for the voice-overs. He came to try to finagle a job out of Gary, but Tess just convinced him to take her back to LA.”

Pike’s brow furrowed. “What? I thought she was adamant about not going back there.”

“So did I. I’m beginning to think the past three or four months have been a cry for his attention. Maybe he’ll finally understand she needs some guidance.”

Pike rubbed his forehead. “You’re going to have to

give me a minute or two to wrap my head around Doug providing guidance."

She touched his hand. "Pike, I want to tell you that I'm sorry about last night. I regret, well, things."

He looked down at her, desire pulsing through his veins like acid. "What exactly do you regret?" he asked.

"We'd all had such a lousy couple of days. I wish I hadn't dumped that on you, too."

"So you don't regret walking away from me exactly, just the way you did it?"

She nodded.

"Water under the bridge," he said. "Have you made plans to return home?"

"Not yet. I was waiting for Tess to decide what she wanted. Now that it appears Doug is back in the picture I'll make arrangements."

They stared at each other. He could not bring himself to break the connection until she raised her hand and touched his cheek so gently it stopped his heart. He nodded once, opened the front door and left.

As BEST MAN, Pike dressed in his good suit, a tailored black ensemble with a longer-than-average jacket and country tailoring at the shoulders. He didn't wear it very often; in fact, he found a folded wedding invitation to Gerard's first wedding in the pocket. The joy of that day had been eclipsed a few years later by a tragic accident. Pike tossed the embossed paper into the fireplace before he fed Daisy, made sure she was comfortable and took off for the main ranch house. The dog had been acting squirrelly that day. He had a feeling motherhood was impending and he hated leaving her alone.

On the other hand, he wouldn't miss seeing Gerard and Kinsey tie the knot for the world.

He found the outside of the barn illuminated with tiny white lights, and when he walked inside, he realized he was the only one there. For a second, he stood inside the door and gazed around at what the film crew had done to ready the space for a country wedding.

Lanterns hung on every post, casting warm yellow light. A few parabolic heaters kept the space warm. Bales of hay had been lined up in rows to act as seats for the guests, while wedding bells consisted of his dad's collection of old cowbells strung together on ropes. A makeshift arch had been draped with evergreen boughs and a lopsided but charming cake, decorated with what appeared to be cookies, sat amid a small sea of twinkling champagne flutes on a trestle table covered with a gingham cloth.

He sat down on a hay bale and folded his hands between his knees. His eyes closed for a moment, but he found no relief from his ping-ponging feelings. As happy as he was that Gerard had found love a second time, he couldn't help but wonder if he would ever find it even once.

A voice came from behind him. "What do you think? Looks pretty good, doesn't it?"

Pike jumped to his feet and turned to find Ogden and Leo walking into the barn. Ogden carried a guitar. "Yeah, you guys did great," Pike said.

"Going to be a nice wedding," Leo said. "We took the precaution of locking the dogs in another outbuilding. Frankie said we couldn't trust them with the cake."

"Good thinking," Pike said.

Over the course of the next thirty minutes, members of

the household filtered into the barn while Ogden played the guitar and Oliver filmed the arrivals. Chance and Charlie stood with Pike for a while before sitting down. Doug made his trademark big entrance, but not alone this time. Instead, he carried Tess to a bale of hay, where he helped her sit. There was a blue walking cast on her foot now, but what was really different was the smile on her face. For the first time in a long time, his little sister actually looked happy. As did Grace and Harry, who arrived holding hands.

Sierra showed up at last wearing a slim skirt and an ivory-colored scoop-necked sweater. He recognized Grace's green cashmere shawl draped over her shoulders. She looked stunning.

"This is lovely," she said as she paused in front of him. Her hair was gathered at the nape of her neck, but glistening tendrils fell against her cheeks. Her sparkling eyes gave the diamond pendant a run for its money.

"Beautiful," he said as he stared at her.

"I talked to Detective Hatch this afternoon. He had big news. I haven't shared it with Tess yet. May we talk after the wedding?"

"Sure," he said.

Frankie and Gary ushered in Gerard at last. Gary was still protecting his shoulder and chose a bale of hay near the back on which to perch. Frankie found a seat next to Chance and Charlie as Pike and Gerard walked to the arch.

"You ready for this?" Pike asked his big brother.

Gerard's blue eyes danced. "I can't wait."

Holding a modest bouquet and dressed in rose, Lily entered next and slowly moved up the makeshift aisle. Oliver changed position to catch everything with the camera. Ogden played the guitar until Lily stopped to stand beside Pike. Then he began strumming the familiar tune of the wedding march.

All eyes turned to witness Kinsey float into the barn, a vision in white. As pretty as the dress was, it was the way she looked at Gerard that fascinated Pike. He glanced at his brother and saw the same look of anticipation. His gaze moved to Sierra, whose head was still turned.

Leo began the ceremony and Kinsey and Gerard didn't take their eyes off each other's faces until they finally exchanged vows, rings and kisses and Leo pronounced them husband and wife.

Again, Pike's gaze strayed to Sierra and this time he found her looking straight at him.

"RAOUL RUIZ IS DEAD?" Pike said a little later as he and Sierra stood off to the side, their heads bent in conversation.

He was so close she could smell his aftershave, a scent she hadn't realized until that moment had earned a spot in her subconscious. "He apparently overdosed," she said. "Detective Hatch says he's been dead at least four days, maybe more. They found his body in Tess's blue car parked in a remote way station out in the desert. The speculation is that he decided to take off for parts unknown after he killed Dwayne."

"Then he couldn't have been in Idaho when you and Tess were attacked," Pike said.

"Nope. And they found his phone on his body. He hadn't sent any texts to Tess. It doesn't appear he had a thing to do with the mine."

"Did you tell Officer Hendricks?"

"I called him. He'd already talked to the LAPD. He said the techs found a few interesting things in the mine, including a gas lantern and a matchbook that was apparently used to light it."

"Did they find fingerprints on the lantern?"

"None. He thinks they must have worn gloves, which makes sense considering how cold it was."

"What about the matchbook?"

"It's for a bar called The Pastime. Why does that sound familiar?"

"We parked across the street from it the day we took Tess in after her overdose," Pike said. "It's a local hangout."

"I didn't realize I had even noticed it. Well, the matchbook was apparently ground into the dirt and damaged. The lab is looking at it."

"And that's it?"

"Besides footprints and things like that, pretty much. He said he'd be in touch."

Pike nodded but looked distracted. "I guess the million-dollar question, now that Raoul has been eliminated as a suspect, is who else wants you and Tess dead."

"Me? Oh, no. I was an afterthought."

"Were you? You're forgetting how spooked you were when you arrived on this ranch. You were looking over your shoulder, remember?"

"I kind of forgot about that," she said. "But that has nothing to do with here. That started on the last night I worked back east."

"Maybe that's where it started. A couple of things have bothered me all along. Why did they ask Tess to bring you with her? And why not just shoot you? If the purpose was murder—they had guns—why risk throwing you in a pit?"

"Good questions. But maybe those facts fit with it

being the old LOGO employee. In that case, the intent wasn't murder, just sabotage."

"How would someone like that get Tess's number?" Pike protested. "How did he know to call himself Danny? How in the world did he find the mine in that weather?"

"Tess could have told him, or he could have looked it up. Information is easier to get than it used to be, you know."

He shook his head.

"And one of the crew could be involved," she said.

"I can't believe that. I know, I know, I'm the one who suggested it, but it just doesn't make sense. There were two men in the mine and the entire crew has an alibi for that time period—they were all out with us at the hanging tree. So now you have a snitch, a crazy ex-employee and someone else all in on a reckless act of sabotage?"

"It looks like it," Sierra said.

"I don't buy it. Anyway, I mentioned all this to Officer Hendricks and he said he would contact Seattle police and see if anyone has a record. Have you remembered anything else about the attack? Have you figured out what they said that bugged you?"

"No. But I had another dream about a bald guy."

He raised his eyebrows. "What?"

She'd apparently never mentioned her recent nocturnal preoccupation with hairless men. "Never mind," she said.

"Did you book a flight to New York?"

"I'm on standby."

"You'll need a ride to the airport."

"Doug and Tess are flying out very early tomorrow. I'll ride to the airport with them."

"When are you going to tell Tess about Raoul?"

"In the morning, during the drive. No need for her to lay awake all night trying to figure things out."

For several heartbeats they stared at each other. This was it. They'd caught up with the news. There was no more to say; it was time to walk away and not look back.

Pike took the first step. "Then this is goodbye."

She swallowed. "I guess so."

He touched her hair and kissed her forehead. "Have a good life," he whispered, then turned and walked over to join his brothers. Sierra told herself she was exhausted and went to bed.

SOMETIME AROUND MIDNIGHT, she gave up trying to sleep. Not knowing who would be up and wandering around the house, she dressed in jeans and a sweater, grabbed what she needed and quietly exited the room so as not to wake Tess. Parking herself on a stool in front of the counter, she opened her laptop and typed *breaking news* into the search engine.

This time, the philandering baseball players had been kicked off page one and replaced by a trio of photographs. One was of the murdered call girl, the next was Ralph Yardley and the last was the blonde Sierra had trailed to the back of Tony's Tavern in Dusty Lake, New Jersey. Natalia Bonaparte, the article reported, was wanted for questioning in the murder of Giselle Montgomery. Police had found Natalia missing and her apartment ransacked.

How in the world did these two women tie in together?

And look at poor old Yardley, caught in a scandal. She almost felt sorry for him.

She wanted to talk about all of this to someone, and with a start realized that someone was Pike. How long would that last?

She admitted to herself that she may have panicked and broken it off before she had to. They could have enjoyed each other for another couple of nights before she left for New York and real life inserted itself between them. She closed her eyes, rubbed her forehead and then stood abruptly, strode to the mudroom, grabbed her jacket, stuffed her feet into her ruined boots and marched outside.

The sky was clear, the air cold, the moonlight reflected off the snow. She made her way to the barn, which was now dark, found a lantern and turned it on. The three dogs ambled out of one of the open stalls and stared at her. The place was still set up for the wedding, and she stood there for a second recalling the touching ceremony she'd witnessed.

To be honest, she'd watched Pike more than the wedding couple. He'd looked so sexy in that suit, so sure of himself, so independent. Frankie and Chance had joined him after the ceremony and she'd watched their fond interaction with a touch of envy. She'd told Pike once that he was easy to love.

She suspected that she was not.

A horse whinnied in a nearby stall and she and the dogs approached it to find the same mare she'd ridden to the mine two nights before. The big animal nuzzled her neck then bumped her cheek with a soft, velvet nose.

Sierra stared into the mare's big eyes. "Are you antsy, too, girl? Looking for some action? I know how you feel. Now, if you and me were in New York, we could clip-clop down to the diner no matter what time of day or night and gab with the night shift. You'd like Billy. He wears a bolo tie, very Western. Or maybe we could go to a bar. I could use a glass of wine. What do horses drink? Water?

Yeah, we could get me a nice pinot gris and you an icy trough of Perrier with a slice of lemon. But here we are in Idaho." She looked down at the three dogs, who were leaning against her legs. "What the heck do you guys do in the middle of the night when you're restless?"

One dog whined, one yawned and one cocked his ears as the mare blew hot air on Sierra's hair.

Sometimes it didn't pay to think things through. Sometimes, a person just had to rely on their gut or whatever it was that propelled action, no matter how ill-advised.

She quickly saddled the horse, doused the lantern and led the beast outside. Once astride, she took off on a moonlight ride. She'd only been to her current destination one time before, but she was pretty sure she knew how to find her way.

PIKE OPENED THE door on the first knock.

Some part of him had known it would be Sierra.

"Is something wrong?" he asked. It was a natural question given the past several days. Her cheeks were pink and her teeth clattered together.

"No, no. I put my horse in your barn. I hope that's okay."

"You rode over here?"

She nodded. "I saw your lights on—"

"What are you doing here?" he interrupted. She bit her lip. More than anything in the world he wanted to usher her inside, but not until he understood what her presence meant.

"I was wrong," she said, darting a glance up to his eyes. "I don't want it to end like this. I don't know, I think I got scared. I think I started worrying that I was getting in over my head and that you and I—"

He took a step outside to cup her face and draw her to him. He kissed her into silence and then he kissed her again. She grabbed his shirt at the shoulders and pulled him closer. For a moment it was LA revisited, the sensation of her body pressed into his, the sweet smell of her skin, heated desire overwhelming everything.

"Come inside," he finally said, and pulled her though the door, where he wrapped his arms around her and kissed her again and again.

She finally pushed him away. Her lips were hot now, her eyes filled with the same lust that swelled in his body. And then she said, "What's that noise?" and reality flooded back.

He stepped aside to reveal Daisy lying on her dog bed, the proud mother of nine tiny, snuffling, mostly yellow puppies, although there were a couple of brown ones, as well. Sinbad had flown up to the mantel when Sierra knocked and now surveyed the proceedings with his superior yellow gaze.

"Oh, my gosh," she said. "When did this happen?"

"During the wedding. Daisy had to usher her family into the world all by herself."

"Maybe Sinbad offered emotional support," Sierra said.

He smiled. "Somehow I doubt it."

Sierra released his hand and walked over to sit down next to the dog bed. "Look at you with your babies," she said to Daisy, who appeared a tad bewildered. Sierra touched one tiny ear with the tip of her finger. "So soft!"

"Go ahead, pick one up," Pike said as he kneeled beside her and rested his butt on his heels.

"They're too tiny! I might hurt it."

"You won't hurt it," he said gently.

She carefully lifted the plump puppy with both hands and cuddled it against her chest, under her chin. "It's so sweet, Pike," she said and her voice held a note of tenderness that raced through his veins like a shot of whiskey. Daisy's ears perked up when Sierra put the baby back where she'd found it. The dog immediately began licking away all the human cooties.

"I was just about to go to bed," Pike said, curling a tendril of Sierra's hair around his finger. "It's been an awfully long day."

"May I stay here for the rest of the night?" she asked, looking up at him.

"It depends. Where do you want to sleep?"

"With you," she said. "I want to sleep in your bed with you."

He stood, then reached down and grabbed her hands, pulling her to her feet. He slowly lowered the zipper on her jacket and peeled it away from her sweater, dropping it onto an armchair, then he lifted her into his arms. The master bedroom was at the far end of the barn, a huge room filled with his grandmother's antique furniture. He set her down in front of the four-poster bed.

"We didn't turn off the house lights," she said, gesturing toward the hall.

"To hell with the lights." He pulled her sweater over her head and discovered she hadn't worn a bra. The sight of her beautiful skin and the perfect globes of her breasts shot heat into his groin. "Let them burn all night," he whispered as he lowered his head to taste each pebble-hard nipple.

SIERRA'S RINGING PHONE woke her the next morning and she sat up straight like a shot, yanked from yet another bizarre dream. It was still dark outside, but a houseful of lights shone through the open door into the bedroom, and she dug her phone from the pile of discarded clothes on the floor.

"Hello?"

"It's me," Tess said. "I saw that you texted in the middle of the night on Pike's phone. Where are you?"

"I didn't want you to…uh, worry about me," Sierra stammered. It was cold standing naked outside the covers. "I'm at Pike's house. His dog had puppies and I wanted, well, to see them."

"Oh," Tess said, and if she saw through the flimsy lie, she kept it to herself. "Well, Dad says to tell you we're leaving in one hour."

"I'll be there."

She clicked off the phone and prepared to turn to face the bed, but before she could move, Pike grasped her from behind and tugged her back under the blankets. Both of them laughed until the blazing awareness that flared between them stole the smiles away.

"I have to get back to the ranch house," she said as he covered her body with his own. His strong arms pinned her in place and she rubbed her hands over his muscles.

He looked down into her eyes. "Do you have ten minutes to spare?"

"I can give you five," she murmured with a slow smile, distracted by the way their bodies melted together.

"Then we'd better get to it," he said, burying his face in her neck.

PIKE STOOD ON the ranch road and watched Doug's rental turn onto the highway and speed off toward Boise. He thought he saw Sierra wave through the back window, but he wasn't sure. He got back in his truck and headed to the main house.

He'd wanted to drive her to Boise himself, but she'd refused. Better they should say goodbye at the ranch, she insisted, and besides, she had to talk to Tess about Raoul. She had a point.

The best antidote for the uneasiness that just wouldn't go away was work, and that was why he'd made plans with Frankie to help pack up the film crew, who were also leaving today. First he went home, fed Sinbad, checked on Daisy and her brood, saddled Sierra's mare and rode her back to the ranch. When he got there, he found the crew still eating breakfast. He went out to the barn and helped Chance clean up from the night before, until Lily asked him to drive Charlie to his school bus. For a few moments, Pike stood alone.

He and Sierra had made no big promises, no vows of undying love, no plans to ever see each other again, and yet he knew he wouldn't last long before he needed to hold her in his arms. However, there was a very real concern in his heart that she would get home, that her life would consume her and that as the days and weeks passed, she would write him off as a fling she once had with a cowboy.

The crew eventually started hauling their equipment out into the yard. Once again as Pike joked around with them and helped them with their things, he could not wrap his head around one of them feeding information to that disgruntled former employee. He asked a couple of semileading questions as he helped stow their gear, but no one rose to any kind of bait.

After they'd left, it was Pike's turn to drive out to distribute hay to the cattle with Frankie and his dad. By the time he got back to the ranch, the day was getting old and he checked his phone. One text from Sierra since her phone had obviously started working once she got back to "civilization."

Caught an early plane. Thank goodness. Have stopovers in every little Podunk city between here and home.

Not in the mood for company, he declined dinner at his dad's house and drove home. He hadn't seen Gerard and Kinsey all day—hadn't expected to. This was their honeymoon, after all, or the only one they would get until a break between calving and summer chores would take them to Hawaii for two weeks. He envied them and not just for the warm weather.

The barn was very still. Daisy roused from a nap as he built a fire and contemplated the evening ahead. A knock on the door served as a poignant reminder of a similar knock in the middle of the night, and he opened it with his heart in his throat. Officer Robert Hendricks stood on the threshold.

"Come on in. I'll get you a beer while you admire Daisy's new family," Pike said.

"I'll take water instead," Robert said. "I'm still on duty. Hey, look at all of these cuties. Do you have homes for them yet?"

"Nope."

Pike handed Robert a glass of water and took a swallow from a beer bottle while Robert peered at each of the babies. "Save me one," he said. "The girls have been clamoring for a puppy."

"Maybe you should take two, one for each of them.

They'll be ready to go in eight or nine weeks. Bring the kids over anytime to choose which ones they want."

"Deal."

"What do you want to talk about?" Pike asked. "I assume it has something to do with the attack in the mine."

"Yeah. I went by the ranch house hoping to see Sierra Hyde."

"She left this morning."

"That's what I heard. Did she mention we found a matchbook in the mine?"

"From The Pastime on Seventh, right?"

"Wrong. Techs were able to lift the area code from the phone number on the back cover. The place is in New Jersey."

"New Jersey!" Pike said. His throat closed and he set aside the beer.

"It turns out The Pastime is a popular name for a drinking hole. Without the rest of the phone number it leaves three establishments as possibilities."

"Was one in a place called Dusty Lake? Sierra was there recently."

"No." He rattled off three towns Pike had never heard of. "We're looking into it. Should know more tomorrow. I sure would like to speak with Ms. Hyde. Do you expect to talk to her?"

"She's flying standby. She could be anywhere. I'll phone her and leave a message."

"Do you have any idea at all who would wish her harm or who had all that information about her and her sister?" Robert asked.

"None," Pike said. "Did the Seattle police have anything to say about the LOGO crew?"

"Clean as a whistle. The local police apparently

weren't aware the company had a continuing problem with their former employee, who is currently interviewing for a job in Alaska, by the way. It doesn't rule him out entirely, but I have a feeling what happened here is out of his league."

Pike's gut told him the same thing. He shot to his feet and paced up and down the room. He'd told Sierra last night that with Raoul Ruiz off the list of suspects, he thought it possible the attacks had been centered on her. She'd dismissed the whole idea.

What exactly awaited her when she stepped off that plane?

Chapter Twelve

As soon as Sierra hit the influence of the airport cell tower, she found a new string of texts from clients and friends, but nothing from Savannah.

As she waited for a flight, she checked the news on her phone. Yardley had gone on the attack, swearing to anyone who would listen that he was an innocent man being framed by the Jakes camp. He threatened lawsuits. The picture of him this time showed an enraged red face behind a sea of microphones. There were no photographs of the two women.

Sierra had written Pike that her flights were taking her to every pit stop between Boise and New York, but it was actually only three. For the final leg, she had to run between terminals and arrived out of breath. Anxious to relax, all she wanted for the next hour or two was to close her eyes, but her seatmate was a real chatterbox. His only redeeming quality, as far as Sierra was concerned, was his accent. It was pure Jersey shore, and reminded Sierra of Rollo Bean and summers with her father.

After the plane finally landed, she turned her phone back on to discover that Pike had left her a voice mail. The thrill of hearing his voice was followed by alarm at the urgency of the message. She dialed his number while the plane still taxied down the runway. "Sierra, Robert—Officer Hendricks came by. The matchbook from The Pastime is from New Jersey!"

"Where in New Jersey?"

He told her the three towns.

"They're close to Dusty Lake but I've never been in any of them," she said.

"He'll keep me updated and I'll get back to you."

"Try not to worry about me, okay?" she said.

"I'm afraid worrying comes with caring," he replied as they hung up. By now, she longed for the peace and quiet of her own four walls, where she'd installed the requisite two locks on her door and bars on her windows.

She caught a cab and gave her home address. The driver was from Bangladesh; his English was minimal, but his musical voice fascinated her. What was with her and accents lately? She'd always liked them, had always been good with voices. That's why Spiro's spoken demand to the bartender that night had surprised her, or maybe more accurately, that's why learning he could turn off his Greek accent, and do it so completely, came as a shock. In her experience people had trouble doing that. On the other hand, Savannah said he was an actor.

She warily let herself into the locked lobby of her apartment building, looking around for ne'er-do-wells with murderous intent. The only ones in attendance were the two candidates for mayor in the form of campaign posters plastered to the foyer's walls. Someone had drawn a mustache on Max Jakes's face and someone else had sketched devil horns and a pitchfork on Yardley's leering visage.

She pulled the suitcase up two flights of stairs instead of taking the elevator, because it had a habit of stalling and she wasn't in the mood. The familiar sounds of crying babies and televisions came from behind her neighbors' closed doors. She'd been looking forward to returning to her real life, and here she was and it all fell kind of flat.

But that was because Pike wasn't here and suddenly she understood he would never fit into this world; he could never be more than a visitor. What would he do in an apartment? Where would he put his horses and his dogs and that impossible cat? The man was busy just about every minute of the day and from what she could see, every day of the year. She'd never even seen him watch television or check email. City life would never suit him.

She unlocked her door at last. The relief at being safely home disappeared when she switched on the lights and saw the mayhem her apartment had become in her absence. For a second she just stood in the open doorway and stared at the mess. She examined the locks: they looked perfect… This B&E was the work of a pro.

It didn't appear the intruder had overlooked one item in his or her search for…well, for what? She didn't have expensive art or jewelry. Her television was so old her friends made fun of it. The only thing she had that was worth money was in her head, the gun cabinet or on her computer…

Stepping over and around overturned boxes and emptied drawers, she hurried to her office. Her dad's big, old, wood desk sat where it always did, but the desktop computer was gone and the file drawers were empty. She stood there with her heart in her stomach. Almost everything on the desktop was also on her laptop. It wasn't that she'd lost much besides sentimental files she hadn't transferred, but the scope of the information about herself and her clients the robber now possessed made her queasy.

And the email. Every communication she'd sent or received not only recently, but also going back years, was accessible on that computer. Luckily she used passwords. The opened drawers and ripped books instantly chided her smugness—why else had the thief ransacked things if not to find the passwords? She made her way to her bedroom, intent on pulling the double bed away from the wall and securing the envelope of passwords she'd taped to the wood frame. The bed was already moved aside and the envelope was gone.

Even without the passwords, someone with enough expertise could get what they wanted, but with them it wouldn't even be a tactical feat. And that meant, depending on when this robbery took place, someone knew about Tess and Danny and all the rest.

And Savannah. Face it, Savannah's quietness nagged at her. After checking to make sure the revolver was still where it belonged in the gun case, she opened her laptop and plugged it in, then looked up Savannah on the search engine. There was a recent photo taken of her at a theater opening and a couple as a former Miss Georgia. Her life was summed up in a couple of paragraphs. There was also a link to Spiro Papadakis, the man Savannah had married, and Sierra went to that.

She hadn't realized he'd been such a successful businessman in Greece. She guessed she'd just assumed Savannah had all the money. Then she read that he lost everything and soon after married Savannah and it began to make sense. There were all sorts of further links, but there was absolutely no mention of him being an actor in any capacity. Even his time in New York as a relative nobody was detailed, but again, no mention of acting.

Something didn't add up.

After reporting the break-in to the police, she found the TV remote on the floor among the scattered contents of an upended box of memorabilia. She sat wearily on the sofa, flipped on the television and turned down the volume as she began recollecting the bits and pieces of her dad's campaign souvenirs littered around her feet.

A flyer from 1999 had been crumpled beyond repair, but she did find the big button imprinted with his smiling face and the words "Jeremy Hyde for Mayor." She put that back with a few of his books; he'd been partial to Robert Service poetry. There were several loose photographs scattered about, as well. She was in a couple, either with her dad or sitting at a table stacked with posters. Rollo Bean and her dad were in another. She'd forgotten how tall and straight her dad stood and how overweight Rollo was. There were other differences, too—some obvious, like Rollo's baldness and her dad's thatch of graying black hair, and others internal. Her dad was a peaceful, listening man who cared about people as people. Rollo was a plotter, a born politician.

As she started to set aside the photo, she caught a glimpse of a ten-or twelve-year-old boy standing by a tree behind the two men. It appeared he was eavesdropping. She looked closer and smiled to herself as she recognized Rollo's son, Anthony, who was doing exactly what she'd told Pike he did. There he was, caught on film being, well, creepy.

The past kept surfacing in the form of a half-dozen small items that brought back memories: a menu from Jersey Dog, another from Bee's Fish and Chips, a pennant from the Dusty Lake Bullfrog Labor Day Race and a paper coaster embossed with a line drawing of a building. With some surprise, she realized she'd seen this building recently. The big fish over the door gave it away. She knew it as Tony's Tavern, but The Pastime was printed on the coaster.

Tony's Tavern must have once been called The Pastime!

The apartment buzzer jerked her from her thoughts. She glanced at the television as she stood in time to see a man pop up on the screen. Ralph Yardley, coming out of a hotel, shading his face from the cameras. Things looked to be sliding downhill for him.

Two officers buzzed from downstairs and seconds later knocked on her door. She was stunned they'd actually reacted this quickly and invited them inside, where they shook their heads as they perused the mess. As one grabbed a notepad from his pocket to take information, the other gazed at the television.

"Can you believe that?" he said, elbowing his partner. "I arrested that gal once for soliciting. Who knew she was the Broadway Madame?"

Sierra looked at the screen. The footage of Ralph Yardley was over and now there was a still photo of Natalia Bonaparte. "Wait a second," she said. "The woman on the television right now is *the* Broadway Madame? Are you positive?"

"Yeah. It's all over the news. Apparently the murdered girl, the one who was drowned in a bathtub or something—"

"Not the river?"

"No, that just came out a few hours ago. The water in her lungs did not come out of the Hudson. Anyway, she called Bonaparte the night she died. Police went to Bonaparte's apartment to talk to her and found that she was missing."

"I knew most of that. How did they decide she was the Madame?"

"They came across a secret book filled with women's names and a code. Who knew people write things down nowadays? Giselle Montgomery was on the list along with a bunch of other girls."

"And all of it seems linked back to Ralph Yardley," the other policeman said. "Whether or not he has anything to do with what's going on, that guy's goose is cooked. I bet the Jakes camp is as happy as a bushel of clams at high water."

"Max Jakes strikes me as someone who'd rather win on his own merit than because of something like this," Sierra said softly.

One cop opened his mouth, looked at his partner and shut it without speaking. He looked around the apartment and cleared his throat. "About your problem. Tell us what's missing. Do you know when the break-in occurred?"

Sierra sat down because her knees felt weak. The state of her apartment seemed secondary to everything else swirling around in her head. Why was she increasingly sure Natalia and Giselle's fates were linked with hers? She answered the police questions woodenly, so preoccupied she couldn't think straight, relieved when they left. Damn it, she wished Pike was here to help her sort through all of this or maybe hold her tight and make the cold sweat go away. She'd missed him since the moment she left the ranch—him, Daisy and her puppies, the mare and those three silly dogs. Even Sinbad.

Angry at her scattered thoughts and growing sense of uneasiness, she went to work putting things back in drawers and on shelves, then pushing her bed against the wall. Eventually, she collapsed in front of the TV. Somewhere during a lengthy weather report, she fell asleep and didn't rouse until a pounding at the door awakened her.

And thank goodness it did because she'd had another dream featuring bald men. This time she was tied naked to a chair and four of them stood around throwing lit matches at her.

Honestly, this was getting old.

She looked out the peephole before opening the door and found a big man wearing a blue jacket stretched tight over beefy shoulders. He also wore a cap with a black visor pulled low on his forehead. A bushy mustache occupied half his lower face.

"Yes?" she asked.

"Delivery," he said, holding up a large cardboard-like envelope.

"What is it?" she called. He hadn't buzzed from downstairs, but that wasn't terribly unusual. People often held doors for each other or buzzed someone with a good story inside.

"I don't know, lady. It's from Internal Revenue. Come on, I ain't got all day."

"Put it in my mailbox in the foyer."

"It's too big for that. Anyway, it says here you have to sign for it."

"I'm not opening the door," she said. "Stuff it in the mailbox or tell me where I can go to pick it up."

"I don't have time for this," he said as her door rattled and the knob turned.

What was he doing? "Go away," she yelled.

The door rattled louder. Apparently, the deliveryman's antics drew attention because she heard locks sliding and then the voice of the fireman who lived across the hall. "Dude, quiet down," he called. "I got a kid asleep in here."

The deliveryman told him what he could do with his sleeping child. She peered through the peephole, but she couldn't see anyone. She ran across her apartment and pushed aside the drapes. Her living room window looked out on the street, and she waited for a minute until a man came out of the building. He turned to look up and she stepped back but kept watching. He spoke into a cell phone as he stood on the curb with the big envelope still in his hand. Within seconds, a long white car rolled to a stop on the street in front of him and he slid into the passenger seat and drove away.

That was no deliveryman. For the first time in her life, she was afraid of being alone in her own home.

"Think," she told herself.

Okay, there had been way too many bald men in her dreams lately. The only hairless man she'd had any meaningful experience with in her life was Rollo Bean. She hadn't seen him in almost fifteen years, so what did he represent to her? The past, obviously. Her dad. Elections. New Jersey.

And what about The Pastime? Did that bar have any significance? She'd probably seen it as a child, but if it had always been a drinking establishment, she might not have actually gone inside. But then she recalled the feeling of déjà vu she'd experienced sitting at the mahogany bar that night… She'd attributed it to the fact that many bars looked alike.

Who would know? Who could help? There was only

one person she could think of and that was Rollo Bean. Where was he now? How could she find him? She opened her laptop, but the first thing she did was write another email to Savannah asking for details about Spiro's acting experience. To her utter amazement, Savannah wrote back at once. There's quite a bit to say, she said. Come to my place in an hour. Now that you're back in the city, we need to plan what to do next.

Sierra responded positively, adding a warning to be cautious until she arrived. Finally, she could start getting answers, but first she took the time to change important passwords.

Next she searched for and found Rollo Bean's contact information. She doubted she'd be able to get straight through to him but she tried, anyway. Sure enough, her call went to voice mail and she left a message and went to wash up before leaving for Savannah's.

Her cell phone rang as she ran a comb through her hair. The number was unfamiliar. "Hello?"

"Is this Sierra Hyde?"

"Yes."

"Sierra, this is Rollo Bean. You just called me on the other line. My goodness, it's been years!"

"I know. Thanks for returning the call so promptly."

"No problem. What can I do for you?"

"I have some puzzling questions about a bar that used to be called The Pastime in Dusty Lake. Do you remember it?"

"Yes, sure."

"Do you know if I was ever in the place?"

"Maybe. They served food so it was okay for minors to sit at a booth with an adult. You're not going to believe this, but these days I live very close to there. It's called Tony's Tavern now."

"How long has it had that name?"

"It changed hands a few months ago. Why?"

"It's complicated," Sierra said. That's why the dropped matchbook still had The Pastime printed on the cover. "Rollo, may I drive out to Jersey and pay you a visit? There are some questions—"

"Of course you can," he interrupted. "I'm on my way home right now. Gave a speech out of town last night. I don't know if you're aware of this, but I'm involved in Max Jakes's bid for mayor of New York."

"But surely those people don't vote for the mayor in New York City," she said.

"True, but they do vote for governor of the state and that's where Max is headed next."

"Wow, Rollo, that's the big-time."

"I know. It's been a long time coming."

She paused for a second before adding, "I hate to be a pest, but is there any possibility I could see you today?"

He paused for a second. "My schedule is pretty tight. Heck, who am I kidding? I can't say no to Jeremy Hyde's daughter. I could fit you in, say in an hour or so?"

"Great," she said. "I'll be there."

"Why don't you meet me in Tony's parking lot?" he added. "It'll save you trying to find my place."

"Okay."

"Gosh, I miss your dad."

"I know, so do I," Sierra said. "Can't wait to see you."

"Me, too, kiddo."

She'd no sooner clicked off the phone than it rang again. "Sierra?"

"Pike? Oh, man, is it great to hear your voice. How are Daisy and her babies? Are you just getting up?"

"Not exactly. I've been traveling all night. I just landed in New York."

"You're here?"

"I'm here. I'm in the process of renting a car. Give me your address, honey."

"Pike, you'll never be able to find parking here, you should just take a cab."

"Don't worry about it, I'll figure it out. Just give me your address."

She gave him her address but had to add that she was literally on her way out the door.

"That's okay," he said. "I'll probably get lost a time or two. I'll catch up with you when you get back from wherever you're going."

"But what will you do while I'm gone?"

"I'll figure it out, don't worry. Where are you going?"

"I'm going to meet my father's old friend at Tony's Tavern and go back to his place for a chat. I'll be honest with you, Pike. My apartment was burglarized while I was away. Then, this morning, a fake deliveryman tried to get me to open the door. There's a dead call girl all over the news because of her possible connection to a guy running for mayor…and then there's a missing woman called the Broadway Madame who is the same woman in those photographs I showed you taken at Tony's Tavern, which, get this, used to be called The Pastime. I'm not sure about Savannah… Oh, drat! I forgot all about her."

"What about her?"

"I made arrangements this morning to talk to her about her husband. Frankly, I just want to make sure she's okay. She kind of disappeared for a while and I'm worried."

"Where were you going to meet?"

"At her place."

"Do you want me to go and make sure she's all right?"

"Would you really be willing to do that?"

"Why not. Where does she live?"

She gave him Savannah's address. "Confirm that Spiro was really an actor. Ask her where he was on stage," she added.

"Okay."

"I wish I had the time to wait for you."

"I wish you did, too. I don't like you going out there alone."

"I know, but it's what I do."

"You'll take a gun?"

"Pike, it's early. The tavern won't even be open for regular business."

"Take a gun."

"Okay."

"Seriously, sweetheart. My gut tells me you're in danger. Don't forget what happened in Idaho, okay?"

"I haven't."

"Sierra, I want you to know that I love you. That's why I'm here."

His comment on top of the past hour of overload jolted her. She mumbled something in response and disconnected. Her heart pounded in her chest.

He loved her? Why hadn't she said it back? Because she didn't love him? Because she didn't know if she did or not?

Was that true?

Face it: she wasn't sure about anything.

*W*ELL, PIKE THOUGHT to himself as he navigated the traffic out of LaGuardia, *you aren't in Idaho anymore, that's for sure.* His beloved open fields dotted with cattle had been replaced by miles of blacktop crowded with every kind of vehicle imaginable. After a few minutes, he detected a certain rhythm to the flow and eased into it himself.

Could he live here? Sure, if that's what it took. He had a degree in agriculture. Maybe he could teach. Everyone always teased him that he looked and sounded like a professor. Maybe they had the right idea.

It didn't matter what he did to earn a living. They could visit the ranch for vacations. All that mattered was that Sierra and he were together. She might not have been able to say she loved him when he blurted it out, but he knew in his heart that she cared and that was good enough for now.

It was important to keep his mind on the road, but it was impossible not to worry about what was going on with her. He couldn't shake the fact that she was in danger but he couldn't imagine why. What did she have to do with dead and missing women and politicians, and what was with the delivery guy?

Eventually, he found Savannah Papadakis's building a few blocks from Central Park. He pulled up to the curb in front as a doorman immediately shot through the doors and waved his arms. "Sorry, sir, you can't park here," he said.

"Do you have visitor parking? I don't think I'll be long. I'm here to see Savannah Papadakis."

"She's not here."

"When will she be back?"

The doorman looked around as though to make sure no one was listening to him. "We're not sure. See, her hubby moved out a while ago. Mrs. Papadakis is kind of a quiet lady, doesn't socialize very much anymore. But a few days ago, a deliveryman shows up here with an envelope from her husband's attorney."

"What did this guy look like? What company did he work for?"

"I'm not sure. Big bushy mustache, wonky eyes, blue uniform."

"Wonky eyes? What does that mean?"

"They was two different colors. Brown and gray. Made it look like he was staring at you and the guy standing next to you at the same time. Anyway, I called Mrs. Papadakis and she said to send him up. Then she calls down for her car, a big old Cadillac she hardly ever drives, and they both take off, her in that red cape she wears like Little Red Riding Hood."

"Did she say where they were going?"

"Neither one of them said a word."

"Did she have a suitcase?"

"Yeah."

"Did you check her apartment when she didn't come home?"

"The manager did. Everything looked fine."

"Have you since called the police?" Pike persisted.

"Why? It ain't illegal to take a trip. She's a private kind of woman and she's rich. You don't mess with her type."

"So, she's been gone several days with no explanation. You need to take a chance of annoying her and tell someone. At least call her husband."

"She'll kill me if I call her husband."

"Then call the police. Something is wrong." He took a card out of his wallet. It showed green pastures and cattle. Pike's name and phone number occupied one corner while the other said: Hastings Ridge Ranch, Falls Ridge, Idaho. “Tell them to talk to me.”

“Idaho?”

“Just do it.”

He eased back into traffic and drove until he found a place he could pull over for a minute. He grabbed his phone and called Sierra, alarmed when she didn’t respond. By now, he’d been driving around New York for ninety minutes; surely she’d had time to reach her destination and could answer a phone call. Even if she was still driving she would have put him on speaker.

Maybe reception was bad at Rollo Bean’s house.

Think.

Sierra had been robbed. She said they took her computer. If the mail on all her gadgets was connected like his were, that meant every message she sent and received was visible to the thief and that meant this person would know a whole bunch about her movements.

Grace had mentioned seeing a map of Hastings Ridge Ranch on Sierra’s phone. If she’d taken the picture with her phone and sent it to her laptop, then it would have been on her desktop as well and that meant the people in the mine could have known of its location by studying the map. They would also know whatever Tess and Sierra wrote to each other while they were in LA. That meant they knew that there was a question about Danny being dead or alive, but not that his body had actually been found.

And they’d know all about Savannah Papadakis.

All along, it had worried him that the attackers didn’t kill Sierra and Tess outright. He’d seen no point in trying to stage an accident instead of getting the job done unless the point was that no one dig into possible motives for murder.

What else was on Sierra's computer? All her work-related information, including the pictures she'd taken with her eyeglass camera at the bar in Jersey—the bar she was headed to right now, the one that used to be called The Pastime, the place the matchbook in the cave had to have come from. And she was on her way to meet Rollo Bean, her dad's old advisor, the man who had fathered a calculating kid with different-colored eyes.

Too many coincidences; too many questions. He programmed his phone to find out how to get where he was headed and pulled back onto the street, his jaw set, his mind focused. Logic said they'd pass each other without even knowing it. His gut told him to go, anyway.

The car was a hell of a lot faster than a horse, but he sure wished he had a shotgun and a better idea of what he would find when he got there.

And he hoped against hope that he wasn't too late.

Chapter Thirteen

Sierra hadn't spent much time in Dusty Lake since her father died. Rollo Bean had been out of the country and unable to come to the funeral so it had been even longer since she'd seen him.

Her dad had loved it here, had hoped to become the town's mayor, but that hadn't worked out. The race seemed to sour him on politics and he took up fishing when he lost the election. He'd told her the week before he died that he wished he'd figured out fishing beat politics all to hell a lot earlier in his life.

This far into the winter, the tree branches were bare and ice shimmered on the lake surface. The skies were as gray as the water and laced with threatening clouds promising showers. She parked next to a large white car sporting two Maxwell Jakes for NYC Mayor bumper stickers and assumed it belonged to Rollo Bean. He wasn't in the car. There was a van parked next to that and a big truck across the lot. The sign hanging under the painted fish over the door said Closed, but that was about the only other place to look. As she approached, the door opened and a man stepped out.

"Sierra Hyde, you haven't changed a bit," he called.

Her mouth almost dropped open. "Rollo?"

"Rolland now, please. Tony came in early, saw me sitting out there in my car and insisted I come in out of the cold." He glanced at his watch and added, "I'm running late so let's just talk here, okay?"

"Sure," she said and brushed past him as she entered the tavern. It was hard to reconcile this trim man with the chubby Rollo Bean she'd known as a kid; he'd lost about half his body mass. "You look very dapper," she said when they faced each other. He wore a crisp white shirt and a black vest with a blue tie. A gold watch sparkled on his wrist.

"Your dad gave me this watch," Rollo said when he saw what had caught her attention. "Do you remember it?"

"No," she said. "I don't. It's very attractive."

"And distinctive," he said, pointing out the four rubies set into the face, one at each quarter hour. "I thought for sure you'd recall it when you saw it. Come sit down. I took the liberty of ordering something hot to chase away the chill."

He led her back to a table across from the booth Natalia and the man who looked like Spiro Papadakis had occupied a week before.

So much had happened in such a short time.

Rollo—she just could not think of him as Rolland—poured them each a mug of coffee from the gold carafe sitting on the table. He took a sip of his and emitted a satisfied sigh. "I'm glad you called me," he said. "I've heard you're working as a PI now."

She was surprised that he'd kept up with her career. "Yes," she said.

"Do you remember the time I brought a lady friend to your father's place? She said she was from France, do you recall? But you told me privately that you thought she was from Quebec. There was something about her accent, you said."

"I was just a kid," Sierra said. "Apparently kind of an obnoxious one."

"On the contrary. You were absolutely right about her. You have a knack for accents and voices, don't you?"

Her brow wrinkled. As a matter of fact, she did, but what was this all about?

"Like my Jersey accent, right? It's distinctive and regional. Like my son's."

"I suppose," Sierra said.

"Combine that with a naturally curious mind and, well, I can see why you're successful at your craft. Now, what exactly is bothering you?"

Quite a lot is bothering me, Sierra thought as she bought thinking time with another swallow of coffee. Things like the feel inside this tavern and Rollo's out-of-context comments that nevertheless were right on point. There was a shrewd look in his eyes as he stared at her, a familiar look that made her wish she'd waited for Pike. It also telegraphed caution.

"You look confused," he said.

She sipped again and wondered if she had the audacity to just get up and leave.

"About that curiosity factor of yours," he said when she remained seated and thoughtful. "Did I mention that besides having my stomach stapled and plastic surgery on my nose and chin I also bought a fantastic wig straight from Paris? Do you wonder what I look like in it?"

Not really, she thought, but managed to mumble, "I'm sure…you…look great." The warmth from the coffee sliding down her throat felt good in part because her head had started to swim. And then her thoughts flashed back to the old gold mine. The men were talking to each other. They had Jersey accents, just like Rollo's. That's what had been bugging her.

She blinked as she met his gaze. She was in trouble and she knew it, but she wasn't a hundred percent sure why. Her gun was in her purse, which was hanging by its strap from the back of her chair. "What's going…on?" she said, alarmed at how difficult it was to speak. She looked at the cup in her hand and then at his. He took a healthy swallow… Had he put something in her mug before he poured her coffee? "You're… Dad's…friend."

"Friend? No, there are no friends in politics. Frankly, it was a relief when he quit. He didn't have the stomach for it. I'm on to bigger and better things and nothing, or no one, is going to ruin it. Now, about my new look. Let me satisfy your curiosity." He opened a box that sat on the chair beside him and took out an expensive-looking wig of shiny white hair. He pulled it over his head, adjusted it quickly and peered at her. "Did I get it on straight? I'm used to a mirror. Okay, what do you think? Do I look distinguished?"

She stared at him with wide eyes. His surface resemblance to Spiro Papadakis was nothing short of amazing. Maybe their mothers could have told them apart, but in a bar at night—it could throw anyone off.

Did this mean Savannah's friend had seen Rollo in this bar and jumped to the conclusion it was Spiro? Was the whole thing nothing more than a giant mistake? But wait, if it was Rollo, then he'd been sitting here with Natalia right before she disappeared.

All those dreams about bald men taunting her, tackling

her, calling her an idiot—had she somehow recognized Rollo despite the changes to his appearance?

Sierra put the cup of coffee down too hard and it slopped onto her hands. Rollo shoved a napkin toward her and she stared at it, unable to make sense of what was happening. Her eyelids drooped; her muscles felt spongy. The gun might as well be hanging from the Statue of Liberty's upraised torch.

She looked at the coffee staining her fingers then back at Rollo. He had two faces now and she internally groaned. "You—you..." she sputtered but the rest of the words wouldn't come.

He lowered his voice and leaned toward her. "The minute I saw you wearing those photo glasses, I knew you were up to no good, and what else could it be but to catch me with Natalia? That was bad enough, but later that night when the other whore...died...well, your fate was sealed. When I found out you were leaving town, I stole your computer. Isn't the information age grand? Your whole life, the past, the present, right there before me and actually moving forward as you scurried around like a busy mouse telling all your buddies every little detail of everything you saw and thought and did. I deduced from all your communications that you didn't know it was me in here that night, but I also knew you had questions and that meant you'd keep digging and eventually you'd put two and two together. And if you ever wised up and looked closer at the watch, I was dead meat.

"Tony and his stupid idiot pal were supposed to get rid of you in Idaho, but Sierra, dear, you're like a cockroach! Then this morning you wouldn't open your door to let him in. And just when I was trying to figure out what to do next, you announce you're going to the Papadakis apartment. I responded to you by using Savannah's tablet. It wasn't a perfect solution, but I thought I could work with it. And then, you actually call me! What a lovely turn of events. The fly came to the spider."

Another man walked up to the table. This one was a bulky, clumsy-looking guy about Sierra's age, meaty through the shoulders in a too-tight plaid shirt. The flagrant mustache was gone, but she knew she'd seen him last in front of her apartment talking on his phone. The white car in the parking lot—Rollo's car—must have been the vehicle that picked him up. The man smiled as he gazed down at her and she cringed. Those eyes. Anthony. Tony.

"Welcome to my tavern, Sierra. Sorry the coffee… disagreed with you."

That voice! She pushed herself away from the table and tried to stand, but her knees started to buckle. She grabbed for her purse and missed it. Anthony hoisted her to her feet and flung her across one shoulder.

Her head just about exploded against his back. "You know where to put her. We'll take care of…disposal… later."

"How?"

"I don't know yet. Just get her car out of the parking lot in case someone comes looking."

Sierra was conscious of being carried across the room, her dangling hands hitting the backs of chairs. She blacked out for a while and came to when she landed on a hard, cold surface. She had somehow acquired tape around her ankles and hands, and a gag in her mouth. Her eyes sprang open. Another woman lay beside her. Natalia!

And then a loud rattling noise heralded darkness and a welcome return to oblivion.

PIKE PULLED INTO Tony's Tavern. The place had a Closed sign on the door even though it was almost four o'clock in the afternoon. He'd hit a bad accident halfway between New York and here and had been held up for what seemed like forever. He'd called the Dusty Lake police as he waited for traffic to clear and asked them to check out the tavern and Rollo Bean's residence. They hadn't sounded real motivated but someone had eventually called him back and told him there was a sign on the tavern saying it was closed due to illness and no one named Rollo Bean lived in or around Dusty Lake.

While he'd waited for the police to call him back, he'd looked up Rollo Bean's number and called him, too. No answer. Where in the hell was everybody? Now he tried one last time to contact Sierra, grimacing when the phone switched directly to messages.

What did he do now?

He got out of the rental, grateful to stand after hours of sitting. There were two other vehicles in the parking lot, a newish gray van and a large white truck, both with New Jersey plates, which meant Sierra's car wasn't here. As he walked by the van, he checked the interior through the window and saw fast food wrappers and a clipboard. No sign of Sierra.

He walked over to the box truck. It appeared to be about fifteen feet long and had seen better days. Pike wouldn't want to take it out on the interstate. It was also outfitted with refrigeration. The low hum of a compressor kicked on as he examined the solid lock on the rear door. He continued on to the tavern, read the sign the police had mentioned and knocked loudly, surprised when the door actually opened and a man appeared.

He was a big guy in his thirties and he looked a little sweaty despite the cold. He wore a green plaid shirt buttoned all the way up to the beginnings of a double chin. His hairline had started to retreat up his forehead, emphasizing his eyes. One gray, one brown, both narrowed.

Again the cold hard facts presented themselves: Sierra had come here to meet a friend and that friend had a grown son with different-colored eyes who was now standing in front of him.

Pike's original intention had been to ask around and see if someone had seen Sierra, but now he decided to be more casual about it. This guy had the look and smell of a cornered bull.

"Sorry to bother you," he began with a smile. "I have plans to meet a buddy here for a beer but it looks like you're closed."

"We are," the man said and started to shut the door.

Pike tried stalling. "Can I wait here for my friend?"

"What? No. We're closed."

"How about I buy a beer and wait inside? It looks like it's going to rain."

"What part of closed don't you get?"

"Maybe the owner—"

"I'm the owner and I say get lost." The door slammed and a lock clicked in place.

Okay, so that was Rollo Bean's son. Someone matching his vague description had left with Savannah Papadakis. This was the place Sierra had come to meet Rollo Bean and since announcing that intention, she hadn't responded to any of his calls. He could almost feel her vibes lingering here. He wanted desperately to get inside that bar.

In case he was being watched, he walked back to the rental and drove out of the lot, pulling in behind an abandoned bait store a half block away. He got out of the car and sprinted back to the tavern, this time approaching from the rear and keeping low. There was a door at the back that was locked, but there was another around the corner next to the garbage cans that was open. He slipped inside the tavern and found himself in an empty kitchen. The place was poorly lit and ominously quiet except for the sound of Anthony speaking on the phone somewhere deeper inside.

Pike had worked in a similar joint during college and could guess the layout of this one. He methodically began searching for some sign of Sierra. She wasn't in the basement, where food was stored, nor was she in the walk-in refrigerator or freezer. He peeked through a window connecting the kitchen to the main room. Anthony held a phone to his face as he paced up and down between tables and chairs. There was no one in there with him.

Pike pulled off his boots and carried them as he made his way down a dark hallway that connected to another, where he discovered the bathrooms. Empty. All this time his heart stayed lodged in his throat because his head kept telling him Anthony was coming apart at the seams, and if Sierra was here, she was probably hurt or dead.

The thought bruised his heart so deeply it made breathing hard, and he pushed it away. He ducked through an open door and found himself in an office lit only with a gooseneck desk lamp. He checked out the closet. When he turned to leave he noticed a strap of black leather jammed in a file drawer built into the desk. He pulled the drawer open.

A woman's handbag had been stuffed inside. Sierra carried one much like it, but so did a million other women. The zipper was open, and using one hand he moved aside the scattered contents until he saw a bright pink wallet. He recognized that immediately. There was no sign of a gun. In the next instant he realized the voice out in the tavern had gone quiet. A creaking floorboard nearby sent his heart into overdrive.

There wasn't time to do more than slide the drawer shut and hide behind the open door. Things were going to go sour fast if the man closed himself in the office.

The room suddenly came alive with the sound of footsteps and heavy breathing. Furniture moved, a chair squeaked. Next came a grunt and a muttered oath. The door suddenly flew away from Pike and his heart leaped into his throat, but Anthony had closed it behind him as he left and now his footsteps receded down the hall. Pike cautiously let out his breath and walked to the desk. The handbag was gone. He quietly turned the handle on the door and peeked into the empty corridor.

A door slammed some distance away and the building instantly took on the silence of abandonment. Pike ran to look out the front window of the tavern and saw Anthony walking toward the big truck, Sierra's handbag in his hand. He unlocked the back of the truck, threw the handbag inside and relocked it. Then he walked to the driver's door and opened the door to the cab.

Pike pulled on his boots and hightailed it back to the kitchen, letting himself out the way he'd come in. He peered around the corner of the building, expecting to see the truck rolling out of the lot, but it hadn't moved at all.

His phone was in his hand. He'd get the police onto that truck no matter what he had to tell them, but he wanted a license number. He started circling closer, threading his way through the lakeside trees. It started raining and big, cold drops hit his bare head.

Anthony climbed out of the truck, patted all his pockets and began walking back to the restaurant. He kept his head down as he moved, obviously preoccupied. Pike kept moving so that by the time the guy was back at the tavern, Pike was right next to the truck.

As soon as the door closed behind Anthony, Pike checked the lock on the back. He pounded his fist against the rolling metal door and called Sierra's name. There was no response and no time to think—he had to trust his gut and his gut said that the truck had some connection to Sierra. He ran around to the open driver's door and climbed inside. The engine wasn't running and there wasn't a key in sight. The truck keys and the lock keys must be on separate rings.

The old vehicle had a lot in common with the tank truck back on the ranch. How many times had he and his brothers had to hot-wire that old beast? He reached into his pocket for his multitool and then remembered he hadn't been able to bring it on the plane. A rusty toolbox on the floor yielded a gold mine. First a pair of pliers that he used to unscrew the nut holding the ignition in place. With that gone, he pulled the ignition unit free, found a pocketknife in the toolbox and cut the wires. He chanced a look in the rearview mirror. Anthony was two thirds of the way back across the lot, headed for the truck. Pike touched the wires to each other until he found a spark. The engine turned over with a roar and actually sprang to life. He twisted the wires together and hoped for the best.

Anthony was at the rear of the truck now and he'd produced a handgun. Just as Pike pushed down on the accelerator, he felt the rear of the truck dip and realized Anthony had jumped for the rear bumper. There were grab bars back there; presumably, Anthony was holding on for dear life.

The trick would be to get Anthony off the back of that truck in case he had the guts to shoot out the lock before Pike could prevent it. Toward that goal, he gunned his way through the stop sign at the edge of the parking lot and drove under the branches of a low-hanging tree, hoping Anthony would be pried loose. He checked the mirror. Damn. Anthony did not lie sprawled on the wet pavement behind him. He was still on the truck.

A refrigerated truck. Handy for storing bodies. It was pretty obvious to Pike that Anthony had abducted or coerced Savannah Papadakis out of her apartment. Why, he wasn't sure. But it was tied into Sierra, it had to be.

Again that almost preternatural sensation of her essence attacked his senses. He had to get rid of Anthony, he had to get the truck to safety, he had to see if Sierra was where his gut told him she was and, if so, what condition she was in.

He ran another stop sign a few blocks ahead and breezed through a red light a block after that. The windshield wipers barely kept up with the rain. He sat on his horn and flashed headlights at oncoming vehicles. It was a strange city to him and he had no idea where the police department was. It didn't help that it was getting dark really fast. He wasn't even sure of the exact location of the city center, as he'd followed road signs to get to the lake and they had skirted around business areas. He couldn't possibly free his hands or his attention to check his phone for directions or even to chance making a call. Instead he drove with all the skill he'd learned since the day he turned ten and his father plopped him behind a wheel of a truck much like this one, with blocks tied to the pedals, and told him to follow the tractor around the field while they gathered huge rolls of hay.

Frankie was fond of saying that it always seemed there were too damn many cops in the world. Easy for Frankie to say as he was talking about scuffles, boyhood mischief and eventually more serious events, where the least welcome thing was the sight of a badge. What Pike wouldn't give for a cop right now, and driving as fast as he was, certainly someone would call one in. For heaven's sake, there was a man holding on to the back of a speeding, erratically driven old delivery truck. What did it take to get someone's attention around here?

More horn honking and this time the driver honked back. Good. He flashed lights again, opened the window and waved his arm. All during this crazy drive, he constantly checked the rearview mirror because of Anthony. The guy had to be half limpet to have stayed on with that last turn. He slowed for a sharp right and that's when his headlights flashed on a sign telling him the sheriff's department was one mile up ahead. At that same moment, a siren announced itself from the road behind and Pike glanced in the mirror to see welcome red-and-blue lights in hot pursuit. He made it to the sheriff department's parking lot and slowed to a stop. He opened the door in time to see Anthony run under the lights illuminating the gate with police in pursuit. More police warned Pike to stop where he was and keep his hands visible. As Pike settled both his hands on top of his head, the cops caught up with Anthony and disarmed him.

"He stole my truck. He's a madman," Anthony yelled. "I'm a businessman here in this city. Arrest him. What are you waiting for?" His face was pasty white, his hair and clothes soaked.

Pike opened his mouth. Before a word came out, they heard a banging noise coming from inside the truck and muffled sounds of distress.

"Shoot the locks," someone said.

"No," Pike said. "There might be a woman in there. That man has the keys."

"Unlock the truck, sir," the officer told Anthony, who looked frantically from one unyielding face to another before producing his key ring and throwing it to the pavement. He closed his eyes and bowed his head. The police set to work unlocking the truck as an officer cuffed Pike and led him to the back.

"Please," Pike said as he paused. "My girlfriend… please. I have to see her. I have to know…"

"Someone get a light," the man with the keys yelled and a bevy of flashlights switched on as the truck door rolled up on its chains.

Sierra sat against the side of the truck, gagged, her bound hands holding a chain connected to the wall. She had no weapon but herself. She must have kicked the truck to get their attention. Another woman in considerably worse condition lay beside her, eyes open but unblinking. Blood stained her blond hair. She stared at the lights as though caught in their glare as men jumped into the truck and leaned over her. A third woman cried out from farther forward, deep in the shadows, and Pike saw Sierra's head swivel to see who it was.

She was older than the others by a decade, tied to cleats, sitting on a box, gagged. She was thin to the point of being gaunt and tangled dark hair swept the shoulders of a red cape. Dark eyes flashed in her face.

Sierra's gasp was audible even through her gag, and as soon as it was removed, she whispered, "Savannah?"

"Savannah Papadakis," Pike murmured to the officer by his side. "I think she's been stuck in there for days."

"Who's the blonde on the floor?" the officer asked as the sound of ambulance sirens wailed in the distance. "It looks like she's in pretty bad shape."

"Natalia Bonaparte," Sierra said.

"She's been tortured," the officer leaning down to tend to her muttered. He looked at Sierra. "How about you, miss?"

Sierra shook her head. "I'm fine. Just, please, help me stand.

It killed Pike not to be able to go to her aid, but soon enough she'd been freed from her bindings and helped from the truck. Sierra peered up at the sky for a second, closing her eyes as the rain pelted her face, then she moved toward Pike in slow motion, officers stepping aside as she passed. She stopped right in front of him, raised her arms and wrapped them around his neck. Her lips against his felt like heaven on earth. When she pulled away to gaze at him, he thought there might be tears on her cheeks, but with the rain streaking her face, who knew?

He just knew his eyes were damp and it had nothing to do with the weather.

"I love you," she said, her voice hoarse but fierce. "I miss Daisy. I miss my horse."

He smiled, a little confused. "Your horse? Which horse is that?"

"The red mare. What's her name?"

"Ginger."

"I miss Ginger. Please, please, take me home."

Unable to put his cuffed arms around her, he kissed her forehead and rested his chin on top of her wet head. "I was just about to say the same damn thing to you," he whispered.

Epilogue

Sierra had heard the tape a dozen times but the fear behind the hurried, whispered words still caused a shiver to race through her veins.

"Natalia? Pick up, oh, pick up. It's me, Giselle. Are you there? I'm stuck in Max's suite. He thinks I left, but we were smoking crack and I fell asleep… Anyway, that Rollo guy is here. I heard him and Max laughing about some man they put in prison on false charges… If they know I heard… Please, Natalia, answer the phone. I—" At this point the voice ended. Someone who sounded a lot like Maxwell Jakes swore. Giselle cried out, "No…"

That was it, but that had been enough. Minutes after she called Natalia, Max Jakes had allegedly held her head under water until she was dead, and an hour after that, someone fitting Anthony Bean's description was seen dumping something the size and shape of a human body into the Hudson River. By the next afternoon Rollo Bean had used his informant to plant misleading evidence in the Ralph Yardley camp. And twelve hours later, Natalia Bonaparte threatened to take the police the tape of the underage call girl she'd sent to Max Jakes's room a half-dozen times…unless a sizeable hunk of cash found its way into her offshore bank account. She disappeared soon after.

All three men were now under arrest and Giselle's voice from beyond the grave had helped make that possible. And that made Sierra very happy.

But not as happy as sitting on this bench in Central Park with Pike by her side. She rested her head against his and he kissed her hair. His arm around her shoulders felt wonderful and safe. He'd been in New York for three days and this was one of the few times they'd managed to dodge interviews, questions and the limelight to find peace without staying inside her apartment. Though it was cold, it felt great to just be outside and alone.

"I have to leave in another day or two," he told her.

"I know."

"I'll come again."

She looked into his eyes. "I know you will but I have a question. Do you think I could go back with you?"

A smile lit up his eyes. "I thought you might have said that the other night because of everything you'd just been through. Of course you can. I'd love that."

"I can't stay long," she added. "Savannah is such a wreck she's asked her husband for a reconciliation. Why in the world Anthony took her instead of just bashing her over the head when he stole her tablet is a mystery. And then there's this case I've been working on—"

He cut her short by picking up her hand and kissing her fingers. "Sierra? Just stay however long you want. That's all I ask."

They stared at each other for a long moment and then both smiled at the same time. "Okay," she said and looked around at the city skyline she loved, then back into Pike's eyes. It was hard not to wonder if she'd ever have the heart to leave his side…

* * * * *

Look for Frankie's story, the final book in
Alice Sharpe's THE BROTHERS OF
HASTINGS RIDGE RANCH *later this year.*